If
Only

Melanie Murphy is an author and award-winning online content creator from a small village in Dublin.

Her YouTube videos have amassed almost seventy million views online, reaching people with her warm personality and life lessons as well as views on divisive topics such as sexuality, women's rights, health and relationships. Also, some silly fun stuff, just 'cause.

Melanie is the author of two books, both Irish bestsellers: *Fully Functioning Human (Almost)*, part memoir part life-guide (2017), and her debut novel *If Only* (2019).

She lives in Ireland with her husband Thomas, her modern family, and her two glorious rescue kitties, Bilbo and Molly Weasley. Her BSc (hons) degree in Education & Training from DCU gathers dust above the fireplace as she writes books and uploads videos to the internet for a living.

Instagram: @melaniiemurphy
Twitter: @melaniietweets
YouTube: Melanie Murphy
www.melaniemurphy.ie

Also by Melanie Murphy

Non-Fiction
Fully Functioning Human (Almost)

Melanie Murphy

If Only

HACHETTE
BOOKS
IRELAND

First published in Ireland in 2019 by
HACHETTE BOOKS IRELAND
First published in paperback in 2020

1

Cataloguing in Publication Data is available from the British Library

Paperback ISBN 9781473691797
Ebook ISBN 9781473691780
Audio ISBN 9781529352085

Typeset in Century by redrattledesign.com

Printed and bound in Great Britain by Clays Ltd, Elcograf, S.p.A.

Hachette Books Ireland policy is to use papers that are natural, renewable and
recyclable products and made from wood grown in sustainable forests. The logging and
manufacturing processes are expected to conform to the environmental regulations of
the country of origin.

Hachette Books Ireland
8 Castlecourt Centre
Castleknock
Dublin 15, Ireland

A division of Hachette UK Ltd
Carmelite House, 50 Victoria Embankment, EC4Y 0DZ
www.hachettebooksireland.ie

Dedicated to my family, my husband, the fond memory of my grandmother and to those who spend far too much time mulling over missed opportunities instead of creating new ones.

Part 1

1
Beggy

It was the springtime I hoped I'd soon forget, Stephen Hawking's last (which deeply upset Granny even though she didn't 'believe in science') and the dawn of my unravelling. There was no chance I could avoid telling Granny and every chance her peace would evaporate when I did, like alcohol: her favourite, brought to the boil.

She won't be a happy woman.

At the end of a long, eventless Wednesday working in Sugar Pot café, I mulled over how to tell her. The worry had consumed me for weeks, as my visit home to Ireland loomed closer. Dad didn't really care, of course. He'd never been Dan's biggest fan. But, unfortunately, 'how to tell your old-school romantic granny you've just called off your wedding' wasn't yielding any useful search results on Google.

It would have been an alright wedding. Lovely pictures, shitty best-man speech, excellent cake and *not awful* consummation. But the marriage? As my best friend Reid had put it: 'like pulling teeth for three years tops till the inevitable, crushing divorce'. Reid Williams's honesty was iron in a world of fragile reassurances.

'Miss? Excuse me, miss? I ordered a soy latte. This is a *regular* latte, with cow's milk.' The café's last customer of the day, with an elegant updo and impeccable eyeliner, looked at me across the counter with the most rested of bitch faces.

'Oh? Um, you sure? I mean – of course. Let me change that.'

Then, as she sat back down with her fellow bitch faces, 'Not again, Erin.'

My insufferable manager, Kenneth. *How many bloody ears does he have?*

'You sure I'm safe to let you close up for me, Beglan? You won't leave the place a pile of ash and rubble? Third slip-up of the day, young lady,' he warned, twirling the few hairs of his meagre beard.

Young lady.

Feigned laughter followed by another meek 'sorry' was all I could afford to respond; my bank balance begged me to continue taking Kenneth's shit and stop hiding in the broom cupboard, virtually scrolling through travel photography online, when the café grew busy. He was definitely growing wise to my extended 'pee breaks', during which I'd imagine being *anywhere* but there.

Kenneth, fancying himself as a thoughtful hero type, offered to help me with the end-of-day duties, but his arm was already stuffed into his jacket sleeve and his body, angled toward the front door, edging to escape. I politely declined. Alone, I cleared up empty cups and newspapers that screamed garbage headlines about the prime minister's body double and all manner of doom and gloom, counted the last of the money in the till, tugged off my grubby apron, turned off the lights and locked up shop. London office workers swarmed around me, everyone with their eyes on pavement cracks and in their own little worlds, as I pulled my phone from my pocket to text Reid. I popped my earphones in with one hand and typed with the other:

Meet in Palace Gardens? Our spot? In half an hour? I need to stop by Dan's house later to pick up some post before I head to the new place. Not ready to face him yet. Shitting it. Please bring calories.

A little blue tick immediately appeared beside my message.

Fine. You're about the only creature I can tolerate right now anyway. But it's your fault I still have no abs and I hate you for it xxx

My lips stretched into the first genuine smile they'd formed in days. Then I closed up my denim jacket, rescued my old bicycle from a nearby lamp post and set off into the bustle of London City's evening, 'Are "Friends" Electric?' by Tubeway Army hammering my eardrums.

It was dull for April – dull and grey but thankfully not wet. I cycled, in no hurry, by traffic jams and the beautiful Royal Albert Hall, where Dan and I had once gone to see ...

No.

Stop thinking about him.

I rode on through the heady aroma of car exhaust fumes, a blooming grove of very Instagrammable pink and white flowering dogwood trees, honeymoon-phase couples strolling along the bike lane with their disgusting public displays of affection.

Although the shadow of my dead relationship seemed to hang over every square inch of London, the Palace Gardens somehow dodged its darkness and I knew that was where I needed to be. The gardens had served as my meeting point with my best friend Reid ever since we'd first met at university, almost eight years ago. It was just for us and our many shared secrets – of crushes, mistakes, sex acts gone wrong and everything in between. One afternoon after getting dumped, Reid had suggested that we *go somewhere pretty*, and, well, *this* is where we'd ended up. This was the place that always reminded us that being out of love wasn't the end of the bloody world. There's still beauty, and there's still one another, and that's something.

I'd never taken Dan there, not once, though today I fully expected to arrive, take one look at Reid and word-vomit about the break-up all over our sacred place, as thoughts of it clenched my brain. I needed that sweet release with a trusted companion who wouldn't judge me for it.

Reid was the only person in all of London left for me to *really* talk to.

Ten minutes later, as I pulled up outside the Gardens, my mind had turned to the mounds of my crap (*and* the crap I'd shared with Dan for six years) that awaited unboxing back in my new shared living space in Brixton. I'd finally secured a room to rent after a few blurry weeks spent sleeping on Reid's couch, where, biweekly, I had no choice but to overhear his sexcapades and lie there wide-eyed at 2 a.m., staring at his ceiling, wondering how I'd ended up in such a ridiculous position. Reid's apology involved helping me to move my entire life across London, though, so I forgave him for subjecting me to the moans and kinky talk I could've done without hearing.

I couldn't say if me from a few months ago would've laughed it off; I couldn't remember her or how she managed to actually live life instead of *just about* coping with it. Physical evidence of an Erin who was planning her elaborate, perfect wedding – photos of pretty locations and set-menu options, and voice messages to Reid of me waffling on about themed centrepieces – just made me feel like the mountain before me was even taller than it probably was. A mountain that had slowly formed only to wedge itself into the timeline of my life, splitting it once again into *before that big, horrible thing* and *after that big, horrible thing;* a mountain I needed to climb. I was lost in a swirly-twirly labyrinth and under orders to find myself. I knew where I was standing and what the bushes in front of me looked like and the colour of the ground beneath my feet, but I hadn't a clue how to describe where I was at from sky view or which turn to take. I knew that I had to exist, right there, but that absolutely terrified me because I didn't know *how.*

Life with Dan was all I knew, but that was gone, and it was all my fault.

I'd *only just* cancelled the last of our wedding arrangements: the venue was unbooked; the dress was returned (well, I hadn't wanted to wear the thing, truth be told – I *hated* dresses, especially that one. It was so bloody itchy). So many deposits lost, and *Granny* ...

She still didn't know that the man she considered a second son was out of the picture, for good.

Exhale.

I chained up my old bicycle between lots of much prettier and newer bicycles before meandering my way through the sunken garden, terraced with flower beds and surrounding a pond with fountains, where tulips and wallflowers decorated my walk to the gate beneath the arched arbour of red-twigged lime.

Knowing that Reid would arrive soon meant that calm could finally wrap itself around me, like a warm cloak; it did, and I realised I'd probably been holding my breath for most of the journey from work. Now, in the gardens, dotted with elderly folk strolling along with their dogs and with pairs of tourists taking photos, I felt safe. I pulled my earphones out and focused on my breath. My chest began to softly rise and fall, and everything was suddenly working properly inside my body again.

And then Reid was coming at me down the grassy stretch ahead, wearing his cheeky grin and jazzy bomber jacket, with a boyish skip in his step and a small box of six doughnuts held out in front of his tiny body, like treasure. My smile reached my eyes.

'I honestly love you right now. Jaysis, gimme,' I said.

'More than you love Louis Theroux?' Reid asked, head tilted. His lively voice was music to my ears.

I'd been reaching for the box, but I snatched my hand back. 'Eh,' I snapped, then tore open my jacket and my white work shirt to reveal an over-washed white tee featuring an expressionless headshot of the British journalist who inspired me more than any other, wearing his trademark glasses. 'He's Dad of Life. *You* just amuse me and feed me and listen to my problems. Are those glazed?'

Reid rolled his eyes and giggled, tongue between his front teeth, as I took the box. 'What do you take me for? Of course they are, you daft Irish bitch. You're losing your lovely plumpness, Beggy, what's that about?'

'I wish,' I said, expertly hiding my glee. 'I'm on the Heartbreak Diet, which consists of inconsistent servings of … cherry Bakewell tarts, mostly.' Although my emotionally wrecked state was the reason I hadn't been eating properly, and so I hadn't shifted unwanted pounds in a healthy manner, I couldn't help but revel in Reid's words, at the fact that he'd noticed that I was a bit smaller. Pride patted me on the back.

A silver lining to this clusterfuck of a situation!

I mean, *obviously* I needed to start eating consistently again. *But still …*

We sat on the old worn-down step in front of our go-to gate and together peeled open the polka-dot box of Krispy Kremes. I absorbed the lip-smacking aroma of featherlight, just-out-of-the-frier doughnuts covered in sugary glaze, and my mouth filled with saliva.

'Go on then, what's He been saying?' Reid asked through a mouthful of beige delight. Reid had refused to use Dan's name since the break-up, referring to him ever since as *He*. Probably to help me to move on and definitely because it was funny. I took a doughnut too, but didn't want to dive right into *that* conversation. I needed a moment out of my own head.

'No,' I said. 'First you've to tell me what happened on the wine-bar date last night. Your last drunk text said you changed the guy's name to "dairy queen" on your phone. Why?'

'Oh yeah, for God's sake.' Reid laughed. 'The twat scoffed some carbonara with his family before our *first date*, even though he's *allergic to dairy*. *"I wanna be a bold boy …"*' he continued, impersonating his date in a try-hard, alluring tone. 'Keeps saying that over and over, then spends half the date in the bathroom with the shits.' Belly laughter punctuated Reid's storytelling. 'Proceeds to tell me all about it, describes the consistency, the smell, while I'm there surrounded by candles, romantic music playing, the works, and me staring at this bloody cheese board I owe twenty quid for *which he obviously can't help me with* and a glorious bottle of equally expensive red. Decided then that he, like your ex, doesn't deserve to be referred to by name, ever again. Erin, why is everyone apart from you and me so very *crap*?'

I swallowed, mid-laugh. Reid had been so excited about this boy.

Being single sounds hellish.

After stuffing the rest of the doughnut into my face, I moaned and curled up into a ball, resting my forehead on my knees through the rips in my jeans. 'Really not looking forward to dating again,' I said, with a toddler-small voice. I rolled my head to the side to face Reid. He sat back into his listening posture and stared at me, putting all his weight onto his hands behind him. I always loved when he did that, though I never told him so. 'I'm too old, mate. Week-old sliced pan, Tesco value bread. I'll be picking from the dregs of London, and even then I'll be lucky if anyone's interested. *The sad, chubby ginger with a journalism degree she doesn't use* – that's what they'll call me.'

'Almost-thirty is the new nineteen, you silly fuck. Besides, you don't *need* to date again any time soon: it's Beggy time now. Also—'

'And, obviously, anyone I *do* manage to pull will take one glance at my stupidly hot flatmate and realise they're insane to be with me. Why eat from Tesco when you can hit up M&S?'

When I first met Rachel a few days ago I was like a person seeing the Northern Lights for the first time. *She's so beautiful.* It was difficult to believe she was a real human being.

'What's wrong with Tesco? We'd be dead without Tesco,' Reid scoffed. 'I thought we agreed that you're going to take some time to focus on yourself.' He delicately picked up another doughnut. Reid was handsome in the traditional sense, yet so very dainty at the same time.

'I will. I mean, *I am.* I'm just saying – well, I'm not getting any younger, am I? If I ever want to have a family of my own I'd want to start bloody well soon.'

'Beggy—'

'And I *know* I'm supposed to go with the flow of life and all that shite, but I just want to be, well, *you know.*' He nodded. 'I'm still allowed to think these thoughts *out loud*, to you, right?'

Reid observed me some more. 'OK. I feel that. The future is scary, and every year goes by faster the older we get. But—'

'Living with a *literal* manic pixie dream girl is pissing on my optimism about my future prospects, is all. The competition in this city makes me feel gross,' I told him, looking off into the distance.

'Elaborate.'

'Rachel – she's bouncy and smiley, but, like, in an annoying way – she never stops. She's twenty-four, so, basically, a child. With long hair that brushes off her *perfect* arse. I bet she's never had a blackhead in her entire life.'

Reid chose not to feed my jealousy. 'What does she do? It's her apartment, right?'

'It is, but I don't know *how* because she's just a dancer, and a part-time art teacher. Neither of those jobs would pay for a London apartment, surely,' I mumbled, all bitter as I picked at the skin around my nail-polish-free thumbs, thinking about how she must have received a big old chunk of inheritance or … something.

'Maybe she dances in the West End. Or maybe her parents are filthy rich. Anyway, you never know, you two could become the best of friends. Maybe she'll even replace *me*, and your dad will rejoice because you've ditched the gay,' he teased.

'Nah. There's more chance of my blog actually taking off than that ever happening. She's far too together for me. And you know I don't have much luck with female friends. Remember Tara?' Tara had used me to help her score better grades at university and then she'd dropped off the face of the earth, along with the entire friend group I'd been sending my class notes and homework to, on her instruction. 'Besides, Dad wouldn't care – I'd be painting over one shade of gay with another. I think Rachel is into girls … or, well, everyone, really.' I recalled my first evening with Rachel during which she took me on a wild conversational ride through her colourful love life. By the end of it I felt like a prudish shrew. 'Forget Rachel, OK? You're here to listen to me vent,' I said, hoping to move the conversation along quickly. I regretted mentioning my blog at all. If Reid asked about it I'd have to admit that I hadn't updated it in almost two months and that my sparkly dream of becoming an esteemed digital journalist was sinking like a stone in the Irish Sea.

'As always.' Reid tilted his head back to look at the sky, and there was a moment of comfortable silence as birdsong and the hecticness of London pulsed around us. When I didn't continue, he gently pressed me again, taking another doughnut. 'Is He still leaving cringe voice messages?'

'He's moved on to writing me *letters*. Propped the last one outside the door to my new place. Rachel gave it to me after her morning run the other day – yes, she actually runs before work, the nutter. Thing is, I never actually told Dan where I moved to,' I said with a grimace. '*You* didn't tell him, did you?' It was clear from Reid's expression that he was mulling over his words.

'Well, you *did* spend years with him, Erin.' I just stared at him, so he'd know that I was fuming. 'OK, look, hear me out. *He* showed up, banging the door down, while *I* was trying to … bang a beautiful boy. To distract myself from the fact that the love of my life, *who also happens to be my boss*, just got married.' Reid explained it as though Martin's wedding wasn't something he'd talked about a hundred times since it had happened. I grabbed another doughnut in frustration, hoping that Reid wouldn't start harping on about Martin again.

Could this be guilt for encouraging me to call off the wedding? Does Reid think I made a mistake? Do I think I made a mistake?

'Beggy, I was drunk,' Reid continued, 'and ... and I figured you just hadn't got around to updating Him. You were *actually* gonna ghost Him?'

'Don't turn this back on me. All I wanted was a clean break. Fresh start, y'know? Like we talked about. I thought you were on *my* side.'

'It's not about sides, it's about—'

'Everyone picks a side when two people break up. You and Dan weren't even friends! All you ever did was slag him off.'

'I slag everybody off.'

'Where's this Team Dan shite after coming from?' I asked. 'Why do you care about his feelings? You won't even say his name.'

'I thought we were on the same page about the whole "vanishing into thin air on people" thing. It's cruel. You didn't tell me you were planning on never speaking to him again.'

'Did I even say that?'

'Not wanting someone to know where you live says that.

Look … I just felt bad for the guy. He didn't do anything wrong. I know what it feels like to be ignored, and it kills, Beggy.'

My ears turned red with fury-heat. 'He's still begging for another chance, though. Promising things will change for the billionth time,' I said, trying to justify my lack of effort at being a decent human being. 'Dan always said he loved me unconditionally, but nah: *he* loved *me* on the condition that I stayed with him. He's not treating me with love – he's making this horrible.'

Reid said nothing.

Then, terrified by the idea that I could be pushing my only friend away, I changed the subject: 'The only other person who has ever written me letters is Granny Beglan, because she's ancient and she won't let me *or* Dad buy her a phone.' Success – Reid pulled his incredulous-with-a-hint-of-a-smile face, the one he always pulled when I told him tales of my granny. (*Like how she drinks about a bottle of wine a day and smokes like it's going out of style but apparently is somehow still in good health.* Her doctors dubbed her Inishbeg village's 'medical marvel'.) 'Funny, though, Dan will go to *all that effort* of leaving letters for me at work, at my new place, at yours, but then won't forward on *my* mail. I'd asked him to forward everything to yours for the time being. That's why I'm so annoyed with him and why I need to go over tonight. I'm waiting on a letter from Granny and some bills …' I jumped from light to heavy fidgeting, thinking about my current lack of funds. I *really* didn't want to ask my dad for another loan. He was off travelling the world with his wife, having a blast.

'I'd love to meet your granny, y'know. Maybe she'll fall in love with me.'

'Nah. "My marriage didn't end when I became a widow" – that's literally a thing she said.'

'Wow. That's the sweetest thing. The cute little bitch.'

'I know. I want *that*,' I said, thinking about the tales Granny had told me over the years about how perfect her marriage to my grandad was. Unfortunately, I'd never met him, but Granny had been sure to paint a vivid picture of their blissful love; of how much Grandad doted on her; of how they maintained the ritual of 'date night' right up until his dying days; and of how she looked forward to spending eternity with him in 'the afterlife', as she called it. I'd basically fallen out of the womb envious of their relationship. It was legendary. I didn't want to settle for less.

'Bet she'll think Dan is super romantic when you tell her that he's been writing to you.' I shot Reid a look. 'Actually, yeah, maybe *don't* tell her that.'

'Granny loves Dan. Bloody nervous about telling her. She'll probably be so disappointed in me – I'm her only grandchild, y'know? Ugh. I *did* love him, right? Are you sure I've not ruined my life?'

'You totally and completely loved him – for a few years, anyway. You made him a cute playlist. You *baked for him*. You. Baked. For a man. And licked his—'

'Ew, stop. That must've been someone who looked a lot like me,' I said with a side smirk. 'But what if I sabotaged a good thing? Something that could've *stayed good*.'

'Then you sabotaged a good thing,' he shrugged. 'Consider it sabotaged. Learn from it and don't sabotage the next thing.' His words curled my shoulders forward. 'Or, maybe you didn't … I wasn't part of it, all I know is it went to shit. Doesn't really matter *why* at this stage, does it? You both seemed miserable, for months. Mainly *you*.'

'Mm-hmm.'

'Especially with his mummy-dearest always shoving her nose in.'

'Josephine. *Don't*. I never want to think about that woman again. What's the opposite of rose-tinted glasses? Black eyes that you can hardly see through, courtesy of life itself?'

Half-laughing, Reid hesitated, then asked, 'You're not *actually* having second thoughts, are you?' His blue eyes darted around, scanning my face.

I defiantly shook my head in response to the feelings that bubbled inside me upon hearing that question out loud: feelings about my ticking clock, about family expectations, the fear of starting over with someone new or being found half-eaten by cats in a flat stinking of loneliness, fear of the empty bed awaiting me in my new place.

A young woman pushed a stroller by us – a single mother, perhaps?

There's always sperm donors.

I had jokingly (dead seriously) suggested going down

that route to Dad, when I'd called him after cancelling the wedding. (Dad was the second-last hurdle. Granny was next, and he'd been warned not to utter a *word* to her until I'd seen her myself.) We'd chatted about life and where mine was headed, and Dad hadn't been at all keen on the notion of me starting my own family. I'd figured he hoped that I'd have a more traditional family, or that I'd at least become financially independent before considering such things. Maybe he just didn't think I had it in me to go it alone. Regardless, I'd dropped it. And I didn't really talk about it with anyone else because most people made me feel like I shouldn't even want a baby *because it's the twenty-first century and women only want babies because they've been brainwashed into* thinking *they want babies, they can't think for themselves … no way! Women's brains lack the capacity to make informed decisions, obviously!*

'No,' I said eventually. 'I'd never go back to him. Well, him *and Josephine*. I could never marry him without marrying them both. Dan would let his ma wipe his arsehole if she offered. I can't be around that woman any more.'

'She's *detestable*.'

'Besides, Dan just rubs me up the wrong way nowadays, even when he's not trying to.'

'Plus he was never really there for you, with your blog and stuff.' This wasn't entirely true, but I didn't want to correct Reid; all of my complaining had likely painted that picture in his mind and I felt bad enough already. 'And he was always so – what's it? – passive aggressive.'

This, I could latch onto. 'Yeah. Ugh,' I said, my face contorting. 'Don't remind me. *I'm not angry, Erin. Fine then, Erin. I'm only joking, Erin* … I was meant to be the one person he could open up to and he'd never just say what he meant. But what if it was my fault that he didn't feel comfortable, y'know, *communicating* – like, what if he never finds someone he can be real with? And what if—'

'Stop feeling bad. Stop replaying every little "what if",' Reid said, tapping my forehead, 'or I'll chuck you off a bridge somewhere. OK?' This Williams boy could paint a smile onto the saddest of faces. 'Go on, have the last doughnut. After all, you're now on – what is it? – *day forty-three* of no sex?'

'Stop. I've had two whole periods since the last time Dan and I even shifted.'

'Shifted?'

'Made out. Snogged. Whatever.'

'Bloody Irish-isms.' Reid kicked at the side of the doughnut box with one of his dazzling white Vans. 'Let's walk and fight over who has it worse right now: you, with your abysmal job and clingy ex, or me, with my STD and my unrequited love.'

We walked several laps of the gardens and laughed so much that we both cried, until we ended up back where my bicycle was chained.

I'd called it Rusty – way back in my teens – because it was *so very*, almost more so than the shade of my hair.

I'd stuck a new basket on the front at Christmas. 'Now it looks even worse,' Reid had said, and he reminded me again now, as always, that he wouldn't be caught dead riding Rusty around London.

I'd grown impatient of his taunts. 'Well, you know, I'm not gonna replace it. It was Mam's.'

'Nostalgic mess,' he half-whispered, rolling his eyes, knowing I'd appreciate the humour. And I did. I truly hated serious chats about my mam's death and avoided them even more than I avoided mirrors during daylight hours. This bicycle and a few old photographs and keepsakes were all that I had left of her. I'd spent 2,982 days (yes, I'd done the maths) with Mam before she passed away, and although I no longer experienced the white-hot, agonising pain of grief, I lived each day with a Mam-shaped hole in my life, and all I could stuff that hole with were the scraps of her left behind for me.

'Look, it's worth looking like Mad Bike Lady to feel like she's still here.'

That awful lump-in-throat feeling.

Push it down.

'Mad Bike *Lady* and not *Girl* is right,' Reid said. 'Can't believe you're almost thirty. When did we get so *old*?'

'When you find out, tell me, so I can start a hashtag in protest of ageing. Maybe we'll wake up twenty-one again. So many wild shags ahead, so much hope for the future!' I forced myself to sound nonchalant; thoughts of Mam, and of the void Reid would leave when he went home, carved out room inside me for tension to set up camp and build a fire.

'I have a surprise for you, Beggy,' Reid said.

'Unless it's a dog, I don't want it,' I joked, suddenly curious. He gave me an early birthday present then – he'd had my gift wrapped and hidden in a tiny metallic backpack hanging from his shoulder all along. My text had alerted him to my need for cheering up, and, besides, I probably wouldn't see him again as a twenty-nine-year-old. I swallowed the thought immediately so it couldn't dry my throat from top to bottom. 'Is it dentures? Coupons? A nose-hair trimmer?'

It was a make-up kit, one of the ones featured all over Instagram, fitted out for a person with green eyes and red hair. I swatched the colours on the back of my hand and poured out thank-yous, all the while thinking about how Mam would've *loved* something like this. We had similar features, she and I. Only she'd possessed more glamour than adult me in her littlest toe – even on her laziest of days, early nineties, when she'd walk me to the schoolyard, heels clicking the pavement alongside me, my hair a cotton-candy tangle in the wind. She'd never owned make-up like this, so fancy and luxurious with beautiful rose-gold packaging. I remembered playing with her cheap blue eyeshadow duo that she'd bought from an Avon lady and her words: 'This is one of Mammy's only nice things – it's not a toy, darlin'. Promise you won't mess with it again?'

Reid and I hugged and said goodbye (I think he knew I was breaking – his eyes flashed with understanding), and I took off on Rusty as the sky turned to pewter, with my thirtieth birthday present in Rusty's basket, thinking about how my own mam never reached thirty herself.

And about my doughnut guilt.

And my new shared flat, complete with painfully perfect flatmate/landlord.

And about Dan.

Ahh, *Dan.*

2
Letters and Loneliness

I played 'Love Will Tear Us Apart' by Joy Division over and over again on my twenty-minute cycle to Dan's house. *Dan's house* … so strange to call it anything other than *our house*. White, Victorian and terraced, with a red door: the house Dan bought with his director's income from the family car firm he'd unenthusiastically taken over when his father passed away, the house that had never quite felt like a home to me. It was just a place where I'd slept for three of our six years together, where I'd kept my things organised and had the odd satisfactory sexual experience and occasional great day between a million silly arguments about everything and nothing.

Well. We'd not always been so unhappy that I'd sit on the side of the bed and tear at my hair while he snored, *begging* the universe for a way out, but that's certainly where things had ended up.

Perhaps he'd heard my bicycle roll up, or perhaps he could feel my presence; nonetheless, I could see Dan knew I'd arrived because I glimpsed his almost-black irises through the front window blinds and an armless fist formed instantaneously, right in the middle of my guts.

My legs were noodles.

He was looking directly at me.

I used to orgasm while looking into those eyes.

Dan was swallowed by shadow as he stepped back, presumably to come and let me in. Flustered and anxious once again, I leaned Rusty against the wall by the door and I waited, fidgeting, with my mind running a mile a second over thoughts of what to say and how to say it, of how to stand and how to move and how to cover up the fact that I was thinking all of these things because Dan would know. He could read me as if I were a billboard with milky limbs dangling from my edges.

Heart hammering, I wrapped my arms around myself when I heard the familiar click of our – *his* – front door, then I twirled, mid-self-hug, to face the tall, unusually gaunt man in the doorway.

Dan.

He looked … terrible.

Even more terrible than me (though I *had* stopped during my cycle over to fiddle with the make-up kit Reid had given me).

Dan's face didn't light up when he saw me. If anything, it darkened even more, as though my presence somehow enhanced his paleness and the blackness under his eyes. He looked defeated. His shirt wasn't ironed, he smelled of sweat mixed with his Brut deodorant, and he hadn't shaved in a couple of weeks. The rugged look never worked with his baby features. I'd told him so a thousand times.

As ever, Dan waited for me to break the uncomfortable silence between us ... with what? *What do I say? How does anyone know how to deal with adult-ish things like this?*

'Granny ...' I inhaled deeply, trying to formulate a sentence for this human-shaped broken heart stood before me. 'Granny's letters, my bills, I ... I came for my post, I ... can I come in? How're you doing?'

Feck. Why am I asking him that? I don't really want to hear his answer. It's not exactly going to boost my low-as-dogshit self-esteem.

Dan pursed his lips and looked at the ground, breaking the eye contact and making me feel terrible. I noticed that the hallway no longer smelled of incense – something our house guests had always said they loved when they visited us. Then, I dug myself deeper: 'I've been worried about you. Sorry I haven't replied to any of your letters or answered your calls ... I've just been so busy with the move, and I wanted you to enjoy your holiday ...'

'It wasn't *a holiday*, Erin,' he began in his impossibly posh British accent that I'd once swooned over. Now, it made my jaw tighten like a vice. 'It was a break away to be with my cousins while you ripped my life apart by moving out. You told me to get out of your way. I wasn't going to stay around when I wasn't wanted.' His voice was cold and monotone, in stark contrast to how he'd spoken to me many moons ago, back when I'd agreed to marry him.

This was *us* now.

'"Wasn't wanted"? I never told you to leave – I just asked for some space to pack. Which isn't unreasonable. And, eh, you didn't seem to mind leaving a lot of *unwanted* voice messages at 3 a.m., or sending *unwanted* letters to my new address ... This is why I didn't want to come over.'

'I thought you were worried about me?'

'I *am*,' I snapped in a whisper, rather than admit that I was just trying to be nice. I took a step toward him, keeping my voice down so as not to attract attention from the nosy neighbours, Luke and Linda. 'But I also decided to move out because of *this*, remember? I can want the best for you and also want the best for myself, y'know? Can I please just come in?' I thought that would defuse the tension, but my sour-as-a-lemon ex wasn't having it. Turning his back to me and holding the door open, moving ever so slowly, he muttered, 'Yes, because this situation really is the best thing for both of us. I'm really *living my best life* right now, and you're positively *glowing*.'

Dan's sarcasm in *that* accent never failed to piss me off. I closed my eyes for approximately three seconds too long, to calm myself down, before following his lead into our – *his* house.

We walked in silence through to the kitchen. Along the way, sadness tugged at me as I realised that all of our photos had been removed from the walls; the outlines of the frames were barely visible in the lavender paint. I mean, I don't know what I'd expected. *Obviously* he was going to take the photos down. But it still hurt. More than I'd imagined it would. The house was so empty now, like a toy store after Christmas Eve. Even though it hadn't felt like home it'd had its own heartbeat once upon a time, and this was just … depressing.

Dan sat down at the kitchen table without offering me so much as a sniff of an Earl Grey teabag. Very unlike Mister Hospitality himself. I remained standing, and the silence became our room's ever-expanding elephant. A moment passed before I found some words. 'Can I have the big picture of us with Turnip?' I asked. 'You know, the autumny one, where we're all in the park? That's my favourite one, of him …' My eyes decided to surprise me then: they filled with tears for our adopted, gastrointestinally challenged greyhound. He'd died so long ago now. Perhaps it was the finality of seeing that naked wall – where pictures of Turnip had lived, when the house had been alive with his quirks and our gooing over him – making me want to cry. I refused to allow the tears to fall, though, and I wouldn't look at Dan.

Instead, I quickly observed the chaos that was the kitchen countertops: they were littered with empty packets of chilli Doritos and brown paper bags from the takeaway; with hollow cans of cider and dirty dishes; with boxes half-filled with our shared household items that I'd asked him to give to the local charity shop. (I could see a lime-green hand mixer I'd bought sticking out of one of them, which I'd used just once to do some 'healthy baking' that Dan hadn't been too enthusiastic about, moaning about how much he missed my 'dirty brownies'.)

After a moment of consideration, he replied, 'That's my favourite photo of *all* of us, together.'

'Yeah. Happier times.' I turned to look at him again. I met his eyes, and for milliseconds it was as though no time had passed since Turnip's death. We were a family. So much love. Comfort, and security, and routine, and sturdiness, and—

No.

We're not a family.

Turnip's gone.

This relationship is a skeleton.

Don't get sucked in.

Dan must have felt my demeanour flicker. 'I'd honestly rather keep it, Erin,' he said, folding his hands together.

'Well, can I have a copy of it, then? Please?' An awkward silence. 'Do you have to make everything so difficult?'

'I'm not making anything difficult. It just *is* difficult. How you can't understand that … For heaven's sake, just because you're fine doesn't mean I have to be, Erin.'

'Can you please stop saying my name like that? You always say my name too much when you're being dramatic. I'm not fine, and I'm also not here to fight with you. I'm here for my post. And … and to ask you to, to please stop asking me to get back together. We've had our second shot at this already, and our third – there comes a time when, when …'

Fourth time lucky?

No.

Dan leaned forward onto his lamp-post-long legs and placed his head into his hands, burying his almost-black eyes as he spoke. 'I don't want to fight either. Your letters, they're on top of the bread bin. Take the photo of us with Turnip. And … I just, I love you, OK? I can't imagine a future without you.'

Deep breaths. The distant buzzing of the next-door neighbour's electric shower. Fidgeting.

The 'I love you' didn't so much as make me flinch.

Why?

Am I heartless?

Why am I noticing Linda's feckin' shower noise? Dan's pouring his heart out. Listen to him.

'Ever since you left, I've felt like there are dozens of knitting needles sticking out of my brain. I'm not trying to be difficult, I just want a chance to prove to you that we can be happy again. I still want to marry you, despite it all … This love I feel for you, it's real. I'd never give up on us like you have.'

There it was again, that awful lump-in-throat feeling. I leaned against the rickety bookcase beside the chair Dan sat on and rested my head back on a shelf. There were no words left in me for our lost love. My head told me to flee, but habit was begging me to get down on my knees and embrace the man I'd agreed to marry on a weekend break to Disneyland Paris last year, where we'd bickered over every *where to eat* and *which ride to go on* and *shall we buy a pair of €25 Minnie Mouse ears for an Instagram picture* decision.

Everything about the atmosphere was sticky, rotten, uncomfortable.

I had all these thoughts but no desire to share them with him. Because I already had, over and over. And it hurt him when I shared my real feelings about us. I noticed Dan playing with his bottom lip as he studied me, waiting for me to respond. Then, 'I like your haircut. The fringe really suits you.'

This made me feel good, and I hated myself for it. I got the fringe cut because I was desperate for the attention of a stupidly attractive man with floppy hair and full lips who frequented my café. He smiled at me once, and another afternoon I saw him check out a woman who had a short, charming Parisian fringe and so I wanted one too, thinking he might like it. But of course, all I said to Dan was, 'Thank you,' before going silent again.

Why couldn't he have given me compliments when we were actually together?

Is it really too late?

'You know I still care about you,' I began, 'and that our time together was important because, I dunno, we learned stuff, I guess, but I just can't—'

A deep sigh. 'I don't want to hear it, Erin. Just take the letters, *please*. I'm dying here while you just pass some time.'

That's not fair.

This is awful for me, too, you arse.

'Please stop making this harder than it needs to be. I'm trying so hard, I am. I don't know what's left to say.'

Dan stood up to face me, feet away but still too close for comfort. 'Look me in the eye and say you don't miss me and mean it,' he demanded. I didn't want to. I just wanted my letters (and the picture of my dead dog, and some closure – that'd be nice). But I did it: I looked at him.

And I couldn't say it.

Deep down, I did miss him, even though I didn't completely *want* him. The confusion was cruel, the familiarity warm, and I really could have kissed him then. So many of our later kisses came after a back-and-forth like this. But I straightened my back, marched over to the bread bin and snatched up my letters. Then I dug through the stack of framed pictures, searching for Turnip's long, stupid, beautiful face, with all kinds of *um*s and *ah*s escaping my lips.

'This really is it, isn't it? The wedding isn't going ahead.' He said it this time like it was a fact he'd just learned. 'Mum's been so excited, Erin, she—'

I'm so done here.

'Dan, sod your mum, and sod this. I think we've had this same conversation about *a dozen times*. I'm sorry, I really am, I – I can't get married to please your mum. Look what I turn into when we talk? This clearly isn't good for me. I don't know *why*, I don't know where we went wrong. But—'

'Erin, since when do you say things like "sod it"? That's such a Reid thing to say.' He was right. And his rightness enhanced the wrongness of everything between us. My heart rate sped up and my stomach tightened – visceral reactions to Dan's distaste for Reid, my favourite one. 'I mean, who *are* you?' He was disgust, veiled with love. 'What happened to my sweet Irish girlfriend? Why are you *so* horrible to me sometimes?'

And then I left. I clutched the small bundle of envelopes to my chest, and, without the framed photo of us and Turnip, I darted through the hallway, where the ghosts of my memories watched me slam the kitchen door, hacking off the infected limb that was us.

'How did we get here, Erin? I don't understand!' he shouted after me.

Neither did I.

All I knew was that I needed to be anywhere but there, and that I wished with everything in me that I felt differently.

Feeling emotionally drained and with my rescued post propped up in Rusty's basket, I stopped by Freddy's Food Court on my way to my new home to pick up a freshly made salad from one of the cute food stalls, thinking it might undo the fact that I hadn't eaten a proper meal in days or weeks, opting instead for random bursts of anything smeared in icing. I was really starting to feel the lack of nutrition. My cells were crying and each one bloated.

There were two rows of stalls, selling foods of every variety, beneath strings of white fairy lights and surrounded by wall spaces covered in beautiful street art. Reid had recommended the food court as soon as I expressed my food-shopping-related apathy earlier that evening, and he knew better than anyone alive that the act of wasting money that I didn't have on dishes I could probably make myself came easily to me in times of *what am I doing with my life? Eating is good, I'll just eat now and fix things … some other day.*

One of the stalls offered up buttermilk chicken burgers smushed between brioche buns with all the fatty, flavourful trimmings. They smelled delicious.

Screw the salad.

Dan won't be seeing me naked ever again.

Why am I basing my burger-buying decision on Dan, or a lack of Dan? It's just a burger, Erin – get it and eat it, right here. Enjoy the shit out of it.

Nobody knows you here.

Starting over, again.

Again.

Alone.

Ugh.

3
Thirty

My phone alarm woke me the next morning in Old Willow – an unremarkable apartment block at the corner of an equally unremarkable street – where the scent of a fresh paint job in my newly rented bedroom hammered in *how much* I actually missed Reid's couch and how drastically everything in my life had changed.

I stared up at the high ceiling of Rachel's spare – *my* – bedroom, at its bare cream walls and the mountains of cardboard boxes that decorated it before noticing that I hadn't even pulled a cover onto my duvet before falling into bed. Regretfully high on burgers (and the blistering fear of starting over), I'd unpacked nothing, nor had I opened my post. With my duvet pulled tightly to my naked body to warm myself up in my cold sweat, I reached for the stack of five letters on my bedside locker.

The top white one, smeared with burger grease, had a

clear window on its front – most likely my phone bill. Then there was a small brown envelope with *Erin* scrawled across it, in Dan's blocky scribble, with a little love heart replacing the dot above the letter *i*. He'd probably slipped it into the pile long before my visit, outlining how perfect we were for each other and how wrong I was for thinking otherwise. I flung it across the room. Two more bills then that I didn't even want to open.

The final letter was medium-sized and fat, inside a pink envelope – the kind that comes free with cheap birthday cards. It was from Granny: I knew straight away by the flowery handwriting and the Irish stamps. Joy like Christmas morning poured over me then, like milk and honey dotted with warming cinnamon. My fear of telling her about the break-up was momentarily overshadowed by how terribly I missed her and her croaky singing after too many white wines; her home-baked apple tarts; the musty, smoky smell of her clothes. I shoved my apartment key under the envelope fold to tear it open, with far too many feelings prickling against the inside of my chest. The page inside (wrapped around a bar of Dairy Milk, my favourite chocolate) had been ripped from a lined copybook, which Granny had stacks of around her house for all of her word games and quizzes. The words were scribbled in blue biro:

Erin,

I'm really looking forward to the big day – the countdown begins! All the girls do be going on about it down the pub. Over the moon for my Erin and her Dan, they are! We're all doing well, myself and the pub group – all save for Chrissy, she needs herself a new hip.

I found myself a lovely lime-coloured frock in the town for the wedding, the kind of thing your grandad loved to see me wear for a dance when he was still alive, God rest his soul, and a new shawl. Thought I'd splash out for the special occasion!

Just writing to make sure you're still planning on coming home to celebrate your thirtieth with your oul' granny in two weeks? There's something I've been waiting almost thirty years to give you, and I'd like to do it before you're wed.

PS: It's not a wedding gift – something a little more special.

Love,

Peggy xxx

I didn't notice how much my hands were shaking until I'd read it three times over, and the last paragraph about five times over. 'There's something I've been waiting almost thirty years to give you, and I'd like to do it before you're wed.' It wasn't excitement at the prospect of a special gift making me vibrate, though. It was the knowledge that I had to drop a bomb on the poor woman. A new outfit? Granny *never* bought new clothes – she must have been living for the wedding.

I rummaged through my unpacked things to find my old tin biscuit box in which I kept paper, pens, envelopes and stamps – almost exclusively for Granny correspondence – and quickly scrawled out a reply. (It couldn't wait: my flight home was booked for nine days from now; this letter had likely been sitting atop our – *his* – bread bin for far too long.)

> Granny,
>
> I really can't wait to see you! New Year's Eve feels like a lifetime ago now ... To answer your question: YES, I'm still arriving on Saturday evening. I'll get a bus from the airport! So much to tell you ...

I considered including a forewarning, but I couldn't bring myself to write the words. If I wrote them, it meant that they were real, that there was no going back. Their echo would confirm that I was even further away from playing happy families now than I was only months ago. So I finished the letter there:

> All my love,
>
> Erin xxx

Then I shoved it (all stamped and addressed to Granny's beachside cottage) into my handbag.

I brushed my teeth while trying to fix the cow lick in my fringe and considered how very miserable it was that I didn't have enough friends to have a big thirtieth birthday party; that instead of going to London's biggest gay nightclub with Reid and his gaggle of mates, I was gasping to chill out with my alcoholic granny in her eighty-sixth year. Rachel's sprightly hum from the hallway snapped me out of my wallowing, though I couldn't help but roll my eyes against her zest for life. Then I resolved to get my arse to work before Kenneth fired me, rendering me a total failure. With no time for make-up, I pulled on my unwashed work uniform of white shirt and black trousers, scraped my hair up into a short ponytail and made my way to the kitchen.

While I rummaged through the cupboards looking for teabags and anything edible, Rachel bounced into my peripheral vision with what looked like a yoga mat.

Who actually wakes up and does yoga?

Who?

My new flatmate, apparently.

'Morning, girl,' she said, her voice like velvet. She wore her hair in braids, and there was a glow about her that made me sick with comparison. I could smear myself in Vaseline and I wouldn't glow like that. 'There's some sprouted grains soaking in the fridge, in the pink bowl ... some stevia mixed in there and some walnuts, too ... even some pink salt for digestion ... help yourself.'

I'd rather die wanted to jump from my lips, but 'I'm good, thanks. I'll eat in work' did instead. I glanced her way, caught one eyeful of her taut abdomen against the neon band of her yoga pants and immediately looked at the floor. The woman was simply standing there, in the apartment she owned, being kind and looking great and smiling a smile that could light up the world, but my envy buzzed around me like a fly that I couldn't swat. I couldn't let her read the frustration on my face. Keeping my eyes on my scuffed shoes, I wished her a good day and practically legged it out the front door and down ten or so

flights of stairs. (The lift was still broken – yes, moving in
had been a party.)

I cycle, I don't need to do yoga.

Maybe I should do yoga?

Might quell the constant fidgeting …

Granny still thinks I'm marrying Dan.

Feck.

I blundered down the stairway, handbag flailing behind
me, and crossed paths with a strangely familiar side profile
that I couldn't immediately place, not without seeing his
eyes: a man about my age and built like a mattress, broad
shouldered yet soft, in the process of trying to edge an
armchair up the stairs. I slowed down, noticing there
was very little room for me to get by. He turned to me to
mumble apologies for being in the way. His eyes were like
two bits of night sky, each with a moon melted in the blue;
they lingered on mine, and I was a teenager again.

'*Beglan!* Erin Beglan. A ghost of teen rejections past.
What've I done to deserve this?' He smiled the world's
biggest smile from the other side of the massive armchair.

'*Finn!*' I beamed, I couldn't not – his booming voice and
Irish accent, endless waves of nostalgia. Finn had been
part of my old group of mates from school. He'd nervously
asked me to be his date for the debs (our end-of-school
prom) one day, under the bridge where students gathered
to smoke cigarettes and drink alcopops and anything else
they could get their hands on, and in front of all of our
friends, too. I'd turned him down, partially because I was

mortified to be put on the spot like that. I'd never even *kissed* anyone at that point, and I didn't appreciate having so many people from school watch on and giggle as my boy-who-was-a-friend publicly declared his crush on me through a mouthful of brand new braces and cheap cider. Though the main reason I'd told him I couldn't be his date was the unfortunate fact that Finn's father and my father didn't see eye to eye. *At all.* The people from our village would only ever invite the Kellys *or* the Beglans to a Christmas get-together or a summer barbecue, never both families at the same time, for they'd refuse to breathe the same air under the same roof. It always bothered me that I had to lie to Dad about where I was going when Finn would invite me around with the rest of the gang to his converted attic (which, back then, we all thought was *incredibly* sophisticated), and I used to wish I could sneak over to the Kelly house more often. Pets included, their family boasted enough members to make up a Gaelic football team. Their place felt so much more *alive* than mine. There were always dirty plates everywhere and piles of folded-up clothes brought in from the line outside, and the one-toilet-between-ten-people situation caused chaos, but I loved it there. I lapped up the madness. And, sure enough, when I told my dad that Finn Kelly had asked me to the debs, 'over my dead body' and something about Oscar Kelly proposing to my mam while she was dating my dad spilled out of him in an angry rant.

'Well c'mere,' I said, 'I did save your suit from my

vomit, which I'm sure is a stain my debs date Georgie never washed away. What're you doing *here*?' My accent had suddenly turned up to eleven on the Irish dial.

'Georgie! Don't remind me about that gobshite,' Finn said, laughing. 'Well, as I'm sure you can see, I'm wrestling everything I own up these never-ending stairs. This is the last of it.' Standing at his full height, Finn put his weight onto his fists, leaning them on the top of the armchair in a power pose – a big change from his body language as a teen when he'd be forever slouched in school so as not to be noticed. 'I've just moved into the building,' he continued. 'Got myself a shiny new teaching post at King's College, so I'm mid-transfer from Brighton to grotty co-living here in the big smoke.'

A teacher.

How boring and anticlimactic. He used to boast about how he'd be the next Steven Spielberg.

God, I'm judgemental.

'Brighton? What brought you there? I always figured you'd have stayed in Dublin.'

I couldn't even remember when we'd fallen out of touch, though I'd never made the best effort to keep up with my old friends.

'Ah, I was … working. In Brighton. What about you, then?' Discomfort slithered across his face, and he evidently wanted to change the subject. 'Well, I knew you were in *London*, of course.' Confusion forced my mouth open. 'Facebook. I have the odd cheeky stalk …' he went

on, raising an eyebrow. His smile looked like it could save
lives. It was infectious. I couldn't relax my face, not even
to cover up the gap in my front teeth, which I usually did
my best to hide. But it was just Finn. I didn't need to be
self-conscious. No desire to impress him existed in me.
'You're the envy of all the gang back home, you know,'
Finn continued. 'Off living it up in London. I'm still in a
group chat with a load of them.'

Suddenly uncomfortable, I crossed my arms. 'Oh yeah?'

'Yeah. Sarah regularly shares your Instagram updates
with us all, adding comments like "lucky bitch" and "I'd
sell my soul to live somewhere where there's actual stuff
to do."'

'Ah yeah, life here is pretty fab,' I lied. It was about as fab
as a kick in the vag, but my beautifully curated Instagram
feed more than likely suggested otherwise. I only ever
shared pictures of art festivals and colourful meals from
hipster cafés – they were smooth, blonde highlights on a
head of dull and brittle off-brown hair. 'Well, eh, welcome
to Old Willow, I guess. How bloody *random* …'

Welcome to Old Willow?

Bitch, you've been here less than a week.

'Figured it was just Inishbeg that was small, but nope.
The whole of the world is 'n' all,' Finn said. We each
scrunched our lips up at the same time, then: the socially
inept person's go-to expression when there's an awkward
silence.

'Mm-hmm. *Anyway*, I've gotta go live it up, in … work,'

I said and did some batshit-mad version of jazz hands. His booming laugh. It was lovely, but what I said *really* wasn't deserving of it.

I bet he still fancies me.

That's cute.

'Ah yeah, go on. Sure we're neighbours again! We'll hang out soon?' He said it as though it were a question.

'Please, that'd be nice,' I said, nodding my head. 'I'm on the tenth floor!'

'Ah. I'm right under you.' Finn's ink-blue eyes flashed with mischief when it dawned on him how the words sounded.

He absolutely still fancies me.

Ego: stroked.

Don't get his hopes up, though. Don't flirt back. Withhold flirty banter for stupidly attractive customer at work with the floppy hair and full lips.

'I'm sure I'll bump into you,' I mumbled, awkward as a standing, breathing smear test, then, 'I really need to get going. I start work at 9 a.m., and I've to cycle, and—'

Finn held out a slightly-more-tanned-than-mine hand to help me scramble over his armchair. He was still no more than an inch taller than me but so much wider than when we were eighteen. His bulk matched his height now, and his pimples had been replaced by more freckles, which decorated the faces of all of his family members. I'd always loved the Kelly freckles. ' "Póigíní gréine" means freckles in Irish, but directly translates to "sun kisses"', his mam once told me.

He's certainly not my type, but he looks well. Good for him.

'Have a nice day, Beglan. Lovely surprise to see you.'

'You and all.' I meant it. Friendly faces were few and far between in London. We kept smiling at each other for a moment until I said goodbye and continued on with my blundering run. Outside, he quickly evaporated from my mind, like mist, and I mounted Rusty's wet saddle. It was time for another day of drudge in the Sugar Pot café.

I turned up 'Enjoy the Silence' by Depeche Mode to full blast and texted Reid before heading off, as I so often did:

I know you have herpes and Martin doesn't love you and all, but ... swap lives? I'd swap lives with my flatmate instead, only I think I'd hate myself if I were that perfect. She was doing YOGA.

He replied, as usual, almost straight away:

Stop being a jealous bitch and go to work. I love you xxx

Kenneth decided to hold my five-minutes-late over me all morning. His snarky comments amid showers of rude, blank-faced corporate heads had me almost worn down to the bone when the stupidly attractive man with floppy hair (wet from the day's rain) and full lips materialised at the counter before me, looking for an espresso. Today he wore matt Ray-Ban glasses and a pink shirt under a black suit. Androgynous could've been his middle name with those cheekbones, that jawline, those balmed, pouty lips, that walk – or, indeed, his first name, for I didn't even know that much about him, only that he seemed to be cast from a different mould than most people, boasting a perfect blend of masculine and feminine energy. He was Dan's complete opposite, and it intrigued me. I had those tingles that you get when something you want is within reach but you're not quite able to reach out and grab for it, like the desperation for dessert to arrive in a restaurant.

I hoped he would smile at me again.

So what that he's a firework?

Reid had talked about Martin from his office being a firework only last week – said he possesses the kind of beauty that's probably most beautiful from afar, just like a firework in the night sky, and that neither he nor I should *ever* reach out and clutch a firework. 'We need to admire those things from a distance if we want to stay intact, Beggy.'

You see Martin every day, I'd wanted to say, but not enough to actually fuel the conversation or Reid's defensiveness, of course. I was sick to death of talking about Martin, and I always did my best to change the subject.

But Reid's words had got to me, even still. I feared destroying this stranger's spell by making him human, by talking to him, but I was hungry for his want. My fringe wasn't looking anything even *close* to cute, but I ached for a distraction from Kenneth's incessant barking and mental images of my granny's face when I told her I'd probably die alone. The brief bit of attention Finn had given me that morning had picked me up, too – so much so that I *actually smiled* at the beautiful stranger before he could smile at me. But Stupidly Attractive immediately looked down at his phone and waited for his order. My cheeks warmed. Disappointment burned my chest. When I realised he wasn't going to return my smile, preferring a device without a pulse, I flattened my fringe and retreated into myself to make his espresso – a duty that didn't fall under my job description, but Kenneth was useless at hiring new people so he'd shown me how to use the machine on days when the full-time barista wasn't working.

'Owen!' some rowdy voice called. I turned around as Stupidly-Attractive-who-didn't-find-me-attractive beckoned me to bring the coffee to a table by the window, where a circle of suited men now waited for him.

Owen.

Owen and Erin.

Erin and Owen.

One of the suits raised a hand to catch my attention and pointed at a spot on the floor by his side, as if to say *bring his drink over here, peasant, also come hither and serve me, too, for I couldn't be arsed going over to you.* I watched Owen sit down and cross his legs, as though he moved in slow motion while the rest of the world couldn't go faster if it wanted to.

He didn't look back in my direction.

What about me is unappealing to him?

Why didn't he smile back at me?

Probably noticed my weird shape, my undesirable proportions. The hint of muffin top. The slight double chin. The Heartbreak Diet probably hasn't made as much of a difference as Reid let on.

Maybe he's just busy, Erin, how about that?

I wondered what his job was, and how many people he'd slept with, and how they looked naked, what they weighed, and whether or not he kept his socks on while he had sex, like Dan did, as the coffee machine churned out his espresso. Then I delivered it to him and his disinterest, only to stand there while several swanky-looking fellas fought to order with me first. I hoped he'd look up and give me the slightest bit of eye contact – a bubble of hope that he'd be my next chapter in Mission: Get-Over-Dan – but he didn't.

Usually, when I'd enter a room, Dan would look up at me and he'd smile, just because I was there. That had always been enough to make him happy. Why hadn't it been enough for *me?*

Days passed, a whirlpool of Kenneth and scrolling and rain and Rachel's happy-person humming.

Then it was midnight, officially my thirtieth birthday. There was no stir in the air, no something-fun-is-about-to-happen feeling, and so I hushed the part of myself that huffed internally over how much less meaningful this moment was than I'd hoped it would be. Nevertheless, that part of me didn't grow silent. It huffed louder against the bitter disappointment that was *everything*.

I was alone in my new bedroom unpacking my childhood drawings and cursing myself for being such a hoarder. As my bad mood peaked, Reid came to the rescue – as always. He sent me a happy-birthday video via WhatsApp. I watched him dance for me, shirtless and drunk in his swish hotel room (he was away on a work trip, rendering me Reidless for my birthday) and singing 'I Want to Break Free' by Queen, my favourite. He followed up the video with a text:

I hope you have a lovely time in Ireland, you disastrous cow. PLZ send me a photo of Peggy, for lolz xxx

I read it, smiling, but with no urge to reply. Reid already knew that I disapproved of how regularly he'd been drinking since Martin's wedding and of his brand-new addiction to dating and hook-up apps. All I'd reply, if I were to reply, would be a laughing face emoji, so I left him on 'seen'. Dad had messaged from abroad, too, but there were none from anybody else.

No message from Dan.

Maybe he's finally … given up?

That's what I wanted. For him to move on.

Right?

And there were no messages breathing life to my

barren wasteland of a Facebook profile either, aside from the generic 'Happy bday' posts from people I'd met about once in my life and who likely felt obliged to comment by Facebook's nudge of *hey, this person is one year older and that bit closer to death, so go congratulate them.*

Even the people I'd chosen to pad out my wedding with weren't messaging me.

The cheek. As far as they're concerned, I'm broken-hearted.

What would happen if I needed to go to hospital right now? Who do I have down as my next of kin?

Dan.

Dan.

Did I just never have friends – apart from Reid, *obviously* – as an actual adult? Or had I shoved my head so far up my relationship's arsehole that they were simply forgotten about?

Rachel, who I'd *not* informed about my birthday because I'd been avoiding her like someone with a snotty flu, sounded like she was having the night of her life next door with a female caller (some girl called Fiona – that's as much as I picked up by eavesdropping as they paused multiple times for sloppy-sounding kisses along the hallway, from the front door right down to Rachel's bedroom). My jealousy of her sexual liberty clawed at me. I put my things away in silence as her bed frame rattled against my wall and noted the proverbial dust that had gathered on my vibrator as Rachel moaned in apparent ecstasy. Then I placed the glittery, pink bullet in my top drawer and covered it with knickers – a habit I'd formed while living with Dan. He'd always been a little bit intimidated by the pleasure I could give myself with its buzzing plastic contours. I wondered if I'd ever meet someone adventurous enough to allow me to use it while they watched me, and then I felt guilty for *yet again* thinking about the Next Man chapter and imagined Reid wagging his finger at me.

After unpacking, and with my mind half-cleansed of love and sex daydreams, I checked in on my blog. The terrible pixelated artwork and the clunky interface made me wince. Even though I was very alone in my room, I pushed my tongue out in a performative faux-vomit expression at the 'content' I'd been posting.

Erin's View ... ugh.

What a perfectly manky blog name.

It was full of farted-out, out-of-date social commentaries on whatever was trending that week on Twitter: celebrity meltdowns, pro-life marches, who got butt augmentations and what butt augmentations tell us about society at large. Dan always seemed completely disinterested when I'd chat to him over dinner about ideas for my blog. Maybe he was trying to do me a favour.

Why would anybody read this?

How did I think I could turn this into a career?

Even I don't want to be here, and I wrote the damn posts.

I had four new followers. Four, in three weeks.

Who are these mad bastards?

I wondered what kind of content I'd be posting if I hadn't blindly turned down the internship as a photojournalist with Miracle Media, if that experience would've squeezed some drips of talent out of me. Dan had advised me to try and go it alone, and while I'd appreciated his vote of confidence at the time, I often wondered how differently life might have panned out if I'd taken them up on the offer. Maybe Dan would've enthusiastically nodded along as I talked about my blog posts; maybe I'd have been much happier not having to rely on him, and my dad, for handouts. Maybe I'd be proper famous right now, with my own Netflix documentary series. 'You'll make it all on your own, Erin,' Dan had said.

I've made it, alright.

Made it to thirty with fuck-all savings and a CV fit for use as toilet paper.

After lamenting that I had no birthday cake and no gifts to open, I dragged myself into the bathroom (which stank of Rachel's weird 'natural and home-made' bath products: lavender and something else too strong and powdery for human noses) to shower to 'Don't You Want Me' by The Human League and to have a little 1 a.m. cry.

I won't even get to see Granny until tomorrow night because I booked a stupid late flight. I'll be spending most of my big birthday all alone.

Good.

Standard.

This is thirty.

4
Granny's Surprise

It was the next day, the day of my birthday, and the day that would lay to rest my wondering how Granny would take the announcement of my wedding's demise. I expected her to be sad. And a bit (or a lot) drunk. I anticipated that she'd tell me to rethink my decision to leave Dan, to hold on and sort things out, *Because for better or for worse, till death do us part, Erin*, and I wondered if I'd nod along and agree with her before calling Dan up and saying, *This has all been a big wobble and I'm sorry and please forgive me.*

But my gut told me to prepare for a queer day of peculiarity.

With my red luggage on wheels stowed above my head, I nervously took off in an Airbus to Dublin as the day approached sunset. The window seat in my row was empty as the plane lifted into the air so, after ordering a ham and cheese sandwich on white bread from the overly friendly air hostess, I dragged my bum to plant it by the window so I could look out upon London's lights, to watch the buildings shrink to the size of bits of Lego.

My travel anxiety melted away over the course of the hour-long flight. Eighties classics kept me company via Spotify, drowning out the cries of small kids as their ears popped, and the sandwich really hit the spot; it sat solid in my belly, gurgling away as the sky turned delicious shades of orange and pink. Home's outline gave me that lump-in-throat feeling as it always did, even from that distance and especially that day.

This was my first trip to Ireland without Dan in years.

Although I couldn't make out the beautiful greens of the fields in twilight, I knew they were there and that the island was welcoming me home with open arms, an older, still unsuccessful and now also very lonely me.

I silently cried into my denim jacket sleeve as the plane descended and hoped that nobody would notice, and I tried to remember what ten-year-old Erin had imagined she'd be doing when she turned thirty. She had spent hours creating drawings of the loving family she so desperately wanted, drawings I'd sorted through while unpacking and that had made it into last night's nightmares. I was pretty sure little me never thought her adult self would be stupid enough to end up almost married to the wrong person, plating up cupcakes most days and taking orders from people who looked right through her as though she were a window. *At least I lived to see thirty, unlike Mam ... Be thankful for that at least.*

Bit morbid, Erin, my inner Reid said. *Look, I'm your family. Me, your dad and your granny. That's your lot. Deal with it.* And then my face, bloodshot eyes and all, relaxed as I gazed out the plexiglas oval upon Dublin Airport.

Forty-five minutes later, I arrived outside Granny Beglan's cottage in Inishbeg, along Dublin's coast. Her home stood short, wide and smeared in ugly cream pebble-dash under a pitch-black sky, with a view of the quaint harbour and the glimmer of all its pubs and restaurants. Her garden was wildly overgrown with grass and shrubbery, though Granny's weeping cherry-blossom tree right in the middle distracted from all that with its pale-pink magnificence. Granny was a bit obsessed with trees; she'd planted this one in her late sixties to represent the fragility of life (or something soppy like that) after my mam's death. She'd even named the tree after Mam: Áine. After all, she'd treated Mam like she was her own child, though the gesture had mostly been for Dad. Mam's passing broke him. A copper plaque inscribed with her name hung a few feet up the trunk.

Once upon a time, I couldn't look at the tree without falling apart, but now it warmed me and put a smile on my face against the night's drizzle.

I stepped into Granny's porch and knocked hard on the peeling blue paint of the front door three times, fizzing with excitement, the lamplight in the porch like the glow inside me, knowing I was about to see my favourite person in the entire world.

Her windows were blurred with net curtains and raindrops. I couldn't tell if she was coming to answer the door, so I knocked again, eager to see her face. Then, a crash from inside the house. 'Granny? Granny, you alright?' Her deep, croaky voice burbling; the sound of fumbling: I was close to throwing my suitcase through the window beside the door to get in, to make sure she was OK, but then I heard her remove the chain from the latch, and I could breathe.

My fidgeting stopped completely.

Seconds of ghost-quiet.

The door creaked open to reveal a wisp of a woman with a wizened face whose tired green eyes drowned in folds of skin, thin as paper. The sight of her white whiskers and the silver-blue tinge of her freshly dyed hair brought the biggest gap-out smile to my face. She came at me, walking stick in hand and cooing my name, then she threw one twiggish arm around me for a brief moment. (Granny's hugs were half-hugs and always brief – Dad had once said 'our family don't do hugs'.) Her left-hand tremor shook against my neck before the strength in her arm went and she wrapped her free, tiny hand around one of mine. Her fingers were fridge cold.

'I've missed you *so much*. What was that big bang?' I laughed.

'That was Meryl, dear. Meryl and Molly, the two bitches,' she said of her beloved tabby cats, who were nowhere to be seen. 'Knocked over one of me candles, Meryl did ...' She looked down at the hem of her long, shapeless dress, and it appeared she'd just almost been set ablaze.

'How many times have I told you *not* to leave candles burning when they're in the house? For feck's sake, Margaret!' I always called her by her *full* first name when I was trying to get a serious point across, especially when that serious point pertained to her drinking problem and the repercussions that often resulted (like the time she passed out in the bath and somehow lived to tell the tale). But she just laughed, and I couldn't help but laugh too as we looked from the black burn mark on her skirt back to one another with a special fondness.

My nose quickly picked up the scent of Granny's stew. She asked if I had room inside me for 'a little feast', and I responded with all the enthusiasm I could muster, but then she added, 'Let's get in 'n' get warm, and you can tell me why there's no engagement ring on this here finger.'

I realised that my left hand was intertwined with hers.

My skin prickled with shock, but then absolute calm seeped through my veins: Granny was still smiling, and her voice was knowing. After a few seconds of wordless communication – the kind you can only experience with family and close friends – together, we headed into the cottage.

I'd been a child in these rooms. The familiar brocade

wallpaper and carpets along with the heavy, dusty feel of
the dark oak furniture brought me right back to my youth,
hiding in the house's nooks and crannies while playing
hide and seek with my parents (and then just Dad, after
Mam died when I was eight). I had no siblings and no
cousins, and so the adults (and the invisible characters
born of my mind) had been my companions for many
years.

'Wine? Tea?' Granny asked, after pottering ahead
to the distant hum of Lyric FM on the radio. She was a
hunched silhouette against the blast of orange light from
the kitchen.

'Ooh, tea, please, and one … *two* sugars,' I replied,
holding back to peer into the living room and up the
stairway at Granny's little universe and all the eyes gazing
down on it from the walls.

'Two, now, is it? Troubled times are giving ye a sweet
tooth, I see.'

I looked at her, biting my lip.

'Oh, ye would've loved the sugar sandwiches we ate
back in my day on school lunch break, Erin,' she continued
from the doorway, then croaked, 'Go sit by the fire, get
warm. I'll bring ye some stew and sugary tea.'

I couldn't believe how *normal* she was being,
considering …

I thanked her before looking back up at the walls.
Multiples of the same few faces: mine (at various ages)
and my mam, looking like a well-fed goddess with her

cascading ginger curls and the full figure that had famously been the envy of every woman in Inishbeg. I certainly knew where I got my wide-as-a-horse's-saddle hips. There were portraits of Dad, too – tall, thin and very *Dan*-looking, but with a moustache and a receding hairline. And, of course, old photos of Granny and Grandad together, like the kind of couple you see in the pictures that come with picture frames in shops: burning with happiness and in perfect harmony with one another. Their chemistry was legendary amongst Granny's friends down the pub. 'Johnny Cash and June Carter didn't have bugger all on Peggy and James,' Chrissy-with-the-bad-hip once told me, sherry in hand.

As I sat by the dirty fireplace and its dying embers, Granny piled into the room with a cup of tea and a too-full glass of white wine for herself before scurrying out and returning with our supper. Stacks of buttered batch bread accompanied by lamb stew. I salivated and then tucked right in. After some small talk about my flight and bus journey while we ate, I cupped my tea in my hands and pondered how to bring up everything about Dan and the wedding, as Granny explained (in great detail) how she'd long forgotten what it felt like to have her joints move freely and without the throbbing pain of arthritis. 'But it won't kill me, I tell ye. Nothing will. Doctor Andrew confirmed I'm a medical marvel.'

Here we go again.

'My aches and pains are like old friends, but I manage,'

she said knocking back the white-wine elixir that had likely pickled her insides over the years, apparently blessing her with this long life and relatively decent health. Then she lit up a menthol cigarette.

I had to say something. It had been eating me from the inside out for too long – it was climbing up my throat, but I didn't know what *it* was—

'He wasn't the one, then? Your Dan. Well, not *yours* any more,' she said, her eyes kind. She glanced down again at my ringless finger as she sucked on her minty death stick.

'I don't think so, Granny. But, I don't, um … I don't really *believe* in "the one",' I began, surprised to hear myself say this, considering my upbringing (injected with Disney-movie endings and Dad's endless love-ballad renditions as Mam watched him with puppy eyes, smitten as she always was), but Granny cut me off.

'Jim was the one for me, the only one. I wish he'd lived long enough to have met ye … Ah, if you'd seen us together, Erin—'

'I know you really liked Dan,' I said, eager to change the subject before she dived into her soulmates spiel.

'Loved that boy, I did. The way he looked at ye. Having him around was like having another son of me own,' she said, genuine disappointment etched into her face. 'I've only one boy, Erin. We wanted so many babes, me 'n' Jim, wanted a farmhouse full of babes. I was fierce old giving birth to yer da, and …' Granny looked into the fire and I heard the words unsaid.

Suddenly it hit me just how sad it was that Dan would no longer be around for our Irish Christmases of Cadbury Selection Boxes for breakfast, Christmas cake, Dad falling asleep from turkey overload during Granny's recordings of *The Late Late Toy Show*.

I wanted her to understand, though. Her, more than anyone.

'It was like drowning, Granny. You and Grandad … it always sounded like it felt right, for both of you. I know it can't always have been easy, but it *worked*, right? Dan and I just stopped working.' She was still watching me as the fire crackled. I could tell she wasn't going to interject again. It was as though she could feel how difficult it was for me to purge these words from my brain before her. Each word was heavy as a brick leaving my mouth. 'I would lie awake at night thinking about having his children. He was dying to be a dad, you know that—'

'He was. He asked me if I'd knit their first jumpers.'

'But I couldn't see it in my mind, you know? Us having our own family. Me being Mrs Fernsby, with mini Fernsbys following me around the place. Like, I couldn't picture him as a father to … to *my* kids, anyway.' Meryl (or Molly – they both looked the bloody same) came in and interrupted me. She purred and meowed and curled up on Granny's lap. Granny stroked her, and I sipped my tea. I went on: 'When I'd visualise my wedding, the person I was marrying was all blurred out as if, subconsciously,

I knew it wasn't going to be Dan. That *we* weren't right, and – I felt this way for so long – but you know me, all I've ever wanted is—'

'A big family of yer own,' she finished for me, as I caught my breath. '"Granny! Granny! I want four daughters, like in *Little Women*", ye used to look up and tell me every time you visited, when ye were small.' I welled up. 'So ye stayed with him. Ye wanted to put things right. But ye couldn't.'

'Yeah. Pretty much. All the rest wasn't worth it for sole access to his ball sack.' Granny howled. I loved her laugh. 'Anyway, yeah, and I figured, *I've given it so many years, what's one more?* But as I get older I'm realising a year is a long feckin' time.'

'Wait till yer my age. Ye blink and yer a year older.'

'Oh, Granny,' I half-cried, half-laughed. 'Everything is crap. I miss him, but we're all wrong for each other. And my job is a pain in the arse. What if I've missed my chance at, well, being happy? What if … what if I never have my own family?' The words caught in my throat like shoe tips on pavement edges as they came out. 'Or a job that I actually like? What if I always feel this way?'

'Ah, yer only a young thing. I used to think that way about the ballet, at your age. Always wondered how life would've been if I'd followed that dream …'

A delicate stillness.

'I thought you *were* a ballet dancer?' I asked. She didn't answer me. Her jowls pulled back into a small smile as she looked down at the grey ball of fluff lying on her bony knees on its back, tummy out for the rubs. I started worrying.

What if she's finally losing her marbles?

Alzheimer's?

No!

Can't be.

Though, I haven't seen her for months …

'You … you told me all about it when I was young. By the beach, remember? We were having a picnic.' She remained silent. 'The pain you had in your toes, you described it in such detail it made me *hate* the idea of being a dancer. You talked about the diet you were told to stick to and the competitiveness. With the other girls … Florence was given the part you wanted …'

Hoarse laughter. 'I'm so glad I never went and did that. Being a farmer's wife is nothin' to turn the nose up at. 'Twas a good life, mine.'

'Were you lying to me, then?' I raised an eyebrow. She continued to laugh and smoke and pet the cat. 'Granny. You won a medal. I told everyone,' I said, tightening up in my chair. I considered calling Dad when I left to go to bed. Suddenly Granny stubbed out her cigarette, threw it into the fire and bundled herself out of the room.

'Where are you …? What are you doing?' This was so unlike her. I didn't follow her – I was frozen. My mind galloped on ahead of itself. What if I needed to move home to look after her? She'd sooner walk into a heavy tide and drown than go into an old folks' home, and Dad was off living his best life with Sienna, the 'free spirit' who simply 'can't' live in one place for long or she'll 'lose her sparkle'. Who else *is* there?

The curse of the tiny family. Fewer people to rely on when shit hits the fan.

She was back within moments. The walking stick was in the door before she came in after it, an unopened bottle of white wine under one arm and a small olive-coloured cardboard box with a cheap, plastic red bow stuck on top – the kind you put on Christmas presents – clutched in her free hand. I just watched her, clueless as to where her head was at. The big burn mark on her skirt combined with her forgetfulness had me fidgeting once again.

She's supposed to be invincible. A constant. One of the four legs holding up the table that is me.

'Yer thirty years old now, love. It's finally time for me to tell ye. Have some wine – wine took the edge off when *my* ma told *me*.' She opened the screw cap bottle with her tiny, trembling-with-age fist and held it out, prompting me to hold out my empty tea cup.

'Should I … go get … a glass?'

'This can't wait any longer,' she replied, struggling to hold up the bottle. I allowed her to pour some wine into my cup, but I was too on edge to drink it.

What's going on?

'What's in the box?' I asked. 'Is this the *thing* you mentioned in your letter?'

She gathered her thoughts, drinking more wine. 'This is

going to sound a bit mad, Erin. Drink up and bear with me.'

'Granny, I don't want any wine.'

'Well, ye will in a minute.' She opened the cardboard box to reveal a pendant – a black stone wrapped in copper wires that were tightly shaped into a bare-looking tree. Slowly and carefully, she took it out and held it up to show me how long the chain was. By the firelight it looked age-old, but at the same time like something you'd see hanging in a trinket shop while on holiday in the south of Spain.

'A tree-of-life necklace? You and your trees!' I laughed. I didn't want to sound unappreciative, so I continued, 'It's, eh, really pretty.' That was a lie. It was clunky and old-fashioned, unlike any of the minimal rose-gold chains I usually wore.

'This is a family heirloom, passed down by the women in our family for centuries,' she said, displaying the stone part preciously against a veiny, wrinkled hand. 'My ma, Mary, gave it to me on me thirtieth birthday. She received it from her ma when she turned thirty, and so on!' She was way too excited to be talking about a pendant. Her voice was animated, as though she'd rehearsed this a thousand times. 'Erin ... *this*,' she clutched tightly at the copper-wrapped stone, 'gives us Beglan women the ability to live out a day in another life – one we could've had based on decisions we made in the past. It gives us a sight into how our lives might've played out had we done things differently. It's a gift from God Almighty.'

I just stared blankly at her.

I'm losing her.
Should I play along with this talk of alternate realities?
No. Don't encourage it.
Ignore it.
And don't mention the devastating void of religious faith.

'Ehm, Granny, have you spoken to my dad recently? When is the last time he actually visited? We really do need to get you a phone, y'know ...'

'I told ye it would sound mad, but ye need to trust yer oul' granny!'

OK, so ignoring it doesn't work.
Lesson learned.
I'll need to buy some books on Alzheimer's back in London.

'If that's true, show me then. Use it,' I ordered, deadpan. I had no idea where this was going, but it didn't feel like it was going somewhere good. 'I can't. Not any more, love. Only you can,' she said, as though she were telling me that leaves are green or that she loves wine. She lit up another minty death stick.

'Why?'

'Well, ye see, it can only be used seven times by each of us.'

'Why seven? Why not ... eight?'

She considered that for a moment. 'Why any?' she replied, giggling like an unwell, choking schoolgirl. Confusion tickled the inside of my chest. The anxiety butterflies took flight.

'OK, so, if you're *not* talking shite—'

'Which I'm not.'

'*If* this were real it would be, like, time travel?'

'No, love. Listen to me now. Ye experience a *vision* of what effect a different choice in the past might've had on yer current life, the only life ye know. No time will've passed in this here *real* life, while ye can spend up to *one full day* experiencing this other reality. And after, it'll feel like a vivid dream,' she excitedly went on, eyes flittering as though she were telling me about last night's episode of her favourite soap opera.

This was all oddly elaborate to be coming out of her sheltered, very religious brain. Very *Doctor Who*.

But wait, no, it's not time travel. Not the past, or future, but ... a different present? Where in the Bible does it say actual magic is a thing? 'You said this pendant is a gift from God, Granny. Why?'

'Well, He created everything,' she said plainly, certain of her words. 'There's rhyme and reason to His actions. If you use the gift wisely ye may find peace, and if ye use it foolishly ye may meet regret. Which'll give ye more wisdom – *or not*,' she warned, pointing a crooked finger at me. There was sense in her babbling, which made me feel even more anxious. She wasn't confused about where she was or who I was, like your typical character with dementia in a TV show or movie; she was saying things that she'd never, ever say. I stood up to pace a little. I needed to move my body. Worrying about my own health messed me up enough, but worrying about Granny's – that was a bath overfilled.

'Where did it come from, then?' I decided to keep her talking, hyper-focused to see if she'd say something to confirm that her memory was crumbs.

'Great-great-grandmother Beglan was given it by a blackbird from Lighthouse Island.'

Here we go.

'She talked to the birds when she felt she'd made all the wrong turns in life. We suspect the bird was *actually* a—'

A bird?

This is far worse than I thought.

I cut in, panicked by how in-depth her story was becoming. 'Eh, how do you use it? To ... see other ... life paths or whatever?'

'Ah. Just you watch!' She was so *utterly* enthusiastic. 'Ye clutch it tight in one hand, like this,' she demonstrated, 'and express a wish to see an alternate version of yer life, with the magic words, "If only". Ye hold the thought in yer mind, real hard. My first one was "If only I'd emigrated to become a ballerina, instead of marrying my James".' She looked up at a portrait of them together and smiled a thin-lipped smile that was lost in skin that hung with age.

I couldn't stop pacing, and I didn't want to look at her any more. Instead, I glanced at my handbag and wondered if I should just skip the phone call to Dad and call a doctor instead. She wouldn't stop. 'Now, remember, what ye say has to be based on a decision rooted in yer own past. Don't think yer gettin' anywhere with "if only I won the Lotto".'

How come she never told me stories like this as a child?

This is some quality stuff.

'But ye can leave sooner than a day if ye like, by clutching this, like so, and visualising yerself coming to, snappin' back.'

'Oh yeah? It's that easy?'

'It's that easy,' she said, mid-puff of her ciggy.

'Um, well, why do we only get handed down this heirloom when we're thirty?'

'At thirty, a woman should almost know herself like the palm of her hand, and this helps with the *almost*. In the hands of someone younger, such a gift could be catastrophic.'

I don't know myself at all.

I'm as lost as I was when I was eighteen.

'Why don't the boys in the family get the chance to try this baby out, huh? Why not Dad?'

'Our brains work differently,' she concluded, after thinking on her answer for a few seconds.

Wow. 'So you were told *not* to give this to Dad?'

'Well, no, Erin. My ma just told me it was intended for the women in the family. Women, because of our female intuition.'

2019 Twitter would truly despise my granny. 'What if I want to give it to my future son?'

'See what happens.' She smiled, eyes flashing. 'But first, ye need to use yer own seven sights.' She held out the pendant to me. So much love radiated from her. I rolled my eyes and took it from her. It was much heavier than

I expected. Then I plonked myself down on the couch, feeling defeated.

This is it.

This is Granny now.

I either play along or make her feel terrible and chance sparking some kind of … fit.

Does that happen in senile people?

Random fits?

I don't want to find out.

'Right. OK,' I began as I threw the copper chain around my neck. Immediately I noticed that it didn't feel like a cheap pound-store piece. Not at all. It felt important, otherworldly. 'Granny, you do realise that in about ten seconds you and I will be having some serious words?' She grinned at me and popped her top denture off and on to her gums to make me laugh, like she'd done for years. 'I mean it, ha. If you're trying to make a fool out of me, which you obviously are for some mad reason, I'll be telling all the girls down the pub tomorrow that you're awful, that I'm disowning you.'

'Oh, ye won't be saying a *word* to them!' Her expression turned grim. 'This is a family secret,' she said, so sincerely, reaching across and gripping my knee with a cold, gnarled hand. '*Our* secret. Your da doesn't even know. He can't know. Nobody can.' I chose not to reply. I didn't think I could keep a lid on the condescension ready to erupt from me. 'Try it. Go on! Hold the words yer about to say in yer mind, like ye would a newborn in yer arms,' she finished.

I sighed and decided to speak the first relevant thing that entered my brain, to play along – play, as I had done for the first chunk of my life in this very room. *What would make the biggest difference to my life right now?* I thought of what Reid had said about me losing weight and how it had made me feel. *What if I were skinny?* I brought the thought and others like it to the forefront of my brain from where they lived, rent-free, in the depths, chipping away at my self-esteem for all these years. *What if I were fit?* What if I looked like the women on Instagram and in magazines? Thin and toned, like the woman with the cute Parisian fringe that I'd caught Owen gawping at in the café …

Before I spoke, I contemplated how she'd react when nothing happened. Then, to the purring of cats and the flick of Granny's lighter and the snap of the fireplace, 'If only I'd stuck to the diet and exercise routine that I started in uni … '

5
Thinner

My phone alarm: 'Sweet Dreams' by Eurythmics.

I floated up from a black sleep. For a moment I lingered in that place between dreams and reality before stretching myself and picking the crisp gunk from the inner corners of my eyes. I grabbed my phone to shut it up and noticed the time.

6.00 a.m.

What? I'm not due in to work for three hours.

Something felt off inside me. I was an alien. Pins and needles, briefly, everywhere. I was old and young and right and wrong, all at once. My throat tightened as I worried I was coming down with something and that I'd have to miss a day of work (and a day of much needed pay).

Rachel's voice: 'Hey, birthday girl, get that booty out here right this instant – there's *a man* joining us this morning, and he's waiting. I've filled our water bottles, let's *go* so we can earn that birthday cake!'

Why am I not in Granny's living room any more? Why am I in bed? And why is this bitch talking to me before I've entered shared territory?

'Eh, coming,' I said, confused as a cat covered in strips of tape. I hopped out of bed then – it came naturally to do so, though I hadn't done that in years. Getting out of bed was usually a tedious process, involving multiple snoozes.

I looked around and choked. The scattered morning light that tiptoed through the blinds showed me that there were no cardboard boxes piled around my room any more. Almost everything was packed away, apart from my old CD collection, which was stacked in front of my shitty IKEA shelving unit. I noticed workout gear that *wasn't mine* neatly folded on top of the wooden stool of my dressing table and a pair of trainers at the foot of it, along with a small, open backpack.

Instinctively, I jolted a few feet to get a mirror view of myself. Every hair on my body stood on end as I looked at my reflection.

That's not me ... is it?

No.

Yes!

My birthmark – on my upper left thigh, shaped like a map of Australia. There it was, unchanged. But, Christ, my legs were more shapely than they'd ever been – even more so than during my stint lifting weights for a few months during uni. The skin on them was pasty as ever, but taut, pulled over semi-developed muscles. I examined them in my low-rise knickers and noticed that my upper thighs were still covered in silvery stretch marks, but there was much less of my lumpiness, less cellulite. My legs looked longer and more slender than I'd considered possible and, somehow, my thighs no longer touched.

Curiosity pulled my strings and made me tug up my old baggy *Star Wars* T-shirt for a peek. My waist, it was … *there*. It existed. I had a waist. The love handles that Dan had so often brought my attention to, calling them *lovely*, were gone; my hips were now the widest part of my lower body. I had no abs, but a hint of core strength winked at me through two lines stamped into my obliques.

I kept tugging at my shirt to see all my parts in the mirror.

Fuck, my arms – toned, slim, with no jiggle – hanging from defined shoulders.

My chest was a graveyard: RIP, tits.

However, everything else looked how I'd always dreamed of it looking. I was still nothing like the girls on the covers of magazines, but I was the image of the photoshopped version of myself I'd created during photo-editing classes at the University of London. I'd edited myself skinny while I was supposed to be editing the background of some generic urban-landscape shot. And now, somehow, edited-me existed, right before my eyes.

After I'd finished ogling my body with my mouth

hanging open, I focused on my face's reflection – my hands out before me as though to protect me from a fall. My hair was long and up in a high ponytail that brushed the skin halfway down my back. I took a step closer to the mirror to appreciate the length, as though I were momentarily in a lucid dream and *un*confused.

I didn't recognise myself.

Rachel, again: 'Babe, if we don't leave now, we won't be able to do the full 10K! You be long?'

10K? K as in kilometres? Is she having a laugh?

My thoughts swirled like a masterfully cut flashback scene in a film. Then I noticed the pendant hanging from my neck. An image came to me, of me sat snug in Granny's cottage, clutching this pendant. It was like a fleeting memory from my teenage years – the kind you can't catch hold of and keep, the kind that vanishes as quickly as it comes.

Maybe Granny wasn't lying. Or maybe I've just ... passed out, somehow, and I'm imagining all of this fuckery. Do I just wait until I wake up? No, no, I can go back ... she did say that, right? If I clutch this and imagine myself back with her?

Everything was foggy ...

'I'll be one minute – eh, I got my period,' I called to Rachel. *How am I meant to know if that's the kind of thing I'm comfortable saying to Rachel in* any *reality where we've fast become friendly? Sod it. This obviously isn't happening. There won't be consequences – or will there be?* I couldn't remember exactly what Granny had said – I'd been too busy worrying that she'd start calling me by my mam's name, not that maybe she was actually handing me *literal magic*.

What've I gone and done?

Why am I not having a panic attack?

Was the wine she gave me spiked?

Erin, it's not real. It has to be a vivid dream or something. Go through the motions.

Getting undressed and then dressed with this body was stimulating. I was playing with a human-sized doll: I could have stood there for hours – pulling up and down a pair of tight jeans, zipping them up so that they actually sat right on my waist for once and didn't dig into it leaving deep red indented marks on my skin, my usual dressing-room experience. I turned this way and that, admiring my sculpted, lean figure as soft orange-hued rays from the window contoured my bare skin.

But Dan loves my curves. This worry came and went – of what *he'd* think – within seconds. *So what if I'm too-straight-up-and-down for Dan? We've clearly broken up, regardless, in a world where I'm skinnier because … I'm living here with Rachel.*

And I look bloody fantastic.

I desperately wanted to take a nude on my phone to show Reid. I'd seen his nudes. They were glorious. *Nobody* had seen my nudes because they didn't exist. 'I don't want blame for causing distressing night terrors,' I'd told Reid when he questioned me about how I'd never taken or shared a naked photo of myself.

'Erin! Hot man. Waiting. Downstairs. I'll leave without you,' Rachel yelled, her voice dripping with cheery seriousness. And with that I was dressed in thirty seconds. I cupped the empty sacks of skin that had been my breasts and mushed them into the sports bra, hid the pendant amid the mush, then checked out my perky arse in the mirror before bundling myself out of the apartment with a stranger to real-world-me who seemed to be well-acquainted with skinny-world-me.

Perhaps I'm – friendlier – in this other life?

Maybe we bonded over something?

Together we bopped down the stairway through foreign gym-bunny small talk when all of a sudden I felt it: a deep hunger pang, radiating through my entire middle. 'Will the Starbucks around the corner be open?' I asked, as though the fact we were going running together was completely normal, 'so I can get a muffin or something before we start? My insides are screaming at me for a feed.'

'Um, a muffin?' She raised an eyebrow. 'Girl! I thought you don't do carbs? Thought you don't even like sweet things? I mean, I *did* offer to prepare my raw date and almond energy bars, but then you were all "dates cause diabetes ..."' she slagged, her doe eyes confused.

'Oh, ha, yeah, ah – I'm having a laugh: Irish humour. It'll take you a while ...'

I hope she's stupid enough to buy that recovery.
'You're funny. A *muffin*.'
She is stupid.
'I would actually *love* to see you get some porridge into you. It's healthy! Honestly, those cravings for processed carbs will go away if you just eat real carbs. Wholefoods. And speaking of Irish humour, I'm hoping to spend a *lot* more time with Mister Ireland from downstairs. So maybe soon I'll get your strange jokes,' she said, laughing. Damn, this girl is wild; just two days ago she was splitting open in orgasmic delight with Fiona, and now she's on about some new guy. 'Hope you don't mind me inviting him, by the way', she went on. 'It's just hard for me to fit in dates, y'know, with both my jobs. All work and no play … I'm not about that life.'

The whine of my empty stomach distracted me from what she was saying.

I guess in this reality I run 10K and don't eat first?
Well … shit.

Rachel and I pushed through Old Willow's entrance doors to meet her morning date outside.

'Mister Ireland.'

It was Finn.

He sat on a metal bench, soaking up the morning dew, all bed hair and legs on show. *Ugh. Of course Rachel fancies Finn, and of course he fancies her, because look at her: she's gorgeous, toned, constantly in a good mood, the kind of woman who loves to clean and wants to save the planet but still manages to be sexy at the same time. Nauseatingly perfect, really. She must have some massive messed-up habit, some kind of flaw – maybe she's manipulative or a thief; maybe she has irritable bowel syndrome and could kill cattle with her farts.*

'Morning, girls,' Finn said, barely looking at me before standing up and immediately puffing his chest out while taking in the goddess herself next to me. I pulled my thoughts away from how empty my stomach was and how *gangly* I felt walking around in this body long enough to notice how profusely illustrated with tattoos Rachel's back was. A sketch of a phoenix decorated the entirety of her upper spine and shoulders: delicate black strokes swimming in red ink looked so beautiful and striking against her dark skin. *So* badass. I fidgeted, thinking about the embarrassing scut of an arrow tattoo on my foot. I'd got it on my eighteenth birthday, somehow thinking I was being cool, even though it was the most basic thing I could think of to get and in the most out-of-sight place on my body. It had no meaning. I just wanted to be able to say, 'I have a tattoo'.

My stomach growled. I immediately tried to silence the rumbling by hopping from side to side as Finn and Rachel hugged, dragging my trainers across the path. I glanced up and down the street to distract myself from my third-wheel status.

Brixton is so unapologetically unpolished, so higgledy-piggledy. The perfect place, really, for a newly single mess like me.

'Nice to see that not all of London sleeps at the most beautiful hour of the morning,' Finn said, eyes fixed on Rachel. He was beaming. Such warm energy, all directed at her. 'It's like zombie town at this time back where I'm from. *This* is great.' He looked around. 'I've already seen a few people out jogging, cycling ... good incentive to move a bit more; watch too many films while sat on your backside like I do and you'll end up with a gut like this!' He patted his tummy, which really wasn't *that* big at all, and I realised he was doing the same thing he did when he was sixteen years old and conscious of his breakouts: he was pointing it out, as if to say *look, I know this exists and now you know I know, so there's no need to judge me*. It was mildly endearing.

'Erin and I love getting in an early sweat,' Rachel said, nodding at me while bouncing on her tippy-toes. 'Finn, this is my new flatmate! Another newbie to the block, like you.' He caught eyes with me then, and his smile somehow stretched even wider.

We've already met, but we haven't, but we have.

Rachel went on: 'We've been running every morning this week. My last roomie spent months fermenting away in that bedroom, so I'm delighted to have—'

Finn stopped listening to her and came at me for a bear hug. '*Beglan!* Be still, my beating heart,' he boomed, lifting me off the ground in an embrace.

'*Finn!*' I mirrored his airy tone, just as I'd done in right-side-up land. Assuming we hadn't run into each other yet in this life, I acted surprised, like I hadn't instantly recognised him.

'How many years has it been? Goodness, London suits ya, missus.' His eyes scanned me.

I didn't know how to respond. Nervously, I glanced at Rachel. She seemed lost, without looking the least bit threatened. 'Old friends?' she asked. 'Aw, this is great. A ready-made running squad – all I've wanted, all year long!' She leaned an elbow on my shoulder and arched her back, placing her other hand on her hip and expertly drawing Finn's attention back to her.

'Erin is an old school friend of mine,' Finn told Rachel, his voice dancing with excitement. He looked back at me. 'I'm over the moon to see you. I don't know anyone in London. Well, apart from this lovely thing, of course.' He nodded at Rachel. 'Rach helped me get my stuff moved in as the lift isn't working. Absolute gem.'

And then they were gazing deep into one another's eyes.

Rach?

Ew.

Already onto nicknames.

Next, it'll be 'ickle baba', and I'll be found strangling them both to death with my skipping rope.

I have a skipping rope?

My real thoughts were blending with my alternate-world thoughts: I could see a green rope with purple handles – clear as day – in my mind, at the foot of my bed upstairs, and it was the weirdest feeling. A bit like when you're in the dentist's chair and you know the bastard is drilling into you but you can't feel any actual *pain*. Something's going on inside you that you're half oblivious to.

Dizzy with befuddlement, I used words to inch myself between them and dampen the sparks that were flying. 'Yeah, Finn and I go *way back*. It's mad to see you after all this time. Um, we'd best … chat and run. *Rach* and I both start work at 9 a.m., so … eh, which direction we heading off in today?'

Hopefully the way I said 'Rach' didn't scream scorn too loudly.

I followed them along Electric Avenue, which emanated energy as people prepared their stalls – fruits and cheap handbags galore – and on to Brockwell Park. As we jogged, Finn – breathing heavily and drenched through with sweat – filled Rachel in about our teenage shenanigans (while conveniently sidestepping his massive crush on me). He told tales of the mad house parties, of our Catholic upbringing and our daily reciting of prayers in school *as Gaeilge* (using the Irish language), of me being the butt end of cheap jokes for wearing trousers instead of the pinafore dress that girls were expected to wear.

He remembered so much more than I did.

It was lovely to hear him reminisce, and Rachel appeared to be loving his stories, but I couldn't help becoming distracted by my body's cravings: for a dirty big breakfast roll with sausage and egg; for a big chunk of carrot cake with cream-cheese frosting; for four-cheese pizza. Strange breakfast cravings. But those aside, all this movement felt surprisingly ... *good*.

I was ... enjoying running.

Finn attempted to engage with me several times as the three of us flew through Brockwell Park – by its emerald-green clock tower, its water garden, its oak trees – but I couldn't concentrate on the conversation. I was so hungry it hurt. The jog became a blur of Rachel's round arse in her pink running shorts and of Finn's voice and of an indescribable gnawing emptiness.

Eventually, I popped in my headphones and played 'Take on Me' by A-ha on full volume.

Eighties synth soothes all.

I don't think either of them noticed, or cared, when I sped up, leaving them behind.

An hour later I waited for them to catch up, to get the key from Rachel. I'd forgotten to bring the backpack that other-world-me had packed, containing my own freshly cut key. Then I left her and Finn downstairs with their gooey eyes, ran upstairs to the fridge, *gobbled* Rachel's block of cheddar and peed.

Everything was all so bloody realistic. Human anatomy and all.

This can't be a dream.

No chance.

This thing around my neck, coated in a film of actual

sweat – it's unnatural. None of this should be possible. But it is, it's all happening. Skinny me is having a pee. I can feel myself peeing, only there's way less flesh protecting my bones from the toilet seat than usual.

I collapsed onto my bed and I wondered if in this body I still worked at the Sugar Pot café. Perhaps, with this bod, I've wiggled my way into a more exciting, better-paying industry?

My thoughts came in wafts.

I had coveted a figure like this for as long as I could remember. I'd always wanted to know how people atop the human pyramid lived, those who got the golden stamp of approval for winning a genetic lottery or for practising discipline to look a certain way. Thanks to Reid, I was always aware of my privileges: 'Bitch, you're white, young-*ish*, able-bodied and you live in London, so shut the fuck up,' he'd snap when I'd complain about my figure. And I'd argue with him that men don't wank over 'healthy and normal', they wank over whippet-thin and curvy in the right places. Everywhere I turned – on every billboard and every cinema screen, on every blog header and bus shelter – lived idealised versions of me. 'Not me,' he'd said, 'I'm a man, and I wank over Martin and Martin alone. Besides, since when is being "wank material" something you care about? You've been overhearing too many assholes objectifying women, Beggy.'

Now, weighing at least ten pounds less and looking like a 7/10, had I done life differently? Had my view from the pyramid changed much, if at all? I ran my hands along my tight body and then my question was partially answered by an anticlimactic text from Kenneth:

Hey, you free to open up today? Jen called in sick, and nobody else is available. I know it's your birthday but it's an emergency. I'd really appreciate you working a half day today, will pay double time. Ken

Bitter disappointment.

Noting that it was now 7.45 a.m., I realised I'd have to get ready and go right away if I was going to make it on time.

Then it hit me: *none of this is even happening.* There would be no consequences.

So I lied:

I'm not well either, something must be going around. So I won't be in. And cheers for the birthday wishes.

Next, I texted Reid:

Mate. Look I know you're probably knackered from your work trip but can you please meet me at our spot in Palace Gardens straight from the airport? It's really, really important.

Instantly:

This better be good, birthday girl. I was planning on going straight to bed. Peanut-butter protein shakes on YOU today, plz. Don't forget my straw again. Need to keep these teeth white for the boys. xxx

I wondered if Reid thought I looked better like this; if I was happier, like this. *What can I possibly learn in one day, though?*

Déjà vu, direct into my bloodstream as though through an intravenous drip. My bike, Rusty; the step in the sunken garden where Reid and I had met just days ago in another world. Only today the sky spat rain on and off, and the grass squelched beneath feet, and puddles formed wherever they could.

I'd not known where to pick up a peanut-butter protein shake for Reid because *who the fuck buys protein shakes on the go at this time of the day*? Instead, I'd bought two massive salted-caramel cookies from a corner shop down the road, freshly baked, and I exercised every ounce of my self-control *not* to devour my one before he appeared. I sipped at a black coffee like a well-trained dog faced with beef jerky, waiting on its moment to pounce.

Shortly, across the pond, Reid: a backwards cap and ankles on show, carrying a stylish beige overnight bag (tag from his flight still attached), his smile gleaming and his eyes piercing as ever. I knew that I was going to tell him everything, just as I knew how sore my bum was in that moment. I could feel the cold step against my skeleton. 'This is a family secret,' Granny had said. I'd never purposefully disobey Granny, but *this* Reid didn't exist. And I needed to allow my feelings to explode out of my mouth to Reid, like they always did. Either he wouldn't believe me and would try to have me sectioned or he'd know but the news would die with this version of him.

Fingers (and arms and legs) crossed, anyway.

I stood up and darted at him, then, propelled by coffee and gnawing hunger, 'Feast your eyes,' I said, waving the paper bag of cookies in his face. 'Take yours, I'm gonna die if I don't eat this *right now*. You owe me for being polite and waiting on you,' I said, breaking off a chunk of lukewarm cookie and almost forgetting where I was and what I looked like mid-chew. I demolished it.

Nothing matters, only calories.

Reid tentatively took the bag and slowly shoved it into his back pocket. 'OK ...' he said, his voice hesitant, '*who* are you, and *what* have you done with my best friend?' He flinched back as he spoke. His eyes were so wide I could see the outer whites all around the ice-blue centres. Surprise held his mouth open.

'I figured I'd see a female prime minster twerk in a gold leotard before I'd *ever* see you eating ... *that*. Is the dry spell really that bad?' My mouth was too full to reply: cookie halfway down my throat, stuck to the roof of my mouth and smushed between half my teeth.

Is this really that shocking?

He went on nervously: 'I mean, I'm delighted to see you indulge.' His eyes flickered. 'For once, it's not just me. This morning, I literally *licked* the last traces of cheesy tomato sauce from the box left over from the *enormous* pizza I ate by myself last night. Wank, cry, pizza, Netflix: the Friday combo.'

It was weird, as though he was saying something to me that he wouldn't normally say for fear of judgement, like a boulder was being lifted from his broken back. I swallowed and hugged him, and hugging felt different without my squidge. I couldn't get my body very close to Reid's body, as now we both owned concave chests. When I pulled away, he held onto my hands as though he were worried about me.

'It's just a cookie. What do I usually eat?' I asked, genuinely curious and remembering Rachel's raised eyebrow from this morning.

Reid stared, eyes still showing too much white, then injected his voice with his usual cheeky animation: 'Firstly, are you OK? Secondly, *why* did you ask me to come out in this abysmal weather instead of going straight home to my warm bed?'

'Listen,' I said, taking his hands in mine. 'Y'know how … you always talk about … the universe and other dimensions and ghosts and *all* that other bullshit?'

'Of course,' he said. 'And you always roll your eyes because you're a cynical Irish potato. Ghosts *are* humans from the future glimpsing the past through some crazy, futuristic technology. We're their museum. Fight me.'

'OK, *listen to me.*' I thought hard on how to word it so it wouldn't sound ludicrous, but it was impossible. 'I – I woke up in a different version of my life this morning,' I said, the words rocketing from me. 'I look different. My body is slim, but everything else seems to be pretty much the same so far.' His grip on my hands loosened. I bit my lip and patted my foot, looking around, hoping something or someone would materialise to back me up.

'This is a *weird* joke, Beggy. I know I'm probably meant to laugh, but—'

I squeezed his hands tightly. 'Look at me. I'm *not* messing,' I said. 'This is all some kind of … vision. I think. I don't know. But for some reason, I'm not afraid. It's just all … happening, and everything is so graphic and, and … lifelike, and, like, look!' In a moment of wild senselessness, I pulled his hands to my chest, right there in the middle of the Palace Gardens. 'My boobs are gone! I'm a *double D*. But there's nothing there!'

Reid pulled his hands away immediately and looked around to check if anyone had seen. Then he gripped my arms and tried to read my face. 'Beggy, what are you talking about? Bra sizes mean nothing to me. I like hairy pectoral muscles. I don't know anything about tits and you know it. Are you telling me you asked me to leave work so you could tell me that your bras no longer fit?'

'No. I'm telling you that this is *not* my body. I woke up in this body. I'm not me. Well, I am. But I'm not! Oh, *please* don't look at me like that. I'm not mad, I'm just – I'm *experiencing a thing*, and I want you to experience it with me, OK?' I felt strange and sad and, somehow, less close to Reid than before, even though we were physically touching.

'You're experiencing *what,* exactly? Carbs?'

Our faces scrunched up and we howled with laughter.

'Granny Beglan,' I said, still laughing. 'This is all her.'

'That mad bitch? Ha-ha ... I thought you were going over to her tonight, for your birthday?'

'I am. I mean, *I did*. In the real world. So, basically, she gave me *this* pendant.' I pulled it out as I spoke. Words spilled from my mouth, sharp and fast.

Reid was dubious. 'She put you up to this, right? You told her I wanted a picture of her so I can laugh at the hairs growing out of her moles, and now she hates me, right? I thought she doesn't have a phone. How have you two been chatting?'

'Listen! This pendant is why I'm here. I wanted to know what would've happened if I'd actually stuck to something ... for once.' My explanation wasn't working. Reid's words kept catching in his throat as he tried to respond, and his expression told me that he couldn't make sense of anything I said. My relentless hunger forced me to give up, to make the most of the time I had left in this bizarre situation.

'I need you right now,' I said gently. 'Can you just be here for me today? You're all I've got.'

A loud exhale. 'Yes. OK, good. Normal talk. I'm here, always, any time, *obviously*. Shall we sit down, and talk and—'

I cut him off.

I felt somewhat cracked.

And, all of a sudden, *giddy*.

'Let's go clothes shopping in Selfridges, on Oxford

Street! I wanna try on all the clothes that I've never been able to wear. I want to *not cry* in dressing rooms today.' I linked arms with him then and dragged him back in the direction he'd come from. 'I need more food, I need 'Girls Just Want to Have Fun' by Cyndi Lauper playing on your phone right now, please, and I want no more questions asked. I just need this. Please.' Silence sandwiched between us. 'OK?'

'OK. You crazy, crazy bitch.'

We demolished herby scrambled eggs on sourdough toast in a nearby café, then walked through the streets of Soho, licking mint-chocolate-flavoured ice-cream cones, as we so often did.

'I think I feel a "dairy queen" coming on,' I told Reid afterward, recalling his recent tale of the diarrhoea date disaster. This new version of my body couldn't take much fun.

'What?' Reid asked, as I massaged my belly (which, while still tight, was now bloated and gurgly). He was definitely not himself: tense and on edge.

I mean, he's got every reason to think I've slipped into psychopathy. What did I expect?

'I think I'm going to have the shits, mate,' I said casually. 'Food isn't agreeing with me today.'

'Well, you never eat stuff like this, Beggy. Don't blame me. You wanted the bloody ice cream … What's a dairy queen? You said "dairy queen" just now …'

Hmm …

This world may not be totally identical to the real one. Small things here and there may have happened differently in this version of events. Maybe Reid met the dairy-queen guy on a dating app, and the smallest interaction between us (like a phone call) could have meant him not coming across Dairy Queen at all. Man, the fact that I even exist is a miracle. A different sperm and … never beginning nor ending nothingness.

'Oh, nothing. I just … don't feel well. However, trying on ridiculously expensive bodycon dresses will make me feel better, methinks. Bit of craic.' I pulled my denim jacket tight to my chest as a thin veil of rain fell, but it didn't solve the issue of the ridiculously small cropped T-shirt I'd decided to wear because it looked hot.

'You're the only Irish person ever that actually says *craic* instead of *fun*,' Reid said, swirling his cap around to keep the rain out of his eyes.

'Just you wait till you meet Finn. He never stops with the Irishisms.'

'Who?'

'I forgot to tell you, actually! Remember years ago I told you about my old-flame-that-was-never-really-a-flame, from school? Well, he just moved in downstairs, in my new building. He used to be mad about me when we were teenagers back in Dublin, but he wasn't my type – I mean, he's *not* my type – but you'll have to meet him.'

'Straight men and I don't mix, we've established this. I'll show up, all enthusiastic like, and he'll just be there in his dad jeans, waving his straight pride flag that's all shades of grey and it'll be *shit*. It's always the same when I try to make straight-boy friends.' I sucked my teeth and wrinkled my nose, thinking about various straight men that Reid had crushed on over the years. 'Well, yeah, either we won't get along or I'll fall for him. Which wouldn't be the worst thing in the world ... *straight* has got to be better than *married to an Adonis*.'

'How do you know Finn's straight, anyway? You read minds now? You keep making assumptions about strangers. I'm disappointed in you. You used to be my most progressive friend.'

As far as I was aware, Finn *was* straight, but I liked to give Reid a taste of his own medicine sometimes.

'Firstly, I'm your *only* friend. Secondly, stop challenging my hypocrisy. I'm allowed to assume and to stereotype because I'm always on the other end of it – that's law.'

'If you say so.'

'Look, if the man says *craic* then he's not queer enough for me. Even if he's bisexual, I don't care. The B in LGBTQ stands for Bastards.' Reid held his chin high in the air and giggled.

I rolled my eyes, glad to see him feign normality. Then, to slice through images of Finn and Rachel having rampant sex, I steered Reid toward Selfridges. We edged our way through throngs of pedestrians, their umbrellas slanted against the light drizzle that frizzed my hair.

And there was no doubt about it: more heads turned for

me in this slim, fit body. Businessmen, men with women on their arms, women in lipstick and others too beautiful to ever notice me normally: face after face examined me as they passed, and, as they gawped, I couldn't decide if I loved the attention more or less than I despised people for their predictability.

Joy is a woman in a high-end department store living an alternate version of her life. When finally faced with rail after rail of skintight dresses in each and every colour, I came alive like a kid high on Skittles and fresh air. My brain briefly stopped analysing how others were reacting to the new me, how strangers – such as the fitting-room attendant in Selfridges with the cascading curls – scrutinised my shape, perhaps wondering if it was genetic or about what I eat and how often I work out to look this way. My self-perception took over as I dressed this version of me up in outfits I'd usually gaze at from afar.

While wrapped in my real body, I'd often tell myself that I couldn't get away with wearing dresses like these, ones that clung to me. The kind the shops always dress the mannequins in. I lived in T-shirts and jeans, and if I *had* to wear a dress for a formal occasion I'd stick to A-line and skater style – anything that cinched in at my smallest part and hid *everything* from the waist right down to the knees.

As I tried on a fourth dress, Reid waited on the changing-room sofa with his legs crossed, clearly and sufficiently freaked out by my behaviour. I knew it because he furiously chewed on the inside of his cheeks.

It's not real, Erin. Stop worrying about him.

This dress, on me, looked just as it did on the mannequin. It was long, strapless, skintight and deep red, with a slit up one side that showed off a bit of leg and robbed attention from my flat chest with its delicate detailing around its middle.

'Reid! Look at this one,' I hissed. Seconds later, he stuck his head through the chink in the curtain. 'Take a picture of me, here, on my phone,' I asked before he reacted.

'Christ. I mean, I didn't think you were … into dresses,' he said. 'It's *gorgeous*, but not very *you*, is it? Besides, where would you even wear something like that? We don't go anywhere fancy, ever.'

'Doesn't matter, mate. It actually fits me. I just … I really want a picture of this.'

Once again, I checked out my own arse.

This needs to go up on Instagram.

Maybe Finn will like the photo.

He's already admitted to stalking me on social media, in the real world.

'Well, the lighting in here is like a hospital,' Reid said with a grimace. His eyes then darted around the room behind him, like those of a master photographer already establishing the finished shot in his head. 'Come out here and stand next to this hideous rich-people plant. And for goodness sake, *take off* that pendant thing. I can't imagine that'll go with anything you try on in here.'

'Eh, don't tell me "how to: fashion", you like mesh.'

I shimmied out, smiling maniacally, and followed him to the front of the changing rooms, wondering what would actually happen if I removed the pendant from my neck during one of my seven tries. And if the Selfridges lady could offer me a pair of high heels to wear, just for the picture. And—

An unexpected sight stopped me dead.

The stupidly attractive man with floppy hair, from the café – *Owen* – waiting in line for the men's changing rooms and somehow lighting up the place. A coat and some knitwear draped over one suited arm, a briefcase hanging from the other and a pout carved into his perfect face. He glanced in my direction and held me in his gaze as though gently peeling my dress off with his eyes; they caught mine and told me that he recognised me. My heart hammered. His lips parted, then he glanced at Reid before looking back at his queue, like he was considering how much time he had before a room would free up.

He was so obviously checking me out!

Reid stood between us, his back to Owen. 'That's the guy, isn't it?' he whispered. 'I'd recognise that jawline from Neptune.'

'You *know* about him?'

'Beggy. We ran into him when we all went out for my birthday, soon after you cancelled the wedding – remember? And you guys always flirt at work. Or so you said ... What is *wrong* with you today?' In real life, I'd felt lousy about myself that night and I'd made up an excuse not to go because I'd wanted to stay on Reid's couch and mope with fudge brownie ice cream.

'Refresh my memory, quick,' I snapped.

'Eh … you came out with me and the boys. Club BED, remember? And you dropped your pint, like the total fool that you are, and that *delicious* man over there was beside us …'

'And?'

'*And* he said you'd never been so clumsy at work, so, he, like, recognised you, then he led you away from the pile of glass shards and foam while some poor sod cleaned up after you. Then you two were talking for, like, an *hour.* You didn't even introduce me, you were that lost in his pretty eyes.'

He chatted me up. *He chatted me up.*

'Beggy.' Reid looked at me just as I'd looked at Granny Beglan when I thought she was losing her mind.

'We … I—'

'It's a yes from me,' Owen said, from metres behind Reid. He approached us slowly, his lithe body covered in pressed attire. 'The designer of that dress is a good friend of mine. It was made for you.'

Reid beamed as soon as Owen name-dropped. 'I agree. She looks very Emma Stone at the Oscars. Hi,' he gabbled, 'I'm Reid, the best friend. Lovely to meet you.' He extended a hand to Owen even though Owen's hands were full. Then he awkwardly shook his own hand and rolled his eyes at his eagerness.

Owen's brows raised ever so slightly; he seemed relieved to discover that Reid was just a friend. 'I'm Owen, I frequent Erin's café.' I was annoyed that he didn't share his surname (so I could stalk him online and find out more about him) but the fact that he actually knew my name in this version of events served as the sweetest distraction. 'What's the occasion?'

Something inside me seemed to be very comfortable with flirtation in this body. The words, and the confidence needed to wield them, simply existed in the moment, and I was swept up by it. 'Well, y'see, I need something fancy to sit around in next Saturday night. Was thinking I could also clean my apartment in this, maybe wear it to the gym …'

Owen smiled, showing all his teeth. The energy between us was immediately amped up. 'That's an outfit for Sketch right there. Have you been?'

Reid swallowed, while I maintained my cool and said, 'The restaurant? One three-course meal in there would cost me a week's wages. I've seen the outside of it, though. Delightful front door. Also, I've seen pictures of it on Instagram. So you could say I've been because I know that the seats are all plush and pink and that it looks like it's run by Dolores Umbridge.'

Reid giggled.

The Harry Potter reference was lost on Owen, though. 'Until you've tried the food, might I insist you know nothing.' Dimples deepened either side of his smile. 'How about you, and that dress, join me there next Saturday? On me. If you say yes here then you won't ruffle your boss's feathers by picking up dates while you're supposed to be working.'

Ruffle Kenneth's feathers. What an old-person thing to say.

'I suppose you're right. I kinda *have* to say yes, don't I?'

'Yes.' Reid said it first, not Owen.

'I'd rather you want to say yes and not *have* to. But it is a lot easier to hit on you here, so ...'

'I'll be there. Sans dress ... this would cost me two weeks' wages. I promise I won't be naked, though, I mean, I'll obviously wear *something*.' The three of us stood in a sort-of circle while Owen and I examined one another's faces, and Reid looked back and forth between us like a dog waiting to be walked.

I'm not even going to get to go on this date.

Why is this-world me so keen to make a date that real-world me can't attend?

This is torture.

'Anyway, speaking of Instagram, Reid is about to take some shots of me in this lovely thing. I want to show off your designer friend's lovely work. Let me follow you so we can make plans?'

'No picture of you in this dress will do it justice. No worries, though. Have it all up here.' Owen tapped his temple, his arm heavy under the clothing he was waiting to try on. 'What's your Instagram handle? I'll follow you when I'm done here.'

'She's @ErinsView2!'

I felt my anus clench with embarrassment. Drowning in worst-possible-username cringe, I sought to save myself. 'I keep meaning to change that. At least it's so bad that you'll *definitely* remember it.' Then I flashed Owen a cheeky smile and thought, *Who are you, Erin, and what have you done with … me?*

'I like a girl who can see silver linings,' he said, holding my gaze with his.

'Anyway, I need to …' Owen nodded his head backwards toward the queue.

'Yep. See you next Saturday.' The words dripped from my tongue like butter in heat and I couldn't quite believe myself.

'See you … on Instagram,' Reid said. 'I creep on everyone she follows.' He held his chin high in the air.

Owen glanced back over his shoulder as he walked away. It was the sexiest thing I'd seen in months. This was all going way too smoothly. The clumsy, nervous energy that usually followed single me around didn't seem to exist in a world where I was thinner.

Am I actually more confident simply because there's less of me?

Or could it be that more people hit on a me that looks like this and I've just grown comfortable with the attention?

'OK, Casanova,' Reid teased. 'Pose.'

After Martin called unexpectedly, Reid insisted that he

drop in to the office where he worked, under Martin, as a social-media marketing director. The job came with a cushy office chair, a delightful assistant and an impressive pay cheque, and the thought of it alone – how interesting it sounded and how well it paid – turned me green as grass with envy. I'd become skilled at hiding that, though, like Mystique from *X-Men* when she'd hide away her natural blue form. Reid seemed exhaustingly worried about me before he left, but I knew the day would end soon and that version of him would be gone forever.

Along with this version of me.

So, after a cuddle and farewell in Piccadilly, where a faint mist blurred the neon enticements for rum and coke, I embraced the time I had to chill out alone with my new body. I wanted to soak up the attention, to be the fit girl munching on the Cornish pasty that everybody glares at, their jealousy like pheromones.

Is that so wrong?

This is all so unimaginable, yet I'm smiling to myself and wolfing a pasty, like life's a painting awaiting the shredder.

On my way down the Tube station's escalator (where I posted the best of around fifty photos of me to Instagram), a beefy, purple-faced man a step below me turned to check me out; he leered, smelling of whiskey and grunting at my navel. I tried to pretend that he wasn't there and kept refreshing my newly posted photo, to watch the likes flood in, but I could hear him mumble 'lovely' about me, in his voice – like gravel. This wasn't innocent curiosity like the peeks along the street had been, and I imagined how things would go down if I came across this guy in a quiet alleyway in the night time.

Thank God we're surrounded.

Again, on the platform to Brixton, another man – spindly, attractive, with sandy blonde hair – leering. 'After you, doll,' he said, licking his lips as the Tube doors opened. His lip-licking didn't cease when I sat down, and then the majority of eyes in the carriage were on me too, like flies.

Just like that, I wanted to be invisible.

It's not like I never experienced sideways glances (and catcalling and unwelcome bum squeezes in nightclubs to boot) while residing in my normal body – far too many had claimed ownership of my body for brief moments over the years, even when my tits and arse lay buried under layers of jumper, overall and coat, but this was in some way different: I was a rabbit chased by greyhounds *trained* to chase it. People learn that *this* is the body of someone to be looked at, all throughout life: *dribble over the flesh furniture, cum looking at it, spend all of your money so you can become it.*

Usually, I blended in more.

Usually, I hated that. So much so that one of my first instincts in a skinny body was to share pictures of me *standing out*.

The teen boy opposite me kept adjusting his belt then and grabbing his balls while he watched me.

I looked down.

If I can't see it, it isn't happening.

I flicked through a newspaper, absorbing fragments of all that was going on in the world – scientific breakthrough, war, injustice and all the rest – and I couldn't help but feel hot with shame for my small self-serving thoughts.

I've used up an entire one of seven chances to see how I fare having made different choices on this.

Earphones.

'Hungry Like the Wolf' by Duran Duran, extra loud – a blanket to cover the mortification with.

'Tell me *everything* you know about this gorgeous Irishman,' Rachel ordered as soon as I arrived back to our spotless apartment, drenched to my skin and dizzy with otherworldliness. I welcomed the distraction from the uncomfortable cocktail of feelings boiling in my stomach and joined her on our squishy green couch. She sipped red wine and shoved a bar of dark chocolate in my face, and, unusually, I couldn't stomach it. As she spoke, she poured me a glass of wine instead. 'I can't believe you already know him. He's so sexy, Erin.'

Sexy? Finn?

'And he lectures in film studies. Couldn't be more ideal.'

That sounds very Finn, alright.

Film studies.

I recalled cold Irish winter nights during which he'd

screen various cult films on the projector in his attic bedroom for the school gang and me. He'd always want to sit next to me, up front, to watch my reactions up close, to relive movies through me as we inhaled popcorn and vodka mixed with cola. More often than not he'd be disappointed that I didn't 'get' the masterpiece he was sharing with me. I just didn't care about films like he did.

'Um, well, like Finn said earlier, we went to school together,' I told Rachel. 'His family lived just around the corner from my family, so we hung out a fair bit. Eh …' I didn't want to rub the years of mostly one-sided flirtation between us in her face, even though it ultimately wouldn't matter because this situation wasn't real. I just couldn't find it in me to be cruel, even if just for a social experiment in a fake universe.

'And?' she pushed, swirling her wine, hanging on my every syllable.

'What do you want to know? My opinion of him?'

'Exactly.'

'Like … his quirks? He, um, wears mismatching socks … He—'

'No,' she stopped me, and narrowed her eyes. 'Come on, girl. I want the juicy stuff, like, does he respect his mother? Is he loyal? Was he ever arrested for drunk driving? Any notable ex-lovers?'

This was when I first learned that 'perfect Rachel' loved to gossip.

Dan hates gossips.

Wait. So what?

I forced a laugh and reached for the glass of wine she'd poured for me, the TV light glinting off it – again, distracted by how flawless every minute detail of this vision was.

How much do I tell her? They're relative strangers.

Erin, it doesn't bloody matter, it—

'Finn shared all kinds of opinions on *you* today,' she said, breaking my thought in two.

'Oh yeah? Such as?' I sat up, wine glass in hand, all ears.

'Well, first he asked about you a lot – y'know, "What does she do? Is she with anyone?"' The thought of Finn fishing for information behind my back excited me. Just for a moment, I felt somewhat interesting – not because of the answers Rachel would have provided but because someone had cared enough to ask about me at all. 'And then ...'

'Yeah?'

'He sorta went into elder-brother mode. Talked about how he wasn't surprised that you called off your wedding. He said—'

'What?'

'For one, that you bore easily.'

The big shit.

'And that you've always been a little emotionally unavailable because of your past.' She said it earnestly, but I still felt my guard come up; it inched around me, like bubble wrap employed by invisible hands.

Did he tell her about what happened to my mam?

She went on. 'That you need someone who can "penetrate your fortress". Also, goodness, the man couldn't believe that you have a degree now – he was delighted to hear it. But—'

'But what?'

'The reason he seemed so pleasantly surprised … well, he said you never really stuck with things when you were younger. That you'd make up all kinds of excuses to get out of horse riding and art lessons.' My posture shift likely informed her that I was growing more annoyed with every word she fed me, so she said, 'I can't believe you two rode horses! So *Irish*, haha.'

I stuck with my diet and workout plan. He only knew me when I was basically a foetus.

He doesn't know what he's talking about …

My guts churned. 'How much did you tell him about me, then? So, the degree. What else?'

He said, he said …

Rachel is a bit of a cow. That's her flaw: her big mouth.

'Only what I know, which isn't much.' A defensive tone of voice. 'He said you guys were old friends. And he clearly thinks of you as family.'

Family?

Elder-brother mode?

I said nothing. I couldn't hide that thoughts of Finn and Rachel discussing Erin the Loser made me want to smash things.

'While running the other morning, I dunno, I got the impression you *hate* being a waitress, and … I like you, Erin. I just wanted his advice on how to encourage you to—'

'So he was bitching about me, then?' My cheeks burned.

'That's not fair. He was being honest about his impression of you, which I found refreshing. I mean, that's what has me so curious about him – he's *so blunt*. Like, he challenged me on—'

'Finn was insinuating that I give up easily on … stuff,' I half said, half asked.

She ran her fingers through her braids, and it pissed me off just how stunning she looked, even in pyjamas, even when overstepping.

'Don't you? Give up easily?' she asked, her doe eyes alive with the spirit of enquiry. I really didn't want to answer her. I didn't want to talk about *this*, with *her*. Already limp with the discomfort of creepy men undressing me with their eyes and of how *direct* I was in this different, toned body, I needed to retreat to the shower, to my safe space. Hearing how Finn talked about me to Rachel – like I was his silly younger sister – crippled me more than I expected.

'I'm annoyed. I don't want to talk any more. It's just … hormones, OK? I'm sorry.' I lied to her not only because I didn't want her to follow me, but because I knew deep down she hadn't done or said anything wrong.

She's telling you what someone else said about you, Erin. That's what friends do.

*

An hour later and wrapped up in a big white fluffy towel after a scalding hot shower (I liked to climb out strawberry-coloured), I checked to see if Owen had added me on Instagram to organise the date we'd never have. He hadn't. My heart sank. Then I checked the likes on the photo Reid took for me that day. It had 247, with 1 from Finn. My average picture in the real world garnered an average of 10 likes, with 0 from Finn.

People are idiots. They're sheep.

Evidently, so is Finn Kelly.

Owen, too. He's not been flirting with me in real life, where I'm less cheekbones, more cushion – he's been flat out ignoring me.

In a huff and feeling conflicted about how the day had transpired, I went to gather clean underwear. In my undies drawer, full of strange, fancy pants I'd never seen before, I came across a journal. The purple cover was worn, battered and covered in illustrations of doughnuts.

I didn't recognise it at all.

Inside it, in my handwriting, 'food log' was scribbled across the first page. I didn't know what to expect as I flicked through the pages (dated with days from last year), but nothing could have prepared me for the journal's insight into life after sticking to my original weight-loss plan, which I'd found in some random forum accompanied by before and after pictures and glowing testimonials.

<u>8 November 2017</u>

400 jumping jacks/200 squats before work

breakfast: black coffee

lunch: packet of cooked turkey breast

dinner: apple, ½ jar of peanut butter

(extra: chicken stock cube in hot water)

<u>9 November 2017</u>

8 mile run before work

breakfast: two black coffees

lunch: nothing

dinner: Zizzi's Italian, with Dan (antipasti platter to myself, Sofia rustica pizza, baked lemon and raspberry cheesecake, entire bottle of white wine)

(extra [binge/purged]: packet of Jaffa Cakes in bed, half a sharing bag of spicy Doritos, crackers with cheese and butter – unknown amount)

<u>10 November 2017</u>

no workout (feel sick from last night)

breakfast: coffee

lunch: coffee, lollipop (cherry flavour), packet of chewing gum

dinner: chicken pot noodle

(extra: two cans of Diet Coke)

<u>11 November 2017</u>

spinning class with Reid before work

breakfast with Reid: avocado on toast and poached eggs, cappuccino

lunch: nothing

dinner: nothing

(extra: two cups of jasmine green tea at night time, 1/2 packet of mint-chocolate-coated rice cakes)

12 November 2017

2 hour gym session

breakfast: peanut-butter protein shake, banana

lunch: beans on toast, salad

dinner with Dan: Chinese takeaway (chicken balls, tray of egg fried rice, bag of chips, prawn toast, beef with black bean sauce, vegetable spring rolls)

(extra [binge/purged]: half a sharing bag of spicy Doritos, full tube of sour cream and onion Pringles, 2 litres of lemonade, strawberry straws from the sweet shop)

13 November 2017

fast day

20 mile bike ride

I had to stop myself from reading more.

The journal revealed a day-to-day battle with binge eating, restriction and … bulimia?

'Binge/purged' it read, over and over again, every few days under a new entry. The entries implied that I hid vomit-flavoured behaviours from people in my life too – according to *it*, I'd eat around Dan and Reid. The idea of some alternate version of me shrouding a huge part of my life in black cloth was like a blade to swallow. I expected desolate sobbing of myself but no tears came – just a shiver up and down my spine as I read words that had come from me, but *not me*.

Memories of earlier that day came to me then, without their disguises on: more than a year on from *these* journal entries and skinny-world me is off carbs entirely. *What's next? A diet of chewing gum and sparkling water with a filling side of lemon wedge?*

I was frightened, temporarily existing in a body hiding a multitude of dark truths behind its mask of health.

This is why I was so fucking hungry this morning.

I ran to the mirror and inspected my teeth. They were discoloured, yellowish. While up close and personal with my new face I noticed how dry my skin was compared to normal; there were dehydration lines around my eyes and peeling skin on the tip of my nose. And I had under-eye bags for days.

Ugh.

If I had to surrender to an eating disorder to look like this, I'd rather spend my days as a severed head, perched on a bakery-shop shelf, a tongue's length away from frosting.

The pendant rested against my towel. I realised that I very much wanted to check out early. I wanted to be in the version of my body that hadn't been starved, force-fed and exhausted on no calories. And I wanted cake, with frosting.

The journal discovery was just too much.

With the tree of life that dangled from my pendant clasped in my fist, I visualised myself, clear as water, opening my eyes by Granny's fire, then I slid away into the blackness at the edge of my brain.

6
Tree of Life

I held on to the sofa for support. The world had turned to liquid. A figure hovered over me in a cloud of cigarette smoke, cackling as if demented, and then everything was still and exceptionally ordinary. The fire burned, the cat purred and in Granny's right hand was a wine glass.

'Only seconds have passed, dear ... and, my, ye have been on some journey, tellin' by that face. White as milk! Ha! Happy birthday ...'

I blew out all of the air in my lungs and grabbed at my tummy rolls to be sure they existed. They did. Soft and spongy as ever. And my boobs ... they were back! I looked up at Granny's face. Hundreds of questions for her filled my mind, but I was so shaken I couldn't talk.

A panic attack was on its way.

She could tell. She'd seen this all before, as I suffered terribly from random bouts of panic as a teen. Granny, stable and forever direct, had been the only person who could calm me down. She sat beside me. 'Focus on the fire, love. Breathe deep in through the nose and out the mouth, like me and yer da showed ye.'

'What … *what* just happened?'

'Do as I tell ye.'

Hyperventilating, my hands tingly and legs shaking, I turned from Granny to the fire and watched the flames sway. I practised my breathing techniques to dampen the panic, but I couldn't keep my fingers away from the pendant, from the thing that scared me so yet momentarily sent my hopes soaring high as the moon that lit the sky outside. Every hair on my body stood against the clothes that covered it, against the hair that brushed the back of my neck, as one thought pervaded everything: *Maybe I can use this to see Mam again!*

What had just happened was so detailed and razor-sharp and real …

Is it possible that I could use this to spend a day with Mam?

If only she'd lived …

I thought through every 'if only' I could say that might bring me to my mam's side, to a life in which she was alive, older, with more smile lines, and my dad, and our old house, and all of the memories that never came to be. I had nothing. Then it hit me. Hard.

That won't work. Because no decision I made contributed to Mam's death.

My heart dropped from the sky right through the earth and out to space on its other side. All of my limbs fizzed and my brain crumbled in pain.

'What are ye thinking?' Granny pressed, gentle as a butterfly landing on the back of my hand. Then, replying to something I didn't have to say, 'Unfortunately, ye can't. That's not what this is for. But sure anyway, she's with ye *now*, in there, and always will be,' Granny said, pointing at my chest.

Don't bloody cry. Talk. Like normal. Like you would to Reid in the Palace Gardens …

I leaned forward and gripped my shins. 'Granny, how did *you* use this? I think I completely wasted that … turn or whatever that was – I …'

'No matter what, it wasn't a waste. The first sight is never a waste … now ye know the value of this,' she said, softly patting the pendant's stone which hung from my neck, brushing my knees. 'Ye didn't believe me. But now, I assume, ye do. It had to happen as it happened.'

'Don't ignore me, please. I want to know how you used this … thing,' I repeated through deep breaths, turning back to face her.

'Ah, love.' She swiped a hand at the air in front of her. 'If I tell ye how I used the gift, it'll sway your decisions. I don't want to do that.'

'Tell me. Please.' My eyes glassed over.

Granny compromised. 'Lookit. I saw myself in rags, with riches, other jobs, other friends, *off the drink* – don't let me muddy it for ye. My ma wouldn't tell me anything about how she used it. I'm glad of it. I want ye to figure things out yerself.'

'Figure what out? This is the most bizarre thing that's ever happened to me. I was ready to call the men in white coats to come and take you away before …'

We both laughed. It relaxed me instantly and soothed the pounding headache slamming away at me from the inside.

'Which is why ye can't tell anyone about this, not a soul. It's not of this world. People can't know. "We each need to figure out for ourselves why this pendant is a gift and not a curse": that's what Great-Great-Grandmother said.'

'It definitely seems more like a curse, Granny.'

'Maybe right now, but take my word, it—'

We spoke over one another. 'I'm honestly afraid to use it again, *ever*. I felt … so light, like a gust of wind would blow me away. I felt more comfortable … *naked* than I do here, in reality.'

OK, don't go into that part with your eighty-six-year-old Jesus-loving grandmother.

She listened, her face hovering close to my own.

'I enjoyed running in this other life. Me! And I was … flirty. And people checked me out a lot more. No boobs, but … whatever. Basically it was all bloody mad. And I had so much energy.'

'That could've just been the pendant at work. The fatigue of real life can't exist in a day that lasts a second.'

'Oh. Oh, right.' I stared into space for seconds or for moments, as though time had stopped. I couldn't process everything. Fragments of memories from my first sight danced like tiny flames inside my head. I was so aware of how solid the floor beneath me was and how the ticking of Granny's clock tied everything together, giving me that deep, knowing feeling that *this* was real and that all I'd just experienced hadn't been.

'Did yer dalliance with the gift tell ye that looking after yerself a bit better is something ye should do? To be happier?' She tapped her cigarette ashes onto the little wooden table in front of us, paying little to no attention to what she was doing. Some of the ash fell onto the carpet, and I noticed how dirty it was and how very old she really was, packaged up in a kind of excitement she'd probably not experienced in years.

The journal flashed in my mind then. 'Well, yeah. You could say that.'

'Tell yer granny.'

I didn't know how to say the words out loud. I was embarrassed and ashamed of a life I hadn't even lived. 'I had … eating problems. In this other life. I, eh—'

'Eating problems?'

'I found this *food log* in my knicker drawer, and, well, according to *that* I was, um, making myself throw up sometimes after eating.'

'Ah. Yes. Ballerina-me was fond o' talking to the giant telephone, too. *Ick.*'

'Giant telephone?'

'Sticking my head down the toilet to throw up supper. That's what we called it in our day. My fellow ballerinas of that life, they'd say, "Margaret, do it fast, or ye'll get fat and be fired." What a waste o' food, I thought. So many poor babies in this world starvin' to death.'

Granny didn't seem to understand the significance of my discovery. In my real life I was overjoyed when my best friend noticed I'd lost some weight – however unhealthily – and my jealousy of Rachel's body was bordering on disgusting.

Maybe I'm still in danger of going down that path … maybe I need to talk to a professional, or, or …

'This is overwhelming,' I whispered.

So many questions.

'But now ye know,' she said softly.

'Know what? I don't know anything, Granny. I'm more confused than I can even *begin* to explain. I—'

'Don't be blind to yer own mind. Now ye know what could happen if ye take things too far, and to watch for warning signs. That – that lookin' different isn't a plaster for yer problems. A lesson! Ye need to look out for the lessons …' Granny stubbed out her barely smoked cigarette and stood up to poke at the fire. 'One life's fault is another life's lesson. The less we covet, the more we cherish,' she whispered, as though reciting prayers or reading from a book. I assumed she was talking to herself, but she could very well have been addressing the portrait of Grandad hanging above the mantelpiece. Fuck knows.

I want answers.

'What's the point in the pendant, Granny? I mean, how much can we really learn in one day in another version of life? How am I supposed to know what's worth using this for and what isn't?'

'It'll show ye the answers. It'll help ye discover yer truth. Ye need to trust it, and trust—'

'What just happened taught me *nothing*. Only that I look fucking fantastic in dresses when I'm skinnier but the price I pay is to be hungry and sweaty and—'

'Ye look fantastic in dresses now, dear, just as ye are.'

'And that people are creeps, that Finn Kelly is a knob, that—'

'Love, listen t'yerself. The grass isn't always greener, ye see. But sometimes it's a different shade of green, and we've been gifted the chance to glimpse it, and isn't that a wonderful thing?' She looked far too pleased with herself.

'Stop speaking in tongues, Granny. I'm not able, not right now. Why should I ever use this thing again?'

'Ye don't *have to* use it, but when the time is right, it'll call yer name. And ye will.'

I went quiet. I thought hard on all I'd experienced in the vision, or whatever it was, only recalling key moments in snippets. I laid down my life before me, in my mind, like an unfinished jigsaw puzzle. Perhaps, using the right questions, I could make the most of this. Perhaps it could really help me out …

It is incredible, that's undeniable, but oh so easy to say the wrong words while clutching it, to set opportunities alight.

I pictured my life branching out before me, like the tree on the pendant, and me standing at the foot of it, wondering which branch to climb. From each branch hung a different desire: tied to one, a happy home, a big family; from another, an exciting career as a famous journalist; opposite that, every country and cuisine and climate known to humankind. They swung above an orchestra of lovers, all playing me differently, and me, tipsy with adrenalin and newness.

What if I never learn to climb? What if I break my leg and never experience any of this? What if …

'Ye see the tree on that there pendant, dear?'

'I do. I was just thinking about it …'

'You are its base,' she said, murdering my analogy with four syllables, sharp as knives. 'Those there branches are how ye choose to spend yer time on God's earth. All the things ye can have and have had. This gift I've given ye is knowledge, it's wisdom … *insight* into the things ye think ye want. That's where ye find the knowledge, the wisdom.'

I fiddled with the pendant as Granny spoke, wondering if things like it are common, only secret, around the world. 'I found contentment in the face o' living life with a family much smaller than I'd hoped for, Erin, thanks to that thing. I had my James, this house, yer father – somehow – the pub group, the two bitches,' she said, turning from Grandad's portrait to gesture to her cats, now asleep on top of one another in her armchair. 'And I had you. Frankly, ye give me purpose to keep on livin'. To keep on truckin' when I get lonely. I always have a visit to look forward to.' I stiffened, and my chest tightened. 'People die when they've nothin' to keep 'em goin', and the thought o' passing this on to you … that's kept me goin', all these years.' I scrunched up my entire face in protest at the tears wanting to fall. 'What ye'll have is largely up to you, love. This is just there … to help. That's all.'

I lay my head back onto the couch cushions and looked at Granny's dusty old chandelier, thinking, *Maybe, just maybe, all my problems will be solved thanks to my bat-shit mental family's heirloom. Maybe this is what I've been waiting for.* I resolved to tread more carefully with my 'if only's' in the future and to try my best to make the most of the power Granny had pushed toward my fingertips.

But I couldn't sleep a wink that night.

I was disturbed and exhilarated and afraid and intrigued, and the worst part about it was that I couldn't tell anyone: I couldn't text Reid; I couldn't call my dad; I'd never see Dan's reaction to any of it, because he was gone; and I couldn't blab to Rachel over a bottle of wine when I got home.

The following day, Granny was straight onto her hangover cure of more alcohol, as usual. My attempts to drag more information out of her about how she used the pendant were like trying to wring a dry towel, so I spent the rest of my visit pondering how to hold myself back from using up all seven sights in one week-long bender and how to avoid letting the Beglan secret escape my lips. I could call off my wedding, I could break a sweat in the here and now after experiencing runner's high, but I couldn't break a promise to Granny – not in the real world, anyway.

One other thing was for certain. I couldn't allow myself to wear the pendant on a day-to-day basis. I'd have to hide it and only allow myself to dig it up when I really, *really* needed it.

Intention determines outcome, after all … right?

Part 2

7
But ...

Months passed, and my single life as a server-come-barista established itself as somewhat more pleasant than my old one as Dan's twenty-something girlfriend, in spite of the unspeakable happenings of spring gone by. The Beglan pendant was long buried inside an old shoebox full of other things I wanted to forget about (but not be rid of) at the back of my wardrobe: ex-love-letters, birthday cards from Mam before she died, uni relics ... The memories of my first experience with Granny's gift had spooked me enough to put 'Mission: Turn My Life Around' on the back burner until I could figure out how to trust myself to use it properly. But the simple knowledge of its power acted as a comfort blanket on the down days. When nothing and no one could hold me still through the emptiness, the pendant's existence, and Granny's letters about it, did.

Now, in the heady heat of August, I often woke to the perfume of roses and other flowers gifted to Rachel by hopeful suitors and randy Tinder matches – males, females and everyone in between wanted her, and she got to play Eeny, Meeny, Miny, Moe. She'd often pass the odd bouquet on to me to freshen up my bedroom, knowing full well that I wasn't accumulating such romantic gestures in my own singledom – which we loved to laugh about.

To my pleasant surprise, Rachel and I had grown close over the months since I'd moved to Old Willow. She was the first female friend I'd had since college – it was strange new terrain for me. Aside from her fondness for tittle-tattle, she was pretty much the ideal flatmate: she was fun, she cooked, cleaned, and when she wasn't making me laugh, she provided a strong, firm shoulder to cry on.

These days (minus boyfriend), I had much more free time on my hands, and Rachel's healthy lifestyle was rubbing off on me. She often encouraged me to join her for yoga in the living room; it's like she sensed my desire for a body as tight and bendy as hers and sought to transform my jealousy into something that would bond us – a sort of let-me-show-you-the-way kind of deal. It was sweet, really. We'd do a 'full body flow' from YouTube in our living room together before work; I'd usually struggle while she guided me in her majesticness, and she'd shut me down any time I talked shit about my body or what it could do. 'You're only a beginner, babe' and 'You're so sexy, look at those assets – damn, I'd kill for them' and all the rest. Rachel always knew the right things to say to make me feel better about myself. I was worried for a while that her capacity to be attracted to women would lead to awkwardness, and that her compliments indicated a possible attraction, but I had quickly gotten over myself; I realised that Rachel was just treating me the way she treated everyone.

The best thing about my new life as a single, though? Rachel and I would spend random evenings with *an actual friend-type group* that had somehow formed between us, Reid and Finn, chatting about life on our balcony under an azure sky.

Reid and I never invited the other two to the Palace Gardens, though – that would always be *our* secret world, where we'd completely take our guards down and bare our dirty, lost souls.

Granted, it wasn't how I imagined thirty. I still hated cycling to my shit job on workdays. I felt wobbly over thoughts of the future, and the ability to wish my life away with a magic necklace beckoned from the depths of my bedroom. But it sure beat living out my nights bickering with a man I wasn't sure about …

Summer's sun beat upon my back as I lay on my front one Saturday afternoon, listening to 'Africa' by Toto – massive classic. I had spot cream dotted around my face and my laptop open in front of me. The screen displayed the receipt of a cheap-as-chips online clothing haul I'd just ordered. (Unwillingly, I added the most affordable version of everything I needed to the virtual basket, knowing the shoes would soon fall apart and the tops were the kind of material needing to be ironed *four bloody times* before being wearable.)

Ugh.

I need to call Dad and ask for another loan.

Dad answered after three rings. I turned the music down. Before he spoke, I could hear his wife, Sienna, blabbering in the background, and distant crowds and flamenco music.

'Darlin', howya!'

'Howya, Da. Where are you two now?'

'We're on a cruise ship. Just havin' breakfast at the mo, continental, croissants 'n' all ... lovely. Have sea breeze on me face. I tell you, selling that land was the best decision I ever made ...'

'I bet.' I was sure Sienna had convinced him of it. An image of my old horse, Clementine, waved like a flag in my memory. He'd sold her, too, along with everything I grew up with – from the bed I slept in to the blankets that had kept me warm at night as a small child. The Big Cull, I'd called it, when explaining everything to Reid one day over brunch: Dad's final attempt to move on from the painful memories of his life with my mam. I couldn't be angry at him for it. Especially not now, as an adult; the thought of going through what he did shook me to the core. I'd probably have done the same thing. But my empathy didn't stretch as far as Sienna. The fact that this random woman was swimming in money earned off our family history didn't sit well with me; it never had, and it never would. 'Sounds nice. Not my thing, obviously. You know me, I'd be curled up in a ball, terrified we'd sink, haha.' Dad chuckled. I missed Dad, but I never told him things like that, so I skipped over *feelings* to update him on work, how shite it still was, and the rest.

'So, you're tellin' me that Oscar Kelly's boy and your queer mate are best friends now?' Finn and Reid had bonded like brothers during the months since Finn had moved to Old Willow, and, thankfully, Reid *wasn't* in love with him. 'Are you sure Finn isn't a bit, you know … bent the wrong way?' Ah. Casual homophobia. My uncomfortable laugh, (*because Dad is set in his ways and his concept of humour will never change*), then, 'Finn is still as into women as ever. Actually, I *think* there are some sparks flying between him and my flatmate, Rachel. But if I asked, they'd probably deny it. Rachel has no trouble in that department, anyway, and neither does Finn.'

'Well, I'm glad to hear you have more friends over there now. I do worry … loneliness can creep through your bones, like a disease.' I stopped breathing for a few seconds, remembering how bad things got after Mam died. Dad wouldn't leave the house – sometimes, he wouldn't even come out of his bedroom, knowing that he had Granny to look after me while he grieved. 'You haven't got an eye on anyone new yourself, then?'

'Nah,' I said, before gulping down some air. 'I think

I need more time by myself, Da. In a big city like this, loneliness ... it can kinda be a luxury. If anything, I don't get *enough* time alone.' I couldn't tell if I was lying or not. And as I said the words, Owen and everything about him rallied together inside my head. We'd had a few clumsy exchanges over the past few months at work, but I still hadn't discovered his surname, nor any more information about him. Unfortunately, I couldn't mirror skinny-world-me's confidence. I'd not worked up the courage to speak to him, and he'd not asked me on a date. I imagined how much more fun being alone would be *with him*: his divine cologne, his exquisite features, his distinctive laugh that I'd now heard countless times during his coffee breaks with suited colleagues in the café, and his expression when he'd seen me in Selfridges, wearing the red dress ...

Didn't happen.

Stop it.

But that version of Erin ... she obviously lives inside me, wrapped up tight in the same old skin. I need to find her.

'Well, all I'll say is, you aren't gettin' any younger, darlin', and I say that because I love you. Back in my day ...'

Sienna's posh South Dublin accent cut in: '*Oh,* are you speaking to *Erin*? Tell her hi from me ...' I could almost see Sienna now, beside my dad: bleached blonde, extra-freckled from the Mediterranean sun, acrylic nails like talons, honing in on the fact that Dad was about to give me an earful.

'That woman couldn't be any more unlike yer mother,' Granny had whispered to me in the hallway over Christmas, while Sienna and Dad were in the kitchen getting drunk. Granny called Sienna *The Witch*. 'Loves the drama, that one. Always looks up t' no good.'

Granny wasn't wrong. I liked to blur out my late-teenage memories from the home Dad had sold, where Sienna would look through my phone behind my back under the guise of 'looking out' for me and would convince Dad to go harder on me when I'd done the slightest thing wrong, always encouraging him to gang up on me with her: two against one. She even tried to wedge herself into my social circle during sleepovers, to show me up and embarrass me by telling my friends sex stories about her and Dad. *Sensational* Sienna, that's what they called her, because she described sex with my dad as such. And they never allowed me to live that down …

'Sienna says hi,' Dad cooed. 'Sure, take this one as an example,' he said of Sienna. 'Waited too long, always wanted a family. Now she's stuck with me. Isn't that right, pumpkin?'

Pumpkin. Possibly the grossest term of endearment.

Silence from The Witch.

'Tell her I said hi. And Da, listen, I'm fine, OK? I'm all good. I'm figuring things out.' Time to hit him with it. 'Though, you know what would *really* help me while I figure things out?'

'Ah, let me guess,' he said, his voice light and knowing.

'I've purposely not asked since Christmas ... I was hoping I'd be in another job by now, but—'

'Are you even looking for one?'

No.

'Of course.'

'And do you know what kind of job you want?'

NO.

'Yeah, just – *anything* that I can use my degree for, that pays better than minimum wage and that isn't completely thankless.'

If I get a new job, I'll likely never get to perv on Owen again. But also, begging for fatherly scraps at thirty isn't a good look for anyone. Owen would hardly get rock hard over my tales of ugh I can't pay Daddy back ...

'Righ', will two grand do you, like last time? That tide ye over?'

'Ah, Da, you're a legend. Thank you so, so much. I'd be lost without you.'

Literally lost. And homeless. Even still, it was hard to fully mean the 'thank you' knowing that Sienna was living off Dad full time, treating herself to constant meals out in fancy restaurants and weekly massages – even lip fillers – and dog sitters during their travels ...

That poor dog.

They're away more than they're home.

After Turnip died, Dan had suggested that we adopt her.

'Anything for my only child. So, what's your plans for today, then?'

'I'll see where the day takes me. Probably no further than the kitchen, to be honest. Being on my feet all week at work leaves me shattered.'

'You're a good girl. Hard-working, like your da. You just need to put that hard work elsewhere – you're too bleedin' talented to still be scrubbin' plates for a few quid a week, Erin. Those Sugar Pot buggers could close up shop anytime and you'd be out on your arse.'

Aside from his choice of second wife and his dinosaur-esque views on gays, Dad was never wrong.

We said our goodbyes. I finally got myself ready to face the day before texting the group chat that Rachel, Finn, Reid and myself had going, called Destiny's Child (a private joke between us about how the only thing that could be worse than being the Michelle of the group was to be the one who missed out on the fame – the band went from four members to three when they hit the big time. We loved to fight over which one of us was Beyoncé):

I'm feeling a pizza party tonight, anyone down? Pizza and a film? Break out some wine?

Rachel replied first:

I can't, guys! Dance classes booked up until 10 p.m., and then I'm seeing Big Max for a bit of winky winky at his place! xXx

Of course she has a date. Then, Reid:

Beggy, it's Saturday. The only pizza I'll be eating will be my post-sex munch, and the only film I'll be watching will involve loads of beautiful boys

performing delicious fellatio, while I perform it on a delicious, beautiful boy (I'll be around for such boring activities mid-week) <3

I see right through that faux enthusiasm, mate. Fool yourself all you like. Finally, about half an hour later, Finn:

I'm free as a bird tonight! I'll be up in ten minutes :)

My heart jackhammered. I immediately wanted to change into less revealing pyjamas and to burn some incense to cover up the smell of the toast I'd burned.

Reid interjected:

Disgusting. Filth. NO FILTH permitted in this chat, Finn. Keep it clean plz

Finn's response:

Takes you ten minutes to get it up? No wonder you're single! At least I'm single by choice.

And Reid, finally:

The balls on you. And the SASS. I love that straight boy sass ;)

As I dug through my pyjama drawer, looking for the unsexiest friend-date thing I owned to change into (an XL yellow T-shirt with Marge Simpson on the front), three steady knocks sounded from the front door.

That was quick.

I muttered 'Fuck,' gave up on the hunt and went to let Finn in. He wore a salmon-coloured T-shirt. 'You're looking very London, lately, y'know that? I'm disappointed in you.' I'd got so used to Finn being around that I no longer tweaked my accent to be more Irish, as I did when he first moved in. He followed me into the apartment, a bottle of red wine cradled like a child in his arms.

'Loving the unicorn shorts, Beglan.' He ploughed on by me. I glanced down at my cartoonish too-short shorts, speckled with drawings of unicorns that clung to my dimpled thigh flesh, and imagined myself in Rachel's position – *I* wouldn't really like it if the guy *I* was into was alone with *her* while *she* wore shorts *this* revealing. Rachel, however, was that rare breed of woman who wouldn't feel jealous if Ariana Grande herself hung out with her crush, and, besides, she'd opted for Big Max, and it was only *me*, so …

Finn made himself at home. We settled at the kitchen table, as we always did when it was just us. I always felt weird about the idea of inviting Finn into my bedroom, my private space, to hang out, or of cuddling up on the couch with him and only him. So I always opted to spend apartment time with him on high-backed, uncomfortable dining chairs.

'What banger are you kicking off tonight with, then?' he asked, pouring me a glass of Malbec. Its red-cherry scent greeted me with wistful affection.

''Eyes without a Face' by Billy Idol, duh,' I said, finding it in my eighties playlist.

'You know, I love that you choose to ignore the near three decades of music that's been released since you were born.'

'It's all shite, mate. All of it.'

'I'll prove you wrong, one day. Tellin' you. Christ, I need this … long, long day …'

We drank, caught up on work, and talk quickly turned to reminiscing about the past. I was only half there as thoughts of my last interaction with Owen clouded over Finn's voice (he'd thanked me for leaving a little mint chocolate beside his espresso yesterday) when the word 'divorce' slapped me in the face out of nowhere.

'You … you were *married*? You've never said.' I felt my face do a weird dance between empathy, pity and confusion to reflect my inner monologue. 'Never saw any Facebook updates.'

'I'm not a Facebook kind of guy, Beglan. I only really use it to share the odd film trailer, the odd song …'

Shit songs. I always scroll past.

'And, well, you never told me about your engagement. Heard about *that* from Rachel. You were a stone's throw away from landing yourself in the exact same situation.'

'Hey, don't change the subject,' I said, trying to be coy.

'Well. I moved here, mid-divorce, just months after my da died. Met you down on the stairs, and you told me life was great. Could *feel* the wall around you. No fooling me. There was a kinda sadness in your eyes. Didn't exactly invite open conversation, Beglan.'

Oh no.

No no.

This isn't light-hearted fun with a friend any more.

I mean, I knew Oscar had died – his body was probably

still warm when Dad called me up to tell me. I remembered Dad's jokes about how Inishbeg could 'rest easy' now that himself and Oscar wouldn't be shooting each other daggers across the streets any more, but his jokes were layered with guilt and sadness. The call was like a really screwed-up trifle.

I miss talking about who the best Batman actor was, and about our teen years, pre-technology. It had been embarrassing enough to admit to Finn that I wasn't, in fact, living it up in London …

Why did I dig?

Shine the torch back at him.

'I'm sorry about your dad. I know we've never talked about it, but, I'd … heard.' I meant it, too. The memory of the terror and pain of Mam's death sparked me somewhere deep inside my stomach. I'd found it hard to understand how the boundaries of human suffering could extend so far. I could remember gagging and gagging and crying and screaming and scratching at my flesh so hard I broke the skin all over my arms, my face, my legs. I had absurd nightmares during the weeks that followed, in which my mam climbed through the dirt that buried her to come collect me after school; others where she cooked and served me dinners as she rotted and turned black; nightmares that began as dreams and ended in night sweats, where I'd wake up in Mam's coffin beside her and she'd still be alive, and we'd scream and scream and nobody would come to help us. 'Losing a parent …

nothing and nobody can prepare you. I can't imagine it's any easier when you're an adult.'

'Part of me wishes that I lost him years ago. At least then I wouldn't have so many memories to haunt me. But, hey, your da probably popped a cork when he found out. The pair of them went head to head over your ma, so I've been told.' He glanced at me, then immediately focused his gaze back on his wine glass.

'Nah, I think he felt bad, actually. For wasting so much energy.' *And thank you for making a joke.* 'How long were you married for, then?' I asked, digging myself an even bigger hole. 'What happened?'

'Four years. We were together for just about seven. Met shortly after you left to come live here, actually. It was mostly brilliant, me and her. Then—'

'Then, you got bored of her,' I said without thinking.

'Then, she cheated on me with some guy she worked with.' I stopped breathing. 'She left me for him and, eh, the end, pretty much.' When Finn finished talking, he looked straight at me. Heavy eye contact. 'Why did you call off your engagement?' He sipped at his wine, waiting for an answer.

Balls.

Twice today, conversation has manifested images of Dan in my head. I didn't consent to spending my Saturday drowning in memories that make my chest hurt.

'Burying things doesn't help, missus. I can say that confidently,' he said, prodding me in my silence.

'It's been working so far.'

'Talk. Go on.'

I took in a bellyful of air. 'OK. The ex-fiancé's name was – *is* – Dan. We were together for six years, and were engaged for, eh, less than a year, actually. Wow. We – we were happy enough. *I think*. Until …'

'Until yous weren't,' he finished for me, after a pause. *Spot on.*

'What was your wife's name?' I asked. 'What was she like?'

'Róisín. She was the best thing in the whole world, really.'

'Until she *wasn't*,' I repeated him, hoping to put him at ease. It worked. His body melted into calmness.

'I haven't said her name out loud since things ended.' Finn's eyes focused on a spot across the room then. Maybe so he could imagine his ex in vivid detail. Something like jealousy scratched at the back of my heart. I leaned forward as he spoke again. 'Ró was my best friend. Loved film as much as I do. Worked in TV production as a make-up artist. That's how we met: on set for an Irish soap opera. I was working there one summer for some extra pennies. Christ, it was shite – the show. But after one date, I was smitten. My ma loved her. I loved her … too much, I think.'

'*Can* you love someone too much?'

He sat quietly with his thoughts as the hum of the building took over from Spotify in the brief silence between songs. 'I was willing to stay with her after I found out about the affair. She was my priority, always. Well, her and ...'

'You weren't her priority?'

'I was just the option she'd temporarily landed on, I think. And I didn't respect myself enough to hold her to any kind of standard. Just ... wanted her to stay. To choose me, over ... him.'

Heavy.

Fuck.

This was the realest conversation *we'd* had, well, ever.

I remembered how Dan and I found fault with each other every day after the honeymoon phase ended, how our standards for one another shattered in time. 'Take My Breath Away' by Berlin came on my playlist then, and I mentally cursed it for being there.

Not a romantic song ... not while he's opening up about this Róisín bitch.

Do I skip the song? Too obvious?

Ignore it.

Talk about Dan.

'My ex, Dan, was like my dad in a lot of ways,' I said. 'Which I know is weird and Freudian, but whatever.' Finn's face warmed up. 'I mean ... he even *looked* like Da. Tall and thin. My nickname for him was Beanpole,' I said, laughing.

'I called Róisín "Mouse" – she was absolutely tiny. All of four foot eleven,' he said, a small smile curling up the edges of his mouth.

Why did Finn ever find me attractive? I'm basically a giant by comparison.

Dan had no long-term relationships before me. I liked that. Less to compare me to.

'The main reason I don't talk about Dan and me any more is because when I do I can't help but get kinda anxious about the whole thing. Like, what if it was a mistake calling off the wedding?'

The pendant, with its tree made of copper wires and its stone, black as the night sky, flashed in my mind.

No chance.

'Why do you say that?' Finn asked. 'Why did you leave him?'

'That's the thing. There wasn't one big reason, like him cheating or – I dunno, violence or anything like that. We bickered a lot, but so do half the married couples I've met.'

'Sometimes people just fall outta love. It happens.'

'Ah, I know. But Dan still wanted to marry me. And after I left him, I still missed him. Even now, as much as I like to tell myself I don't, I *do* miss him.' I needed to shift the tone of the conversation, and fast. 'Y'know what he says to me? As I'm moving out?'

'Go on. It can't be worse than Róisín's the-person-you're-still-in-love-with-doesn't-exist-she's-dead speech.'

'How very Taylor Swift,' I said, laughing. 'Well, right, you be the judge. Dan says ... Ready for this? He goes, "You'll spend life searching for my love in someone else, but you'll never find it." I mean, how cruel can you be?'

'Brutal! Ohh. *Desperate!*' Finn choked on his wine, mid-laugh.

I giggled.

This is nice.

As I poured myself another glass of wine, I went on. 'I told Dan I didn't want his "love" any more. That it was wearing me down and rubbing me out like a bloody eraser on the end of a pencil. All those lines I'd drawn in were disappearing before my eyes. I was losing myself in the thing. Yes, the man adored the ground I walked on, and, yes, he looked after me. But ...'

'You did the right thing. The thing that demands a lot of strength. If there's a *but*, that's all that matters. You'll forever be focused on the *but*. With Ró and myself there was never a *but*, at least for me.'

'Seriously? Never? Surely you had some doubts, at some point?'

'Nah. Mouse never cleaned up after herself, and she was insecure, and I *hated* her mates, but all the downsides were never deal-breakers because we'd just talk and sort them out before they snowballed into anything problematic. I never questioned whether or not I was in the right situation.'

My insides were popping bubble wrap as Finn spoke. For some reason, I'd always assumed that *I* was his *but* – that he'd always wonder about me; that I'd be the shadow his future girlfriends lived in.

I guess there's not a person in this world pining for me, after all.

'It was the right situation at the time, anyway,' Finn said, interrupting the storm that was my thought pattern. 'I don't regret a second of my time with Ró.' Sentimentality fogged up his eyes. 'She taught me what it means to love someone. Just as *you* introduced me to the crippling reality of one-sided puppy love.'

I smacked the table, secretly pleased. 'So you *did* love me.'

'Haha, ah, c'mere, we all have that one all-consuming crush at that age. It's got the "puppy" prefix for a reason.' Finn playfully pushed his tongue out.

'What d'ya mean "at that age"? I have one *right now*.'

'Is that so? An all-consuming crush, eh? Tell me about the lucky thing, then. Spit it out.' Genuine curiosity moulded his features as another song started, which I barely noticed – my brain once again turned to all things Owen. I probably looked high. I wiggled in my chair, excited to talk about my ultimate passion.

'Right. Every time I see this guy through the windows, on his way into Sugar Pot, it's like all of my insides are being tickled, y'know?'

'Mm-hmm. It's the best feeling,' Finn said solemnly.

'I do be almost on the lookout for him, mate. Like a dog waiting for its owner to return. I know what times he usually pops by at, and the minutes drag till the clock tells me he's nearby. When I see him I instantly start biting my lips, to make sure there are no, y'know, gross bits of dead skin clumped on them, haha, and, ugh, I can't focus on *anything* else while he's there ...'

I'm getting tipsy already.

These are drunk confessions.

Beggy the lightweight strikes once again.

'Who is he? Some randomer?' Finn asked.

'His name is Owen. I don't know his surname yet. I've toyed with the idea of asking him to sign the back of a receipt while he's on a phone call ... *hopefully* he wouldn't ask why ... at least then, I might find him online ...'

'You're mad, woman.' Finn laughed, stretching himself to take up as much room as possible as he played with his wine glass. 'Go on. So, you don't actually *know* him, then.'

'He's been coming to my café for months now. I know that he's from Northern Ireland, because of the accent, and that he's the CEO of ... some company.' The glorious prize I'd won by eavesdropping. 'That he loves basic-bitch food like avocado toast, and that the way he moves and smells and laughs makes my ovaries squirm. He wears suits, like, all the time – it's so hot – and he's got that kind of charisma you only ever see when actors do their press junkets to shift movie tickets. He gleams, y'know? Pulls off glasses instead of opting for contacts, which I *love* ...'

Finn narrowed his eyes.

Am I in conversations-with-Reid territory?

Should I maybe not talk about my ovaries and sexy men?

'I'm not sure he's that into me, anyway,' I hammered on.

'He's smiled at me once or twice … makes little jokes here and there … gives me the eye. He's not very forward.' I felt the guilty itch. I was lying: I'd encountered a *very* forward version of Owen using the pendant, but I was describing the Owen I'd really met, so it was an off-white lie at most. 'It's a lovely change, though, to *not* be heavily hit on at work. That's probably why I fancy him.'

'So, hang on. Northern Irish. CEO. Wears suits and glasses. What does he look like?'

'Ehm, floppy dark hair. Just … stupidly attractive. There are no other words.'

'Surely you're not on about Owen Brown, Beglan?'

'What? Back up. Who?'

A tremble. Gooseflesh.

'The head of Paradigm House?'

'What's that? How d'you know him?'

Finn stiffened. 'The lad I'm on about gave a lecture at King's College a few weeks back. I went along with some of my students who're interested in how social media is changing how we find out about and consume film—'

'Yeah, yeah, OK, to the point, mate!'

'Jaysis, you're really keen on this chap.'

'An understatement. Now talk.'

'Whoever you're on about sounds like this Owen Brown guy. Wore a suit. Northern Irish. Was fairly shy after he finished his talk … I asked him a few questions. He's a CEO, too … Could be your man?'

'I need to know all that you know.' I was dying of thirst,

and Finn was holding an open bottle of water over my head, ready to pour. The table became my safety raft as I spread myself across it and held on for dear life.

'Ah, look. He's a rich yuppie and must be ... what, near a decade older than you?'

'No way!' He only looked about thirty. 'I mean, so what. I like older men. Dan was four years older than me.'

'Google him, go on. Guarantee you he's near forty. Seems to me the type to get a stiffy over social-rights marches.'

'What's that supposed to mean?'

'Ah, just ... he seems like a busy, ambitious fella, with little in common with you.'

'Hey, I like activism.'

'You *like* activism?' Finn forced out a mock laugh. 'Beglan, you're no activist. You won't pull the wool over this lad's eyes. Mad into his internet analytics and *campaigning*.'

'I have a blog, y'know. We'd have *loads* in common,' I sneered, as I ran a Google image search for Owen Brown on my phone.

'Ah yes, this mystical blog I've heard so much about that you won't even share the name of ... *That* blog. The short stories you wrote when we were younger were great. I don't *get* the secrecy – around the blog.'

But I wasn't listening. I'd hit the jackpot. A professional photo of Owen that led me to *his very own website*. 'It's him! You beautiful bastard, Finn, you've just saved my life!' I clicked out, deciding to save the website for later. I wanted to get a better idea of how much info Google had on him.

I bit my lip as I scrolled through various articles about Owen attached to glorious HD photos of him, completely forgetting that Finn was sat at my kitchen table waiting for me to come up for air.

His Wikipedia page had no spouse listed. *Score*.

I sat up straight. 'So, OK. Explain to me why you think he and I wouldn't hit it off,' I said eventually, with my best impression of someone who wasn't bothered by her friend's lack of encouragement.

'Oh. Good. You're still alive. Well, it's simple. He's like … the movie *Inception*. There's a lot going on, y'know? And—'

'I've *got* to hear this. Seeing as you've got me all figured out and all. I'm what, exactly? *Dumb and Dumber*?'

Finn laughed his booming laugh. 'OK. You're right. I don't think we're close enough for me to give you a movie label just yet.'

'But you know Owen enough to give him one, yeah?' I pushed my tongue into my cheek.

'I'm just saying. Chalk and cheese don't go off and get married, do they? He's a somebody, and you're … you're—'

'Excuse me? Firstly, who says I want to marry anybody, ever? And … a nobody, am I? Mister lecturer who lives in a bedroom in someone else's apartment?'

Ick. Maybe that was a bit mean.

I'm just drunk.

Need to slow down on the Malbec.

No, fuck that. He's being mean.

'I obviously didn't mean it like that …'

'In what other way could you possibly have meant it? Enlighten me.' I knocked back the last of my wine before tightly folding my arms in fierce defence. Every cell in my body wanted to throw in his face that I knew what he thought of me because Rachel had told me that night as we chatted on the couch. But that had happened when I'd first used the pendant, in a non-existent timeline, so I repressed the urge.

That pendant is far more hassle than it's worth.

'I just mean … Well, you said yourself you've a massive crush on the lad. And I got the vibe when I met him that *he* has a massive crush on himself. Kept tooting his own horn during his talk. *You're* not like that.' Finn seemed to be genuinely annoyed now.

Someone sounds jealous of Owen's success.

'Were you always this judgemental?' I asked him.

'Everyone is judgemental. Some hide it, and some are honest about it.'

'Your truth isn't *the* truth, Finn.'

'You said yourself, you don't even know this guy. Look, I just don't wanna encourage your romantic notions, when—'

'You're not my big brother, OK? Don't worry your willy about me. Just help me out. What does his company do?'

He sighed. 'They link online creators, film-makers, influencers – all those types who make money online – with big brands. To fund their projects. I *think*. He runs events for stuff like that, awards shows and all, from what I understood from his spiel on campus. It's a bit of marketing, bit of this, bit of that. Like, he's way ahead of the game. He's—'

'He sounds *brilliant*,' I said, sneering again.

'Beglan, I know I've no say,' Finn began, a tense sideways smile across the table.

'Correct. You don't.'

'Just saying, well – I dunno – what would yous even talk about on a date?' He playfully nudged me. 'Would you fill him in on the splendour of washing dishes for seven quid an hour? The *sheer joy* of having nobody reading your blog and being so ashamed of it that you won't even show it to your mates?' Finn poked fun with just as much love as Reid usually did, but, still, I wasn't so comfortable with Finn saying these things, for some reason. His words stroked my skin the wrong way, like a lover's hand rubbing at your stubble before you can smack it away. My expression evidently screamed discomfort because then he said, 'I'm only winding you up, Beglan. I just don't think you're making the most of your time, or your talent. I remember when Miss White would make you read out your English essays in school. You've really got something.'

I gulped. 'It's not like I plan on being in this situation forever. I'm just getting back on my feet after Dan and all we've just been talking about: the loneliness, the *big life change*.'

'Loneliness is the worst reason to go chasing more heartbreak.'

'Awfully pessimistic way to look at things, don't you think?'

'I'm one of the most positive people you'll ever have the pleasure of knowing,' he teased, 'but running the gauntlet again? So soon? I don't think so. No, thanks.'

'You date. You go on dates. All the time. You're the biggest flirt I've ever met in my life, ever.'

'Yeah. I date. But I always make it very clear that it's casual, straight up. That I don't want anything serious. I don't string people along, and women always know what they'll be getting before they confirm that they want it. So there's no crossed wires. No hurt feelings,' he said, avoiding my eyes.

That's why he's not made a real move for Rachel. Limited flirtation for the one he knows would cut too deep. Self-preservation.

'Maybe I want something casual with Owen,' I challenged him.

'And maybe tears aren't made of water,' he scoffed.

He's not wrong.

'Well, look. How about I show you my blog and you give me some tips? And then I take it from there. I'd like to at least *talk* to this guy. I've not been able to get him outta my head for months. The blog might be my one chance at having any common ground. Help. Me. To. Impress.'

'You don't need to impress anyone but yourself. So let's just work on that, Beglan.'

We moved onto the balcony, home to two plastic chairs and a small plastic table. We sat out to enjoy the evening's coolness beneath a light-polluted sky, overlooking great bursts of leaves from street trees. I had a nosy at the loud drunken louts below us – starched shirts, crisp and pressed; shaved back and sides; football chants – then I huddled in my duvet (that I'd tipsily dragged from my bedroom while Finn 'broke the seal') on one of the chairs, with Finn by my side. He scrolled through *Erin's View*. Embarrassment enwrapped me.

'People Are More Likely to Have Twins as They Get Older, Apparently.'

'15 Things Every Foreigner Goes Through as a Twenty-Something in London.'

'A Handful of Ways to Make Chocolate Rice Krispie Cakes (Easy and Quick).'

'I'm Reducing My Use of Single-Use Plastics and You Can Too.'

He's being very quiet.

This is a bad idea.

I'm only letting him see it because WINE.

'It's shite, you can say it,' I said quietly, fidgeting. 'It's all just practice, really, and—'

'It's pretty shite, yeah. The titles are terrible. And there's *no* consistency.'

'I know, *I know*—'

'But, it's shite mostly because I can't really see *you* in any of these posts.'

'What?'

'Your personality is completely missing. These could've been written by anyone. Also, you're being *extremely* politically correct. What's that about?'

'Isn't that ... a good thing? It's the internet ...'

'Yeah, and people appreciate honesty online as much as they do in person. You're watering yourself down in these posts, anticipating the worst reactions. That really comes through. I can't relate to any of this.'

'But people will get all down my throat if I...'

'Tell things like they are? Fuck 'em, then. You can't make everyone happy. Listen, we had this chat in a lecture the other day about how casting directors go about finding actors that look the part for the roles they need to assign ...' Finn lit up from within when he talked about anything to do with films. It was adorable, in a dorky kind of way. I loved that he'd remained the same after all these years.

I don't love anything as much as Finn loves films.

Not even eighties music.

Unless Granny counts.

'Sorry, I won't bore you with all that. Just ... share your truth,' he said. 'These topics, too ...' He eyed the laptop screen. 'Do you really care about any of this?'

'Um, like, women's rights, you mean? Of *course* I do, I—'

'In the context of what you're actually writing about *here*, though. None of this stuff really relates to you.'

'So? It's important for people to know more about, eh, child brides, and, and ... transgender issues, and—'

'But you're basically just regurgitating existing facts or thoughts without *adding* much. Who needs that when there are plenty of huge publications covering these topics, with so much more heart? You can do better than this. I know you can. You're interesting. This isn't.'

I'd wanted directness and advice, but I don't think I was really ready for it. My inner child pouted and thought: *Admire me! Tell me how great I am!*

'Why not focus more on things that directly impact you? Experiences you've had or, eh, you could interview people who've gone through things. You have to share something real – a bit more informal. Conversational, even. It's a *blog*. That's what blogs are for, right?'

He was trying so hard to help me.

Dan never did this.

I picked at the hard skin around my fingernails and listened to the distant whistle and jeer of some man (likely one of the louts I'd glimpsed) shouting at some young woman out for the night with her friends. *Catcalling* ... *objectification* ... I could write a whole bloody essay on *that* from my own perspective.

'I modelled the blog on Louis Theroux,' I admitted. 'How he tackles issues bigger than him. I love him.'

'Louis Theroux immerses himself, Beglan. The man got plastic surgery during one episode ... went to a swingers' party in another ... spent loads of time with *actual paedophiles* ...'

'I know. He's so great. How can I be that cool and, I dunno, pioneering?'

I showed Finn a clip of Louis Theroux getting a massage from a prostitute in a brothel, and we giggled at his discomfort.

'So, you want to be a female Louis Theroux?'

'Well, no. Don't reduce me to my bits, mister.' I hated being called *female*. Or *lady*, as Kenneth called me at work. It didn't sit right and it never had.

'Haha … ah, g'way. Ye know what I mean. You want to do the same kinda thing. You want to explore meaningful stuff and have an impact on people – have fun while doing it. Do something new.'

'That. All that, exactly. Owen would eat me up, I bet.'

Finn rolled his eyes. 'If you want to impress *him*, this blog ain't the way to go,' he said sincerely. 'I mean, if you want to lead with this as the big conversation starter, I'd put a fair bit of work into jazzing it up. But forget him for a minute. This could be the foundation for something really bloody great.'

'Do you think I could do it, then? Make something outta, I dunno, online journalism?' I curled the toes of my right foot over those of my left, like I always did when I felt vulnerable, ready to be judged.

Finn looked at me, eyes alive with a thousand unsaid things, holding his breath in the moonlight. 'I believe *you* can do anything you put your mind to. I always did, and I always will. But you need to believe it yourself, and you need to do it for the right reasons. I just want you to grab your life by the balls, Beglan.'

I exhaled, and thought of Granny, the night I'd used the pendant, and how she'd somehow seemed to want to shake my whole body into action. 'I wish I knew how to do that.'

'One day at a time, as with anything.'

One go with the pendant at a time might get the job done.

There are so many things I could use it for, but what if I say the wrong words? What if I use it and nothing is different, and I throw away another opportunity? What if a different version of my life is so good that I can't face this existence? Or, worse yet, what if I'm bloody dead in another reality? What would happen then? Would everything just be black for what would feel like twenty-four hours?

I shuddered.

Finn blabbered on, with no idea of the thoughts that were swallowing me whole. 'I won't be working on a film set anytime soon, for example. But one day, I'll have my beachside house, full of stray dogs, and a few credits to my name. I will.'

I wish I could be so certain of my future.

Get out of your head, at least until he leaves.

'You're a dog man, then? I prefer cats. See, that's why we'd never have worked. Cat people and dog people mix like oil and vinegar, my friend.'

'Ah, I've enough love to go round. I love cats and all,' Finn said, biting his lower lip on one side.

We talked about my blog and my dreams and his dreams

until the early hours of the morning, polishing off the last drops of wine we could squeeze from the apartment after two hunting sessions for half- or near-empty bottles. Rachel returned from her midnight romp with Big Max at 4 a.m. She interrupted my careful rendition of 'Under the Milky Way' by The Church, then she and Finn got talking right away, as usual. I took the opportunity to leave them to it and slide off in my intoxication, carrying my laptop and hot-dogged inside my duvet, which trailed along the cheap wooden floors of the apartment behind me. I yearned for privacy so I could Google my obsession without disclosing my absolute creepiness.

'Lovely night, Beglan – such a laugh …' Finn's voice sounded from somewhere far off. I couldn't say from where – nothing around me was solid any more.

Bet he's in Rachel's room. Bet they're getting up close and personal. Bet he wishes she'd been here all night instead of me.

I was hammered. I soon found myself on all fours on my bedroom floor, holding my phone inches from my face and blinding myself with bright artificial light so I could read blurry snippets about Owen and his acclaimed media company, so I could absorb him from all angles on Google Images once again. Drunkenness gobbled my pendant apprehension whole.

What if I use it to see if Owen could be into a non-skinny me?

I may never experience anything with this majestically interesting specimen otherwise …

Wait. I'm proper pissed.

What am I doing on the floor?

He's so fucking sexy.

We probably have loads in common.

I love the sound of what he does for a living. I need to be around actual, real-life successful people – it might give me the push I need … and—

Screw it. Last time wasn't that terrifying.

I mean, I didn't end up with post-traumatic stress disorder.

I'm doing it.

I crawled to my wardrobe on my hands and knees, inebriated and in my unicorn shorts, a pile of hair and slurred words peppered with laughter, with all caution thrown to the wind. I grabbed at shoes and books and camera equipment and all manner of hoarded items and threw them behind me or pushed them aside until I located the old shoebox where I'd hidden Granny's gift.

Before I knew it I was on my back with the soft synthetic fabric of my shag rug cushioning my skin and the pendant wrapped around my neck, its tree-of-life-encased stone in my right hand.

OK, let's go.

It might not even work.

You only live once, isn't that what Reid always says before he does something stupid?

In my clumsy, drunken voice: 'If only I'd gone out for Reid's birthday …'

8
Girls, Plural

The bed was a puffy cloud of white. Its pillows and duvet hugged my body into consciousness. I'd never woken up anywhere so bright, or quiet. Everything was still, like a schoolyard before the rush of screams at lunch break. Through sleepy eyes I saw walls the lightest shade of blue and paintings of boats and of children feeding swans. I rolled my head to peer out the room-wide window and was shocked upright when I saw through to the other side: a mesmerising lake of still water and forested hills on the other side.

Within seconds my face hovered an inch from the window. I stood there, wearing nothing but the pendant, looking down at a woodland garden leading to private lake frontage and a boathouse and a patio adjacent to ... wherever I was, strewn with cosy outdoor furniture.

And I recognised the distant sights visible beyond the

tall trees to my left, from a childhood holiday with Dad and Granny. They'd brought me on a guided tour of the World of Beatrix Potter (I was obsessed with *The Tale of Peter Rabbit* growing up) in a place called Bowness, a scenic fishing village on the shores of Lake Windermere.

Is this the Lake District?

Has to be.

Why am I here?

I pulled my eyes away from the view outside and glanced around the room, searching for a clock. Ornate hands above the bed informed me it was only 10 a.m.

The room was cute but void of any personality. Very holiday home, with its generic, beachy decor: wicker baskets, anchor wall hangings, random shells strategically placed on top of shelves – Dan's vision of hell on earth, basically. 'The sort of place you go to live when you're about ready to die,' he would have said.

When will I stop relating everything back to Dan?

Unlike the first time I'd used the pendant, I wasn't feeling at all disturbed or unhinged by the fact that I'd woken up in a new life because this time I knew what to expect. I was at peace but with the same strange pins-and-needles sensation I'd experienced during the last vision. Mild excitement crawled over my skin like static – probably because I knew how authentic this day was going to be. At least I knew that, if nothing else. I was also acutely aware that real me lay drunk on her bedroom floor and would remain there for this entire 'day'.

And it didn't freak me out one bit.

White floorboards creaked beneath my feet as I nakedly tiptoed back to the foot of the strange bed. My clothes, handbag, phone and ballet pumps were messily stacked on the floor beside two empty condom wrappers. The sight made me smile a smile that reached my eyes.

Sex! I can't even remember what that feels like.

Twice in one night?

I've still got it.

I grabbed the bed's grey throw and wrapped it around me so I could explore the unfamiliar house/cottage/ wherever I was. Then, as I was about to turn the doorknob, a male voice called from downstairs in a Northern Irish accent.

Owen.

It bloody worked!

'Get that lovely bum down here. You're in for a breakfast extravaganza of the Irish variety! Was about to take it up to you on a tray, but I hear you creeping around up there …'

Slowly, enraptured, I opened the bedroom door as Owen continued to say glorious words, each one a shooting star. I peered through to the landing. His voice rose up from the bottom of the staircase.

'Bet you can smell it … I'm drooling here, missy. Come help me demolish all this before I go. And *don't* brush your teeth first. We've got freshly squeezed OJ on the go, and you know how mint makes it taste all funny.'

Curiosity turned to fearlessness, so – naked, wrapped in the blanket – I scurried across the hallway to the top of the stairs. He stood at the bottom, looking up at me, his eyes alive in a way I'd not seen them before. And he wasn't wearing a suit. It was the first time I'd seen him dressed in regular human clothing (a grey jumper and fitted jeans), and his floppy hair was wild and untamed.

'Look at you,' he said, through a content smile. 'Call me an old sap, but I'll dream of that face for the whole eight-hour flight.'

Goodness, compliment me some more – go on …

Wait, what flight?

I'm supposed to get a whole day with you!

I've used up one of seven goes with this pendant thing to see if this is worth pursuing, and to get laid by you, and, and—

'Where are you going? Do you *have* to go? Today?' I walked down the steps toward him, treading carefully so I didn't trip and pile down on top of him in my excitement, all the while enjoying the food smells that took me right back to childhood. He wrapped both his arms around me when I was close enough, then lifted me up and placed me down on the floor beside him.

'New York, of course. I told you the other day, you sleepy thing.' He twirled a random piece of my messy red hair. 'Ten hours horizontal in bed wasn't enough, then? Did I tire you out?'

He said that last line in a hush and leaned closer to me. My scatty, other-world memory showed me slivers of us in the throes of passion at the bottom of the bed in the

room I'd come from – and on its white floor, and against
its white walls …

Standing this close to Owen and recalling things I'd
not really done with him was detachment folded up with
closeness, intimacy without the sense of belonging you
expect to feel in such an exchange. Just plain proximity,
like you feel while getting a professional massage or
having a facial. From here I could see his forty years
mapped onto his face in soft lines, mostly around his eyes
– detail I could never make out from across the café when
I'd watch him.

'Um, yeah, I'm wrecked … New York, I just, um …
forgot,' I said, struggling with thoughts of *Can I put my
hands on him? Is that OK? Why is he going to America?
And what about me? Why do I care so much?*

Before I could think straight, Owen took my hand in his
and led me through the bright open-plan room we were
standing in to a kitchen area, where some kind of soft doo-
wop music played from his mobile phone. I followed along
behind him, like Bambi taking his first steps. Owen then
proudly held his hands out toward the island jutting out
from the back wall. Its marble top was laden with plates
of food and condiments – *so* many things I liked to eat
in one place: sausages, bacon, black and white pudding,
baked beans, fried tomatoes and mushrooms, scrambled
and fried eggs, toast, creamery butter. My eyes couldn't
absorb everything at once.

'I even conjured up Irish soda bread for you, from

scratch' – he pointed at a mess of mixing pots and ingredients by the sink – 'because, well, you mentioned how much you miss it. And look – Lyons teabags!' His voice was raw enthusiasm. My mouth fell open. I picked up the box of *my favourite tea in the world* and shoved my nose in past the cardboard opening to get a good sniff.

'Mmm,' I moaned.

'I drove over the border for this tea last time I was home, visiting friends. This is another reason I wanted to get you out here. I don't stock such, eh, *interesting* ingredients in my own house. We have guests staying here a lot, and so ...'

He looked and smelled and sounded so good.

Tired of waiting, I reached up to touch Owen's face as he spoke, soft as it looked, and the rest of his words were lost against my lips. My first kiss with him was perhaps his thousandth with me, though that didn't take away from it one bit; he kissed me back, long and gentle, searching into my eyes as he did. A mighty wallop of ultraviolet madness. It was so hot. He knotted his fists in the throw wrapped around me as though he wanted to pull it off, to reveal my nakedness, but he didn't. Instead, after giving me a few soft kisses across my face, he held his forehead against mine, for seconds or for hours – time may have paused itself.

The eternity of a moment like that. I think the universe's heart skipped a beat as it all erupted between us, at long last.

'I'll miss you,' he said, nose to nose with me. 'Y'know,

every time I get out of bed you do this intake of breath in your sleep, a kind of reverse sigh. It just kills me. One night here and there is never enough.'

How long have we been seeing each other in this world? And why is our time together so scattered?

With no idea how this-world-me would respond and with every desire to learn how to make this a reality in the real world, I said simply, 'I'll miss you too,' and I wrapped my fingers up in his. 'Now, let's eat – look what you've *done*.'

'You're happy?'

How myself can I be with him? I mean, he's obviously not put off by my actual body, like, at all … Him chatting me up wasn't just an isolated event in skinnyland – it would've happened either way.

He likes me.

Test the waters …

'Am I happy? About *this*? Do farts smell like shite? Of course I'm happy. I mean, look!'

He's laughing. Good. I can talk about farts in front of him. Humour, looks, money, maturity and he cooks. This is promising. I'm all for this.

'I've never seen a better pile of food in my life,' I went on. 'Well, apart from my granny's Christmas displays. That woman is a force to be reckoned with.' I threw him a cheeky-but-also-cute look through the curtains of my bed hair (at least I hoped that's what it was). 'Food really is the way to my heart, mister. Ten-out-of-ten impressed.' I sat down on one of the high chairs by the island and started to plate up, choosing a little bit of everything he'd laid out, weak with hunger.

And with lust.

I can't remember the last time anyone surprised me like this.

'I'm near dead after last night,' Owen said, running a hand through his hair and pushing it all off his face. 'Need energy. This jet lag is going to stick the final knife in. But it was worth it.'

'What was?'

'You! So rampant. I love it.'

'They do say us females experience our sexual prime in our thirties,' I said, disregarding the likelihood that this was a myth and hyper-focused instead on the thudding of my heart upon hearing Owen say the word *love*. I'd thought he was going to say The Three Words, mid-preparation of a cup of tea, and I wasn't ready. Not only because I hardly knew him in reality, but mainly because something deep inside me told me we weren't *there* yet. Granny would tell me it was my intuition doing a dance to catch my attention.

'Are you excited about your trip? What's on the agenda?' I pried, wearing a poker face and smearing the perfect ratio of butter to marmalade onto a slice of the bread he'd made for me, hoping he'd elaborate on the New York thing without picking up on my lack of knowledge. But he seemed taken aback by the question.

'Since when do we talk about work?'

Shite.

His words were devoid of all the warmth he'd expressed when showing off the breakfast spread. All was still for a moment, save for Owen's fifties music that made me think of Italian American mobsters. I pulled the blanket tighter to my chest, conscious of the pendant resting there – the culprit responsible for my dizzy understanding of our relationship. 'I'm over there for half of each month only because I *have* to be. Anyway, what are *your* plans for the rest of the day? Think you'll hang about here?' Before I could shrug in my disappointment, he added, 'I'll leave money for you for a taxi to the train station, of course. But I think you should make a day of it. Stay, relax, work on your blog, read …'

Way to pivot the conversation. I munched on my buttered soda bread, holding back compliments on how great it tasted because I was confused why asking about his trip was such an issue.

'Or you could head into the village,' he continued. 'It's gorgeous. I spent a lot of time here as a kid. Mum moved here after she split with Dad.'

Well, he's open about his past.

That's got to be a good sign.

'You'll be able to get lovely Instagrams. Of the old houses, the cute cafés and inviting pub fronts and all the narrow streets that flow down to the lake, like rivulets. Magic. Show the place off!'

Why does he speak like he's a hundred years old? I don't

*think I've ever heard someone say the word 'rivulet' in casual
conversation.*

And I don't want to wander around on my own.

Why can't you just not fly today?

'You can leave the key with Wendy, the cleaner. She's
a friend of my mother's. She'll be along soon.' Owen
reached across then and stroked my thigh through the
blanket. 'That nice?' He nodded at the remnants of my
slice of bread, trying hard to re-engage me. I'd retreated
into my shell and it must have been obvious. 'Worth the
brawl I had with the wooden spoon?'

'It's lovely. Thank you for all of this, really.' I meant
it. 'Especially seeing as you're ... busy and stuff.' But I
couldn't hide that I wanted to know more than he was
willing to share. It came through in my tone of voice.

Stop being a selfish bitch.

This guy is fantastic.

*He's away a lot – so what? And he's guarded about what
he gets up to when you're not with him – who cares? Why
should it be a problem that he has a life of his own? That
he's busy. That he can compartmentalise. That he doesn't
want to throw a red dress in with his white wash. Isn't that
part of the attraction? He's got an amazing career and he's
so bloody attractive and ...*

I'm making excuses, aren't I?

I do care.

My desire for romance battled my self-respect as
Owen's hand continued to caress my leg before moving
up to my shoulders.

'Good,' he said, as it all roared inside my head. 'I really wanted to do something special for you. Because I won't see you again for a while, and you deserve it.' Then, with his free hand, he reached for a fresh newspaper, which he folded out across his lap. 'Enjoy! Eat to your heart's content, gorgeous thing.'

I was really out of practice at being all soppy with someone – I didn't know what to do with my face. And people didn't call me *gorgeous*, not ever.

'Your skin glows so much in the mornings,' he went on, 'especially after …'

A good shag?

He leaned forward and continued to pet me like I would a kitten. 'I just love your face.'

There's that L word again.

And goodness, he knew how to make me feel good. I enjoyed his diction, the way he said things with such focus on the choice of words. I don't think Dan ever said anything other than 'you look nice today' to describe me or his opinion of how I looked. Dating Dan was like eating porridge boiled in water for breakfast every day, with so many other exciting flavours and textures of foods to choose from, all left untouched. Sometimes, I'd will Dan to grab me out of nowhere and tell me that he found the curve of my back sexy or, well, *anything* other than that I 'looked nice'. But he never did. Maybe it just wasn't his way. He did say 'I love you' a lot, though. And he always told me where he was going and what he was up to …

How do I literally erase Dan from my memory?
Stop holding other people up against him.
He's irrelevant – or he should be.

I was just kind of staring at Owen, then, lost in thought, when he asked, 'Everything OK?' He stopped stroking me and instead planted a concerned grip around one of my hands.

'I'd just … I'd like to know what you'll be doing in New York. I'm interested. I've never been, and, well, yeah, I'm curious,' I admitted. 'I'd actually love to – to go with you.' I thought about how quickly Dad-of-this-world could transfer me some travel money and about how I'd only get to enjoy the flight before the day was over, but how that was better than having all of this cut short. But Owen's eyes didn't widen with joy when I said it or while I sat there getting way ahead of myself. Instead, they glazed over.

Regardless of how lovely Owen was being, the fact that he didn't want to tell me anything about what he'd be doing on his trip – where he'd be staying, or with who, bothered me.

'That's not possible, I'm afraid. Look: I'm here, with you, *now*. Can we just enjoy being together?' He flashed me a closed-lip, insincere smile. Then he turned his music up and proceeded to read the latest headlines while poking at his plate, sealing up my boxful of questions in the process.

What's the big deal?
Why can't we talk about your work if we're together?
Or … are we together at all?

To be honest, this reeks of eau d'affair.
But Google said he's not married …
Oh, what does flipping Google know about anything?

Owen's head bopped along to the music that throbbed from his phone on the countertop, and I couldn't help but gaze at him like I did when he came into work. It was like staring into the sun for a second too long. *A firework.* And regardless of the damage staring too long could do, in this private moment that I might never have witnessed without Granny's gift, Owen lit up my otherwise grey existence with a curious light.

Enjoy it while it lasts.

We didn't say much to one another after eating. I peed, washed my face with a bar of soap that smelled like an expensive sea-themed scented candle and dressed myself in the yellow playsuit that had been balled up on the bedroom floor. Then I offered to tidy up (seeing as Owen had prepared everything) only to regret the offer about ten minutes in when bean juice made its way into my hair and meat fat mixed with breadcrumbs along with fuck knows what else solidified under my fingernails. Owen showered as I sorted out the mess, then, newly dressed in a fresh pressed suit, he responded to emails on the L-shaped sofa while I sat across from him and watched like a spare tit.

I couldn't tell if the dried-up mood was my digging's doing or if it was work-related time pressure he was experiencing.

Things had become a tad … awkward.

Even more so when someone called Zoe phoned him and he chirped on about how excited he was to land, to catch up with her.

The wife?

Does this-world-me know about her?

Or am I so desperate for Owen that I'm ignoring all the red flags flapping inches from my face?

From the call, I picked up that this Zoe person would be meeting Owen in JFK Airport and they'd then drive to Manhattan together. With me in his peripheral vision, Owen cut the phone call short. Knees to my chin at the edge of the sofa, a fire roared in my brain, a fire with a voice that screamed: who is she?

Maybe I'm just being nuts, maybe she's just a co-worker.

Before long, after a brief and near-wordless kiss and cuddle session, Owen was on his merry way in a taxi he'd booked for noon to go to Manchester airport. And I was left alone, with my phone from a life not yet lived.

Goosebumps erupted all over my body the second the door closed behind him. An adrenalin rush, a special alertness, gifted by the fact that I was about to spy on somebody (even though that somebody was *me*).

I knew the cleaner was coming, but I wanted to buy as much time as I could to stalk through my own phone so I dashed upstairs, taking three steps per stride and emitting micro squeals. I dived onto the master bed where we'd slept, on my front, and reached for my phone, now resting on the bedside locker.

Let's get to work.

The first port of call was my photos folders. Scrolling through them felt how I imagined floating out of my own body while on the operating table might feel. Between batches of twenty or so selfies, one after the other, were pictures of Owen, or Owen and I together, the pair of us all dressed up against exciting backdrops – maybe work events of his or fancy dates and trips he'd taken me on. We looked like a couple of happy suckers in love, sipping cocktails and grinning like the Cheshire Cat and his twin. There were photos of us lying in bed together and standing beside national landmarks like Windsor Castle and Tower Bridge, broken up by the odd shot of Reid pulling a silly face or views from my dad's travels that weren't much different from photos I'd been sent from him in the real world.

And then there were the nudes.

Nudes Owen had sent me – dick pics galore, impressive in their unexpected nattiness, and even naked mirror selfies, though all had his face cropped out. There were nudes I'd taken of myself, too, also with my face hidden, though I'd recognise those ginger pubes and violin shaped hips even if I were blind. I could tell I'd taken them for Owen because all the naked shots of the pair of us were grouped together in piles of flesh and arousal, clearly from various messaging sessions we'd indulged in over the months since we met.

I couldn't believe the screen.

In my real self, I'd never felt confident enough to

capture photographic evidence of all the dangling, all the squishiness going on underneath my clothes.

Erin, I thought you decided that sending nudes to anyone ever *was a terrible idea?*

But a gut feeling tugged at me as I zoomed in and out on the nudes, examining every crevice of us both, telling me that Owen had unleashed something in me, that he massaged my self-esteem and never pressured me to send him pictures like this. That I'd decided to do so myself.

After looking through hundreds of photos, I clicked into my Facebook app to check if we were at least listed as being 'in a relationship' – something I always argued was important to do in this day and age. 'Consciously deciding *not* to declare your relationship status on Facebook is the modern equivalent of removing your wedding ring on a night out, except it's even worse,' I'd said to Reid one day in the Palace Gardens, to which he'd responded with a rant about how *some people don't like sharing private information with the world, Beggy – besides, Facebook steals your data, blah blah* ...

As my profile loaded up, I held my breath in anticipation. Then ...

Nope.

Still single as a Pringle.

'Oh, piss off,' I said to the empty room.

Then I checked Twitter to see what I'd been tweeting about while involved with Owen.

Ugh, it was bad.

Bad bad.

Cringe quotes and song lyrics about being crazy into someone one week, then, the next, posts that were all 'I'm a strong, independent woman who don't need no ring on it', and sprinkled between those utter gems were memes I'd retweeted with captions such as: 'When u see bae liking someone else's pics and you're trying to play it cool.'

This is gross.

Embarrassing.

I'm obsessed with someone who isn't so obsessed with me, and I'm posting passive-aggressive tweets for all to see.

Finally, it was time for Instagram.

I couldn't get over the fierce oddness that was looking at pictures of me that shouldn't exist.

Back in right-side-up land, my most recent post was of a pretty coffee beside my laptop's keypad, with a caption about how I was 'working hard on my blog'. (A lie. I'd figured posting it might give me the push I needed to make it happen for real, but I'd continued to procrastinate while the virtual world thought I was being mega productive.) In *this* world, my newest post was of a beautiful castle's turrets and towers with the caption '#wreycastle #cutedate'.

There were no pictures of Owen on my Instagram at all. Which made something about our relationship smell … off. I'd basically come up with the pics-or-it-didn't-happen mantra myself. I shared so much on Instagram, always, from well-plated-up dinners, to Granny's two bitches, to couple shots of Dan and me smiling (never us fighting, because *duh*), to sunsets gilded with smog, to candid shots of Reid.

Owen's Instagram was at the top of my most recent searches.

I clicked in, and my jaw dropped.

Seventy-three thousand followers!

What?

There were photos of him on red carpets, inside expensive-looking cars, wearing Ted Baker suits, volunteering at animal shelters and with an array of stunning women – none of whom were me.

What kind of CEO becomes semi-Instafamous?

Before I could virtually delve further into his career, I heard a fiddle of the front door downstairs.

It must be Wendy, Owen's cleaner …

Begrudgingly, I made my way downstairs to find she'd let herself in. All five foot of her stood dressed head to toe in hues of purple under a nest of frizzy dyed-blonde hair with silver roots. A set of keys twinkled and clinked in her hand as she caught me walking toward her.

'Oh! I didn't realise he'd have someone here this weekend … Hello! Hi!' *Someone,* she says, voice like a foghorn. 'He told me we've guests arriving tomorrow, but failed to mention any radiant company.' Wendy's deeply creviced face was warm with affection as she eyed my outfit, and the pendant too. 'Beautiful necklace. So, where's the master of the house, then? Last month he mentioned New York …'

'That's where he's headed. You just missed him.'

'Irish! Lovely,' she said of my accent. Then, flustered, 'I see ... ehm, OK, well, I best be off, then. He wouldn't want me in your way. I wasn't expecting anyone is all, but I can come back later—'

'No, goodness, don't leave on my account,' I started. 'I kinda fancy sticking around for the day. Owen said I could, and he did say you'd be coming along. I won't mind you doing your thing.'

She beamed. 'You'd be mad not to stay on. Shame *he* gets so little time here himself.' Wendy looked around the spacious, spotless living room, brimming with pride. 'I like to keep it spick and span for him between his stays. So, long stay?' She placed her hands on her hips, vibes as comforting as chicken soup.

'No, just a short getaway,' I lied. I hadn't a clue how many nights I'd been here. There was a small suitcase belonging to me up in the wardrobe, but other than that I hadn't the foggiest. 'Wendy, would you like a cup of tea? Before you get to work?'

'I'd adore one. Y'know, you're the first of Owen's girls ever to give me the time of day ...'

Girls, plural.

She's met the exes, I take it.

I glanced down at the pendant as it glistened in the natural light of the most holidayish holiday home to ever exist, and I mentally prepared myself for a *very* enlightening exchange with Wendy over some Earl Grey.

*

Two women, two cups of tea and an oasis on the lake. After proper introductions, I learned that we were in Owen's 'only spare property in the UK' and that I'd guessed correctly: it was situated on the outskirts of the enchanting village of Bowness.

Now, how do I drag every bit of knowledge about Owen from this lovely lady without sending her running for the hills? I need to know more about him: if he's married; if he's worth it, after what I went through with Dan ...

Wendy and I sat out on the patio, on a two-seat sun lounger beneath a wide blue sun umbrella. I admired the scenery as she admired the house some more; she wore it like a badge of honour. 'I love the dark local stone,' she said, as though talking about an oiled-up well-hung lover. 'Don't you? And see those potted flowers there? My idea. The contrast, with their bright colours ... just fabulous.'

'Really pretty,' I said, staring up at the house, wondering how much it must have cost Owen, and if he paid Wendy fairly, and, still, about *girls, plural*.

'Sometimes Owen lets my partner and me stay here, for free, with the children. It's much nicer than my own home, and *right by the lake*. My job is a blessing,' she said, beaming.

'How many kids do you have?'

'Five natural births, one adopted. The youngest is eight – our adopted boy, Peter.'

I choked on my tea. 'Six kids? Wow. How, how do you ...?'

'Cope? Haha. Just about. I haven't stuck my head in the oven yet!'

Part of me wanted to ask Wendy if she felt differently about her biological children and about how difficult it was to adopt, but most of me didn't care and selfishly just wanted answers on my crush and alternate-me's situation. The day wasn't over.

I still have time to make the most of this drunken turn.

If I can find out as much as possible, this won't all have been for a kiss and a fancy breakfast spread …

Wendy continued, yanking me out of my thoughts, 'Chaos has been my way of life for over two decades now.'

Maybe that's why she shout-spoke – she probably couldn't get a word in edgeways at home.

'It gets easier after the first couple. We have lots of rules in our house, y'see. A solid system.' She sliced through the air with a wrinkled hand, heavy with clunky rings. 'They go to bed when they're told; they eat at the table when they're told … that helps. Plus, they're only as expensive as we allow them to be. No iPads in our house, no gourmet dining – it's stew and library books!' She talked on about motherhood like a composer talking about music, and I was entranced. Her life sounded so *full* compared to mine and jealousy pricked me.

This woman has her shit together.

'People are kind and helpful, too. I don't do it all by myself,' Wendy added, with her fluffy eyebrows raised, as though to render herself mere mortal once again – probably sensing that I couldn't relate or my overall social ineptness.

'It must be nice to have so much purpose – at home, anyway,' I said, immediately regretting how unintentionally condescending a thing it was to say.

'Work gives me purpose, too.' She brushed her words over mine like she was painting gloss over cracks. Before I could interrupt her with, *Oh no, of course, goodness, that didn't come out right*: 'I know I clean toilets for a living, but I clean for my well-being, not just for money to feed mouths at home. I've always loved a good scrub, me. Really look forward to coming here every couple of weeks ... it's not the only house I clean, but it's my favourite one. The best view. Nice and quiet. I can just dive into my imagination and work out all my frustration with life on the tiles, with the duster ...'

'I'd love to have a job that I like that much. I hate being a waitress.'

'I had a ball waitressing in my youth! And you're only a young thing. Maybe the problem isn't your job. Ever think about that? Maybe it's how you perceive it. Your mindset.'

Maybe the problem is me, *you mean.*

Well, I could at least try to enjoy the café. After all, I've put more effort into faking orgasms than I have into Sugar Pot and my life there. And it is in bloody Kensington – Kensington is beautiful! But ...

Wendy had planted her seed, and she knew it, and she was moving swiftly on. 'Do *you* have any?'

'Any what?'

'Kids.'

'Oh, ha! I mean, no. No, no. I'm still a kid myself, up here,' I said, patting my temple.

Am I just saying that, or do I really believe it?

Wendy pulled her shoulders back and crossed her legs under her long purple skirt. 'Sure aren't we all? Sometimes I catch my reflection and think, *Christ, who's she?* It just comes to you. Raising them. Like riding a bike. You learn how to do it by doing it. I'm guessing you don't want children then.' She said it like it was somehow an obvious fact, and I wondered why any mother would assume such a thing of a young woman.

I don't look older than I am, do I?

Do I look like someone who couldn't handle it?

The right words wouldn't come to me, but she seemed to read *why would you say that?* from my face. 'I only say so as, well, you're involved with Owen. And ... wait, how long have you two known each other?'

'A few months,' I said, my voice flat like a lid in an attempt to hide my inner explosions.

'Ah. Then you'll know he loves to brag about how he's had the snip.' Wendy hesitated, waiting for a reaction of some kind. My eyes widened, but I tried to hang on to my cool. 'I love him dearly, but Lord knows I'll never fully understand the man. How he thinks he's "helping to save the planet" by fathering no children.'

Act normal, you already know this, control your fucking face, Erin ...

'Oh, yeah, his – vasectomy.'

'Forgive me for prying, but is it serious? You and him?'

I nervous-laughed and figured I'd just say exactly what was on my mind as it would have no consequences for real-life me. 'To be honest, I'm fairly confused. He's kind and affectionate, and we *seem* close. But I get the feeling he's …'

Wendy raised her eyebrows again. 'Go on?'

Just say it. This isn't real life.

'Cheating.'

She shifted uncomfortably in her seat.

'He won't talk to me about work,' I continue, 'and he posts pictures of himself online with other women … He was talking to some girl called Zoe on the phone earlier. I don't think I'm the only person in his life.'

'Do you want to be?'

Yes.

He's perfect for me.

So what if I'm not perfect for him? I can't lie …

'Well, usually I'd demand up front to know whoever I'm seeing is as committed as I am. What's the point otherwise? I'm confused by what I'm doing here.'

Would I be saying any of this if I actually lived this life? Have I dived into this fully aware that Owen's not available in the ways I want him to be? Am I over Dan in a world where Owen's involved with me?

'By what you're doing with Owen, you mean?' Wendy pressed.

'Yeah. Spending a weekend in my non-boyfriend's holiday home isn't very *me*.'

Wendy chuckled. 'OK, right. Wow. Look here. I need to say something because you seem like a lovely girl. What I'm about to tell you … can it remain between us?'

'I promise,' I said, clutching my teacup with such force it could have cracked and seeped milky warmth all over me.

'You appear to have "entered the fold", so to speak. But frankly, I'm baffled. Because for some reason he doesn't seem to have told you everything. He's usually very upfront and honest about his … situation. That's what I understand of it, anyway.' I looked at her, open-mouthed, grasping at plausible responses. 'He brought you here. That's something, really. Between you and me – Erin, is it?'

'That's right,' I told her, forcing a smile, hoping to encourage the free flow of her words.

'Erin. Well, between us, he only brings two of the others here. And they're not a patch on you. Faces like smacked arses when they were introduced to me, the pair of them. They always look down their noses when I clean during their stays …'

Who, Wendy? Who?

In this reality, has he told me he's dating other girls?

Sure sounds like it.

Could I be OK with that in any reality?

No. I don't even like sharing the bloody bread basket.

Or is a casual relationship exactly what I need to get over Dan?

The questions and their half-formed answers pierced the area behind my eyeballs as I tried to concentrate on Wendy's words. 'I'm telling you this, woman to woman, because I don't want to see you wounded. Our Owen was in a relationship for fifteen years, long time – a girl called Emma. And one day he woke to find she'd packed her bags and left. Never recovered. Never speaks of it. His mother was the one to tell me.'

I stopped breathing.

'Now, according to Brenda,' she explained, 'he openly dates ... a few people, but prioritises his work.'

A few?

We used condoms, calm down.

And, wait, this isn't even real.

Relax!

When will I get used to how realistic these ... happenings are?

'I've never judged his lifestyle since ... what happened. Hell, I was born in the sixties myself,' she said, winking at me. 'But I have found myself judging his taste in women. Until today.' She nodded in my direction then. 'That air-hostess one, though, with the curly hair – twit of a woman, she is! I'm just ... I'm surprised he's not told you. Odd, that. Doesn't sound like our Owen.'

Wendy sat back in her chair and gazed up at the sky as I fought the urge, once again, to check out early, to return to my real body. Guilt caressed me. My brain was scrambled egg.

May as well have stolen his password and be reading his private emails.

This surely wasn't how Granny Beglan had hoped I'd use her gift, after all the years she held on to it for me. But I couldn't help myself.

I pulled on my best lying face.

'I have a confession. He has told me – about the others. I'm just surprised that *you* know. It's true, I've been feeling jealous and wanting him to myself. But, well, how much has he told you about his relationships?' I implied surprise at Wendy's awareness, hoping it would make her feel the need to explain herself and divulge more of Owen's secrets.

'Oh! Oh, no, don't worry about *me*, I only know the basics – enough that I don't grow dizzy from the, eh, *rotation*.' She said it in a reassuring tone. 'I'm sorry, I understand … why – *well*, you know. Just know that I'm not judging him, or you. You can't reach my age without learning that monogamy isn't for everyone. In my day, monogamy meant one mate for life. Nowadays, it would appear to mean one at a time, and some can't even do that. Owen prefers to be forthcoming. Phew – I'm glad you know. You had me worried there!'

I hate it that she's right.

Every monogamous person I've ever met has gone from partner to partner, or cheats, like it's to be expected.

Well, except for Granny and Grandad, and Liz and Alan from school, and—

No, fuck this.

I'm not down with this at all.

What if, in this existence, I'm just going along with things, hoping that Owen 'picks me'?

'I imagine you're not the jealous type.' Wendy's eyes studied me as she said it. 'I envy that. I'm not so independent, me, but, y'know, I'll act it. I'll try it on sometimes, wear it like a nice coat, mainly when Martha's having her own problems and it's up to me to be the strong one for both of us. For the family. But I depend on Martha like I do on air. I need as much of her as she can give me, most of the time.'

'Martha?'

'My life partner. My wife.'

As she said it, my expression twisted with confusion.

'Oh, sorry if I misunderstood, but, how did you … your pregnancies …?'

Wendy drew in a lungful of Lakeland air and flattened her skirt across her lap. 'I've been married twice,' she said, trusting me with every word. All thoughts of Owen abandoned my head as I clung to each and every one. 'Even after you've been married to someone for a thousand years, doesn't matter how many layers of dirt you're both buried under, they'll continue to surprise you. There'll always be aspects of one another we don't know about. I married a man, Ian, in the spring of 1988. Dripping with infatuation, we were. Head over heels. Lucky for us, infatuation grew into love and brought us our wonderful children.'

My mind, again, slipped off to thoughts of Dan.

'But one day, many years later, Ian … he hit me.'

The sentence swallowed images of my ex immediately in a deathly silence.

'He knocked me flat on my face. Bloodied my lip. Then somehow convinced me it wouldn't happen again. But it did. A few times.'

The silence lingered, broken only by the distant chirp of birds in trees.

'Then, he hit our eldest, late one night after we'd all been to the cinema … That's when I got out. With the kids.'

'Wendy, I…' I didn't know what to say.

'But love found me again,' she said, toying with the rings on her left hand. 'And she's everything I've ever wanted in a partner.'

'I guess you never really know how life will pan out.'

'You're telling me!' A thunderous laugh. 'I was in my thirties when I first realised I could love another woman in that way. A big shock for the kids, mind. But they love Martha.' When she said 'they', I could feel the 'I' in how she said it. 'There's this old picture, Erin, by René Magritte, of two people kissing with bags over their heads. I bought a replica on a holiday to Belgium and hung it above our bed at home – as a reminder of our … unknowability to each other. We never really know a person. I mean, do we ever *really* even know ourselves?'

I thought about Owen.

And Dan.

And how much I gave up when I left Dan.

And how much I expected of Owen.

All while having very little grasp on myself, and who I was, and what *I* could offer a person who wanted to share their life with *me*.

I hunched my shoulders and thought about how many versions of myself I'd been in the past decade alone, as though I were in a costume shop the night before a Halloween ball, trying on different Erin-shaped masks. In this reality, I'm an Erin who'll seemingly put up with other women for (some of) a man's time. In past realities, I've been the conflicted fiancée, an Erin who cries herself to sleep after uploading a smiling selfie. I've been the girl who loved to ride horses but often sacrificed practice to go stand in a circle by the mill with girls from school, pretending to enjoy smoking fags, just so I wouldn't slide any further down the popularity scale. I've been the university student who felt the joy of being touched by great art but who had nobody to talk to about it and so lived a double life online as 'cellarddarling89', who wrote passages of great length in forums full of strangers in the night. I've been an Erin so unhappy with her body that she threw away a chance to peek into any number of possible realities just to feel, briefly, what it's like to look like *hashtag goals* …

What I wouldn't give to know myself.

'Martha is a lucky lady,' I said, 'and your children are lucky, too … two mammies. I didn't even have the one mammy for very long …'

The words just fell out.

Wendy had loosened my hinges.

Seems the lump-in-throat feeling still comes to me when I'm using the pendant.

'Sorry to hear that,' Wendy said. She reached across and touched my arm, a simple thing that instantly made me feel as though my troubles were halved. I missed human contact. Dan had been liberal with affection …

'I was eight when I lost Mam. Breast cancer.'

The C word.

I hated saying it out loud. Doing so gave it more power, more life.

'Ghastly thing, that,' said Wendy. 'No child should know that pain, of waking each day and, for just a split second, forgetting they're gone, then remembering. And the awful numbness that follows. It's unspeakable. Indescribable.'

She told it perfectly. That realisation had punched me in the face with fists the size of baseball gloves every morning for three entire years after Mam died.

'Only months ago, I lost my own mother,' Wendy went on. 'Old age. Martha got me through it.' She watched a flock of wading birds as she spoke. 'I try to be grateful that she lived a long life, that she met all her grandkids. But … so many worries came to me after. Of my children losing me before they're ready, as you lost your mum. Frightening thought.'

'She was younger than I am now,' I said, realising, as I

spoke, how deeply that knowledge terrified me. My bones itched with a dread that I couldn't scratch away.

'Ach, life can be wicked. Truth be told, I would've had ten more children if I knew I'd live to be a healthy ninety. But none of us have that guarantee, do we? We have to make the most of the day that's in it.'

'I think I want a family,' I said, out of nowhere. 'No, I definitely do. I want to be surrounded by babies I've made, with someone I love unconditionally, like how you love Martha. Like how my granny loved my grandad and how my dad loved my mam.' My voice wavered. 'I thought I was on the way to having that life, but, ah, I'm so lost, Wendy.'

If I were in my real skin I'd have cried a waterfall then, but tears wouldn't come. I felt all the feelings but they were blurry and dreamlike, as if they existed out of sight, right under everything tangible that held me together. It was a side effect of the pendant I'd also experienced the first time I used it. And, honestly, if this had been happening in the real world I doubt it would've tumbled from conversation to free therapy session so fast, but that it did.

Much like Reid, Wendy really listened to me, rather than just waiting for her turn to speak. There was no cutting over one another like the chat I grew up having with Dad and Sienna. Patient and warm, she permitted me to spill my guts as though she had a mop and bucket at the ready to clean them all up when I was done.

I admitted to her that I was drowning in life itself, in its scalding hot water, and while I could see the surface, I no longer felt I'd ever reach it. That I might just be one of those people held down and destined to turn red and die from asphyxia.

'This can't be *it*,' I said moments later, wincing.

'What do you expect to find?' she asked. 'What does not-drowning look like, in your head?'

'Doing a job I actually like, for a start.' *How do I know I'm not, in this life?* But all I cared about was ironing out the real world, so I carried on as though the thought hadn't crossed my mind. 'Waitressing – well, it started as a temporary thing I did part-time during uni, but I've not been able to escape. I've been stuck in the same place for years. Working at the Sugar Pot feels like something to do while you're learning how to do something else, or waiting on the chance to do something else.' I hoped she wouldn't ask me why I hadn't applied for other, better jobs, and, thankfully, she didn't. 'And I hate relying on my dad to look after me. I'm a big girl – I shouldn't be relying on anyone financially. My ex used to give me loans to get by, too. I still want to pay him back.' That was true, but I knew Dan would never take money from me.

'A lot of people nowadays still rely on their parents for help at your age. It's tough out there.'

'I came to London to make my dreams come true – big, naive head on me at twenty-two. Going to work every day physically hurts.' I hadn't realised how strongly I felt about my lack of a career, my Groundhog Day existence, until I uttered those last two words and realised I wasn't exaggerating. A kind of agony wrapped me in its razor-edged wires every day as I cycled to the Sugar Pot, to Kenneth and to my hideaway cupboard. It was dull, like my skin was smeared with a strong numbing cream. My fear of knowing how much better life might be now if I hadn't taken a job there held me back from using the pendant to simply check and see; I worried I'd be crushed under the weight of regret. 'I get nothing from the job at all. It's like ... drinking fizzy water instead of Fanta Orange, y'know? And I'm stuck there. Right now, anyway. I've got to pay rent. I don't even know what I'd be good at doing.'

'Not ideal. It's a means to an end, sure, but without an identified end you can't move forward, can you? You need to make a decision ... to figure out what you need to do to get from A to B – and, of course, what B *is*,' she said matter-of-factly. 'Has any good come of working in your café? There's gotta be something.'

I thought hard. 'It's where Owen first caught my eye. But maybe he was just a welcome distraction from the mundane. From the boring routine I'm stuck in.' I paused to allow Wendy to interject, to share some more things-about-my-non-boyfriend-that-I-don't-even-know-myself, but she didn't. She gave me space to spill some more. 'And I doubt I'll get to have kids at this stage,' I threw in, casually but not casually at all. 'Hearing stories about your home life, it makes my heart swell. I know I probably don't seem like a typical mammy,' I said, poking fun at myself and my non-togetherness, 'but every part of me just wants to finish the job my own mam never got to finish. Having gammy ovaries – it's like someone's playing some cruel joke on me …'

'Gammy?'

'Um, dodgy … broken, maybe.' Wendy waited for me to go on. 'PCOS.' I rested my chin in my palm and said the words I hated saying out loud, for the third time ever. 'My doctor told me two years ago that I have polycystic ovary syndrome, which affects my hormone levels.' *Erin*, he'd said, *you produce higher than normal amounts of male hormones, and the imbalance leads to your skipped periods and excessive hair growth along your arms there.* I recalled him pointing at me like I was a map, like he was showing me the rivers I could very clearly see myself. And then came the lightning after the thunder. *PCOS can make it more difficult to fall pregnant. It's not impossible, but it can be more complicated.*

A knowing sigh. *'Tut tut tut.'* Wendy made the noise by tipping her tongue to the roof of her mouth, behind her front teeth, and pulling it away, over and over. 'He could have been a little more reassuring. I mean, it's *very* common, pet—'

'That's what my dad said, too. "Ah, Erin, it's really common," but like I said to him, so is cancer, and I don't want that shit either.'

Why is this news so throwaway to people?

Well, at least Granny had drunkenly comforted me over whiskey-soaked Christmas pudding. She understood. She had it herself.

Step away from the PCOS talk. She'll just keep telling me I'll be fine, as if that helps at all.

'My relationship with Dan – that was such a huge chunk of my life, and it ended, and, like, I couldn't put kids through a messy separation like that. I'd need to get to know a person for years before getting married, let alone pregnant, and it's supposed to be dangerous to try after a certain age, so they say—'

'Pish-tosh, a myth. I know someone who had their first biological child aged forty-two. Besides, who says you'll separate from someone you decide to raise a family with? If you decide to be with them, and they decide to be with you, why bother worrying? That's all anyone can ever do, all anyone has ever done: choose someone.'

'How can you ever really *know*, though – for certain? How do you know you're safe, with…?'

'Martha? I can't know for sure that she won't leave me. I just have to believe that she won't, based on her words and, more importantly, on her actions. But also the piece of paper that says *married* doesn't handcuff the other person to the end of the bed.' She laughed to herself. 'This is my *second* marriage. People part ways all the time for all kinds of reasons. I don't know that I'm safe with Martha, not a hundred per cent. I never will. But I believe that I am right now. Because she makes me feel safe.'

I wondered how anyone could make someone feel safe. *I've become so narrow-minded and cynical, Christ.*

'Martha sounds amazing,' I said, imagining what she

must look like and how loving she must be. 'I think I stopped making Dan, my ex, feel safe pretty early in our relationship. During big arguments I'd always threaten to leave. I was a pretty shite girlfriend, really.'

Ew.

I really mean that.

Ew.

Not a nice feeling.

Why did I run away? And who was I really running from: Dan, or myself?

And even though I was awful, still Dan had seemed completely blindsided by the break-up – maybe because he could recognise how much good stuff there was between us, and I'd become oblivious to it, as things weren't ... perfect. He could see past all of my flaws and wanted me, and a family with me, in spite of them, yet there I was, sleeping with some guy who probably knew none of my flaws because he was too busy swanning off to New York with *fucking Zoe*.

Did I bolt too early, even if Dan and I were never going to last the distance?

'These things happen,' Wendy said, oblivious to my mental juggle. 'Some people don't fit, and sometimes we push a good thing away because we don't feel like we deserve it. If I may ...?'

'Yeah?'

'Well, seeing as you want children so much, and you didn't have any with your ex, it's just, I think there are worse things a child can go through than growing up with parents who aren't together any more. Even just *being* in an unhappy home with two miserable pillocks for parents can be worse than divorce. At least, that's how my older kids felt. Once they got used to the situation they were as happy about the divorce as I was!'

'How did you cope with the … the fear that, well, what your kids experienced … might, y'know …'

'Fuck them up?'

The *fuck* out of her mouth was a clap in a dark room.

'Can't wrap young ones in armour, can you?' she said, smirking. 'Has this fear-of-separation stuff got anything to do with Owen, by any chance? I know his parents are divorced, and, you know, he's adamant to never grow too attached after … everything. I hope you don't think I'm *meddling*, I just—'

My big secret stretched my mouth into a smile. 'I promise you that Owen's views on relationships have absolutely nothing to do with my own.'

I'd not known about Owen's feelings on commitment and his penchant for multiple simultaneous relationships until today. In that moment, I really wanted to tell Wendy about the pendant. She seemed like someone open to all kinds of possibilities in life, but, even still, the memory of Reid's mini freak-out the last time held me back. Talking to her was a tonic, and I didn't want to scare her away. I wanted to sit with her for as long as she'd stay and to enjoy her motherliness.

And I did.

For a short while, before returning to my drunk self on my shag rug, Wendy filled a five-foot-six-deep hole in my heart.

9
Tinglies

Sunday was a blur of dry mouth, puke-flavoured saliva, the sway of rooms along various trips to fetch fresh water (and to throw up) and a pounding in my skull *so* fierce I could've discovered an axe planted in it to no surprise at all. My stomach burned, and I fell in and out of a dreamless oblivion all damn day.

But then it was Monday. I was alive again. Back at work in the Sugar Pot café. Wearing cracked lips and limp hair I took orders, made coffee, delivered teas and cakes and sandwiches to tables, washed plates, hid in the broom cupboard intermittently to breathe, with my mind's eye all the while on the time. I knew Owen *might* be in around ten minutes after noon and I was sick with post-pendant cringe.

I shouldn't have reached for it while drunk and lonely.
The guy doesn't even want babies, and he's non-committal.

Surely I could've found that out without dancing through realms?

But the way he kissed me ...

I'd written to Granny about it, mid-hangover. About how desperately I'd projected my hopes and dreams onto this man only to discover that we didn't want the same things in life at all. About how I felt guilty and embarrassed about my desire to be enough for him even still. About Wendy, and how much I missed Mam, and how much I longed for home. Every cell in my body wanted to visit Granny again as soon as possible, but I couldn't afford the flight – my next trip home would likely have to wait for the winter.

The café-door bell sounded as I sat on my haunches in the dark, cobwebby broom cupboard, mulling over everything for the billionth time while I stalked through who'd been liking Owen's Instagram photos (a curious thing that I felt like others must do too, but never in front of people – only in private). My phone's clock read 12.08.

'Jen? Erin?' Kenneth called for us.

What is Jen doing? Why can't she serve them?

I didn't want to go out there, just in case.

He's probably in New York right now. No, he's definitely in New York right now. His plans didn't change when I was in the picture, so they've hardly changed without me in it.

'*Girls*,' Kenneth snapped, in the tone that meant 'I'm overrun with orders and there's someone waiting and I want to scream at you both but I can't.'

I carefully stepped over the hoover and some boxes of

cleaning products to peer through the crack in the doorway. This was my usual routine to ensure that Kenneth (and whoever else was sharing my shift that day) didn't see me leaving my hideout, so they'd assume I'd just been in the bathroom all along – the place where stuff-you-don't-talk-about-at-work goes down. With the coast clear, I quietly stepped out into the corridor bridging the café and the kitchen. I could see what looked like a woman's arm – the sleeve of her red jacket and her French manicure – hovering in the little bit of counter visible from where I stood.

It's not him.

Exhale.

I stood tall and walked out front only to meet with a sideways glare from Kenneth. He stood with his back turned to the lady who was waiting to order, frothing milk for someone else.

'I only have two hands, y'know,' he said under his breath. A tiny pool of sweat had gathered above his top lip. I remembered that time on a staff night out when he wouldn't stop coming on to me after four too many shots of tequila – that same pool of sweat had glistened in the flashing light of the nightclub.

My stomach turned.

'Sorry,' I mumbled. I wanted to make up some crap about not feeling the best, but the customer impatiently tapped her nails on the countertop to catch my attention. I pulled on my work mask: a friendly, cool-headed smile. 'Apologies for the wait. What can I get for you?' Her jawline-grazing bob was glossy and almost black. She didn't crack a smile, but I couldn't stop staring at her. Everything about her screamed 'chic' and 'impish' and 'look at me'.

Stop staring.

'A green tea, and an espresso, please. And two of these.' She pointed through the glass. 'What are they?' she asked in an American accent. (I could never figure out which part of America customers were from, only that they spoke with that American twang.)

'Oh! Great choice. They're salted dark-chocolate truffles, my favourites. Apart from our banoffee pie, of course.' I pointed to the pie, hoping to tempt her. Even though I didn't do the baking or come up with the recipes, I always encouraged customers to try the banoffee so they'd be hooked and would tell their friends about the café. It was the one minuscule goal that kept me going through a working day: to ensure I did enough while in Kenneth's general vicinity to avoid getting the sack.

'You've tempted me. Alright, your biggest slab of *that*, and the truffles, and the drinks. Can we pay after?'

Sophisticated, elegant, beautiful figure and room for dessert. Is there some kind of finishing school in America where parents send their daughters to ensure they turn out like this, and can I go there as a thirty-year-old?

'Of course,' I said warmly, to blur my insecurity, 'where are you sitting?'

'In the corner,' she said, pointing to the table by the window with the yellow cushions and …

It was him.

The espresso she'd ordered was for Owen.

He waited, on his phone, with his legs crossed and his eyes firmly planted on Glossy Hair's behind.

'I'll … be right over,' I told her. Within seconds of her walking back toward Owen I felt flushed, faint, short of breath.

Nothing bad is going to happen.

I turned away from them and held my head down so my hair obstructed Kenneth's view of my face.

He doesn't know about the pendant.

I reached for the green tea.

In through the nose, out through the mouth.

The woman was probably Zoe. Maybe she came to visit Owen in this version of events, instead of him going to New York.

She's jaw-dropping.

When am I going to stop feeling so intimidated by other women?

I'm as insecure as a thousand-year-old footbridge, and all I've figured out so far is how to hide it.

Hands shaking, I stole a glance or two at them as I placed their chocolates on little porcelain plates – couldn't help myself. They were all over each other with soft touches and tender face kisses. She was ice, melted, and he was the glass.

That woman could be – *was* – me.

My anxiety turned to electricity: power that coursed

through my every artery as I approached them, knowing things I shouldn't know. I took in everything in front of me and tried to make some sense of it. This couple, surely not in a serious relationship, sitting tall and confidently displaying their affection publicly, with their bodies intertwined and not a morsel of but-what-if-people-see? My small-town brain struggled to imagine them being OK with one another having other relationships on the side; to think of their passion, so in-your-face it may as well have its own name, as something shared, diluted. *There must be some level of rivalry.* I couldn't contemplate competing with someone else for a partner's time and affection, nor could I put a partner through that.

They look so happy, though.

Am I the one missing out?

Are my expectations too high?

I want him, and for him to only want me. Is that really too much to ask? And, ugh, I miss being like that, with someone who is mine. Jealousy is telling me to rip this Yank apart from Owen even though I've absolutely no right to care that they're so tied up in love. I'm nobody to him, and I shouldn't know otherwise about his carry-on …

My next letter to Granny will be as long as my bleedin' arm.

'Oh, thanks,' Owen said, smiling up at me like he so often did. 'And, hey, quick question. Do you know of any really gorgeous bookshops around here?' he asked, his voice full of enthusiasm.

'Book*stores*, sweetie,' Glossy Hair corrected him.

'Aye,' he said, eying her lips. 'This lady here is on a photography mission.'

'I am,' she said, more to him than to me, a giant grin on her face. 'I'm looking for somewhere *crammed* with books, old looking – it's for a work project.'

Look at me if you're talking to me. Rude.

'And for pleasure, right? We both love a good book,' Owen said, stroking her leg and her back with both hands simultaneously while still managing to meet my eyes with his.

I'd give anything to push Glossy Hair out of the way, to take her place.

'Ooh, let me think,' I said.

I never had the money to spend on books, but Reid loved to drag me to bookshops, usually on a hunt for some self-help garbage to help him move on from Martin. Dan also adored reading, so much so that he verbalised his crushing disappointment in my last choice of Christmas gift: a Kindle. *It's not the same,* he'd said. *I'll be so depressed if the world rids itself of libraries and bookshops.* Then Dan's favourite bookshop manifested in my mind.

'Actually, there's a place just off the King's Road in Chelsea called John Sandoe Books. Really impressive selection, and very Instagrammable.' Owen's eyes flashed with interest. 'Looks like it belongs in a Dickens novel,' I went on, happy to have his attention again at last. 'Not too far in a cab, either.' While talking, I placed their orders on the table in front of them as slowly as possible so I could be in their presence for longer, to take in all the little details of their lustful body language.

'Oh, I know the one! Yes. Creaky, narrow staircase – *yes*, it's so picturesque. Thank you, eh … what's your name, by the way? I've never asked. You lot don't wear name badges.' Glossy Hair smiled at me then, too, eagerly awaiting my reply. They were like two well-fed puppies wagging their tails in front of me, looking for belly rubs.

'It's Erin,' I said, my eyes darting from his to hers, brown to green.

'Erin. I'll remember that,' Owen said. 'And really, thank you. I'd forgotten that place existed. It's ideal.'

'No worries. Enjoy your drinks … I hope you get some great photos,' I said to Glossy Hair. Then I held Owen's gaze just once more before retreating to the familiar safety of the area behind the till where my envy and confusion could drown in Kenneth's top-lip sweat.

I sat in the Sunken Garden once again with Reid, swallowing mouthfuls of Turkish Delight, which I'd pissed away too much money on in the Kensington Palace shop thanks to furious time-of-the-month cravings for sugar. Reid wouldn't eat any because he was trying to shed water weight in advance of Brighton's Pride march. 'Martin will be there – well, *everyone* from the office is going, but obviously I don't give a shit about any of them.'

We admired the exotic and colourful floral displays, which changed throughout spring and summer, and chatted to the Palace Garden's head gardener, Sean, who knew us both on a first-name basis. Then, when Sean was all out of small talk, I thumped Reid with my big update. About Owen and how Finn knew who he was – how I'd googled him and discovered his age, his occupation …

I also had to tell Reid a white lie for the first time. It felt like I had to run out of a restaurant without settling the bill. Shame inside me like a blade. But I couldn't disobey Granny, not in real time. 'And so, last night I found this forum somewhere really random online,' I continued, after babbling for an age, 'tumbled down some huge virtual hole, y'know – and, apparently, Owen dates a bunch of women. Never just one. Because he had his heart broken … or whatever.'

'Is he in an open relationship, or does he have several relationships?'

'I think it's a lots-of-relationships kinda deal. I *think*. Maybe he does have one main person. Who knows. Doesn't really make a difference, though, does it? It's still very much an it-would-never-just-be-me situation.'

Reid rolled his eyes. 'All you need is "loves" – that's what the Beatles sang, right?' he said, smirking. 'What are we, then? Nonogamous? Becasuse we can't find and hold on to any love at all?'

Owen and Glossy Hair, all over one another. Owen's loving gaze in Bowness. His life seems to be more full of love than either of ours.

I giggled, mid-swallow of my period snack. 'Seriously,

though, we've got definite chemistry, me and this guy,'
I said, thinking about all the times Owen had smiled at
me over the past few months and about our other-worldly
love affair. Sure, the chemistry mostly existed in fantasy
land, but still. Reid didn't need to know that. 'Thing is,' I
continued, 'he's also apparently had the snip. So, there's
that.'

'Beggy, every person you date doesn't need to be a
candidate for Daddy. You need to lighten up.'

'Correct.'

'But would you actually *want* to date a guy who has
other girlfriends?'

I didn't even need to consider my response, which
made me sure that I was telling Reid the truth. 'No. If I'm
going to mess around with someone and not get serious,
I'd at least want to hold their full attention in the process
of said … fun. Though I'm so desperate right now I'd
probably sleep with you if you'd let me, so I need you to
talk me down if I ever bring up going for him, OK? Think
of me as a diabetic and you as someone with sway over my
consumption of sugar.'

Reid giggled. 'OK. Let's focus on finding your insulin,
eh?'

'Hear, hear.'

'Have to say, I'm impressed by the self-awareness,
Beggy.'

Me?

Self-aware?

No, mate. Just been world-hopping.

'I mean, remember that time you didn't talk to Dan for days one time after he went for drinks with that what's-her-name person, from his job ...'

'Oh, Becky. Ah, but—'

'He even told you about that, and you lost it! You'd combust if you dated this guy. Or you'd kill one of the other girlfriends, and it would be a Twitter news headline and I wouldn't stand by you because my mother would disown me for associating with a psychopath.'

I need to sort myself out. Yikes.

'That's fair.'

'Jealousy wouldn't be your only problem. You'd also end up dating other people just for the sake of it because *he* does. Like, obviously you're not going to sit at home when you know your man's out with other Sarahs and Samanthas. So much admin, though – bleh. You know my mate Josh?'

'The one with the pierced ear and the huge chin?'

'Him. He's polyamorous, in a "polycule" with four other guys. And they're all dating the other members of the polycule. Josh hosts dinner parties for them and everything! I've been invited, but I never go because I don't want to get sucked in and chewed to shreds – I always imagine the polycule as this big mouth full of pointy teeth. No body, no face, just *teeth*.'

I laughed.

'One of them even lives with Josh. But Josh works full

time, and, I dunno, it sounds super complicated trying to fit everyone in.'

'So open dating doesn't appeal to you? Even though it would be the perfect way to distract yourself from Martin?'

'Erin, my daily thoughts go a little something like this: Martin, Martin, eat, Martin, work, text Beggy, Martin, Martin, wank while thinking of Martin, check Grindr for Martin lookalikes, talk to Martin, or hang out with Martin, or go on a date to get mind off Martin for a while. Then go to sleep and dream of Martin.'

'Exactly,' I said.

'My point is, I don't have any free space in my brain to entertain people who I'm not in love with in any real way, beyond having sex with them – multiple times per month. I like to get in and get out, as you well know. I can't imagine having feelings this deep for more than one person. Being infatuated with one person always zaps me of so much energy. Add in a couple more and I'd die. How do people do it?'

'So, right, Owen came in earlier with one of his women.' Reid guzzled water as I said it and shock plugged up his throat, causing water to dribble everywhere.

'Go on. Were they sitting in silence? Mid-fight?'

'They looked like they wanted to tear each other's clothes off with their teeth,' I said.

'See! Teeth, Beggy. *It's all … teeth.*'

'Maybe there's something to it. To living life that way. Every time we put all our eggs in one basket, we end up…'

'Eggless,' Reid said.

'Mm-hmm.' I plucked the last piece of Turkish Delight from the pretty tin it came in and savoured its taste.

'I think I'd rather be eggless than buried under a bunch of baskets. Right now I could go out and find myself three handsome, caring boyfriends. But those relationships are hardly going to last another sixty years.' *Sixty years with anyone would be an accomplishment deserving of a trophy.* 'With polyamory I'd encounter all of the same rubbish, all the problems I have with monogamous relationships, only far more often. More wet-faced conversations about childhood and broken dreams, more reassuring ... more money spent. *So much make-up sex.* It'd be chaos.'

I found myself nodding along as he spoke. 'And I always get bogged down by where something is or isn't going,' I said. 'I overanalyse everything, probably because, in the end, I want ...'

'What?'

'Y'know. Kids.'

'Bitch, same! Dying to be a dad. That's all about timing, though. You don't want kids on your own, surely?'

I wiped my sticky fingers along the insides of my jeans-covered thighs and considered whether or not it was a moot point because I'd been told by my doctor that I might need IVF anyway.

I don't need a man for that.

'Like, single mothers deserve all of the respect and all, but why would you choose to, say, have a kid and have *no help* from the get-go? Less sleep, because there's nobody there to take turns doing the midnight nappy shift. Less time with friends, as you don't have that one other person to rely on, to look after the baby when you wanna get mad wrecked on a night out. You don't have a car ... Your family is tiny ...'

'Where are you going with this? Feels like you're setting my dreams on fire right now. People have kids with someone and break up, or divorce, all the time, and they figure it out.' I didn't feel confident in my words. I wanted to believe what I was saying, just like I'd wanted to be more like Wendy. Still, defensiveness tainted each and every word, and Reid surely sensed it.

'I'm just saying. Starting a family is a big deal, and I wouldn't like to watch you go it alone.'

'I wouldn't *be* alone.'

Likely would be, Erin.

'Sure, I'd help out – hell, I could even gift you my sperm and be the daddy, but I work a lot and I love to go out *all the time*. You know that.'

'*Have a test-tube baby with my gay best friend' is not on my to-do list for life.* Yet life had landed me in a position where even *that* sounded too good to be true.

'Add a baby into your current situation and ... just picture that for a sec. I doubt Rachel would be dancing for joy. And she's literally a dancer, for her job, because she *loves dancing* ...'

'Ha. Ha. Hilarious,' I said sarcastically. 'I don't want

a kid right now. Obviously. I'm not set up for that. My life is a state. But, one day … I mean, first I need to find myself some tinglies. Owen and Zoe looked like they were experiencing the tinglies. The lucky bastards.'

'You know the girlfriend's name? How much did you virtually dig?'

'Oh no, she, eh, introduced herself at the counter.'

Another lie.

'Yeah, yeah,' he said, poking my side. He didn't believe me. But he didn't hold that against me. 'The tinglies, really?'

That's how Reid and I described the tummy-flips-and-butterflies feeling when you not only like someone but you crave them; you need to kiss them and touch them and talk to them, always, no matter how you're getting along. Reid had brought up the lack of tinglies between Dan and me several times before our break-up. But I was starting to believe deep down that long-lasting love and parenthood existing alongside the tinglies was an extremely rare and improbable thing; that Granny and Grandad were an anomaly and I shouldn't expect to ever be so lucky. That I was living in the shadow of a peak that jutted out of miles and miles of flatland.

'God, I miss reciprocal tinglies,' Reid said with a sigh.

'What if it's a feeling that isn't meant to last?'

'I don't like to think very far ahead in general. I just hate feeling it for someone who doesn't feel it back – it's exhausting.'

I prepared myself for a twenty-minute black hole of chat about bloody Martin, but the conversation took a completely different turn – sharp onto unexpected and bumpy terrain.

'Finn has the tinglies right now. Some girl teacher from King's College. They're going on their first date on Thursday.'

I rolled my eyes. Reid didn't know Finn like I did. 'No, he doesn't,' I said. 'He told me he doesn't want anything serious with anyone when we hung out on Saturday night … Oh, did you know Finn was *married* before? I know we only see him every other weekend but I thought he'd have let that slip by now.'

'Sure, I knew that.' Surprise created wrinkles in my forehead: surprise that I was wrong, that Finn wasn't as close to me as I'd thought. 'How have you two not talked about that? And he *does* have tinglies,' Reid insisted, turning his body all the way toward me on our step so that his knees touched my thigh. 'I think it was his conversation with you that changed his mind, actually.'

I nervously swallowed all of the spit that had unexpectedly filled my mouth.

Reid and Finn are closer than me and Finn. When did that happen?

'We hung out yesterday. You weren't texting us back in the group chat, you hungover mess. So I invited Finn for a cheeky Nando's – we like to pretend we're top lads, and that's what laddish top shaggers do. Anyway, Finn said he realised he's kinda had his love life on pause for ages, and that if *you're* able to move on after a long-term relationship, he should be able to as well. Glad you guys talked. You have a positive effect on him, y'know.'

Sure I do. He thinks of me as his little sister – isn't that what other-world Rachel had said?

'Why can't you have the same effect on me? Why can't I just destroy my Martin shrine, proper blow it up, and make myself available for the right man to step into my life?'

'Shrine?' I ignored all the parts of what Reid had said that I didn't really want to talk about.

'If anyone saw how many photos and keepsakes I have of and relating to Martin I'd be thrown in a cell,' he said, before biting his tongue and scrunching up his nose. 'Anyway, Finn met this woman he's into when he first started his new job over here. They've become closer over the past few months. He said she's great, that they click, and—'

'What about Rachel?' I blurted out.

'She had evening art lessons, Beggy. She always works on Sundays.'

'No, I mean, doesn't Finn fancy Rachel?'

'Maybe a little because, eh, well, she's a babe. Even I fancy her, and I'm as gay as London's air is polluted. But—'

'*Bit* of a bitch, though,' I said, cutting him off.

'She enjoys a gossip, sure. So do we, though. We're bitching right now, you big bitch.'

'Whatever. I just thought Finn "like liked" Rachel, in spite of her being a bit, y'know, bitchy.'

'Nah. That's what I was about to say. For one, his flatmate is into Rachel, he told me, and that didn't seem to bother him. But also I think he knows he shouldn't shit where he eats so he's friend-zoned her.'

'You can't friend-zone someone else,' I said dismissively. 'You can only choose to be in the friend zone yourself, which is what you've done. You're a walking example.'

Reid leaned back onto the palms of his hands and looked up at the sky. 'Explain this bullshit.'

'You're friends with someone who you know only sees you as a friend, even though you love him. You've stepped into the friend zone by choice because you've boyfriend-zoned Martin, but he only ever saw you as a friend. You can't ... put someone there, like, you can't label someone "friend" who never wanted to *just* be your friend,' I said.

'Go on.'

'Right. So if Rachel actually saw Finn as a romantic option and he didn't like her back, I can't imagine her settling for buddy status. She's hardly going to go to the cinema with him on a Tuesday evening if she's mad about him and he doesn't like her back.'

'Like I do with Martin, you mean.'

'You go to the cinema with him?'

'We literally saw a Marvel movie after work last week.'

'Well, yeah then. That's you choosing to hang out in the friend zone, mate.'

He threw his eyes back. 'Anyway, Rachel and Finn are still getting to know each other. You're being reductive.'

'I don't think I am. If I loved someone, I wouldn't accept friendship.'

'Firstly, we're not talking about *love* in Finn and Rachel's situation, are we? Secondly, I'm curious about the view from that high horse you're on. What's it like? Everything must be really black and white, huh?'

I widened my eyes and smiled awkwardly. Reid was pivoting the conversation and was evidently annoyed with me. His eyes were half closed, and he only ever looked like that when there was proper tension between us. He already knew how I felt about his closeness to Martin, post-marriage, but it had seemed like he'd become so accepting of the situation as of late that he'd flipped a switch from 'care' to 'don't give a shit', or so I thought. *Maybe I don't listen enough*. While it did upset me to watch my friend's self-respect slide so far in the wrong direction, I decided there and then that pushing and pulling him wasn't my place. This was a role that Reid was wonderful at filling when it came to me and my romantic life, but nothing I ever said or did seemed to change anything about Reid's addiction to Martin, so I needed to lay off. We'd previously settled on banter as a means to acknowledge how messed up the situation really was, but I worried such banter's shelf life was up.

'I did think Finn liked Rachel,' I pushed on, to avoid confrontation, 'and I did think there was a chance she'd be interested in him, especially after getting to know him.' I thought of Finn's expression that morning before the three

of us went for a run and of the many times since then that
they'd gravitated toward one another in a room, to laugh at
each other's jokes and give each other gooey looks.

'Maybe. I dunno. Not enough to make a move, obviously,'
he said flatly.

Come on. Don't be mad at me. 'Who's this new person,
then?' I tried to stir us through the discomfort by keeping
a straight face. 'He's *never* mentioned any women from
work. I always assumed that Finn went in to talk about
plot and cinematography to a bunch of morally superior
types, then ate sandwiches with the crusts cut off, like he
did when we were in school, surrounded by a bunch of
farty, pretentious old men who get horny reading about
Cannes Film Festival, then, I dunno, that he came back to
Old Willow to his empty bed and internet dating profiles.'

'He's mentioned her a few times to me. Hannah. Lectures
in some kinda engineering or something.' I threw my head
back and made a snore sound. 'Oh, yeah, like you're the
leader of the Army of People with Interesting Careers.'

Fair.

I deserve that.

*Engineering is probably fascinating and lucrative and all
of the things my job isn't.*

'Besides, I don't get why you're surprised he hasn't
mentioned her. You only just told him about *your* crush
this weekend. Maybe spend more one-on-one time with
him. He opens up a lot more when he's not in a group does
our straight-boy companion.'

'I find it a little weird hanging out with him on my own.

We do have a laugh and all, but ...' Reid didn't prod with a 'what'; he just allowed me time to find the words. 'I don't want to lead him on. He used to like me when we were younger. I told you that already, right? Like, he liked me *a lot*. But that ship has sailed, y'know, and—'

'Listen, you narcissistic slag,' he began, his tone returning to standard playful and his eyes managing to hold on to their love for me. 'Your assumption that Finn still sees you in that way, it's a total comfort thing. It's like he's a stuffed animal from childhood that you secretly hope will always be there just in case you want to pick it up. I'm going to say this once, and I want you to get this into that skull because you matter to me, and so does he. OK?'

'OK.' I was uncomfortable. A cat forced to lie down on its back.

'Finn is not to you what I am to Martin.'

Ouch.

I never insinuated that he was.

Did I?

'Like, I know you're trying to walk on eggshells right now so I don't say any more about it. But this is us. Me and you. We tell each other everything.' *Not everything, not any more.* 'Beggy, if Martin ditches the Greek god he's married to in five, ten, fifty years' time and declares his love for me, I'll abandon the world and leave for another planet with him. Seriously. I'll leave you behind; I'll wave farewell to sexual freedom and to whomever it is I've settled with. The hole in my heart that prick has unknowingly scraped out is now deeper than the Grand Canyon. And

Finn – he isn't pathetic like me. You've nothing to worry about there. You two can be friends without you having to worry that you're crushing his heart under your big Irish arse. I promise. Nobody deserves to be anyone's safety net, anyway, but if Martin saw *me* as a safety net, even for a while, I'd catch him. Finn *isn't* your net. Let it go and be a good friend. London is lonely. He doesn't have many people, just as we don't.'

Reid's phone beeped then, and he went to answer the text right away. Probably a message from Martin. I hoped he was right about Finn, though a strange disappointment overshadowed Reid's central point – disappointment that he had placed Martin on a higher shelf than the one he kept me on.

Martin's shelf is probably dusted and uncluttered by miscellaneous objects …

I'm second in line, as usual. Second to Sienna, second to Granny's portrait of Grandad, second to Dan's mum and her wishes for my wedding … Even when I use literal bloody magic to dip into other realities, I'm juggled with girls, plural. 'Erin can't be a priority for anybody' must be universal law. There's no other explanation.

'You're probably right,' I said, pushing the words through teeth that ached to grind while Reid smiled at his phone and typed at lightning speed. He wasn't listening to me any more. Nothing but Martin stood between us. I tried to fidget the building frustration out of me while Reid replied to his number one, but it didn't work, and so, like a daydreamer in an exam hall, I forced my mind onto something I could control: my blog – the one thing that always took me in its arms when I grew tired of playing second fiddle. It didn't exist without me. It *needed* me.

A pretty genius blog-post idea had been slowly manifesting in my mind, and right there and then it solidified into something I could see – an outline.

Excited, I said, 'Anyway, mate, when are you free this week to take me on a night out, so I can do some … um, research?'

'*Research?* What are you shitting on about?' Reid asked, returning to me and pushing his phone back into his pocket.

I clapped my hands together and rubbed them as though to heat them from a chill. 'I wanna observe people who are experiencing the tinglies. For a blog post.'

'Will there be alcohol involved?'

'How else could we suffer through self-inflicted envy?' Reid smiled warmly. 'Finn advised me to put more *truth* into my blog. And he was right, y'know – my blog is awful, and nobody will ever read it if I don't put more of myself into it. I have this idea for a post about dating in the digital age. Think I'll call it "Modern Love". The whole Owen-has-girlfriends discovery kinda sparked the idea, and I have a lot of thoughts – and this could be a way for me to become closer to Finn, *as a friend*, because he did really inspire me with his advice, he'd love it, and—'

Reid raised one eyebrow and pattered his fingertips against his shoes. 'So, you *were* listening. A first! Let's toast, this Thursday, to firsts, friends and future tinglies.'

10
Two Shadows

It was a warm Thursday morning, and I could already smell the freedom of a weekend off work.

To my relief, my post was finally arriving at Old Willow instead of our – *Dan's* – house, so after wolfing down some of Rachel's home-made granola with yogurt and with my hair wet from the shower, I gathered the small stack of letters waiting for me on the side table in the hallway. The only envelope I cared for was the one I fished out first from the small stack: Granny's latest, inside a lemon envelope and scribbled in her unmistakable flowery handwriting. I tore it open while leaning against the island in our kitchen.

Erin,

I learned my lesson about using the pendant while on the sauce, three times no less, and now you've learned first-hand!

A good stab requires a sober mind, love. Tough to get the words right when you can hardly string two together. Though it sounds to your oul' granny like it was a worthwhile adventure! Wendy seems to have left quite a mark on you. Be grateful to have met her at all.

I knew she'd bloody say that. I'd written an entire page to her all about Wendy and how wise she was.

The seven sights will help you to shed leaves and to grow like a tree!

Oh here we go. Granny and her fucking trees.

I'll tell you something Mammy said to me. Imagine that each of the seven branches of the pendant's tree bears different fruits. And what a wonderful thing it is to be able to taste so many of them! You can better choose which seeds to plant! Just think carefully about which fruits to pluck. The questions you ask are lessons in themselves.

Too right. So far, the overall lesson is 'Erin is a self-centred gobshite'.

Feel lucky. And trust your gran! Learning across time and space is just God's way.

God. Again with the God. Might as well be talking to me about Barney the Dinosaur, the purple-and-green tyrannosaurus – well, no, at least I've seen *him*. He definitely exists, in some capacity.

PS: when are you coming back home to me again? I'd go over to visit you but I'm getting along, you know. The boat over would take it out of me. And Chrissy can no longer feed the two bitches for me if I wander off – she's recovering from her hip operation!

    Love,

    Peggy xxx

I wish Granny wasn't so terrified of airplanes.
She's so alone, so isolated.

Guilt stabbed my heart as I realised how much responsibility I felt for her and how much I genuinely wanted to be around for her, to help out and to take some of the weight off her friends and neighbours. After all, Granny was growing more fragile with each passing year, like a fading flower pressed inside a book. I'd been self-medicating with self-forgiveness, though, as it wasn't like I hadn't planned on moving home to Ireland – that's what Dan and I had intended to do, after our honeymoon, but then it all went to shit. I snipped away the boyfriend with the well-padded bank account who was going to help me start a new life back home.

Well done, Erin.

Why can't Dad just move home and look after her?

At least while I try to hang on to my sanity ... while I figure my life out ...

Before heading off to the Sugar Pot, I fetched my Granny-correspondence tin so I could post a letter back to her along my cycle to Kensington.

Granny,

I miss you so much! And you're right. On the one hand, if I hadn't been twisted on wine, I wouldn't have used up another go, or whatever, on a guy I hardly know. Without thinking it through, at least. But I'm really glad that what happened happened. Wendy is a legend I'm glad to have met! And some things are a little clearer for me after our conversation.

I'll just try to make better choices when I do use it. I'm going to start wearing it during the day so I'm more tempted to try it out when I'm in my right mind! I never asked you, how many years did you spread your sights over? Should I only use it once per year? Am I wasting opportunities?

I'll update you about my next 'trip', shall I call it? Holding out for something more ... important.

(And it's OK that you can't come over here — I understand. And I don't want you stressing! I'll book flights for around November, when they're affordable — I'm pretty broke right now. Dad's latest loan needs to stretch to cover rent and bills for as long as possible. My wages are shocking bad. Just about making ends meet! If, by some stroke of a magic wand, I come into money, I'll be with you in a heartbeat.)

All my love,

Erin xxx

I stood there for all of five minutes feeling well sorry for myself because I couldn't go to see Granny sooner; because I missed the tranquillity of Inishbeg almost as much as I missed make-up sex with Dan; because life in

London wasn't how I'd imagined it would be a decade ago when I used to fantasise about it while working in a corner shop back home.

In my pool of pity, I scrolled Facebook to distract myself. As you do.

I searched for Finn's profile, to nosy through his friends, hoping to get a look at Hannah before I cycled to the café. But there were no Hannahs in his friend list.

Maybe she's one of those 'I'm above Facebook, fuck Zuckerberg' types.

Finn had recently shared a link to a song on his page: 'Common People' by Pulp. Not eighties, but not terrible either. I was pleasantly surprised at how it immediately lifted my spirits, and I smiled to myself thinking of Finn's goal to get me into non-eighties music.

I listened to it on repeat along my cycle to the café.

And nodded my head.

And blanked everything out, everything but the catchy British anthem.

I couldn't get it out of my head all day long.

As planned, I met Reid at 7.30 outside a popular cocktail place called Clout Club in Shoreditch, under its neon sign with two interlocking Cs. He'd suggested it, to my delight; we used to frequent the place as students for the spicy discount. It was tucked away on a side street, fairly inconspicuous to passers-by, and I always loved that. From the outside, you'd never anticipate the stunning variety of rooms and delectable award-winning drinks; one time, Reid and I drank a whiskey cocktail from a chocolate egg in this place.

Those were the days.

Reid led the way with his confident strut, and we shuffled into the front room together. It was ever-buzzing with hot twenty-somethings but small – and home to a huge mahogany wardrobe dubbed Cocktail Narnia by Reid, great for first-date impressions. Couples loved to watch one another's expressions when they realised it was actually a surprise entrance to a lounge furnished with plush baroque velvet furniture and retro chandeliers.

Then I remembered: Dan had taken me here for one of our first dates.

The furniture smell brought back memories of Dan and me, years ago, caught up in heavy eye contact; of his kisses on my bare and pale shoulder; of how I once really liked how tall he was and didn't find it a nuisance for hand-holding and missionary sex. I could almost smell his cologne. So many memories.

I'd felt so sure of him when I didn't even really know him.
I guess things were good in the beginning.

'Through the wardrobe? Find a corner? It's probably less crowded in there!' I said, my voice raised above the hum of talk and of my very loud ex-thoughts.

'Well, first I need to go mark my territory in the cassette-tape-adorned bathroom. I've missed this place, Beggy!'

'Right, go tinkle. Meet you in Cocktail Narnia.'

On the other side, where a dull easy-listening soundtrack blasted a much emptier room, I made a beeline for a cosy booth, and I ordered us both Devil Inside cocktails.

'How fitting,' Reid said cheekily after he joined me and learned of the name of our drinks. They arrived to our table, blood red, and we sipped them, oohing at the distinctive combination of flavours: rum, mint, anise, coconut and pineapple.

'Cheers to being nosy devils,' he said, raising his chin and then his glass. I bit my lip, excited to people-watch, and glanced from Reid to the spot behind his head where the entrance was, and my whole body stiffened when I saw two people come through the wardrobe. It was Martin, and Martin's husband.

'Don't look – please, don't look.'

'Already? But it's not even eight—'

'What do you mean "already"? You picked this place because you knew *he'd* be here, didn't you?'

Reid's face dropped, along with the hand that held his drink – it went limp by his side. 'Don't be like that, Beggy. We don't need to talk to him, and, eh ...' He took a deep breath and slowly turned his face to glance over his shoulder. Martin – looking like some museum piece chiselled from marble, in a white shirt that bared sparse chest hairs – had an arm around the shoulders of a vibrant blonde man.

'Fuck. I hoped Gerry wouldn't be with him. Every time I see him I want to smash things.'

'Don't look,' I said, gripping his knee tightly. 'Talk to

me. Ignore them.' My annoyance was swept aside by concern. Reid's entire demeanour had shifted in seconds, like he'd lost control of a car.

'Think I've broken out in a rash all down my neck and chest. This bastard haunts me.'

You're the one doing the haunting here, mate.

I was pretty sure Reid had told me that he hadn't had a proper conversation with Martin's husband before. And yet he stared him down while he ordered drinks at the bar like he were a schoolteacher who'd made his life hell for years, his mouth a line etched into his face and eyes like tunnels, hate on the other end. 'I swear it. Literally can't avoid him. He's always there, Erin.' *He only calls me Erin when he's being really serious.* 'When I scroll Facebook he's tagged in Martin's photos. When I hang out with him, Gerry calls. When I'm minding my own business, he bloody shows up ...'

'Technically, you're not minding your own business – I mean, you decided that we were coming here, you big stalker,' I said, hoping to pull the edges of the line across his face up into a smile, but it didn't work. His long, slender fingers gripped his drink so tightly I feared the glass would shatter, that the Devil Inside would become the Devil All Over the Place. 'He's not going away any time soon. If you're going to keep working with Martin and being around him, you're going to have to get used to—'

'When you experience unconditional love for someone and they don't return it, *then* you can give me advice on this. When—'

'Bit harsh. I'm just trying to—'

'When you've been *this close*,' he pressed on, placing his forefinger and thumb an inch apart, 'to flinging yourself in front of the Tube because you know you'll never get over someone and you'll have to go on watching that person live out your dream life with someone else while you dance in and out of the depression you've been fighting since your teens ... Until *all of that* happens to you, just leave it out, OK? Nothing you say to me helps. It just pisses me off.' He barely blinked as he spoke, all the while looking at Gerry as though willing him to explode on the spot. He moved his leg away from my concerned grip. The silence between us deafened then. Reid had never told me that before – about the train. I'd known he was hung up on Martin, of course, and that he was dissatisfied with life and took low-dose antidepressants, but not that he'd had suicidal thoughts; not that he'd been seeking salvation in this love, however unrequited.

His confession had a chokehold on me.

I couldn't speak.

'Time doesn't fix everything,' he went on. 'Just get that into your head. Please? Some hurts go too deep. Be glad you've never felt pain even close to what I've felt.'

After a minute or so of murder-staring at the love of his life loving someone else, Reid turned back to face me. His sullen expression softened when his eyes met mine, as though he could see through my eyes to my reminiscence of my mam.

'I'm sorry,' he said, nervously playing with a beermat. 'Ignore that last bit. But, well, I never get to talk about any of my shit, do I?'

'I … we …'

'No. Don't.' *Don't talk over me; don't make excuses* – I could hear it in the space he left between the words. 'I've tried to talk about this. But I feel like I'm wrecking your head when I talk about Martin.'

'I wreck your head too, mate. We're best friends. We're supposed to be able to wreck each other's heads.' I said it as fast as I could; I couldn't be silenced when I knew what he needed to hear most in the world.

I've been such a shit friend.

Wow.

'Well, *yeah*. That's meant to be the deal. It's just … well, it's partially my fault. As much as you don't seem to want to hear about it all, it—'

'I do! I—'

'Just let me talk! Please. It … it feels like nobody alive could understand because they're not sharing my brain. Right now it's as if someone has drop-kicked me right in the fucking heart. I feel that a lot,' he said, scrunching up his face and rubbing the top of his chest as though it pained him. 'And I daydream about ways to break them up, even though I'd obviously never want that.'

'You wouldn't?'

'No. Honestly, I love that he's happy. I know that's probably hard to believe, but I do.'

Shit.

I wonder if Dan is happy, and if I could 'love' his happiness – minus me?

I really wish I could let Reid use the pendant.

Then, the question I had to ask, even though I didn't know how to deal with its possible answers. 'Do you think you would've actually ... I mean, do you ... would you have—?'

'Killed myself?'

I just looked at him, eyes wide.

'I don't think so. But it *was* on my mind for a while. Mainly after Martin told me about his engagement to McFucker over there. So stupid, I know, but this was around when you and Dan were trying to sort stuff out, so I was hardly ever seeing you, and I've no family left here, and the guys don't understand, and I just felt so alone and lost and rejected and jealous. One day, I was waiting on a Tube and listening to *Tristan und Isolde, Prelude* by Wagner – know it?'

I shrugged. 'Probably not.'

'It's something Martin and I listened to one time on this striped picnic blanket at, like, 2 a.m., while off our faces.' His eyes focused on a far-off spot as he conjured the memories. 'We blasted it and stargazed together. He kept giving me a certain look that night. Maybe it was the drugs, or maybe he was curious. Anyway, I was *this* close to telling him how I felt. And, of course, I didn't. And, yeah, the song came on my Spotify playlist one day, in the

Tube station, and the hairs all over me stood up. The urge to actually *do it* was fleeting, but it was there. This rotten voice from deep inside. I've never told anybody.' I kept looking at him. 'And I'm fine now, I think. Probably should go speak to somebody. The time I spend with Martin is so fucking masochistic, Beggy. And showing up here when I knew he was coming... But I love my job – you get that, right?'

'I know you do.'

'Literally, I live for it. Not just because of him. Because I'm bloody good at it. It's hard to know what to do. Sorry, this is all too heavy – we're meant to be having fun ...'

'Want me to change the subject?'

'Yes. Also I think I need to throw up, but if I walk to the bathroom he'll see me and then they'll come over, and I – I can't.'

'I'm sure they'll move along into one of the other rooms soon.' I was ever-so-slightly shaking. Adrenalin rushed through me at the idea of losing Reid. That was a thought that had never occurred to me and that I wanted to Tipp-Ex from existence.

Be smooth, be chill.

Don't freak out.

He hates people fussing over him.

Reid was very clearly doing his best to compose himself, to replace the happy-go-lucky mask. 'Can we just stay here and spy on people from afar? For now?'

'Uh, of course, yeah, anything you want ...'

'And you can drop *that*.' I looked at him, my eyes narrowing in confusion. 'The concern. Drop it. I'm fine, honestly.'

You're a liar is what you are.

And what you've just told me has made a bed in my brain and it's not going anywhere.

Then, pretending like Reid *hadn't* just scared the living daylights out of me, I tilted onto my side to look over the booth at groups and couples piling in and hovering around the bar, high on pheromones and the thrill of possibility. Images of Owen and Zoe swam in my mind's eye, the two of them tied up in their chemistry. Like Reid, who just played with his cocktail and whose eyes said it all, I craved that intimacy. I was like someone awake from an operation having fasted the whole morning and evening before and gasping for a piece of toast and a pot of jam. And, just like that, wrapped up in thoughts of Owen and Zoe and Bowness and kissing, I spotted Finn. And his date. They appeared on the far side of the bar to the bash of dark electronica. I'd not seen them come in, but I felt I couldn't even blink for fear of missing a second of them together.

'It's Finn, mate. Oh, God. They're here! Him and Hannah! Why is everyone *here*?'

'Have Martin and *Thing* gone to another room yet?'

My eyes flitted around the room. They were interwoven at a table near the wardrobe. 'No.'

'Right, well, I'm not turning around. But, yeah, *I* told Finn about this place. It's two for one tonight, too – he must've looked it up online. He's a frugal boy.'

'You don't think we should join them, then? Is it not a bit weird, us being here and him being over there?'

'He's on a date. And I'm hiding for dear life. You may describe Hannah to me as I sip this deliciousness with my head in the sand. Go.'

Peering over the high top of our booth, I took everything about Hannah in, like oxygen, and breathed out as much comparison as I could. Physically, she was me, but at the same time, everything that I wasn't. Rust-coloured hair, big eyes and snow-pale – but tall and athletic-looking, with much more than a basic understanding of fashion. She wore glasses, too, which made her look intelligent. I spoke the thought aloud to Reid.

'It's such a stereotype that people who wear glasses are smart, Beggy. My flatmate is the biggest moron I've ever met and his glasses are thick as the bottom of shot glasses.'

'Well, she looks, um, professional, then.'

'Because she *is* professional. She's an engineering lecturer.'

'Are you trying to rub my crap job in my face right now?'

'Just a bit. I mean, lots of people our age have it together, you know. And you do have a degree. A lovely degree that cost you a fortune you've not yet earned back. Just saying.'

'Sure you are.' My job situation seemed to bother Reid as much as it bothered my dad, and Finn. 'How about you stop "just saying"? I'm well aware.'

'What are they doing? How's the body language?' he asked, ignoring me.

'They look like two strangers sharing pleasantries. And – Fuck. Wait. They're coming this way. They're, shit – duck down!'

I swung around and rolled my hips forward on the seat to pull the top of my head down along the back of the chair, as did Reid, so we wouldn't be visible in the booth.

What if they want the corner booth? What if they walk over here and see us? Their date will be ruined ...

Part of me felt oddly OK about that happening.

Finn's laugh grew louder as they approached, and then their voices were drowned by the noise of the room.

'Please, Reid, check how close they are. Please! Just – don't look anywhere other than the row of booths behind us, they're all still empty.'

'Fine. But if *Thing* is in my eyeline I might have a heart attack.' He sucked up the last of his cocktail and inched his forehead to the tip of the seat. 'They're two booths away,' he whispered.

'OK. This is fine. As long as they don't see us or anything. Y'know, this could actually be so perfect for the blog ...'

'What if I have to piss? Holding in the vom took it out of me. I don't know what I'll do if I have to go ...'

'You may piss yourself. Now, *shh*, listen.'

We could hear every fourth or fifth word of their conversation. Like schoolkids, we stole glances and analysed their chat in whispers. It was all fairly boring until we noticed a certain name was coming up over and over again. Bo.

'Who's Bo?' I mouthed.

Reid shrugged in my peripheral vision.

As the cocktail embraced my system, I found the bravery to kneel up on the seat so I could look directly at Finn and Hannah. Reid tugged at me as though to warn me to sit back down, but I wanted to try my hand at reading their lips.

'She's really beautiful,' I whispered to Reid.

'Beggy, what if—?'

'He's showing her some photo from inside his wallet, but I can't see who's in the picture. She's *swooning* over it. Finn doesn't have a secret dog or something, does he? Has he ever shown you the photo inside his wallet?'

'No. Now, quick, *get down*.'

'They can't see me – they're facing the bar,' I snapped. Envy had me in her snare. 'What's the picture of? *Ugh*. She seems so desperate to appeal to him, it's laughable. Probably just a picture of his grandparents or something. So over the top, this one is.'

'She must just really like him. You know how it is. The sight of someone's unflushed morning shit makes you moan in delight when you're into them. Are you *annoyed* because he's showing her something he hasn't shown you?'

'A bit. What of it?'

Reid dragged at my top again, this time with force. I caved and sat back into the booth.

'Do you like Finn?'

'What? Do I fancy him, you mean? No. I fancy Owen, I told you.'

'Cut the shit.'

'I don't see Finn in that way. He's alright … looking, I guess, but not for me.'

'Why?'

'Because he's my friend. Because we don't have enough in common. Because—'

'But you don't believe in the friend zone, correct?'

'Oh, stop being ridiculous. Move out of the way.'

The single drink had really gone to my head. Without contemplating how I'd look if anyone came over to sit down, I scrambled over Reid and snuck on all fours into the booth directly behind Finn and Hannah so I could hear what they were saying, leaving Reid behind with his silly notions.

'I admire that you've waited until you're more established career-wise. More settled. Sometimes I mull over how much easier everything would've been if we'd done that. But, sure, no regrets,' Finn said. I had no idea what he was talking about, but suddenly I clung to his every syllable.

'I can see why,' said Hannah in a soft, breathy voice. 'Did you ever worry that it would hold you back?'

That what would hold him back?

He paused. 'Definitely. Anyone who says otherwise is full of shite.' She laughed at his words with far too much enthusiasm. 'But, y'know, it hasn't. Gives me something other than work to live for.'

' I can't relate. All I live for is work – right now, anyway.'

'I like that.' Another pause. 'I mean, I like that about you – that you're so driven. Busyness is attractive.' She laughed, louder this time. 'It is! That independence. So hot.'

'You think I'm hot, then?'

Yet another pause. I imagined he was doing his seductive biting-his-lower-lip thing. 'I respect the hustle.'

'The six years of study paid off, I guess.'

I thought about my blog and how desperately I wanted to put more time and energy into it, but also scolded myself because the desperation was born from Finn's words and not from my own desire to succeed. Then that name again: Bo.

'I worry about Bo sometimes, too,' he said. 'You want them to have positive role models. She needs to be around people who not only have goals but who work to make stuff happen. People who have interests outside of poxy Instagram.'

'Wonder what she'd think of my banging on about colonising the moon and artificial gravity and the future of airliners and why we need to build higher and—'

'Stop being so sexy. Right now. Or I'll have to kiss you.'

That was enough for me.

Bo's identity mattered far less to me than how little I imagined he must think of me in my current situation, without the nerve to admit it. I crawled back to Reid and placed one of his arms around my shoulders so I could rest my face on his chest.

'We're going to hide out here until the coast is clear and you're going to help me with my blog post. And then, *maybe* a general life plan, too. One for each of us. OK? Because you're an even bigger disaster than I am.'

Reid's squinty grin: my favourite. I couldn't help it – I grinned too.

The next day, however, I barely grinned once.

Kenneth was being impossible. For hours, he spat out sentences like, 'It's work – it's not supposed to be fun'; 'I don't pay you to think'; 'If you don't want the job I'll find someone who does.' We were close to shutting up shop when I felt myself coming apart at the seams, fragile as antique silk. All I wanted to do was hide in my broom cupboard till 5 p.m. and lose myself in extraordinary travel photos posted by people who'd played their cards right, to imagine myself self-employed and circling the Taj Mahal under pastel skies, instead of cleaning pissy toilet seats because Jen called in sick.

How pathetic that I'm wishing a day away because Owen didn't drop by for his usual espresso.

I'm the kind of person I detest.

Dan had a lucky escape.

Even after all I'd learned about Owen I still wanted to stare at him, sad as that was. Doing so had become the sick highlight of most of my workdays. Our brushing of lives thanks to the pendant felt like a private joke I shared with the universe – a star in the black sky of everything else that made up my life – which Reid and I most certainly hadn't made game plans for, like I'd pledged to do the night before. Three Devil Inside cocktails later we'd ended up at a karaoke bar where together we banged out 'I Wanna Dance with Somebody' by Whitney Houston, two cats on helium.

Suddenly the café-door bell sounded, snapping me out of my sorrow, and then Owen was before me, soaked to the skin from the shower of rain that fell outside. What a sight he was. The kisses we'd shared came back to me in HD sensually immersive detail. Kenneth was out back in the kitchen, probably scratching his arse with an ungloved hand, and the rest of the café was empty, so it was just me and my non-boyfriend from a different life. My heart thudded so much I could feel the blood pumping in my neck.

'Double espresso, please,' he asked curtly.

So normal. So ordinary. But in that moment Owen was the red love-heart balloon from Banksy's famous black and white mural, and I was the little girl in the picture, hand extended as wind carries the balloon away.

Is there definitely no chance I can hold on to?

I tilted my chin down to make my eyes appear larger before finding my most alluring voice. 'Double, eh? Someone's living life on the edge,' I said, leaning my body toward him over the edge of the counter, hoping to not only look seductive but to *be* seductive. If ever I was going to flutter my eyelashes it would've been right then.

He didn't smile, though. There was no acknowledgement of my words at all. No magical moment where realities collided. His eyes were glued to his phone, and my fragile ego drooped several inches.

I need to get out of this place.

In a mope, I made Owen's drink, took his money and watched him scurry off into the evening where goodness knows how many women awaited his passion and ten-out-of-ten breakfasts. Then, in the very same mope, I retreated into the broom cupboard, leaving the café completely unmanned – something I'd never done before – so I could use my gift for something worthwhile. Something necessary for my sanity.

I closed the door behind me, using the torch on my phone to guide me to the corner spot I liked to curl up in, and I unbuttoned the top of my blouse to reveal the pendant. I gripped it, soberly and fully aware of its power for the first time before using it. It was light and warm and heavy and cold. It was everything. I thought about the words I'd need to say to actually experience life away from this hellhole, where people with talent and dreams come to waste away amid crumbs and chatter for less than minimum wage. I knew that in reality it would all be over in a split second, but still I spoke softly so as not to blow my cover. I needed to know, now more than ever: 'If only I'd accepted that internship as a photojournalist with Miracle Media ...'

11
Paris

An alarm sounded like a siren, jolting me awake in what felt like billion-thread-count sheets. My eyes opened so wide in fright I was sure the whites would've been visible all around their green irises. Then my blurred vision met with the unexpected sight of a crystal chandelier, which hung from a high ceiling above me and sent my thoughts racing faster than Irish greyhounds chasing a squeaky stuffed bone on a mechanical lure. The alarm eventually slowed them down and annoyed me enough that I smashed my palm against my phone's touchscreen so that silence could help me to figure out where on earth I was *this* time.

I tapped the home button to find my screen covered top to bottom in notifications. Half of them were from people I didn't know – 'Susan', 'Mary', 'Jordan London Office' – but the rest were from a very familiar name. And that name surprisingly wasn't 'Reid'. It was one that inched out on-the-spot tears from a place deep inside me.

'Dan'. With the same red love-heart emoji beside his name that I'd added to my address book when we'd first started out, to set him apart from all the rest.

Did we stay together?

The ecstasy of curiosity took me on its hand like a sock puppet. Clicking into Dan's messages, the swirling whirlwind of possibilities broke me out in small bumps all over.

He'd texted at midnight:

Hey, honey <3 Hope you landed safely! I know you're probably in bed now – you must be exhausted. Mum came over with a fresh apple tart ... think she could hear my loneliness from miles away, haha. I miss you already. The house is so empty without you here. Call me when you wake up, yeah? Really wish I could be there with you. You need to start pushing for +1s on these work trips ;) Sleep well, love you xxx

After the text he'd sent two cute gifs from romcoms I loved as much as he hated them.

Holy moly, this is freakish.

Silent tears the size of Skittles fell, dampening my cheeks and splattering the phone screen. I'd completely forgotten how it felt to read messages from Dan when we were on good terms, when everything was peaceful and we weren't biting each other's heads off over every little thing. We'd been so *off* with one another approaching the break-up, and I'd felt so alone in the months since calling off the wedding ...

Wait.

Did we actually get married, then?

I dropped my phone like a burning coal and twisted my wrist so I could see the fingers on my left hand, nail side up. Sure enough, right there on my ring finger lived two stunning rings: on top was my engagement ring; I'd pined over it after seeing it in a jewellery-shop window back home in Dublin, and Dan had obviously made a mental note of my heavy hinting because he proposed with it just weeks later. It had a simple rose-gold band with a red ruby in the middle, surrounded by mini diamonds. In the real world, I'd made Dan take this ring back when I was moving out by hiding it under his mattress – through croaks, he'd *insisted* that I keep it. But here, before me, beneath the engagement ring sat *the* wedding ring, closest to my heart as tradition (and probably Granny Beglan) dictated. I imagine I'd been happy to play along just to bring her joy. It was also rose gold, and it was *beautiful*, the milgrain detailing giving it a vintage feel.

'Fuck,' I said aloud. 'Me. A wife.' Then I shuddered.

And I decided to call Dan.

I wanted to hear the soft tone of his voice, the way it had sounded during happier times, even more than I wanted to learn where I was, and why I was there, and what I was doing to earn a living in this reality. And so, blanking out the last time I'd seen Dan in our – *his* – kitchen, and the sad atmosphere that had enveloped us all those months ago, I hit 'call', curled myself up into a ball on my side, facing the grand headboard, while I nibbled at my nails. They were much thicker than usual and seemed to be coated in some layer of elegance (gel polish?) that I'd never experienced before. I'd been too busy gazing at my wedding ring to notice such a non-Erinism.

Dan answered almost straight away.

What am I actually going to say to him?

This is crazy.

I—

'Honey! G'morning!'

'Goodness, hey you,' I said, my voice flooded with affection.

'I'm just heading to work in an Uber, was running late for the train, so we can keep chatting. I found it hard to nod off last night without you sitting in your chair,' he said, in that posh accent. I laughed through my tears and visualised his eyes. 'The chair' was a sleeping position Dan and I had coined. Because he was so very tall, when we'd spoon in bed, I, as the little spoon, essentially had to sit atop his thighs, and from a height he'd have looked like a giant human chair.

'I miss the chair,' I said, laugh-crying in the foetal position, eyes glued to my ring finger.

Do I really?

I must.

'Are you crying? Ah, darling, what's the matter?'

'Oh, nothing, I just … I feel like I haven't spoken to you in for ever!'

Because I hadn't.

'I know the feeling. You're away so much lately, especially since you left the magazine. New hurdle.'

Magazine?

'But we're managing, aren't we? Team fuck-the-world-we're-married-now. We're killing this work stuff. Hashtag power couple.'

I laughed some more and then realised he'd said *he* was 'leaving for work', something I'd never heard him say because he'd spent our time together 'working' from home, while he essentially paid strangers to run his late father's car firm. He found no joy in his duties whatsoever, which were few and far between. He spent most of his working hours playing computer games. It hadn't bothered me when I first met him that he didn't have to do very much to earn money, but after a few years I'd started to wonder what it was that got him out of bed in the morning, what his focus was and where his sense of accomplishment came from. One night, over pasta at our favourite Italian just down the street from our – *his* – house, I'd asked him, and he'd told me: 'You. You give me purpose. You, and the family we're going to make together – that's what I live for.' And that had terrified me beyond belief. It was a lot of pressure to take on my freckled, unbuilt shoulders; I'd

had my own lack of achievement to worry about. I was
certain my spine would crumble like dry spaghetti.

'Work ... how's that going?'

Tell me where you work now. Tell me what changed and
why it changed. Did you sell Fernsby Motors Ltd and find a
job you love? Convince me that I made a huge mistake by
calling off the wedding and that you're capable of putting in
a hard day's work and that if I got back together with you
everything would be OK.

'Ah, shit as usual,' he began. 'You wouldn't even begin
to understand how dehumanising it is ... customers treat
retail managers like rubbish. Yes, sir, I am responsible
for all pricing decisions across every branch. Me alone.
Shout at me some more, I beg you!'

I recalled random interactions I'd had with customers
in the Sugar Pot café and wanted to shoot a sassy response
that, yes, I bloody well did understand, but I only giggled.
I was impressed that he was working, out in the real
world, doing something productive with his time, and I'd
so missed his dry complaining.

'Anyway, I know it was important to you that I get out
and live a little, even though selling the company *did* set
us up, but "You can't play *Call of Duty* all day every day,
Dan," I know, ha, *so* I'm grinning and bearing it. Let's talk
about *your* job,' he said. 'That's *far* more interesting. Did
all of the organised transport run smoothly?'

'Um, yep! Got here alive,' I replied, oblivious as to who'd
sent me where.

'Go on. Brag to me about how unimaginable the room is. Fill my head with images of you hopping up and down on the bed like a kid on Christmas Eve in the fanciest hotel that Paris has to offer.'

Paris.

I bit my lip and rolled my body onto its other side so I could see the room. I'd been too caught up in the unexpectedness of Dan that I'd not really looked around me. 'RIP Erin Beglan.'

'Excuse you, it's Erin Fernsby now—'

'I've died, there *is* a heaven, and it's here, and…'

'Tell me!'

'I – I, um, well last night I was so tired that I went straight to sleep. This room is ridiculous, Beanpole.'

I've not called him that in so bloody long.

I stood up and pulled back the curtains, flooding the room with daylight. I had a balcony, and – 'Fuck! Eiffel tower view! *Eiffel tower view!*' I exclaimed, opening the door and sucking in the French air with my nostrils. I'd dreamed of travelling the world from childhood, ever since Granny and I would watch travel documentaries together while she got pissed and I got high on sugar. The first stop on my travel bucket list had *always* been Paris. I'd romanticised it so much (likely why Dan had proposed to me there, in Disneyland).

My heart fluttered.

As he cooed down the phone, I devoured the view with my eyes. Paris was special to me. It was one of the only European cities I'd had the chance to explore on my waitress wage. Memories of our engagement trip came in bursts: couples making out everywhere, brides posing for their wedding photos, cute old men walking along carrying single fresh baguettes like walking sticks that cut off before meeting the ground.

Back inside the ridiculous room, I described to Dan the lovely little sitting area, all shades of yellow and green – olive, gold, jungle, mustard; I told him about the fresh flowers on the desk – orchids, calla lilies and tulips – and about the closet with enough room for a family of ten.

'And there are marble floors in the bathroom! And they've got every kind of beauty essential you could ever need on the go.'

'A room fit for a queen. That's why you're there.'

I snorted. I'd become so unused to compliments that my body seemed to want to audibly reject his kind words. 'This room is a work of art. It's a kiss of grandeur and I'm muddying it up by just being here.'

'Not like you to talk yourself down any more, honey.' Maybe he was right. I caught my reflection, and I didn't look like someone out of place in such a room: I had a fancy new haircut, the kind you'd see on a poster hanging in an uptown hairdressing studio, and my eyebrows were tinted and shaped. I even looked like I could afford facials and skin creams that didn't cost £2.99 in this world – my skin looked glowy without looking greasy. 'But I was being sarcastic, obviously. I can't for the life of me understand how these people can afford to put *you* up in such lavish places. You don't even have to do much. It's mad, is all.'

Am I happy? In this job?

I wanted to ask him, but doing so would probably set off alarm bells and ruin the lovely flow of conversation. Instead, I asked, tongue in cheek, 'What's that supposed to mean, I don't even have to do much? What are *you* doing, brain surgery?' I hoped this would lead him to justify what he'd said, to spill some sweet info.

'Not brain surgery, no. But come on. We both know your job is a bit—'

'What – a bit better than your job?' My words laughed, so as not to intimidate or start an argument.

'A bit ... silly.'

I itched to snap at him, but I didn't. 'Silly,' I repeated.

Then I could practically hear Dan's eyes roll on the other end of the phone. 'You take and edit photographs for airheads who hold up packages and products from whichever brand will pay them the most. You constantly complain about it, you *know* it's silly, and yet you reap the rewards. You're always away ... I know it's fun, and I'm happy for you, obviously. I ... I just ... I miss you.'

It mustn't be easy being married to someone who's rarely home. I let Dan's comments slide and told him, 'I miss you too. But, um, I'll see you when I get back from Paris!'

'No, you won't.' *Don't I know it. The Sugar Pot awaits.* 'You're away again the day you land. Edinburgh, remember?' His words lost strength as he finished the sentence, like it hurt him to confirm the details out loud.

'Ah, crap. I forgot. Are you OK?'

He hesitated. 'We promised each other on the honeymoon that we'd avoid having these conversations when apart.'

We did?

How mature of us.

'But you brought it up,' I said.

'Well, *sorry*, Erin.'

Here comes the every-sentence-ending-with-*Erin* part of the conversation. This reminded me of the Dark Months, and I remembered why Reid had started referring to Dan as 'Him'.

Reid … Finn … Rachel … are they in my life, this time?

With that thought: 'Look, I've got to go. I'll call you later!'

'I'm sorry. I mean it. I didn't mean to drag all that up. It's just hard, you being away.'

'Right, look, don't worry, just forget about it. I've got to go … *husband*. Right, wow, that's weird. To say.'

'I'll never get sick of hearing it. Bye, love.'

With my farewell I realised I'd reopened a wound that went so deep it near pierced me all the way through, like a pen pushed through an apple. Although I didn't miss the bickering, I missed Dan, now more than ever: his sweet texts, his need for me and the knowledge that he was always there no matter what. I pulled the pendant into view and mentally begged for Dan to be wrong about what I'd ended up doing for a living after accepting the internship. I'd often daydreamed over the years of this life path being everything and more, but Dan thought my job here was silly, and apparently I did, too.

I curiously flicked through my phone. The Destiny's Child group chat didn't exist here, and I felt a pang of sadness imagining a world in which I hadn't been reunited with Finn, one where I didn't live with a rather lovely flatmate who made sure to feed me real food. Then I went to message Reid, but my last interaction via text with him had been two months ago. He'd been the last one to reply, and he'd sent two follow-up texts that I'd clearly ignored.

No, no, no, no.

Did we drift apart because of this job? Or did our bubble of closeness pop because Reid and Dan get along like Harry Potter and Voldemort?

I got myself ready in a haze, dressed in clothes I'd never usually wear (but that looked pretty damn good on me): a tailored, check suit, far more glamorous than real-life-me's go-to attire. Then I tackled the messages from the unknowns. 'Susan' seemed to be my point of contact for this trip, and I really wanted to meet with her, instead of running off gallivanting around the Champs Élysées and the Louvre, because she might be able to provide me with valuable information about a career I could've had.

Self-torture, crisp as fallen autumn leaves.

As I read through her email about the day's schedule, she called me. 'Erin, babe, we're in the lobby. Did you not get my voicemail?'

No, confident-sounding-Susan-from-somewhere-in-Great-Britain, I didn't. This is an alternate reality. I don't know right from left.

'Sorry, Susan! Missed it! On my way now,' I said with faux cheer, grabbing at uncomfortable-looking heels laid out by other-world me at the foot of the enormous hotel bed. I cursed the version of myself that would subject herself willingly to *heels*.

High heels are bullshit.

I bundled everything that was strewn on the floor by my travel case into my briefcase-type contraption (a Canon camera, a small tripod, memory cards, adapters and chargers galore) and made my way down to Susan. The hotel was a feckin' maze, mind – thousands of rooms stacked high as a church's spire. On my stilts and wincing, I landed in the lobby inside a lift that seemed to be made of actual gold. A circle of three stood waiting by the revolving glass door at the front of the hotel, their heads glued to their phone screens. One of them – slender, with mousy hair and an overbite – looked up as the lift door closed behind me.

'Hey, love!' she called.

I wanted to respond with a 'Susan!' but didn't want to give my alienness away by it coming out 'Susan?' so instead I said, 'G'morning!'

'How'd you sleep? Well, I hope!'

'Eh – feeling bright-eyed and bushy-tailed, so that's a yes!'

'Ah, that's what we like to hear. *Janet* certainly demands full attention,' she said, then exchanged awkward glances and half-laughs with the others by her side. 'Not having a great start today, our Janet. We had to find someone new on short notice to go to her room to style her hair for the shoot today – apparently the guy we booked was useless.'

Janet?

'Here's the rota for today printed off, Erin,' said a short girl with slicked-back hair, who was presumably Susan's colleague, 'and, as discussed on Skype, you're simply tasked with doing your thing and capturing Janet looking fab in various hotspots here in Paris. We'll let you know when she wants extra shots, so you don't need to worry about … talking to her much. We'd just really *love* if you could almost shadow us and work your magic. Instruct us when you'd like Janet to pose and where, of course, but the key is for us to ensure that the Total Opulence perfume features in at least *four* perfectly captured images with Parisian-themed backdrops.'

I'd smelled a spritz of Total Opulence on one of those cardboard tester sticks while going through the airport to visit Granny, and it was revolting.

'That alright?' she pushed.

I glanced over the rota taking us from 10 a.m. right through to 8 p.m. Head spinning, I wondered how on earth I was going to pass for a professional photographer when in reality I only ever took crappy pictures using my iPhone. Mostly of Reid, upon his request, for him to send to boys he wanted to distract himself with.

'Rota looks great. I adore Paris, this is actually where—'

A vibration sound interrupted my engagement story.

'Sorry, it's Janet,' said the short colleague before she shut down to the outside world to reply on the spot. The third person waiting for me was a guy who looked no older than twenty-one, with corkscrew curls. He seemed afraid to look me in the eye.

'Does Janet have a surname?' I asked Susan, faking coolness and adjusting my feet because they were already killing me. 'Just so I can make sure I'm following her online. I like to follow my … clients,' I let on.

'Janet is just Janet. Like Cher, or Beyoncé, or Prince, or—'

'Oh, I get it,' I said. 'She's super famous, then?'

'She's got over eight hundred thousand followers on Insta,' chimed in Corkscrew Curls as though he were sharing an obscenely exciting secret.

'And what does she *do*?'

Another awkward laugh from Team Janet as Slicked-Back Hair returned to the conversation.

'Peter, Janet needs us. *Now.* Do you two want to head straight to breakfast without us? Janet doesn't want to eat because her first outfit option is skintight, so – yeah.'

'Run along then. We'll be chowing down on the brekkie buffet!' Susan said, smirking wickedly at me. I couldn't put my finger on *why,* but these people made the back of my neck itch. Still, I was glad to spend some alone time with Susan so I could pick her brain about why they'd hired me and who *they* were. We piled our trays high with fresh French pastries before sitting outside to eat and chat.

'Do you three work for Janet, then?' I asked.

A look of concern.

I should already know this.

'Well, yes. Sorry if there's been confusion. *I'm* her personal assistant, then Jen and Peter – from the lobby – that's her brand manager along with her publicist. Busy few days ahead for us, but of course you're just here until tomorrow morning. Today is content day. For the brand. We need to *nail* these shots.' It was a threat dressed up as a statement of enthusiasm, or so it felt.

As we ate, I managed to wriggle out of Susan several details about Janet. Eighteen years old in reality but publicly twenty-one. (Susan didn't say why and I dared not ask.) A 'professional Instagram model' with no prior modelling experience or training. Gained popularity after posting her 'peachy booty workout', which went viral. Is a bit of a diva and lies about having had fillers injected into her lips and cheeks because that's not hashtag relatable or achievable from home for her primarily underage audience.

'Surely, if she's so young, fillers are the *last* thing she should be—'

'You're telling the wrong person, love. I warned her. "Age you, they will," I says to her. But it's the done thing now, isn't it?'

Is it?

'She kicked up a fuss. There was no arguing with her, or her parents. They didn't care. And sure enough the jobs are rolling in, so in the end who's winning, really?' Susan shrugged then pulled apart a chocolate croissant: apathy in human form.

I don't really think anyone is winning here. Especially not Janet.

'How did you get started working with influencers, then?' But before I could make up an answer: 'An old mate of mine put you forward for this gig, y'know. She worked alongside you at *Extra* magazine.'

I choked on my sip of tea.

Play I'm-having-a-brain-fart.

'*Extra?*'

'I hate to admit it, but I got a cheeky giggle out of your "Cancelled Crushes" column back in the day. The things you'd say about those candid celeb shots … you always said what we were all thinking, babe.'

Nausea took me.

'Are you … are you *sure* that was me?'

Reid and I had spent many trips to supermarkets together slagging the people who'd write such tripe. Reid had once said, in the magazine aisle in Tesco, 'I think I'd rather be a pile of mince left on a roadside to cook under the sun for a week than go to bed at night inside the head of someone having written this stuff for a living.'

The pang of sadness for our lost friendship panged once more.

'You sure you got enough sleep?' Susan laughed while loudly chewing on her croissant. Its gooey chocolate stuck to one of her front teeth. I didn't want to tell her.

'Oh, no, ha. I know that was me, I'm just … joking. Sorry. I suck at jokes.'

'Well, you didn't suck when you worked for *Extra*, let me tell you.'

Please don't tell me.

'The girls in my old office would be howling at lunchtime reading your stuff aloud! You gave Kim K such a hard time of it. But hey, being self-employed sure beats *that* hamster wheel. Am I right? The magazine industry is dying anyway. The future is online. And here we are, in the most beautiful city in the world, all thanks to Janet! *To Janet.*'

She raised her coffee cup so I'd 'cheers' her. I did, to play along, but something told me that meeting Janet would have me longing to be right back in the Sugar Pot broom cupboard.

The day was hell packaged in a shiny sweet wrapper. Just the right amount of sun, beautiful architecture in browns and golds, busy streets and macarons. But also, there was Janet.

By lunchtime, I'd deduced that I hated her. I hated her hideous strops over having to walk from location to location, even after Team Janet explained that

'Everywhere we're shooting is within a one-mile radius, babe! The places are much too close together to justify car transport!' I hated her incessant comments about how fat she looked, even though she almost disappeared from view when she turned sideways. I hated her cruel remarks about Susan's organisational skills, and her rudeness to pedestrians 'distracting her from working her best angles' and 'ruining the light' and, not least, her (fair) disgust at my photography skills. 'I'm basically paying you to take pictures that I could take myself,' she mumbled, after giving me some heavy direction and asking Susan why I was hired for such an important brand deal. It took me five minutes to figure out how to switch the camera to 'auto', so she had a point there, but, goodness, by noon I direly wanted to text Reid to tell him, *If I ever have a child grow up to be anything like this abhorrent bitch, I'll want to shove her back inside my womb so she can start life all over again, fresh and untainted by fame, fortune and blind followers. Plz come help me get through this without ending up in a French prison cell for murder – thanks.*

But he likely wouldn't text me back. I'd seemingly been a truly shitty friend after getting hitched. Even I wouldn't text me back after a two-month wall of silence.

It was about 3 p.m. when my hatred for Janet swiftly thawed to liquid empathy, and that in itself surprised me more than the sight of Dan's rock on my finger earlier that morning. I'd really thought I had her pegged. Turns out I was no less judgemental than the losers who wrote articles about celeb cellulite, and the minute that dawned on me I decided I was probably the person least deserving of the pendant's power in all the world.

The twiggy young girl, with her bum too round to be natural and her e-cigarette, on a picturesque bridge and on the phone to Mother. I stood a few metres away with no idea what to do with myself while Team Janet looked over my shots, a heap of English accents speaking over one another. Janet's small voice caught my inquisitive nature in its hook.

'Please, Mum. I'm bored. And *all* my friends are going to a party without me, *again*. Can you please just move the flight forward by, like, two hours?' Janet sucked hard on her e-cig while Mother spoke. 'Why don't *you* do it, if it's so great?' More sucking. 'That's what you don't get ... these people *aren't* my friends.' She glanced sideways at Team Janet. It was as though I didn't exist: I was one of many industry folk who tiptoed in and out of Janet's world, each one leaving with heavier pockets and stories to spin. 'It feels like I'm not even here. Like I'm just a prop. What? No, *you're* being ridiculous. I didn't ask for this, did I? Let's replace all of your friends with numbers on a screen and see how you get on, shall we, Mum? Ugh. I'm done here. Yeah, *whatever*.'

Sounds like Mother is pulling the strings.

When she hung up, I inched toward her, hoping she'd look at me and open up to me and relieve me from my bad feelings about how I'd thought of her only moments ago, so I could offer some kind of comfort or support. But she didn't. She sent a voice note to someone about how Mummy was using her to pay off loans and legal bills. And I retreated into myself, feeling like a *massive* asshole.

The charm of this job was transparent as a glass window full of cracks. Its surface opulence was a big, fat lie, covering up lonely people playing pretend.

Hell came to an end in our five-star hotel's Michelin-star restaurant with my head inside a large glass of red wine and those belonging to Team Janet glued to phone screens, once again. Janet ditched us as soon as I'd taken my millionth still of her prancing about with the perfume bottle that mattered more than any of us, and I felt like I was counting down the seconds to return to my normal life.

As food arrived to our silent table, Dan unexpectedly texted:

Sorry, darling. Trying to stick to this honesty thing and to sidestep bickering before it begins. You know I love you and that everything I say comes from a place of love. Mum and I miss you dearly. Hope the day wasn't too tedious ... just try to enjoy the downtime before bed! I love you xxx

Usually after any kind of disagreement, Dan and I would dance around one another for days until he'd text a simple 'Sorry, love you x' while I was at work, to shove a plaster over the gunshot wound that was our communication. A world in which Dan worked hard at conflict resolution, instead of avoiding it like he would a punch in the face, intrigued me, though almost everything else about this world revolted me.

Maybe I am a successful photographer in this life, but, hey: if I found success by slating celebrities instead of being a proper, actually good journalist, then I don't want the busy résumé, the better pay cheques or even the free trips. It cut me to my core to know I'd ever stoop so low as to be one of those nasties Reid and I couldn't bear, and it shredded my sense of stability to know that Reid and I had fallen out in *any* version of events.

Does he dislike who I've become in this life?

Or is it the fact that Dan and I worked things out?

What if a falling out is something we're heading for? What if there's no avoiding it?

I remembered all Reid had divulged to me about his mental state that night we'd seen Martin and Martin's husband, and I wondered how I could possibly be going about my life without Reid while he fought inner demons. I thought about how important his friendship was to me and how no occupation in the world would be worth his loss.

Did I sacrifice him for a happyish marriage with Dan? Surely not.

But I guess even the greatest gift on earth can't tell me everything.

A day is a drop in an ocean.

I glared at Team Janet in my frustration, one sitting at each side of our four-seater table, and realised I didn't even want to stay long enough to eat my forty-euro salmon dish.

12
Bo

My third 'if only' dalliance rotted inside me as the weeks following Paris passed. Soon after I opened my eyes as my real self again, right there from the broom cupboard floor, I googled flights to Dublin, desperate to visit Granny, but I couldn't afford any of them. Even the cheapest available tickets weren't cheap enough. I couldn't stand that she was uncontactable by phone. To cope, I planned out my next fireside DMC with her to talk about the pendant (and how I was choosing to use it) over tea and wine. And as the days turned into a month and more, as I found myself firmly planted in September and its piles of freshly fallen leaves, the scar that bloody wedding ring left revealed itself to be as deep and jagged as the others etched into me by the day spent as Erin who followed her heart over her then boyfriend's advice.

I still can't believe I actually married him in that life, or

*that I miss him now more than I did before. Is it a sign that
I fucked up?*

Ugh.

*Perhaps everyone would feel like they'd made massive
life mistakes if they all had old enchanted objects hanging
around their necks that permitted them little peeps at
various possibilities.*

Perhaps Granny's gift isn't a talisman at all.

Maybe it's just a … a pretty noose.

It was a Thursday afternoon, and I'd called in sick to
Kenneth. Rachel had popped out to fetch us some lunch;
she'd somehow recently become my personal chef, and
I wasn't complaining. I'd pretty much been surviving on
Jaffa Cakes. 'Why don't you do yoga with me any more,
babe?' she'd ask me. 'You were feeling so much better in
yourself!' I couldn't tell her the truth, of course, which was
'Because this noose around my neck is showing me things
about myself that I'm failing to process,' and so I gave her
every excuse in the book: 'I've got period cramps'; 'This
headache is killing me'; 'I pulled a muscle on the bike'; 'I
think I might have food poisoning'; 'Maybe I'm low in B12';
'I'll never be as good at it as you are.' But I was very happy
to allow her to pump me full of good calories. In exchange,
I'd listen and nod along while she wondered aloud about
Finn and Hannah, about the next-door-neighbour-who-I-
didn't-care-about's private life, about her favourite actress
calling off another engagement.

As I spent my 417th hour since Paris scrolling through

old texts between Dan and me – a stinking mess of fluffy socks and messy top knot on a couch that smelled of Rachel's chemical-free room spray – a familiar, steady three knocks sounded from the front door.

Finn.

I'd stopped caring about how I looked (and smelled) in his presence. Gremlin Erin was reserved for my closest humans, and Finn had taken a heavy step inside that ever-shrinking circle. It was now overwhelmingly evident that Finn *wasn't* sitting around waiting to get down on his knees and beg me to shack up with him as Mrs Kelly. I could finally feel completely at ease when in close proximity to him and had released the need to live up to being on the pedestal he'd put me on all those years ago when he was smitten with me.

I slithered off the couch to go let him in, like Gollum from *The Lord of the Rings* – all oily skin and no fucks to give, wearing my cheap grey dressing gown reminiscent of the Irish mammies who'd walk to the shops for teabags of a Sunday back home in Inishbeg, looking like house coats that had sprouted legs and pale faces with eye bags.

The door swung open to Finn holding himself steady against the doorframe. 'If you're looking for one of those weird lemon-cake things she made, don't bother – they've been polished off,' I told him of Rachel's latest kitchen delights.

He looked right past me, searching for sound and movement, for Rachel.

'She here?'

'Gone to the shops,' I said, turning my back on him to go and take up residence, once again, on the couch. Finn silently followed me into the apartment after closing the door behind him.

'You off work today?'

'Half day,' he said. 'Tea?'

'Only if you're making it. I need to not be vertical today.'

'You mean, you *want* to not be vertical today.'

'Oh, shut up. Two sugars. Cheers.'

'Would you not open a window or something? It's so stuffy in here.' My silence was enough of an answer to that. We existed in it for a few soft, slow moments as he prepared tea – the kind you can only experience with kindred spirits. Then Finn sat opposite me in an armchair after planting a cup in front of me.

'Did she say how long she'd be?' he asked, about Rachel.

'Nope. But y'know what she's like. Chats to everyone: everyone with a cute dog, everyone stacking shelves with tins of whatever, everyone at the checkout tills, everyone in the queue ...' I reached across to capture the heat from the cup with my cold-as-death hands and caught a glimpse of a telling expression shaping Finn's face. He looked like someone who'd just remembered a fond holiday memory from years gone by.

'She's lovely, isn't she? Rach?'

'I guess,' I said, 'in that sexy, eco-warrior princess kind of way.' I smirked as I said it. She really was great, but admitting so made me realise how great I wasn't. Making fun of her was my way of dealing with my lack of Rachelness.

'She's a pretty straightforward person, really. And an all-round nice girl. I like that she's chatty to strangers. It's sweet.'

'Is she sweeter than Hannah?'

Finn had told Rachel and me over drinks one evening about his budding relationship with Hannah, after that date Reid and I had spied on over cocktails. He described how he woke up one day knowing the time had come to finally move on from his marriage. But he and I never spoke of Hannah when alone together, and so he flinched at my unanticipated question that dripped with sweet implication.

'Things are off ... with Hannah.'

Tea got stuck halfway down my throat. 'Oh yeah?'

'Yeah. There's something missing. I'm just not feeling it.'

'She seemed great,' I said, remembering the chemistry between her and Finn. 'Really into you, I mean.'

'You never even met her.'

'Oh, I *know* – I just mean the way you talked about her ... to Reid. And, well, Reid tells me everything.'

Thankfully, Finn laughed. I overextended myself reaching for my half-empty box of Jaffa Cakes, figuring it would make me appear like someone with nothing to hide.

'Ah, she was into me. And, I mean, she's a gorgeous

girl with a great head on her shoulders. But it was missing the, ehm, the … fuzzy …' He trailed off, looking for the right words while rolling his fingers across his palms.

'The tinglies,' I said. 'That's what Reid and I call them.'

'The sexual compatibility.'

'A close relative to the tinglies, that,' I said, biscuit in hand and surprised to hear him say the word 'sexual' so casually.

'Yeah, well, I need that. I want it to feel … what's the word? Fluid. And for there to be no holding back. One night, she got weird about me holding her hand.'

'Oh?'

'Yeah. I just wanted to feel close. I like that stuff. Physical affection. With Hannah, I think I was trying too hard to force it. It wasn't coming naturally because she's not really that way inclined herself.'

'Why?'

'Why was I forcing it?'

'Yeah. Why bother?'

'Because she's perfect on paper.'

'You've got a little perfect-partner checklist, then?'

'Absolutely.' A big, wide smile animated his face. It was how he looked when he talked about films he loved. He didn't break eye contact.

'Really?' I pressed him, surprised that he'd become so picky.

'Really,' he said. 'But it's short. I don't care so much about what she looks like, where she's from, what she does or … how she eats her Jaffa Cakes,' he said, eying me closely – I'd eaten the chocolate top layer of one and had just sucked off the sponge base so I was left holding a thin slice of orange jelly – 'only how she makes me feel.'

'This doesn't make you *feel* revolted?' And I dangled the jelly over my mouth, sticking my tongue up to lick the side with flecks of sponge stuck to it. He shook his head, and a close-lipped side smile told me he was amused. 'So, your list is less "ample bosom" and more "doesn't moan when I make her watch *Rear Window* for the millionth time".'

He nodded this time, without laughing at my excellent joke. I waited for the sexual innuendo, for the jokes about how he wouldn't say no to a big-titted mistress, but they didn't come.

'I don't really have a list,' I said.

'Don't bullshit me, Beglan. Everyone has some kind of list.'

'Nah. We all don't have what we want so figured out, Captain Sure-of-Himself.' I thought about why Finn might be here in the first place – Rachel – and then, as I peeled chocolate off another Jaffa Cake, about the few movies Rachel and I had watched together. She'd been engrossed. She wasn't someone to speak during the boring parts of a film or to randomly turn the light on halfway through, to do other things while a story unfolded in the background. I wondered if Finn's rapport with Rachel ran a little deeper than Reid had assumed. 'Does Rachel fit with your blueprint then, eh?' There were a few seconds where our eyes danced together in the gloom of the room like tea lights and Finn wordlessly told me something in a language that I couldn't understand. 'You're intrigued by her, anyway. I know you are. You should spend more of your time off work alone with her, rather than with the three of us, because, well, Rachel's different when she's on her own. Just take my advice. Get to know her better.'

I don't know why I said that.

For the most part, I think Rachel's great.

She'd most definitely be a wonderful girlfriend for Finn.

Her happy-person whistling while she simply exists is the only thing I find truly maddening about her.

She's so together.

But Finn clearly wants someone like that.

'I intend to get to know her more. Don't worry about me. I'm not the type to project onto people I don't know from Adam,' Finn said, clearly taking a dig at my crush on Owen.

'Below the belt.'

'You still want him.'

'I actually don't. I want …' In the silence of the living room I could hear Finn grip his cup extra tightly; his skin squeaked across its ceramic. 'Dan,' I finished, after a pause. 'My ex, Dan. I think. Ah, I don't know any more.'

He didn't say anything, only looked at me and waited for me to elaborate. The space he provided me to continue speaking screamed, *Since when?* And I wanted to say, *Since I witnessed positive change in him in a different world where we actually got married and I was in a* much *more favourable position to make my dream of having a family come true.* But I actually said, 'He's just been on my mind a lot. Does this happen to you?' Finn still couldn't find his voice. 'Why am I asking you that? Of course you think about your ex-wife. You were the dumpee. I – I'll shut up now, sorry,' I said, sensing him plugging up. 'Bit of a mess at the moment, so I am. Miss feeling like my life has some kind of structure. Dan definitely provided that.'

Finn leaned forward. 'What's the story with that blog of yours, eh? You'd feel a sense of direction if you focused some more on it, on getting it out there. How's it going?'

'It's not going anywhere.'

'Why?'

'It just isn't. There's so much to unpack. I've got this one concept and a title idea, something you might like, actually: Modern Love. But I've got so many thoughts on modern dating and modern families and society at large, and I don't know how to express any of it, and I feel like I should just give up on the blog entirely and—'

The far-off sound of a key in the front door interrupted my spiral. Rachel was home. Her happy-person whistling filled the apartment. Finn intently searched my eyes. Then Rachel was upon us, a bouncing bundle of rosy-cheeked joy in a hat, carrying a reusable shopping bag full to the brim, her hair in two thick French braids and her doe eyes on fire at the sight of Finn.

'Hey! This is a surprise. Didn't think I'd be seeing you this week, mister,' she said breathlessly.

Finn's eyes took milliseconds too long to shift from me to Rachel. But as soon as they were on her they didn't veer off again. 'I popped up to see if you fancied coming for a walk, but I see you beat me to it. Fancy a late lunch, on me?' he asked her, standing up slowly. 'There's this new place just down the road. They do all your ... special vegan stuff ...'

I felt like a third wheel and forced myself to zone out, using my phone as an excuse to ignore them. Moments later, the pair of them took off together, leaving the comatose lump that was me in their wake. I didn't feel happy or excited about the thought of them on an unofficial date.

There was only one thing to do. I texted Reid:

So you know how I've been all for Finn and Rachel realising how perfect they are for each other for a million years now? Well, I think he just told me that he's interested in her and I feel weird about it. Why?

Reid replied as I zoomed in and out of pictures of Rachel on my phone, cursing her physical perfection.

You're jealous because you have no prospects and you're lonely and bored, Beggy. Like me xxx

I took a selfie of me sticking up my middle finger and sent it, with no caption.

You know I'm right. You're so desperate that you've started mentioning your ex/Him far too often

for my liking, and now you're getting territorial over Finn for no reason. If you don't stop it, I'll delete your number and remove you as a friend on literally everything. Join Tinder, for goodness' sake xxx

I would, I wanted to tell him, *only the worry of wanting to use the pendant every time I swipe left by accident is enough to prevent me from ever going there.* I wanted to joke with Reid about how I'd probably use up all my remaining sights on bland 6/10 dates only to waste away encased in the regret of squandering my magic. We'd go on to talk about how he'd probably use all seven sights on Martin just so he could spend seven entire days in his company and tell him all of the unspoken truths that grasped his heart through the years, like tentacles.

But my loyalty to Granny wouldn't allow me to share my big secret with him.

I couldn't.

Not ever.

As I gazed, deadpan, up at the ceiling, my busy thoughts chattered over one another and near deafened me. I feared I would lie there long enough to decompose and imagined my flesh melting away, just like the Nazis in that *Indiana Jones* movie that Finn used to make me watch with him over and over back in Inishbeg.

I rolled over to nap and dreamed of Finn watching *Indiana Jones* with Rachel instead of me. That's literally all that happened: just the two of them, inches apart, staring at a screen depicting Nazis melting to the bone. And when I woke, I couldn't figure out why the simple dream's atmosphere had been so nightmarish.

Rachel burst into the apartment all 'Erin, Erin, Erin, girl, you're never going to *believe* what I just found out – I probably shouldn't tell you but I'm going to *have* to tell you I just *have* to or I'll die ...'

I was still half asleep, having spent the entire afternoon falling in and out of a broken slumber. I didn't even have the energy to go downstairs to check for post, for a reply from Granny, and I was in no mood for Rachel's 'gossip mode' – her, high on new information about other people, her pupils turned big as discs any time she poured titbits onto me. She was being that buzzing, flapping version of herself now, pacing the living room in the lamplight against a backdrop of the navy sky through the window and *The Simpsons* on our TV. A beautiful robin with a damaged wing stuck inside a cage, Rachel was manic, unhinged, ready to explode with someone else's secrets.

I often forgot that her need to stir pots was even a thing because she was so good at being bloody lovely, at thoughtful gestures and all the nurturing, comforting stuff that comes naturally to women like her, but, sure enough, every time I decided she was literally the best and I'd be far more lost without her, she'd hit me with a heavy dose of reality. And today's dose almost obstructed my airways.

'Erin, Finn's a daddy.'

I peeled my upper body off the couch. 'Are you saying that in the he's-extremely-attractive way or in the he's-a-gay-man-who-likes-to-date-people-much-younger-than-him way?'

'Sit up, wake up, *now*, and listen to me. He's an *actual* daddy.' Rachel stormed over to her water filter, poured a glass and handed it to me like she was giving a washcloth to someone who reeked.

I took the glass, but curiosity wouldn't let me sip from it. 'What are you on about?'

'Finn. Has. A. Child. He's a dad. He made a kid. He had sex, and nine months later, a—'

'Can you stop yanking me by the nipples and calm down and talk to me like I just woke up? Because I *did* just wake up and I'm not able for … whatever it is that's happening right now.'

Rachel was shaking. And opening her eyes wider than they opened naturally. And saying, 'Oh my God, oh my God' on repeat, each time in a different tone. 'Erin, I'm not playing around. He doesn't know that I know, so keep this between us, *please*, but he's … a daddy. He's got a daughter. A secret daughter!' I could feel the blood pulsing through my veins; I could hear it deep in my ears, and I could even taste its metallic flavour as I bit my lip so hard I pierced the skin. 'So, we were just in Finn's place,' she started, and it was like a kick in the chest because I'd never been invited over to Finn's place – he always insisted on calling up to us. 'And he was in the bathroom, and I don't know what came over me, but I lifted up the lid of his laptop, just to, y'know, to see if I could quickly check his browser history ...'

'*Rachel!*' It came out of me, a knee-jerk response, even though I had no moral high ground to walk on, seeing as I'd eavesdropped on his date.

'Don't have a go at me, babe, please. I have trust issues, I couldn't help it, I—'

'Wait, hold up. Since when? You're the most confident person I know.'

She crossed her arms. 'My ex-girlfriend cheated on me for months. With *two people.*' *Damn.* I tried to imagine how I might be, now, if Dan had put me through something like that. Empathy flooded me. 'It's not that I'm not confident, it's ... that shit hurts, you know?' It was like she was trying to protect herself from what I might think of her admission. She was all closed up, like an armadillo. *He's not even her boyfriend ... he's just ... a flirty friend. She must be embarrassed. I'd be embarrassed.*

'Nope. I don't know. I've never been there, thank God. So I won't judge.' I forced a gentle smile, and she mirrored it back at me. Then, welcoming my understanding, she slowly unfolded her arms. 'What did you see, then? Are you sure you aren't getting things mixed up? There's just no way Finn wouldn't tell me ... us ... something so important.'

Right?

Rachel sat on the edge of the couch. 'His desktop background.' She slapped both her thighs in unison with her punctuation. 'It was a picture of him with his arms around this *stupidly* cute little girl with glasses, and I was, like, huh? Maybe a friend's kid? Or maybe she's adopted. But, no. She's his – he's her ...'

'Daddy. You keep saying that, but how could you possibly know that?'

She looked incredibly guilty. If the word *guilty* had a face, it was the one hovering before me, all flushed cheeks and massive eyes. 'Because there were two folders on his desktop. Only two. One was called "semester two papers", so just, like, boring work stuff. And the second was called "Bo", which caught my attention because those two letters don't mean anything together. It just sounded interesting and weird, and so I clicked it, and ...'

'You're something else. And what? Come on, what?' My voice was tinged with impatience. By this point I was sitting up straight and fully alert.

'The album was full of photos of Finn with this same little girl, and in some of the pictures she was just a baby, or a toddler, and there was this woman in them, this *tiny* woman with curly hair with a personality of its own. It's got to be his ex-wife, Róisín.'

Finn's voice, telling me about how he called Róisín *Mouse* because of her height, sounding deep in my memory.

'I don't know ... I can't – I – I – *how*?'

'My reaction exactly, babe.'

Finn and Róisín had a baby together?
Why would he keep that from me?

Finn has a child! Finn has a child! It repeated over and over deep behind my eyeballs like an eerie fire alarm.

'Now calm down,' I said. 'Just wait a minute. You might be getting ahead of yourself here. Maybe it's just his ex's kid, and … ehm …'

Rachel sat down beside me. 'I've done the maths, babe. He was with Róisín for years. It *has* to be *his* daughter.'

'Tell me more. About … the pictures.' I sounded like I was asking to hear more about the bloodied corpse of a deceased pet she'd found on a run.

Rachel shook her head with her hands out in front of her, palms up, trying to make sense of things. 'The little girl's face popping out of the bath, with bubbles on the tip of her nose; Finn and the little girl by the swings in a random playground; Finn feeding the girl in a high chair; Finn and this tiny woman kissing, while the woman held the little—'

'OK, stop. None of this will compute. I can't … process this.'

'*You* can't process it? Girl, I just ended a date with someone I thought was my pal, and it turns out I don't know him at all. I'm shook.'

Oh, shut the fuck up, Rachel. Finn's not yours.

'I've known the man for ever—'

She wasn't listening to me at all, this stunning, sly thing, and yet Rachel's presence was one of the only comforts I had in the whole world, so I couldn't find it in me to actually fight with her. 'He was so high up on my boyfriend-material list, too,' she went on. 'I don't know what to do about a kid from another woman – like, do I pull back? Do I run for the hills? I don't want kids, babe. I don't. Teaching them about charcoal a couple of times a week is enough for me.'

'Well, there you go. Maybe Finn doesn't want any more children because he already has one.' I felt bitterness shape my lips. 'And you can just be Bo's friend, and you can all live happily ever after, with her only coming around on weekends ... I always wondered why we only see him every other week.' That last part was me thinking aloud. I didn't notice that I was speaking it until Rachel replied to me, but I couldn't focus on a single thing coming out of her mouth. She'd essentially walked into the apartment carrying a grenade and this new information was the pin, pulled.

Part of my heart turned black with rot and decay, and I didn't know why.

Until I did know.

*

Erin,

Well, if you think wearing the pendant every day is a good idea, I won't try to convince you otherwise. Though you'll need to control your impulses and always think about the repercussions when you're considering asking a question with the gift in your hand. I know it's a lonely burden, dear, but do trust Granny – you'll understand why, one day. After all, you're only learning how to live. And I've given you something to help. You asked me a few questions about the gift, but you know

I don't want to tell you about how I used it. But if you must insist on knowing more, I'll tell you this and this alone: I didn't use all of my sights.

What? Why, you mad bitch? You said you couldn't use it again, that it was my turn ... then again, even if you had demonstrated how to use the pendant, I wouldn't have believed you. It all happens in the blink of an eye. There wouldn't have been any visual evidence. Clever old girl.

Now, no more questions. I've done the job I was told to do – I've passed the pendant down my bloodline. The rest is on you to figure out. But I do wish to hear your updates. I remember telling my mam all about my little adventures, and she'd listen, from the end of my bed – the only one who could, obviously. So do write me and fill my head with all that you're learning!

That's OK that you can't get over right now, love. I'll wait. I'm a patient thing, and I'm not going anywhere, I'll be here with the two bitches when you're able to come stay!

Love,

Peggy xxx

How do I summarise everything? How has my life come to handwritten letters about a magic necklace while everyone I went to school with retweets memes about vegan sausage rolls?

Granny,

I really don't know if it's helping. Like, at all. I think I
understand what you mean about anticipating repercussions
now ... So, I used it again. (I know, three out of seven sights
down already. I obviously can't stick to my guns, I'd intended
to try space them out a little more!)

**I thought about what Finn had said to Rachel and felt
that familiar knot of all-the-bad-things-people-think-about-
me-are-true form in my stomach.**

It's not what I expected, but not in a good way. I actually
figured it might push me harder, career-wise, but all it did was
leave me with doubts, mostly about my decision to, well, jilt
Dan. I know I said that my relationship with Dan had stopped
working, but now I'm worrying that it was my fault or that I
could've done more. We were married in my last ... vision, or
whatever, and so many memories and buried feelings have
come to the surface. I'm struggling.

That last go also has me worrying about my best friend
– you know Reid, right? Well, during my last adventure he
wasn't my friend any more, or so it seemed. He's been going
through a lot of stuff in real life, personal stuff in his romantic
life, generally poor mental health, and he covers it up a lot, as
many lads do, and I'm realising I've not been helping him
enough – I've not been fully there for him. But, Granny, I don't
need the pendant to tell me that, or to deepen my fears of
losing him, and that's all it's done.

I'd really love if you could tell me why you didn't use it seven times ... please? I've sat here for twenty minutes while writing this trying to figure you out. Worst thing is, you're not the only one keeping secrets from me. Guess what? Finn Kelly, who I went to school with and who lives in my building – remember I told you? He has a bloody daughter that he's not told us about. I literally just found out. I can't imagine why he'd hide such a thing. So I'm gonna go deal with that bombshell, and post this, and cross my fingers that you'll spill some more beans in your reply. 'Lonely burden' doesn't quite cover it!

All my love,

Erin xxx

I posted my reply to Granny and cycled to the Palace Gardens on Rusty's back in the near-dark, listening to 'The Killing Moon' by Echo and the Bunnymen on repeat. The gardens closed at 6 p.m., as they did every day, but even at night they served as our meeting point. Reid was waiting at the gates when I arrived, and we spent the remainder of the evening walking the streets of Kensington with Rusty between us, attempting to make sense of the news about Bo.

Naturally, I'd texted Reid just minutes after Rachel dropped it all on my head. I figured he'd soothe the throbbing pain of it.

But he didn't.

'It's so massive. And it's fucked. And he probably just didn't know how to tell us about something so massive and so fucked.'

'It's not fucked, though,' I said. 'Loads of parents split up nowadays. He should've told us.'

'He's probably afraid of people's opinions.'

'Our opinions?'

'Well, yeah. He might feel ashamed that he couldn't hang on to the marriage. For Bo's sake.' We'd already taken to referring to Finn's daughter by name, as if we knew her, even though neither of us even knew what she looked like. 'Or, he mightn't have known how to bring it up – maybe she became a secret by accident. I mean, that must be weighing the guy down. He must worry all the time about us finding out. And at the end of the day, it's really none of our business, Beggy. We can't let him know that we know. This news needs to come from him directly – otherwise it's something we *never* bring up, not ever. We can't land Rachel in it.'

My chest hurt and my guts hurt and my head hurt and all I could deduct from all the hurt was that I wanted it to be my business, though I didn't know what that meant or why I wanted it.

'Why did stupid Hannah get the privilege of being told the truth? She was so – disposable to him. We're proper *in his life*.'

'Well, if *you* had a kid, wouldn't you want to make sure anyone you were considering dating was, I dunno, OK with the fact that you're already a parent?' He read my mind's response as we strolled along in silence, lit up by street lamps and headlights. 'If anything will make you believe that Finn isn't holding out for you, this is it. You need to accept that and be there for him.'

'He obviously doesn't trust us, though.'

Reid banged on about how having a kid changes people's perceptions of you and about what it must be like to father a child who doesn't get to see you much but instead spends copious amounts of time with a step-parent. My mind wandered to what Finn had told me about Róisín leaving him for someone she worked with, and to all manner of memories of Finn's eyes and his smile and of how he'd spoken about his dream future, working for a film studio, surrounded by dogs, with no mention of a family, ever.

Now I know why.

He's already walked down that road. And he probably doesn't intend venturing further.

Reid hopped on a Tube, leaving me with my mouth craned open around a Cornish pasty. Comfort calories. I looked around the station as the warm beef and vegetables filled my tummy, and I watched some people dash through the barrier, others flit in and out of shops, and I noticed how many travelled in pairs. Smiling pairs. Scowling pairs. So many pairs. Humans sharing the journey with a somebody – its highs, its lows.

I wondered if I was weak for missing Dan, and then about how Dan was getting on – even about where he was right in that moment and if he'd come to meet me if I texted asking to see him, after all this time.

Just over an hour later, Dan and I faced one another across a corner table in a late-night coffee shop. I couldn't describe the coffee shop if I tried, only that a single fake rose propped up inside a cheap vase stood between us on the table. My awareness was a balloon deflated by Dan's reply to my impromptu text:

Erin. Tell me when and where, I'll be there.

Our first underwhelming interaction since the day I'd slammed the door behind me, rescuing my letters from our – *his* – house. It had me wobbly and blind to all but my racing thoughts.

Dan's gangly arms were crossed. 'Your hair. It's grown so long.'

'Not as long as your beard,' I said. I thanked the stars that he'd never grown such a beast while we were together.

'I don't know what to say,' he said.

An awkward moment. Bated breath. Knives and forks on plates. 'You've been on my mind a lot lately.'

'You never left my mind. Not for a second.'

'Not even while you played *Call of Duty*?' I asked him, forcing a laugh. He shook his head, and he looked into my eyes and then away again, over and over.

'You've lost weight,' I said. 'Are you eating?'

'You know how I get when I'm stressed. Even Mum's cottage pie won't go down.'

'Why are you stressed?' Still Dan continued to catch my eye only to look away.

'I thought you'd deleted my number,' he said.

'I told you that to help you move on. I could never. Just in case.'

'In case what?'

'I don't know. In case something happened.'

'Has something happened?'

'No.'

'Then, what?'

'Like I said, you've been—'

'On your mind. You've not said why.'

Although I'd withstood the tears that held strong on standby since I'd discovered Bo's existence, a split second of weakness came and tugged at them so hard that they glassed over my eyes – a layer of vulnerability I could deny no longer. 'I wish I could tell you why. I do. But I can't tell anybody. All you need to know is I'm worried I gave up on us too easily. I mean, I'm worried about a lot of things, but right now I'm mostly worried that if I'd not given up on us that we would have worked out. And I'm not saying I want to get back together, but—'

'Are you just saying all this because you've been around the block and you've realised I was right?'

'Right about what?'

'About how nobody will ever love you as much as I do.'

I dissolved into tears, but my vatfuls of Dan-doubt pinned me in place and prevented me from reaching for him across the table.

'Erin, stop lying to yourself and hiding from yourself. You've spent your life dreaming of the one – of making memories with the one and making babies with the one. And you're looking at that person. *I'm* your *one*! But you walked out. You left. You almost killed it.' His voice caught on every word of that last sentence. 'You *did* give up on us too easily.'

'It's not completely dead? You still have feelings for me?'

'Look at us. We're sitting here now, so, no, it's not dead. Somehow, it's not.'

'How can you be so sure when I'm ... not?'

'I'm the walls that hold up the roof, remember? Remember you said that to me once?'

I did say that to him.

Well, she *did: the girl I used to be.*

The pendant weighed heavily on my chest under all the layering, as though calling to me with its presence alone. I never left the house without it any more – I slept with it, I showered with it, I served up coffee with it – because I knew I could never predict when an urge would strike, an urge so profound I'd consider chipping away at my limited offering of glimpses into other lives I might've lived.

I reached for it.

I clasped it.

I looked deep into Dan's almost-black irises, and I whispered, 'If only I'd married you ...'

13
Josephine's Son

The stretch of his long body behind me woke me up with a start, five minutes before the alarm by the bedside was due to snap me up and into my work uniform. Something less nostalgia and more muscle memory took control of me and rolled my face to the right, to let Dan kiss my cheek with his familiar lips and his morning *mmm*.

'Morning, honey,' Dan said softly.

'Morning,' I replied, all sweetness and light, because I'd truly missed him, and I'd missed *this,* and I couldn't quite believe my luck, getting to live this out again, this treasured relationship routine.

'I had such a God-awful nightmare,' he said, brushing hair out of my face so he could tell me with his eyes as well as his words.

'What was it about? What happened?'

'You never married me.'

Glimpsing alternate realities there, Beanpole? 'Oh?'

'You left me waiting. You didn't show up, and all the wedding guests stepped into the aisle and started to scream these bloodcurdling screams. Granny Beglan was there sobbing her drunken head off, and I … well, *I* was naked.'

'There you have it. Dream, confirmed. Granny would be cursing you out of it if you were actually stood in front of her with your cock and balls out for air.'

I felt sad reassuring him, knowing my reassurance was a lie.

Why can't I experience these days with zero awareness of reality? Why can't that be the magic?

'I know it sounds silly, but it was *horrendous*.' He squeezed me tight to him. 'It was like you'd died, but I knew you were still out there, living, so I couldn't even grieve.' *Apt.* 'I love you so much. I'm glad you're here,' he went on, nuzzling further into my neck. I felt his thighs, thin as my forearms, against my bum, under our – *his* – duvet, which smelled as it always did: like floral fabric softener. Dan reached around to interlock his fingers with mine then, as he held me close, I caught sight of the same two rings on my ring finger that I'd worn in Paris and bit my lip. He continued to kiss my cheek and the spot right below my ear that always made my nipples harden, clearly looking for his biweekly morning quickie. It had been a core part of our time together, just like pizza Sundays and nightly back scratches. I wanted him, too. For a few full seconds I wanted him, right until he pulled his fingers from mine and ran them softly across my tummy, pulling my focus away from his stiffness and onto what felt like skin stretched tightly around a basketball – only the basketball was my insides and the skin around them was mine.

My tummy wasn't just bloated from a pig-out.

It was completely different, alien, relatively massive.

I had a baby bump.

And it was horror-meets-euphoria as it sank in. It was *bizarre*. I cupped my breasts – they ached against my palms – and, *my*, they'd blossomed. So much juicy mammary tissue: fat deposits laid down in anticipation of lactation. The size of me made rolling onto my back difficult so I went to jump up out of the bed, but Dan pulled back on my shoulder. 'Erin, careful now! Your ankles, remember?'

'Whatever about my fucking ankles, Dan, I'm *pregnant*!'

I can get pregnant.

PCOS hasn't doomed me.

I can make a baby!

Did I get IVF? Oh, I don't even care, I—

He laughed. 'Ahh, my wife: she is beauty, she is grace, she is *observant*.'

I planted my bare feet on our grey carpet and heaved myself up so I could examine the mound filling me out from every possible angle. *I need a hand mirror. I need to film it and watch the footage back. I'm pregnant. I'm pregnant. I'm* ... but before I could make strides toward

the full-length wall mirror that hung at the foot of our bed,
a happy woofing sound from the floor.

Turnip?

Obviously not, Erin. This isn't Back to the Future.

A mongrel pup with black feet appeared below me and
jumped up and down against my bare legs. I stared, agog,
pregnant and in blue cotton underwear, at this strange
and fluffy ball of delight that looked like it wore black
socks. With a whistle, Dan instructed the pup to jump
onto the bed. It dived onto him, then looked back at me
with pricked ears.

'Marguerite, tell Mummy to come back to bed.'
Marguerite. For a dog? Yuck. I thought of how Turnip
would greet us every morning, years ago, by climbing on
top of us, looking for his morning feed. I remembered the
belly laughs we had looking at him and his dopey long
face. I remembered the comfort of my life with Dan and
all the things I'd needed to push out of my mind when
breaking up with him.

Pregnant, married and owner of a new puppy.

*Is this what it is to feel happy and whole and safe and
surrounded?*

Am I all of those things?

'Can you believe this?' I asked Dan absent-mindedly,
stroking my rounded tummy.

'What, the bump? Does something feel wrong today?
Are you dizzy? Sore?'

'No, no, just – how am I …?'

'Is Mummy having one of her I-never-thought-this-would-happen gushes, Marguerite?' He said it in his cutesy voice (reserved just for me) as he held both of the puppy's front paws between his piano-playing fingers. Dan could be so attractive at times. I looked from my bump to him and back to my bump.

My bump!

'Maybe. Yes. That,' I said, feeling the shock morph into elation.

'Ah, honey. Well, I'd best feed our dog child. I'll leave you to your gush – I need to get the house ready for Mum,' he said, scooping up our-dog-that-wasn't-Turnip and making for the bedroom door in his boxers.

'Your mum is coming?'

'Yeah.'

'Why?'

'Why not? You'll be in work.'

Ah, yes. So I'll be on my feet all day growing a human inside me, while you will likely sit here and scratch your balls between 'work' phone calls and eat home-made sandwiches with your mum, then have her watch you play FIFA and tell you how great you are at it.

This has got to be pregnancy brain combining with Erin brain.

Dan hasn't even done anything annoying yet, other than offer me space to be hormonal, and I'm even more annoyed at him than I'd usually have been when we were together.

My face was red hot, and I wanted to shout at him.

Calm down, preggers.

'I thought I'd take the day off today. I'd like to spend some time with my hubby,' I teased, but Dan wasn't having it.

'Erin, you know Mum likes to come over to occupy herself. I like having her here. Don't you?'

'But can't we just … spend some time alone together today? You don't understand. I really need this. I need *us* time – it's important, OK?'

'Why?'

'Oh, for goodness' sake, Dan. She can come over *tomorrow* – what's the big deal? I'm just asking to—'

'Fine, then. I'll tell Mum to sit at home, alone, in her freezing cold living room. The only grandmother our child will have. No problem.'

I closed my eyes in frustration and forced all the air out of my lungs through my nostrils – the noise sounded like it came from a moody teenager who'd had their phone confiscated. Dan's subtle reminder about the mam-shaped hole in my life was completely unnecessary, but it was his tone of voice and how quickly he could shift his attitude that bothered me the most. Why did our interactions flip like pancakes? Had that not changed in a world where we got married? Had I made the conscious decision to have a child with someone who does my head in like this? How had we not killed one another in this life?

Erin and Dan: like Romeo and Juliet, only it's death by mutual murder rather than suicide in the name of love,

Reid had said of us shortly before our real-world break-up. *Don't marry someone you want to throw any object but yourself at, Beggy.*

Where would I be if I'd ignored Reid's warnings?

Here, Erin. Right here.

And pregnant.

Your deepest desire.

Was Reid wrong?

'Dan, look,' I said, faux calm, stood in underwear, 'there's no need for that. The guilt-tripping. I'm not trying to exclude *your mother*' – it was impossible for me to speak of the woman without disdain cracking through my words – 'I just wanted a day with you to … work on things.'

'What is there to work on? You *always* say this, and we always agree to new rules of how we'll speak to one another, and yet neither of us sticks to them. I married you for you, and you married me for me. You know how I am—'

'So we just give up on bettering ourselves? On improving how we communicate with each other?'

Marguerite barked a single cute high-pitched bark from Dan's arms.

'She's hungry. Can Mum *please* just come around as planned? I don't have it in me to let her down, honey.'

His eyes begged me to back down. I shrugged in response and left him with the puppy to go lock myself in our en-suite bathroom, so I could be alone with the baby I'd never have. Even if I got back together with Dan, and even if he did indeed get me pregnant, it would be a different egg and a different sperm and I'd never be growing this specific baby, ever again. That knowledge overshadowed my desire to bicker with Dan about his meddling mother, *Josephine*, who I'd be happy to have already seen the last of. On the contrary, the notion of saying goodbye to this baby by nightfall did anything but make me happy. It pummelled a hole into my chest, and there was no hope of repair.

I spent forty minutes propped up against the side of the bathtub hugging my bump and sorting through the wreck that was my mind.

Then the doorbell rang.

Josephine was the kind of woman who fancied herself an aristocrat, and she always dressed accordingly. Even on the most blah of days she'd swan around in pearls and vintage designer suits, with impeccable posture and unrivalled table manners. The Fernsby family came from great wealth, which Josephine married into, and although she'd not earned a penny of the sizeable sum left to her in her late husband's will, she carried herself with such importance it made me retch. Jo, as I called her, liked to pencil in her eyebrows much darker than her white, straightened hair which she always kept tied up into a bun. She was immensely fond of *The Great British Bake Off*, and she most definitely had a favourite child.

'Dan, *darling*, you need to put some meat onto those

bones for when John Junior arrives. Let me make you some brunch – she mustn't be feeding you enough,' I heard her say as I eavesdropped from the landing. I would've preferred a visit to the dentist for a root canal over an afternoon with Josephine, *even* on a day in another life. No joke. I couldn't stand to breathe her air.

Pots and pans clanged.

'Mum, I've already told you, Erin doesn't want to call the baby after Dad. Besides, we don't even know if we're having a b—'

'It's Fernsby tradition,' Jo cut in.

'I've asked her, and she's said she wants to wait to see the baby before even thinking about names.'

Too right, Dan. Five points to Dan. I like this-world Dan!

'Your father would be turning in his grave, darling. I'm just saying.'

'I suppose I can bring it up with her again.'

'That's my boy!' Jo said, each word packaged in victory. 'Baked beans on toast, and tea? That alright? That's all she has in, food-wise. She'd want to work on her grocery lists and her food prep before my grandchild comes along.'

'She could learn a thing or two from you, Mum, that's for sure.'

Dan, minus ten points. You absolute doormat.

I plodded downstairs to the pair of them minutes later, after dressing myself in a black roomy maternity dress that I found in other-me's wardrobe. Jo appeared surprised to see me, while Dan sat on the very same chair by the rickety bookcase where we'd had our final parting earlier in the year. He was devouring a plateful of his mum's efforts and she was cleaning up at the sink. In *this* universe the house was far more homey and cosy: candles with half the wax not yet burned dotted every surface, the fragrance of incense, the sound of a puppy lapping up water from its bowl, the faceless chatter of people from the TV in the front room. That intangible something that made a house a home was there – only, even still, it didn't feel like home to me. Even though my very own wedding photos decorated the walls.

Dan just stared at me, chewing loudly, while his mum tried to catch his eye, clearly trying to figure out why he'd not mentioned I was staying home from work, and probably worrying she'd been overheard making comments about how I chose to run my – our – *his* – kitchen.

'Oh. Good morning, Erin,' Jo said without looking at me, lips thin as blades of grass. 'Surprised to see you here at this hour,' she said, as though talking about some randomer who'd shown up to her birthday party uninvited. 'Is everything alright? With …?'

'John Junior?' I said playfully, to let her know that, yes, I'd heard her. 'Yeah, everything's grand. I just wanted to spend some time with Dan today, so I texted my boss. Told him I have morning sickness.'

'You can't still have morning sickness, surely?' She looked at me, aghast. 'That's not normal. You *must* visit Doctor Kennedy, my doctor. He's—'

'It was a lie, Jo. I lied so I didn't have to work today.'

Her eyes flashed with embarrassment, but instead of laughing it off, she did 'a Jo'. 'Even still, I'd recommend you to switch to my doctor. I'd feel better about that, knowing the baby is in good hands.' She smoothed the sleeves of her Chanel two-piece and smiled at Dan.

I didn't want to feed her ridiculous megalomania so I changed the subject, looking straight at Dan myself. 'Can we have a nice day out today? I'd love to catch a movie, go for some Italian food ...'

Dan unattractively wiped crumbs away from the side of his mouth and pulled his eyes from me to his mother. 'Mum? That interest you?'

Of course he invites her on a date with us. Of course he does.

'I don't like Italian food. You both know that.' Jo crossed her arms and looked at the floor as she manipulatively raised a dark pencil-thin eyebrow.

'Where would you suggest we go?' I asked her, trying and failing to mask my irritation.

Dan piped up. 'Mum was hoping to prepare dinner for us tonight, honey.'

'Wow. Mind-reader now?'

'We were texting.'

'Let me guess, Jo. You'll be making Waldorf salad?'

'Erin. I love Mum's salad. Mum, please excuse Erin, her *hormones* ...'

I've been demoted from 'honey' to 'Erin, full stop' once again and he's speaking on my behalf.

Fantastic.

Why did my brain paint pretty pictures over all of this?

'Yeah,' I said and threw my hands up in the air. 'I'm pregnant. I'm hormonal. *I* want pasta and garlic bread.' I gave Dan crazy eyes. I couldn't tell if it was me-me or this-world-me or a bit of both, but I truly was a bit cracked.

'Are you trying to test me?' he asked.

'Let my boy finish his meal,' Jo interrupted. 'We can go wherever you like, Erin. I'm sure there'll be *something* on the menu for me. If there's not, I can just sit there while you two eat your meals.'

The apple really doesn't fall far from the tree.

'No, Mum, don't be silly. We love your Waldorf salad.'

'OK, *OK*, we can stay in for dinner,' I said, acutely aware of how much time was being wasted from one of my seven sights. My crazy eyes became puppy-dog eyes, or so I hoped. 'But can we please go see a movie?' I desperately wanted to recreate the early days of my relationship with Dan – the hand-holding, the giggles over buttery popcorn, the analysing of movies we'd just seen together on the journey home – but he seemed insistent on being a hurdle to our closeness.

Dan looked to his mum for approval. 'How about a West End show instead?' he suggested, flicking his eyes between Jo and me.

'Why? Why not the cinema?' I asked.

'Mum's not a fan of the cinema.'

'I'd much prefer that, darling,' Jo said to Dan.

I wanted to comment that my friend Finn would be frankly disgusted to hear that someone wasn't 'a fan of the cinema' and that he'd manage to convince them otherwise, but then I remembered that (a) Finn couldn't be a current friend in this version of events and (b) Finn had a daughter and I was mad at him and I didn't want to be thinking about him any more.

'It's settled then,' Dan said, fresh with enthusiasm. 'Ooh, this is exciting! We'll have to pop along to that booth in Leicester Square that offers discounted tickets last minute. Great idea, Mum. I can't wait!'

'Oh, I do hope we can see *Les Misérables*,' she said, smiling down at her son as though he were a bouquet of flowers all tied up in pink ribbon.

Les Misérables translated to English as *Wretched,* and that also happened to be the unofficial definition for Josephine, so I wasn't one bit surprised – about her choice of show or that Dan was being an overgrown child, that he'd somehow twisted my romantic gesture into his mother's brilliant-day-out idea. That I was giving in and going along with it didn't shock me, either. After all, I'd done so for six real-life years.

A clunky answer-me-now ringtone sang out from Dan's phone. 'Excuse me, it's the office,' he said, and shuffled out of the room to do several minutes of the hour (-ish) he actually worked every day. Josephine's smiling eyes followed him as he left, then, without looking at me, she grabbed his plate and walked toward the microwave to keep his food warm, her shoulders back with purpose, to look after her not-so-little boy.

Now's my chance.

'Is everything OK between us, Jo?'

'Why wouldn't it be?'

'I'm only asking. This baby. Big deal, eh?'

'The biggest.'

'It's important that we get along, y'know, for the baby's sake. I just … I – um – is there anything you want to say to me? It's just, first the doctor thing and then, I don't know, I'm just trying to spend quality time with my husband and—'

Josephine dropped Dan's plate onto the countertop with more force than someone doing fine and dandy would. She spoke, her voice a hush. 'What about the next time you wake up and tell him it's all off, hmm? What then? Who'll be there for him then? My boy needs me. I'm worried about you two. It feels like a ticking time bomb, Erin. What would you have me do?'

I was lost for words. I examined her face, and genuine concern looked back at me from her eyes, from her wrinkled-up forehead, from her lips, flattened together.

Be careful with your words.

I kept my voice low to match hers while Dan grunted in the other room. 'Next time?'

Josephine gripped at a pearl earring dangling from her earlobe with her right hand and clutched her right elbow with her left. 'I know you *say* you won't pack your bags off to Ireland on him again, but how can we be sure?'

I'm obviously not happy here.

I've left him once, but I came back … because I'm having his child?

'You say *we*, but you mean *I*, right? I mean, does Dan think I'm going to leave again?' My real feelings tangled up with my other-world feelings yet again. I *really* wanted to know; it felt like so much hung on Jo's reply to my question, like ten coats were about to pull a too-small hook from the wood that held it in place.

'He says he trusts that you want to work things out, but I'm his mother and I know him. You destroyed the boy that day you barged out of here. Don't look at me like you know a thing … Until you have my grandchild you've no idea what that urge to keep them safe will do to you.'

We stood there looking at each other as Dan said his goodbyes to whoever had called from the car firm. Wordless communication said so much more to me than Jo could in the seconds we had left alone: *if my son ends up heartbroken, I need him to know that I'll always be there for him. I'm sorry to be in the way, but I'm terrified. I'm only doing what I feel is right. I don't believe you're right for him – you probably know I never did, and now you definitely know – but please act like I said nothing when he comes back in here.*

Dan returned to the kitchen. 'Are you ladies making plans? Hey, Mum, you don't need to heat that up. Give it here.'

With fresh, unwelcome feelings of guilt for not being

more understanding of Jo, I walked over to the kettle so I could hide my face as they chit-chatted, and I fought the urge to cry all of the shame out by preparing myself a lovely cup of tea, even though I wished I were in Granny's, where wine before noon would be most acceptable and where I wouldn't have to feel so bad about my icky feelings for my well-intentioned mother-in-law.

We ended up going to see *Wicked*. I adored everything about it so, naturally, Jo hated it. Jo always took the opposite stance to me: if I liked my steak overcooked, she liked hers pink and bloody; if I bought gold tinsel for our Christmas tree, she'd tell me I should've bought silver; if I said the sky was blue, she'd insist it was actually a rare shade of aquamarine; and, always, whoever I voted for was the devil incarnate. In that vein, as we walked out of the theatre, wearing our finest evening wear, Dan stated that he thought *Wicked* was 'just OK', because he probably wanted to avoid a 'fun debate'.

Dan couldn't possibly disagree with Mummy.

With Jo third-wheeling, I couldn't get a sense of how different my relationship with Dan was in this weird time warp because – apart from the fact that I waddled more with my giant belly – everything on the surface was the exact same as I remembered it. Dan was attentive to my needs, but not to my desires; he made me laugh, but not nearly as much as I laughed with Reid; and, of course, all of the things I'd grown to dislike about him were still there, and they ate away at pregnant-me: his constant nose-blowing (fuck knows: allergies, apparently), his cynicism ('Oh, honey, she's probably just a drug addict, don't feed the addiction, that's all these people want,' he said, when I took out my wallet to find some coins for a homeless lady), his pussyfooting and agreeableness around his mother. (I asked if we could stop for ice cream on the way to the show, then his mother insisted that sugar was bad for the baby, so he talked me out of it.) Worst of all, the act of being with him in a romantic way and all that entailed – linking arms with him and smiling up at him and replying 'love you' when he'd say 'I love you' – it was all stuff I was making myself do rather than stuff that I really wanted to do.

I was both puppet and puppeteer, and Dan was this very tall prop on set that lived in the shadow of his maker. And it was all wrong.

I am over him.

Whatever it is I'm not over has less to do with him and more to do with my life being turned upside down and inside out.

As the three of us strolled in silence, waiting for a free taxi, I felt pain like lightning in my lower back. 'Fuck me!' I yelled more than said.

Josephine looked disgusted. 'Erin. Language, please, we're in *public.*' So shrill, so ashamed to be stood in my presence.

'Oh, mother, she's Irish. Is it the leg cramps again, honey?'

'I'm *Irish* – what is that supposed to mean?'

I usually keep my mouth shut when it comes to Jo, but why bother here? I'm clearly not good enough for her, even in this life, while carrying her blood inside me. I always hoped we'd get along, but ...

'Jo, have it noted that your precious pride and joy swears like a sailor when you aren't around. His favourite word happens to be *the c word*. You should hear him in the bedroom.' Her thin mouth opened wider than I'd ever seen it open in real life. I hated how immensely satisfying it was. She'd crawled back under my skin where I'd picked her out from months ago and I couldn't handle her, not in this pregnant body anyway. 'Dan, take me to a ... I dunno, a pharmacy, or a supermarket, anywhere that sells painkillers, please.'

'You speak to me like that, after my son gave you our family name? You should be ashamed of yourself! I *always knew* ...'

I rolled my eyes while rolling my pelvis in a circle to try to ease the annoying pain I was feeling, a kind of cramp I'd never experienced before, as Dan cut Jo off before she said something she'd (he'd) regret. 'Mum, look. I'm going to hail this taxi for you, and I want you to get back to your house and rest up. I'll call you as soon as I get in the door. But I need to help my wife right now. Is that OK?'

'Stop asking for fucking permission,' I spat. 'My back feels like it's going to snap – just get some drugs into me, *now*!'

Dan put his mother into a taxi and wordlessly guided

me into the nearest Tesco while I whimpered with the pregnancy pain that was foreign to me. And as soon as I saw the Tesco sign, I thought of Reid, of the hundreds of times we'd strolled the aisles together since uni. He'd been right when he said we'd be dead without Tesco.

'Hey. Can we *not* fight and instead hang out with Reid tonight? Go to a bar or something, now that your mother has graced us with her absence?'

Dan stopped me right outside the store, where a man wrapped up in a sleeping bag watched on, seemingly intrigued by the whiff of drama. 'Why do you have to be like this? What has my mother ever done to you? I'm worried about you, Erin. You're talking gibberish. A bar? While pregnant and in pain? And Reid? Are you *joking*?'

'Why would I be joking? He's my best friend in the world. I don't know why you two can't just—'

'You mean the *friend* who pulled out of being your man-of-honour and left you in the lurch? The one who dodged your calls for *weeks* before you gave up entirely? *That* best friend in the world? I thought I was your best friend.' Sleeping-bag man snapped his fingers as if to say *he got you there*. As Dan's words about Reid fully absorbed, psychological pain pulsed through me like nothing I'd felt since losing Mam.

'Reid didn't come to the wedding?'

Dan furiously blew his nose in the spare Kleenex he always kept up his sleeve. 'You know he didn't. He thought you were making the mistake of your life. Didn't care about you enough to stand by you in *your* choice. Some friend he was.'

More nose-blowing.

I looked down at my belly. I wanted to use the pendant to wake up back in the real world in *this* body, with *this* baby still inside me. But I knew I couldn't. And I had no words left. The pain was too much – my lower back, sure, but my *heart* and my head – they filled with sour misery.

'I'm worried about you. You're sore, your memory isn't working – will I phone an ambulance?' Dan reached out to touch my bump.

'No. I just need some painkillers and some tea and some cuddles. Can you just … give me those things, please?'

A sideways smile. 'I can indeed, honey. Sorry for today, alright? I know the pregnancy isn't easy, and Mum—'

'No more about your mum.'

'OK. Come on.'

Back in the house, Dan lit the fire, poured me a bath and fetched me sour cream and onion Pringles (apparently my pregnancy craving), and we shared a rather alright last-night-ever together. Morbid curiosity drove me to initiate sex with him on the couch while 'Against All Odds' by Phil Collins played. I could truthfully describe it as bittersweet, tender sex that was more awkward fumbling thanks to the bump and strange familiarity than fulfilling lovemaking. Afterward, we sat naked on the floor, our bodies half covered by the blush-pink throw we always kept on top of the couch for cosy nights in, and we talked, just the two of us.

No Josephine.

No impending marriage because we were already married.

It had been so long since we'd done this, and it was nice. It was what I needed.

We reminisced about the day we'd met during final year, and we laughed at Marguerite doing stupid, not-particularly-funny dog things like yawning and stretching and rolling over. And after I manipulated Dan into the role of storyteller for the night, he inadvertently filled me in on how I'd fallen pregnant after a few weeks of us trying and tracking my ovulation.

The relief of knowing I can get pregnant is worth every moment of today.

'So, are you going to tell me why you brought Reid up earlier, huh?'

I took a sharp breath in through my nose and fidgeted with my thumbs. 'I miss him,' I said, settling on vagueness. I'd become a master at hiding my big secret from the people who occupied my various other lives.

'Never thought you'd miss Reid Williams after those final ugly words, Erin.'

'It's like my brain just *forgets* the bad stuff. What did he say again that was so bad?' I was all big eyes and anxious hands.

'That you have "such low self-esteem" and are "so needy for any affection at all" that you, eh, I can't remember the exact words, but he implied that, that ...' Dan looked down.

'What?'

'That you settled for doing whatever to keep us together instead of facing up to yourself and leaving me to find someone right for you.'

'Bit rich coming from him.' I realised how angry I was as I started speaking – angry that he could abandon me just because he didn't agree with my decision. 'He's obsessed with his boss and he has no intention of trying to get over him. He never listens to me. But, I don't know, maybe Reid thought he was being a good friend by standing his ground, or—'

'Erin, I don't want to talk about him. The fact that you guys got talking again during the week we daren't mention really, really hurt me. That he's basically waiting around for you to "come to your senses" or something – is that what he said? Anyway. What's done is done. Can we drop it?'

'I don't want to drop it. I want to talk about this. I need to talk about this.'

A sigh. Dan's head, thrown back in exasperation.

Reid left a window open for me.

He didn't abandon the friendship: he just needed to leave me to dig myself out of my own damn pit because he's in a different pit. Who does he really have, in this life, if I'm out of the picture?

From the look of things, Reid had been right on the money.

He had my best interests at heart, I knew that. I found it hard to believe that any version of me *hadn't* known that. Reid had said, according to Dan (who continued the conversation and grew more irritated with every passing moment), that he *couldn't watch me slowly poison myself.* 'He said that's what you'd be doing if you married me. Said you'd wake up a completely different person because of me and Mum, and that we'd end up divorced anyway, and that watching it all unfold would be too much for him. *Pfft.*'

It would've been too much for him because he was already living a lie himself, holding himself back from finding happiness. I couldn't be angry at him any more. Actually, I wanted to hug him. Hard. Because even though my heart was broken as I climbed into bed with Dan and Marguerite and baby Fernsby, I knew that it wasn't the life I was meant to be leading. It wasn't our bed: it was *his* bed. Dan wasn't right for me. Just as no life without Reid would ever be right for me, either.

I lay on Dan's chest with my head mostly resting against his underarm hair, and for the very last time, I breathed in his smell, his Dan smell, totally unique to him. I tilted my chin up to kiss the side of his face, allowing the energy of the room and our overlapping life to fill me full, then I patted my baby bump farewell. It was time to wake back up to broken, bearded Dan as lost and lonely Erin; time to tell him that I'd made a huge mistake by texting him, that I was sorry and that I hoped he'd find contentedness without me.

Part 3

14
New Dawn

It was the first Saturday of November, and the Palace Gardens looked enchanting: frost covered the ground, the flowerbeds were invisible under a heavy layer of early, crisp snow, and the passageway was now naked and bare so it looked like an ancient tunnel leading somewhere magical and important. Reid and I arrived to the sunken garden cupping hot chocolates to keep our gloved hands warm, and it was like the setting for some epic swashbuckling sword-fight scene you'd see in the kind of high-budget romance movie that Finn would hate but that Rachel could probably convince him to go and see with one flutter of her luxuriant lashes.

Because Finn and Rachel were now as good as dating.

Well, *not really*.

It was completely casual.

Early days.

And on the surface I was fine with it. I was even texting this nice, relatively cute young doctor called Matt, from Manchester – Manchester Matt – who'd asked me out near the end of a long day at work, bold as brass, but, honestly, I wasn't handling Finchel very well at all. (That's how Reid referred to Finn and Rachel one day, and I liked it because it sounded like a goblin's name.)

Things between them had kicked off with a fumble in the hallway in Old Willow after a group night out, and they'd been casually hooking up ever since – a Netflix and chill sesh here, a jog followed by a shag there – but over the past week it seemed that their relationship was progressing. Not to 'Hey, Rachel, guess what? I have a daughter' territory, but it was moving along nonetheless; they were spending a lot more time together in the evenings, which, to my own dismay, had me close to tearing my hair out in clumps.

'You know Finn's invited Rachel to some secondary-school reunion thing back in Dublin?' Reid asked. 'Said it was supposed to be a ten-year reunion but that the organisers didn't have their acts together in time for the one-decade-on date, so it's more like a twelve-year reunion. You two went to the same school, right? Are you going?'

'He mentioned it,' I said, staring into space and allowing the waves of jealousy to wash over me. The reunion was going to be debs themed, according to the Facebook invite. I'd fantasised about Finn asking me to be his debs date again, only *this* time I'd say yes, and I wouldn't let my inexperience, or my nerves, or even the bad blood between our families, stand in the way. But I felt stupid thinking such thoughts. I was only coming to terms with being fully over Dan, and Finn couldn't be any more wrong for me if he wanted to be. A divorcé, a father and a dear friend, tied to London, too, because of Bo and Bo's mam. *And yet* ...

'Hello? Earth to Ireland's daftest bitch. I asked if you're going to the reunion? You should!'

'I might,' I said, my breath like a fog gun. 'It's happening a week after my next trip to visit Granny, so I *could* just stay on and—'

'Invite *me* as your date,' Reid said, sticking his tongue between his teeth in the cute way he always did. 'You can't bring Manchester Matt to something so important. It has to be me. And we'll get to make ourselves all pretty together!'

'You'd go? To Ireland? Seriously?'

'Of course I would. I'd love to meet Peggy, and to live without technology, and to survive for a few days on potatoes in the wild, and to be surrounded by hot ginger boys who hate me for my nationality and who'll beat me up but in a kinky way, and—'

I gave him a dig in the ribs with my elbow, sipped my hot chocolate and threw him the mischievous side eye to let him know that I was glad of his offer to accompany me to the reunion, despite the attitude he'd need to dampen down around people who didn't understand him like I did.

'Had you considered asking Matt to go with you, then? No?'

'Of course not. We've had *one date*, mate. We sat and poked at chicken wings for forty minutes while he told me all about A&E. I don't want him meeting you lot yet – like, I'm not really sure about him. His laugh is weird, and he sort of smells ... musty.'

'Delicious image. Just asking because Finn thinks it's more serious than it is. The way you went on about Matt in the group chat after date number one ... He, well, it seemed more—'

'I don't really care what he thinks,' I said, knowing full well that Reid could see right through the façade but that he wouldn't push me. Finn's name had, as of late, become the elephant in the room that we tiptoed around so as not to wake it up and draw attention to it; neither of us ever verbally expressed why we thought it had become a source of heaviness between us, but usually all talk of him would last a maximum of two minutes tops because, for one reason or another, I'd clam up and give off shut-the-fuck-up-about-Finn-now-please vibes. 'Let's just go somewhere warm and plan this vaycay to Dublin!'

I spent Sunday afternoon lying on my front on the living-room carpet, tapping away at my laptop keyboard. I'd been working pretty hard on my 'Modern Love' blog post for a couple of weeks and was feeling pretty proud of how it was coming along. An interview with Granny during my next stay would allow me to sprinkle in some direct quotes from her about dating in the olden days – then the blog would *really* come to life. She'd even agreed to it in her last letter, and I was mentally counting down the days until I could see her again.

I couldn't wait to really talk to her about my hopes and dreams and how I was starting to discover the appeal of not knowing how things might have turned out. I shouldn't have needed to spend a day with Dan to know that my gut had been right all along. And I wanted to share my rediscovered passion for blogging with her, even though she still couldn't grasp what 'blog' meant.

Finn's push for me to put more of myself into the blog – to put a unique twist on things – had planted a seed in me that had long since grown to the size of a giant sequoia tree, but I liked to repeat to myself over and over again that I wasn't hoping to impress him with my writing.

Though I'm sure I didn't believe myself.

I finished up a paragraph. Then, wearing my circular glasses that I hardly ever wore (because I thought they made me look older) and my hair in a messy half updo, I paced while holding my laptop. I read aloud the fresh passages I'd written – about changes to marriage that occurred after the glorious women's-rights movement, after the rise of access to contraception, after the legalisation of divorce. I'd weaved in my decision to *not* marry Dan, who I was referring to throughout as Mister X, and how grateful I was to be somewhat in control of my own future. I was well chuffed with how it all flowed.

I'd read this.

An urge for sugary tea struck me. I wandered over to make some, but we were all out of teabags. So I flung on my warmest coat and my headphones ('Nothing's Gonna Stop Us Now' by Starship) and darted out of the apartment, buzzing with a rare sense of accomplishment. Habit stirred me toward the stairs; I'd been opting for the stairs over the lift ever since I'd first moved to Old Willow, when the lift was broken. I watched my feet as I scrambled down the steps then had the fright of my life when I collided with someone broad as a fridge halfway down the staircase. My headphones went flying through the air and my phone along with them; it crashed down the steps, and I could instantly tell the screen was likely smashed to shit and that I'd soon be on the phone to Dad for yet another loan to have it fixed.

As I composed myself, a familiar, booming laugh, broken up with the word 'sorry' and accompanied by the high-pitched giggle of a child, filled my ears. I looked up. It was Finn, and he wasn't alone. Safe in the cage of his arms was a doll of a child, wrapped in layers and wearing a bunny-rabbit hat to protect her head and ears from winter's chill. She was maybe four or five years old.

This must be her!

His kid!

Bo.

'Ah, Beglan, I'm so sorry – where are you running to, you clumsy thing? Almost scared this one to death,' he said, smiling at Bo, who appeared to be laughing at how my phone and headphones now sadly lay metres away from me. His pupils widened between rapid blinks and his smile looked somewhat forced, fake. But he didn't freak out in an obvious way. He was calm in his discomfort.

Maybe he just doesn't want to freak the child out?

Play dumb, Erin.

Shock, horror, come on – make use of all those rip-off drama lessons you took during transition year.

'I needed teabags. You know yourself,' I said. 'But, anyway … who is this one?' I beamed at Bo. And through the bashfulness of youth, she beamed back. Behind her red-rimmed glasses, Bo had Finn's eyes, but everything else was clearly her mother's – skin several shades darker than her dad's, fuller lips and tendrils of curly hair poking out from her hat. A complete dote.

'This is Bo. Bo, meet my old friend, Erin,' Finn said, in that sing-song voice people usually use for infants or young children. And I'd never found myself more attracted to him than I was in that moment. My left wrist went limp in my right hand.

'Hi, Bo! Lovely to meet you. I love your glasses – they're way cooler than mine. Though you might owe me a new phone,' I joked. 'I'm afraid to look! Maybe you can give me your glasses … as payment!' I regretted saying it within seconds – she looked well confused.

The girl won't understand that humour at all you dumb, childless cow. Stop trying to impress her with your shit jokes.

'Well, *you* owe Bo here a brand-new dodie,' Finn said, eyeballing a pacifier that had also fallen to its demise. 'Call it even?'

'Dodie? Don't you mean dummy?' I asked him as I went to pick it up. While down there I rescued my phone. It *was* smashed to shit. I shoved it in my back pocket so neither of them would feel bad.

'Dodie!' Bo said, drawing out the word as if to say *give it back to me.* Finn and I laughed in harmony.

'My ma and da always called those things *dodies*, so it's a dodie,' Finn insisted.

I handed it over. 'If you say so.'

'Need to give this a wash first, Bo, don't we? Icky! What is it?'

'Icky!' she repeated.

'Finn, she's precious,' I said. *Ask the thing. You know nothing, remember? For Rachel's sake.* 'Eh, whose is she, then?' *Damn, I'm good.*

Finn hesitated, but then Bo put his foot in it. No, not just his foot – the kid put his whole wardrobe-wide body in it. 'Da,' she said, pulling at his nose and poking at his cheeks and flicking his bushy eyebrow hairs. 'Da!'

'Ha! She sounds so Irish,' I said, as I attempted to give off an aura of I-didn't-know-this-information-but-I'm-trying -to-act-normal-for-your-child's-sake.

Finn smiled a closed-mouth smile at Bo. But he wouldn't look at me. Then, 'I've got teabags, Beglan. Come over for a while.'

'Are ... are you sure?'

'You're off today, right? And Rachel's teaching.'

'I am. And she is. So I *could* ...' I said tentatively.

He looked right at me. Our eyes were dancing flames in the darkness again, only the stairway was bright as the day outside. Something like electricity between us, but more concrete than that. There was surely something there that wasn't there before.

Maybe that something's name was Bo.

Or maybe not.

I followed him into his apartment, hoping to find out.

He gave me the grand tour, as his flatmate was out. Finn's space within the apartment was as Finn as any place in the world could possibly be: every square inch of his bedroom walls was covered in film posters, all higgledy-piggledy: *Amélie*, *Withnail and I*, *The Rocky Horror Picture Show*, *The Room*, *Donnie Darko*, *Closer*, *Raiders of the Lost Ark*, *Mulholland Drive*, *Her* and many more he'd shown me a long time ago on his old projector back home. Finn's shelves were loaded with prop replicas and character models, and his small section of the living room consisted of a beanbag (to watch films from) and a unit weighed down by a ton of DVDs beneath a framed poster of his absolute favourite film of all time: *Labyrinth*.

'*Labyrinth* got me into film in the first place,' he said matter-of-factly as he unwrapped Bo from her winter wear.

'Finn. I know. I know you. I know everything about you.'

'You so sure about that, Beglan?' He arched his eyebrows at me and gave a quick, purposeful glance to Bo.

'Right. I take it back. Gonna need some calories for this one, Kelly.' I never called Finn by his surname but I felt a strange pull to mirror him.

'Don't worry. I'm well stocked up on Jaffa Cakes,' he said through a grin. 'This little one will show you how to eat them properly,' he said, floofing Bo's hair. It was magnificent hair, like her mother's. (Rachel and I had stalked his ex on social media, naturally, though her profile had been set to private so I'd not seen what Bo looked like before today – my imagination had been running on Rachel's descriptions.)

'Jaffa Cakes!' Bo said upwards to Finn. 'Ma *never* buys Jaffa Cakes. One time, I wanted some, and she said no, they aren't real food.' I loved how transparent she was – how I could see her concentrating on the memory. No walls yet built to the big, scary world. Total innocence in a tiny body.

'Is that so?' Finn asked Bo, stroking her hair with one hand and holding her shoulder against his thigh with another. 'I guess you can't have any, then. Myself and Erin will have to eat them all while you starve ... Dinner isn't for *four more hours*,' he finished dramatically. I was enjoying their ordinary exchange far more than I could ever have expected.

'No! I'll be a *Goonies* skeleton!'

Finn smiled at me. That big smile that could bring people back from the dead. 'She's talking about *The*

Goonies – very eighties, actually, *you'd* love it.' What felt like the wire of an electric fence that connected us both tugged at me then. 'I only showed it to her the other week, and I think I may have traumatised her. There's no parent guide book that says *PG isn't necessarily safe*, ha.'

'I'm traum-um-tised!' She tried to repeat him while chewing on her finger. She clearly had no idea what she was talking about. A cheeky smile emanated from her – like her dad's.

Finn covered her ears for a second. 'They're like sponges at this age. I'll stick on something for her in my bedroom – we can chat out here.' He removed his hands. 'So are you going to have some Jaffa Cakes, then?'

'Ma will kill me. I'm not supposed to have snacks before dinner!'

'She won't kill you. I'll explain to her that I wanted to give you a treat for being so good today in the park. Okey-dokey?'

'Okey-dokey!'

'So. Feckin'. Irish!' I mouthed at Finn as he went to fetch us our snacks. Then he steered Bo into his bedroom to set up Netflix and I attempted to cool myself off before he came close to me again; I was all flustered. I waited for him against the edge of the armchair he'd been dragging up the stairs when he first moved in, hovering there like a lost balloon and wiping the corners of my lips and flattening my fly-aways and secreting *a lot* of sweat.

He reappeared and closed the door over, but not fully,

so he could still glimpse her if he needed to. Then he handed me some Jaffa Cakes.

'Please, sit,' he said, nodding at the couch near the window.

I did so without saying anything. I pulled apart a Jaffa Cake as if I were a five-year-old dismantling Lego after hours of practice.

'You're not going to grill me?'

'I'm waiting for you to explain.'

'I've wanted to tell you. For a long time, actually.'

'Why didn't you?'

'It's not the easiest thing to bring up.'

But you told Hannah.

'Did you want to keep Bo away from me because ... because you think I'm –' I swallowed a mouthful of sponge – 'a bad influence or something?'

He eyeballed me as I moved on to the orange slab of jelly and giggled in a way I'd not heard him giggle in many years. 'Yeah. I kept my girl away from you so she'd never pick up your horrific table manners and your disgusting habits. You got me.'

I almost choked on the laughter that burst from me. 'What, then? Why didn't you tell me about her? You obviously didn't want me anywhere near her because you think I'm some sort of—'

'I thought you'd think less of me,' he said solemnly. He averted his gaze as he said it and focused on an invisible mark on the far wall.

'Think less of you?'

'It was hard enough to admit that I'm divorced. Even that shocked you. You looked at me differently after I said it. "Divorced father": that's not the label I wanted to have hanging over my head in my early thirties.'

'It's a hell of a lot better than "sadistic serial killer" or "bankrupt arsonist" or "the man who never loved anyone more than his DVD collection". To be fair, I half expected you to have that last label hanging over your head by now,' I joked.

'You don't think it's a bit, I don't know … pathetic?'

'What? That you have a daughter that seems to worship the ground you walk on?'

'Ah. You know what I mean. That I couldn't … keep it all together. That *this* is all I can offer her when I get to see her on weekends.' He gestured around as if to point out the shabby, under-furnished and overall underwhelming apartment. I pushed my bottom lip out and moved closer to him so I could rest a hand on his shoulder. He looked at my fingers as I squeezed him; all I could see were his many eyelashes shifting direction. That was enough to make my chest swell.

He's been so alone in all this.

'I'm your friend, Finn. And I don't judge you at all. Not for keeping this a secret, not for having been through what you went through, not for anything. To be totally honest, I'm in awe of you. I don't think I could manage. Right now, I'm imagining having a mini human that I created with

Dan and being tied to him for ever while also trying to navigate single life with the mini human just ... always there, in the background. I can feel my throat *literally* closing up at the thought.'

'You're stronger than you think you are, Beglan. You'd be grand.'

'I'm a mess. I wouldn't cope.'

'A strong mess. Stop putting yourself down. You've not had it easy. Besides, you moved over here, all alone. I only made that leap across the sea for someone else, not to follow my own dreams, like you did.'

We both smiled, and I leaned my head in to press my forehead into his. It only lasted seconds, but it felt more intense than I'd expected, like the sting of a burn caused by a little steam shooting from a kettle's snout, and it was as though I'd popped a joint back into place. Like all Finn needed was for me to be there with him and to understand. Complete oneness. Then I shifted away from him again to ask him the question that was burning me from the inside out. 'Why would it matter to you that I'd think less of you, anyway? Even though I don't, as I said. Why did you care so much about how I'd react?'

'Because it's *you*.'

He didn't need to explain what he meant. His eyes told me all that I needed to know. And then his phone vibrated in his pocket, and it was Rachel. 'Let me tell her, in my own time, please? We ... it's ... I'm figuring things out, and I don't want to dump this on her right now. Is that alright?'

I wondered if that, in fact, bode well for their relationship, *or* if it meant they were completely doomed. Then I nodded, knowing that Rachel already knew and was losing her mind. Finn left me sitting there so he could answer her call, and I was collapsing under the weight of mental dirt that might very well bury me alive.

15
Hurdles

From that day onward, everything Rachel did or said annoyed me, and I loathed myself for allowing myself to be so consumed by jealousy. When she offered me her home-made meals and goodies, a part of me convinced itself that she secretly wanted to undermine my ability to feed myself right so that I'd rely on her for my meals and slowly forget the little cookery knowledge I had. There was no *why* to my reason. But that's what my brain did to me. When Rachel invited me to work out with her, I figured she was making a grand statement about her perception of my body – that she thought I should be more like her if I was to have any hope of finding a partner. *Bitch, bitch, bitch*, I'd think, while I nodded along to her blabbering. When she'd ask me how I was, I'd convince myself that she didn't care and only wanted me to ask *her* how *she* was. And when she talked about Finn, in any context, I'd text Reid about how badly I wanted to smash plates over her likely-carved-from-crystal skull, and he'd tell me to shut up, to get a life and to stop dragging him into it.

'Babe! Guess what?' Rachel called in to me one late November evening after dance class.

I was working on the final edits of 'Modern Love' before making it live on my blog. It had turned into a real passion project, exactly what I needed to distract me from the shitstorm that was everything else in my life. In it, I'd explored so many interesting themes and ideas that Reid had helped me to brainstorm: microcheating, how mental-health problems can impact love and how divorce rates are actually declining. The excitement I felt at the thought of sending Finn the link over Facebook was all that had kept me going that day in the Sugar Pot.

'What?' I asked Rachel, against my will. I just wanted her to leave me alone. To exist in her apartment away from me while allowing me to exist there too, with walls between us, in exchange for the rent.

'Are you decent? Can I come in?'

'Yeah. You won't be getting an eyeful of *my* tits. You've seen enough of those in your lifetime,' I said, hoping to lighten the lousy mood I'd fallen into upon hearing her voice. I didn't want Rachel to notice how off I was with her because at the end of the day she'd not stepped a toe out of line. My feelings were unreasonable, and I knew it.

'One can never see enough tits,' she said giddily as she came in. 'Yikes, what happened in here?' Rachel looked around my room in disgust. Her face contorted into the expression of any vegan looking at dead fish on ice in a supermarket.

'Just some good old-fashioned living,' I said, defending the bomb shelter that was my room.

'Girl, what are you like? Anyway, listen, I *need* to tell you or I'll—'

'Explode. Combust. *Die*. Go on,' I said. 'It's about Finn, then,' I finished, pretending to type to make myself look busier than I was. 'Lksjflksjfejfskjf' and more like that filled out the bottom of the blog-post draft before me.

'Finn wants me to meet Bo! His daughter! Well, not in a relationship-milestone kind of way, like, we've still not really clarified if we're "a thing" or not, but – he wants me and Reid to meet her at the same time. Still! Ahh!'

I could tell my ears were turning red so I pulled my hair out from behind them to cover them up. 'Oh. Cool. *I've* already met her. He introduced us last week.'

She raised an eyebrow and sat at the end of my bed without seeking permission to come so close to me. 'Huh. Finn told me you guys accidentally ran into one another on the staircase.'

Fuck sake, Finn.

'Well, yeah, but then he told me all about her. He brought me to his apartment to hang out with her.'

'He did?'

'Yep.'

Kind of.

Please don't ask him about it, though.

'Are you alright?'

'Oh, um, yeah. Hormones.'

'You're not due, right? We've synced up, remember?'

'Well, sometimes my period is irregular.' *That's not exactly a lie.* 'Anyway. I'm OK.'

She didn't believe me. But, just as Reid would, she let it go. 'So what's Bo like then? I'm so nervous about meeting her, babe. Feels like such a big deal.' I continued to stare at my laptop screen, my eyes unfocused on anything in particular. 'She looked *so beautiful* in the photos ...'

'The ones you shouldn't have been looking at, you mean?'

I could feel Rachel's doe-eyed stare on me. 'I need to thank you,' she mumbled.

'For?'

'For having my back. For not telling him about what I did.'

I wish I had told him.

Maybe I should tell him?

'I'll never do anything like that again. Finn's a real special guy, Erin, and I kind of ... well, I need to deal with my issues if I ever want to give it a real shot with him. Or with anyone.'

'You really do. If you had a nosy on *my* laptop behind my back, I'd slice through your fingers like chorizo sausage.'

'I bet you're not even joking.'

'I'm not.'

'Tell me, then! What's she like?'

'Bo?' I'd not stopped thinking about her ever since I'd left Finn's place. I hadn't seen or spoken to Finn since then, yet the image of him holding her like a bundle of freshly washed towels and her waving goodbye to me down the hallway was so clear in my mind.

'She's amazing,' I said honestly. 'You can tell how much she loves him and how much she looks up to him. He goes all dad-mode around her, too. You're going to fall in love with her.'

'Ha. Hopefully not before I fall in love with *him*.'

My mouth hung open for a few seconds. 'You're not, then?'

'Not what?'

'In love with Finn?'

'*Christ*, no. No, no. Not yet, anyway. That's what I mean, though – that's why I wanted to talk. I feel like introducing the kid is – y'know, a big step forward, right? Almost like a test or something. A test I'm not sure I'm ready for.'

'Probably. Maybe. Yeah. Yeah, I guess.' My thoughts had increased in speed up to 150 per cent. I couldn't keep up with them. I selfishly hoped they wouldn't get too involved, for my own sake – so I wouldn't feel trapped in this ocean of jealousy for the foreseeable future. But at the same time, I couldn't deny that I'd rather see them be happy together than miserable apart, or, indeed, happy apart than miserable together. All of my jealousy aside, they were two of the *handful* of people in the world that I cared about at all, and maybe, on a subconscious level,

I wanted to protect them both – Finn more so, of course, because he was so tied to my past. 'Don't get too attached to Bo, then. Just in case. He's still dealing with his divorce, I think. Deep down.'

Rachel shook her head. 'We talk about that a lot. He's doing fine now,' she said. 'I know I'll get attached to Bo, if I go down that road. That would be bound to happen. I shouldn't hold back "just in case", though, right? That's no way to live. I'm so nervous, though! This feels even more serious than meeting the parents – meeting the *kid*!'

'Yeah. I suppose. Look, Rach, I was *really* hoping to get this done before bed, and—'

'Get what done? A new blog post, is it? You still need to show me your blog – I keep asking—'

'Something like that. Do you mind if I—?'

'Hint taken, babe. I just thought you'd like to know, seeing as Finn's like a brother to you.'

I wore my fake-smile mask. 'Let me know how it goes,' I said.

When she left my bedroom, I jumped up and walked two laps around my shag rug, then sat down on it, stood up, looked out the window and felt like I was about to cry. Before long I was back on my bed, chewing the side of my lip and typing furiously so I could finish 'Modern Love' with some words on fear holding people back from opening themselves up to vulnerability. I slotted them in near the end, in the only place they seemed to fit, and hoped that Finn would make sense of them and act upon

them, cryptic as they were. Because I couldn't. Because
he was the strong one, even though he liked to insist
otherwise.

As I brushed my teeth, my face dotted with Sudocrem
on the few random pimples that had erupted for some
unknown reason, my phone beeped from the side of the
bathtub. I assumed it was Reid. I'd sent him an essay-long
text over two hours before about my blog-post nerves. (I'd
almost sent the link to Finn twice but I kept chickening
out.) My text was topped off with a very necessary 'How
are you?' as Reid was away on a work trip and staying
on the same hotel floor as Martin. Ever since he'd told
me about his dark thoughts, I'd made a daily routine of
enquiring about his mental state. I spat out a mouthful of
peppermint foam and reached for my phone, continuing
to brush.

The message wasn't from Reid.

'Manchester Matt', my screen read. I opened it.

**Hi! Hope you've had a good day. I just wanted to
be straightforward. I've met someone and we've
really hit it off, so I feel it's best to call it a day with
you and to explore things with this other person.
It's been great getting to know you, and I wish you
all the best! Matt x**

It was a violent strike in the guts, yet I was impressed
with his directness.

But still.

The detachment. The inability to pick up the phone. The 'I wish you all the best'.

Maybe it was shock that made me sick, or maybe the text just accelerated my repressed emotions' rise from my subconscious to the fore, but seconds later I threw up the superfood salad Rachel had fed me and I curled up on the bathroom floor in a puddle of my tears.

Why am I crying?

I hardly know this guy.

Why am I crying?

I asked myself that question over and over again, and I realised that my tears weren't for Matt. They were for my loneliness, for my sanity, for the life in London that I wanted to end. Every molecule of hope I had for a self-made career huddled together, waiting for the end; they'd been waiting a while – months back, so desperate, they'd hoped that maybe Owen, as well as showing me the romantic time of my life, would put me in touch with the right media people or that some kind of miracle would strike, dubbing all the years spent in that cold university library 'worth it'. Sure, the blog was a nice little distraction, but did I really expect it to take off? To go viral?

No.

Ultimately, I was seeking catharsis; I was writing 'Modern Love' for me. Maybe for Finn, too, but mostly for me.

On top of all that, the big part of me that relied on Reid for survival sulked in the knowledge that in other realities our friendship didn't make the grade, didn't tough out the storm. I wanted Granny. Familiarity. Community. A quiet life. Real love. Fresh seaside air. Financial independence with a job that would cover the cost of the odd trip to London to explore the Palace Gardens with Reid.

I want to move home.

16
Woman Down

That night, I hardly slept a wink, and when I did, dreams of my teeth flaking from my gums like pastries plagued me. Reid told me before that such dreams represented a terror of ageing or of becoming less efficient or productive.

It must be the ageing thing because I couldn't be less efficient or productive if I tried – I've written one blog post in eight months.

The next morning, I packed an overnight bag so I could stay with Reid after work who would be back from his night away. I texted him a plea to let me share his bed, not just for his bony cuddles but so I wouldn't have to sleep on his couch, where I'd recovered from the Danpocalypse while listening to 'Go Your Own Way' by Fleetwood Mac under heavy blankets and empty pizza boxes.

He texted back:

As long as you agree to hold in your repugnantly smelly farts, feel free to spoon me all night long xxx

I had to get out of the apartment. *Had* to. I just couldn't take any more of Rachel's happy-person whistling, and I really didn't want to talk to her about Matt and my ongoing lack of prospects. The idea of swallowing barbed wire was sadly more appealing than the thought of opening up to her about a romantic knock-back. Her and her line-up of great candidates, where Finn stood all bright-eyed like the rest of them. I needed to be within arm's reach of Reid as soon as humanly possible and for as long as I could – because I'd slept on my decision to move home, and it hadn't changed overnight.

I didn't plan on telling him.

Not for a while, anyway.

But I wouldn't live so close to him for much longer, and I needed to soak up our affinity for one another while I still could. I'd completely given up on London. Aside from Reid, it no longer seemed to offer me anything but anguish.

Granny needs me, anyway, and I'm too old to break into journalism. I can just – eh – write the blog for fun and be a waitress in Dublin. Maybe I could work my way up to management, take a course … I'll be fine once I get away from memories of Dan, from the Sugar Pot, from Finn. Dad started over, so why shouldn't I?

Before I left the apartment to cycle to work, I scrawled out a letter to Granny and paid zero attention to my handwriting.

I didn't even keep the words in straight lines. The look of the page I shoved into an envelope – and then into the postbox – was disturbingly representative of the state of my soul: smudged splotches on half-crumpled paper.

Granny,

I'm writing to let you know that I won't make it home for my planned visit. Not because I don't want to see you – I do, more than anything in the world – but because I've decided that my time over here has come to an end, and I'll be back for good at Christmas. Living here isn't right for me any more. I'm really not happy. I miss home so much and I'm dealing with a lot and leaving makes so much sense, so I can be there to help you out, so I can start over. See, the pendant – or, rather, how I've been choosing to use it – hasn't helped me to solve anything. You could say, though, that it's helped me to realise what's important to me, and right now, that's being back in Inishbeg, away from all of my bad memories here and with a blank canvas to work with. Goodness, there is so much I want to talk to you about! The last time I used the pendant was a big eye-opener, yet I feel like my vision has been smeared with chip fat or something. I need you. I'll probably call Dad soon to plan the move. Just giving you the heads up so you're not sitting waiting for me with the kettle on and a pot of stew at the ready. I need to say some goodbyes and get some things in order. See you soon!

All my love,

Erin xxx

I knew I wouldn't be able to resign from the Sugar Pot until I'd made actual plans to *actually* move. I needed to keep the wages coming in – Dad wouldn't appreciate me living off him until I sorted my life out. I'd have to line up a job back home first – somehow – and, and …

Shit!

Rusty swerved into a kerb as I cycled downhill, accompanied only by racing thoughts. It happened faster than I could blink – I almost flew over the handlebars but managed to hold onto them. Instead, I ended up on the footpath with the bicycle on top of me.

Then I sort of … lost it.

'Fuuuuuck! Fucking fuck, *fuck*! Fuck my fucking life!'

A rotund man in a thick winter coat and pork-pie hat scrambled over to see if I was OK as I clambered up off the path and wiped at the flecks of mud all over my uniform.

'Gosh, pet, that was some fall. Are you alright? Do you need anything?'

'A time machine would be great,' I began, fully aware I'd never see this man again in my life, 'so I could go back and decide against moving here, for a start. That way I'd have nothing here to leave behind. And I could do everything all over again *properly*.' I was clearly joking, but concern twisted his features. To be fair, I probably did look like someone with several screws loose. 'I haven't hit my head, don't worry. It's just, all I really need is a time machine, y'know? Because, y'see, the magic necklace passed down to me by my granny, that's not helped, even though it lets me fiddle with time ... in a way.' *It's fine, to say this, to him, he'll obviously think it absurd, and won't take me seriously.* I had to speak my ludicrous thoughts aloud or I'd burst into tears again, dishevelled road scrap, only this time I feared they'd melt any strength left in me and this stranger would have to deal with my remnants.

If only I'd never moved to London? Should I try that?

If only I'd gone to the debs with Finn? God, no. What if we ended up together in that life? No Bo; possibly no Reid, again ... that would be too much to take.

I grasped at every way to use the magic at my disposal.

'Pet, look – how many fingers?' The stranger held up four fingers in front of my face.

I laughed a manic laugh. 'I'm fine. Honestly. Well, that's a lie. But I'm not *hurt*.'

He glanced up and down along the hill, searching with his eyes. 'Lock up this thing,' he nodded at Rusty, 'and come for soup with me.'

'Soup?' I said. 'At 8.30 a.m.? Not coffee? Not even a sandwich? *Soup?*'

'Aye. Soup and chats will sort you out.' He had such beady, kind eyes.

'My mam would've agreed with you there if she were still alive. She always brought me soup when I wasn't well.'

'Well, there you have it. Maybe she sent me along to help you.'

What a lovely man.

London isn't all bad.

'I'm – eh, I'm actually late for work. Otherwise, I would join you. Thank you. For offering. This place, it can be quite …'

'You're telling me!' He looked away from me and at the ground near my feet. His eyes widened then. 'Imagine what it's like for me – I don't even know how to use one of those.' He pointed at my phone which had toppled into a puddle. 'I sure hope it's not broken.'

It *was* broken.

To compliment the smashed screen from when I'd collided with Finn, it now wouldn't even turn on. Dead as a dodo. But I had no more fucks left to scream, only gratitude for this man and his warm smile and his offer of soup for breakfast.

He can't use a phone himself and he's asking for my company. You're not the only one trying to stay above water, Erin.

We bid one another farewell in the rain and then I cycled the rest of the way to work with my mam on the brain and memories of the flavour of her home-made vegetable soup with brown bread, wishing with everything in me that she wasn't dead, then, second to that, that she'd died some other way, any way other than the big C. Maybe then I could've prevented her passing and could spend one more day with her using Granny's gift. It killed me, knowing that there were no 'if only' words I could say that would result in the chance to be held by her again.

17
The Best and Worst Day

I ended up staying with Reid for the rest of the week. On Saturday morning, I sat at his kitchen table with an emotion hangover like a puffy grey cloud above my head and an omelette, Reid-style, plated up in front of me, made with almost more cheese than egg.

'Get that into you, Beggy,' he said, wearing nothing but a pair of tighty-whities. His entire body was hairless and smooth but he bruised like a peach, so he was dotted with sporadic brown patches, which he informed me were, in fact, hickeys. I was wondering who he'd been sleeping with, and if he was being safe, and if this was some wild form of self-harm, when he asked if I wanted some coffee.

'Please,' I said, counting the bruises.

'Did you sleep OK?'

'No.'

'Figured. You look like trash. Like Queen of the Bins.

Thoughts of Manchester Matt keep you awake? Or …?'

'Definitely the "or".' By 'or', Reid could only mean the fact that Finn had probably read my blog post by now and hadn't messaged me about it, though Reid was keeping Finn-talk to a minimum. Even when I'd mention Finn, he'd stay out of it and promptly change the subject. He probably feared it all coming apart at the seams as much as I did.

Last night, as we lay in bed giggling about how doomed I was in general, Reid had backed me into the Brave Corner and made me read 'Modern Love' to him, aloud, from my laptop screen. (He'd genuinely seemed to enjoy listening to it – he hadn't interrupted me once, he'd nodded along as I spoke, and he'd shed approximately three whole tears.) Then I'd told him I wanted to send it to Finn – Reid knew Finn had advised me to jig up the blog in the first place, but, as to be expected, he was kept firmly out of it and was all 'Oh, right, cool, do. Anyway, as I was saying …'

I'd emailed Finn the link along with a 'let me know what you think'. And I'd buried my face into Reid's back as he nodded off. I lay awake in that position until the early hours, feeling on edge and antsy because I had no way to tell if Finn had looked at my message before bed or not. If my phone hadn't been destroyed I'd have been refreshing our chat box for hours.

Unhealthy, I know.

'He'll *love* it,' Reid said. 'Now, eat. While *I* give you Reid's Review, because I've had time to reflect on what you read to me. And my opinions are always 100 per cent correct.'

The hairs on my arms and the back of my neck stood on end.

Reid cleared his throat, and I sliced into the yellow flap of rubber he'd served me, trying to tell myself that I'd take his words with a pinch of salt when, in fact, I knew I'd hang on every one of them. He raised his fork to his mouth like a microphone. '"Modern Love" by Erin Beglan is a poignant reminder of the passing of time as we search for something we may never find. It explores the messier aspects of love, the clashing of goals that can occur amongst young couples in this new age – where marriage is for love and commonly demands more than one breadwinner.' He said it all in a put-on radio voice, but then he switched back to his normal voice and dropped the fork to say, 'Also, like, there's so much of *you* in it, Beggy – that's what makes it stand out from the rest of the tripe you've posted on Erin's View.' In my zombie-like state, I laughed. His insults were always soft, like face kisses from a pouty aunt. Back to his radio voice, Reid said, 'She hits on all bases – monogamy, monogamish and the generation-wide lack of resilience amongst millennials who often give up when things get tough. She challenges this with wit and hard-earned wisdom.' I scoffed at that. He was completely building it up, probably to encourage me, which I appreciated more than the words he was pulling from his arse. 'It's relatable, with broad appeal. Shows off her writing ability and her unique take on that which affects us all: the search for human connection and belonging. The blogosphere's freshest new voice, or, well, maybe just a woman who's done something proactive for the first time in … is it years, Beggy?' He raised his coffee cup in celebration and bit his tongue between his front teeth, as always.

'You think all that? Really, mate?'

'Yeah. You haven't applied yourself to anything like you have to this post in … for ever. Now I know what Finn sees in you. Usually, all I see is your fucked-up-ness.' He sipped his coffee and sat down beside me to his own omelette.

'What do you mean by "what he sees" in me?' I asked coyly.

'Eh, well – just that, y'know, you're talented. And capable. I don't think I've seen this side of you since we were in uni. No offence. Dan just drained you.'

'Hey! You said his name!'

'Because I'm *so* over him.'

Reid's phone rang, then. And when I saw Finn's name I could practically feel the colour drain from my face.

'Speak of the devil,' Reid said, dropping his knife and fork. He went to answer.

'But, but – wait – *what*—?' I stuttered.

'It's just Finn.' *It's just Finn*, he says. How can someone be right and wrong at the same time? He picked up. 'Oh, yeah, she's with me. The walking shambles herself destroyed her phone,' he said, rolling his eyes. 'Yeah. Here you go.' Reid pushed the phone into my face.

Ahh.

I reluctantly took it from him, as though he'd just handed me a dildo in front of my dad. 'He's been calling you. Didn't know about your phone.'

Could've just bloody emailed, but whatever.

'Howaya!' I said to Finn, twirling a strand of my hair and fidgeting with my feet. Reid grinned to himself.

'Hey, you. Are you free today, by any chance?'

I looked at Reid as though he'd tell me how to respond. He simply leaned back and crossed his arms, waiting for me to put on my big-girl pants.

'Um, I think … yes, I mean, yeah.'

' "Yes" and "yeah" both have the same meaning, Beglan. You're clearly a writer. You know this.' His words were playful. *He read it.* 'I'm asking because I'm bringing Bo to Winter Wonderland today, to the ice rink. She's been begging me to take her since it opened up. Fancy joining us?' Words wouldn't form in my throat. A small croak. 'Bo has brought you up a few times since she met you. "Red", she calls you. Because of your hair. She figured maybe Daddy could convince Red to join us on the ice. You can skate, yeah?' I couldn't tell if he was being real with me or if he was just pretending it was Bo that was dying to see me, and not him.

Reid could hear Finn's voice in the silence of his apartment. 'Do it,' he mouthed. 'Find out what the story is with him and Rachel!'

'Shut up,' I mouthed back, away from the phone. Then, 'I can skate! I used to go with …' *Dan.* 'Well, I mean, I'd love to come along. Only I don't have a phone, as Reid said, so meeting up might be a bit ...'

'I'll collect you in a taxi and drop you back to Reid's, or we can Uber back to Old Willow. Don't worry. You're safe with me.'

'Right. Count me in, Kelly.'

Reid bit his lip and threw his arms into the air, then quickly retracted them, like he'd let something slip that he shouldn't have.

'See you in about half an hour?'

'Yep.'

'*Slán.*' I swooned.

'*Slán.*'

'Slawn?' Reid repeated in his very British accent. 'What the fuck does "slawn" mean? Sounds like the name of some animated lump of flesh with gross body odour.'

'It's Irish—'

'Of *course* it is,' he teased. Then he intertwined his fingers and cutely leaned his cheek on the back of one of his hands. 'Oh, Beggy, I'm glad you two are going to hang out.'

'Why?'

'Because I don't want to see you guys losing your friendship over Rachel. Or for you and Rachel to fall out. I know the *real* Destiny's Child broke up, but not us.'

Ah. Yes. Rachel.

It's not a date, Erin.

You can stop smiling now.

*

I waited for Finn to bring up 'Modern Love' in the taxi, but he didn't. The three of us piled into the back seat and he sat with his legs spread wide – Bo between them, propped up against his chest. The journey to Hyde Park mainly consisted of her and me talking about all the things she'd asked Santa for. Then, while Finn paid our driver, he was stuck explaining to Bo why Santa couldn't *possibly* bring her a baby mermaid.

She was so entertaining.

I wouldn't say it seriously to Finn, but being around Bo reaffirmed my desire to be a mother. So instead, as we approached the main entrance to the park, I whispered, 'Just letting you know, one of these days I might kidnap your daughter.' The pride Finn felt for Bo carved out so many lovely lines in his face – that face I knew so well but that all of a sudden rattled me with its newness.

'Are you happy now?' Finn asked Bo, lifting her up to sit on his shoulders so she could see everything.

'Yes, yes, *yes*!'

In all my years living in London I'd never been to Winter Wonderland during the day. At twilight I knew it to be a burst of neon where couples and people on dates gathered to hold hands on the giant wheel or to sway to live music after some mulled wine. But during the day it was something else entirely. The three of us took a leisurely stroll through the charming Christmas market (at Bo's slow tiny-limbed pace), by the fairy-lit wooden chalets that offered up unique gifts and culinary delights.

I kept a keen lookout for a Christmas gift for Granny. Wine wrapped in a bow was always my lazy go-to gift, but this year I wanted to step it up because I'd missed her more than a nice bottle of wine could express. Some beautiful hand-crafted jewellery distracted me, reminding me of the pendant tucked underneath my warm wool jumper, and then Bo piped up, pointing at the jewellery that had caught my eye, 'Rach, Da! Pressie for Rach!'

My throat tightened.

He's told her about Rachel? But they've not even met yet ... Reid said that was happening next week ... maybe she bumped into them, like I did ... maybe he arranged a separate meeting, without Reid?

Finn brushed it off with a 'we'll see' and steered her away, toward the ice rink.

'Holy moly!' Bo said loudly, when she saw it. The rink was wrapped around a Victorian bandstand and hundreds of thousands of lights illuminated it like fireflies. 'Let's go! Let's go!' she clapped.

'Daddy is going to stand here and watch,' Finn said. 'Erin is going to take you.'

Come again?

'Red!'

'Yeah, you and Red are gonna go skate. I'll be right there,' he said, pointing to the barrier, 'waving!'

'Ah, won't you join us?' I asked without looking at him – disappointment punctured my voice, and I was mortified at how obvious it was.

'I was hoping to take some pictures of her on the ice, to text to her ma,' Finn said, leaning in close to me to say it so Bo wouldn't hear. His cologne was the same one he'd worn years ago. It brought me right back to skipping class to hang out under the bridge, where our friend group had thrown together quite the hooky den. 'Would that be alright?'

'Of course,' I whispered, still looking anywhere but at him. 'We'll have a great time, won't we?' Bo beamed at me and reached out to hold my hand. Or, rather, two of my fingers, one of which would've been home to Dan's rings if I'd married him.

I'd never held a child's hand. Not in my adult life, anyway. Euphoria rippled through me. The blind trust, the sheer excitement she exuded. The kid had my massive heart in her minuscule hand.

'Quick! We need skates!'

'Yeah, Erin. Youse need skates!' Finn said, imitating Bo's voice. 'Have fun, baby.' He kissed her on the cheek. 'You and all, Beglan.' No kiss for me, obviously, but there was that look again – the one where our eyes would catch and then fail to pull apart. It hurt, this time, deep in my belly.

'We will!'

And just like that, I got to play mammy for the first time in my life – to imagine how I might *be* as a mother, to fill Mam's empty shoes. And it was the best feeling in all the world.

Melanie Murphy

Right up until Bo's *real* mammy showed up and took
her home, anyway.

After our antics on the ice, Finn – mid text session –
walked Bo and me to a Viking-inspired pop-up bar in the
shape of a big cone-shaped tent, fronted with a retro sign
that read *Thor's*. I tried to ignore the glaring light of his
phone and the fact that his eyes were glued to it, but I
couldn't. I wanted his full attention. And I wanted to know
who he was talking to.

'Can you wait here for a minute?' he asked, outside the
welcoming tipi that smelled of cinnamon and cloves.

'OK,' I said, confused.

'Time to say goodbye, baby – your ma is here,' Finn
said to Bo. My heart stopped, and her eyes welled up with
tears. It was amazing – how her feelings were so close to
the surface. 'You'll see Red again soon!'

'Today was so much fun,' I said to Bo, dipping down
onto my knee to give her a hug.

'You skate so good,' she said, her bottom lip wet with
spit. 'I only fell two times!' She put up two fingers as
she said it, to reinforce her point in case I didn't already
understand. It was so cute. 'That's better than my friend
Nicola.'

'You were great,' I said with a laugh. 'I think you're
actually better than I am.' She smiled. 'Dry those eyes
before your mammy sees you! You need to tell her about
all the fun you had.'

Finn carried Bo away, and they vanished into the thick

crowd of festive hats and red cheeks. He returned minutes later. 'Right. That was a success. I love handing her over to her ma when she can't stop smiling. You're a natural, Beglan.'

That's the nicest thing anyone has ever said to me.

I think.

Probably.

'Anyway … come on, it's mad cosy in here,' he said with a raised eyebrow, and then he led me into Thor's mouth. The bar was all holly, low lighting, log fires and snuggly blankets where people huddled in small groups to escape the cold outside – everything I loved and more, because it was there Finn finally spilled on 'Modern Love'.

'I'm proud of you. Really. The post you sent along, it was a brilliant read. And I use the word *brilliant* sparingly, honestly.' *Wow.* 'How's it doing?'

'Surprisingly well. Last time I checked, over four hundred people had read it.'

'*Yes.* What inspired it?' Finn asked, and warmed his hands by the open fire as he waited for my answer. Before I could speak, to say *you did*, Finn added, 'Anything to do with that Owen chap?'

'Well, yeah,' I said, blindsided. 'He got the ball rolling, really.'

'He gave you the idea?'

'Oh, no. It was *my* idea. But meeting him sparked a lot of the ideas, and they developed over time. He seemed so experienced with … all this stuff.'

'With love? With sex?'

I blushed, hearing Finn say the word 'sex'. My face was a tomato and I was thankful that it wouldn't be noticeable in the warm light of the dark tent. 'Yeah.'

'Do you still think about him? You were mad about him.'

Why do you care?

Jealous much?

Just chat, like friends.

You promised Reid you'd work on this friendship. Even if it is from the friend zone …

'The odd time. I mean, it was never going to work. But, I guess I did like that he was older. He's, I dunno, distinguished.'

'Is that code for "he's loaded"?'

'No! Well, he is, but that's not why I fancied him. I was interested well before I knew about his …'

'Beds of cash.'

'Yeah.' I folded my arms, fists clenched.

'Ah, well, fair play to him. I just hope he's happy. Teaching might not make much money, but it pays in other ways that are … more important.'

Why do you think I care about what kind of money you make?

'It's cool that Rachel teaches, too,' he added. 'It's a passion thing. That's what matters.'

I curled my toes inside my boots so hard that they easily could've burst through the leather. 'How's that going?' I asked reluctantly.

'Yeah, grand. So, does that – what's his name? – that Matt guy, does he have any children yet? He must want some if you're dating him.' A swift change in direction.

'None yet,' I said. I didn't tell Finn about Matt's text. I was too embarrassed. Besides, his mention of Matt wasn't what stood out to me. 'And I suppose Reid told you I want kids. I've never talked about that with you.'

'No, Reid said nothing. I can just see it in your eyes when you're with Bo. You should.'

'Should what?'

'Have kids. She's the best thing in my life by a mile. I still can't believe I made her.'

'I do hope to have a few.'

'A few? Ha. Good luck with that,' Finn said, sitting tall. 'Have one and *then* decide if you're able for any more. I know I'm not.'

I think, in that moment, it was as if a nuclear bomb had been dropped inside the cavity of my chest, and nobody in Thor's had any idea, for I sat still and quiet and didn't so much as shudder from the blast. I already had a million reasons to stop clinging to whatever was blossoming inside me for Finn. Rachel, a move home to Ireland – but this was the last nail in the coffin, the one reason I needed to hold on, crushed.

A miracle isn't hanging about on the sidelines, Erin.
Talk.
You've been quiet for way too long.
'Bo never asks for brothers and sisters, then?'

'Never. She loves being an only child. She's spoiled rotten!'

'Rachel doesn't want any kids.' As I said it, her rightness for Finn finally sank in.

'I know, she's said.'

'Ehm, I'm bursting for the loo, Finn. Do you know where the toilets are?'

Finn looked startled. 'Oh, sure, over there and then in to the left. Will I order you a drink? Something warm, maybe?'

'No, thanks. I'll actually probably head off after. Reid and I were hoping to catch a movie tonight.' *I just completely made that up.*

'What movie?'

'Oh, some gory one, wouldn't be your cup of tea.'

'Alright.' He sounded disappointed. 'Well, I'll call a taxi—'

'It's fine – I'll take the Tube,' I said.

I didn't want to be dramatic, nor to crumble in front of him, but he must have sensed the sadness welling up. I couldn't fight against my urge to be short with him, my urge to vanish into thin air. Finn's pupils were the size of saucers and his forehead creased. I assumed he knew what I was thinking but that he wouldn't bring himself to acknowledge it. *He probably pities me.* 'Thanks for inviting me,' I said, in the most formal voice I had in my arsenal. 'It's been such a nice day. Bo's great. *You're* great. I'll …

see you around. If not soon, then I'll see you and Rachel at the reunion thing. Bye.'

I walked to the bathroom as fast as my feet would take me there, before he had a chance to say his own goodbye, and I collapsed over the sink. I probably stood there with my sore chest for a good ten minutes.

After pulling myself together, I kept my eyes focused on my feet, walked to the nearest Tube station, with no phone (and therefore no music) to distract me. My thoughts were so loud I had a pounding headache before I could fall in through Reid's front door.

That's when what started out as the best day I'd had in a long time *really* became the worst.

'Beggy, finally,' Reid said as soon as I let myself into his place using the spare key he'd given me months back. He was all on top of me within seconds, trying to help me take my wet coat off and offering me tea and muttering away to himself. I wondered if Finn had messaged him about my weird behaviour. But I couldn't have been further off. 'Beggy. I don't know what to say. I don't know how to do this to you.'

'What's wrong?'

'Can you sit down somewhere? Can you let me make tea?' Reid's hands were shaking like the leaves of a thin branch on a gusty day.

'Reid, what is it? Spit it out, please. I'm not able for this right now.'

'I'm sorry, I … I don't know how to …'

'Is it Finn? What did he say?'

'No.'

'What?'

He wouldn't answer me so I walked through the hallway to the couch and dumped my handbag on top of it. 'My head is hammering, mate. I need an early night. I'm begging you, can you do me a solid and just say whatever it is *now* so I can check out of this day early?'

If today had been a pendant day I'd have bolted back to reality by now, for sure.

Reid slowly entered the room and hesitated before speaking. His arms were crossed, like he was trying to keep his own body safe from the words he was about to say. 'Your dad called me. About twenty minutes ago. I've been wandering around ever since – I didn't know when you'd get back. He's been trying to call you since yesterday …'

Reid didn't have to say any more.

I knew.

There's only one reason my dad would need to contact me so badly that he'd resort to calling Reid if he couldn't get through to me.

Granny.

It was about Granny.

18
Broken

If I was fractured before, I was broken after the moments that followed returning to Reid's.

Granny Beglan died on a Tuesday, meaning no Tuesday would be just a Tuesday ever again. She took a hard fall on a walk into Inishbeg village and was brought to hospital by a concerned passer-by who found her sitting in the mud at the side of the road. Apparently, he said, she 'seemed fine', but he insisted that she go to A&E with him to get checked by a doctor. She'd experienced a blunt impact to the head: 'epidural hematoma' they called it, which Dad later explained to me was a blood clot that pools between the brain and the skull. A few hours after the fall, the complication of her head injury killed her.

One minute Granny was awake and alive and laughing and breathing in the young man's car, the next she was talking gobbledegook, and before long she was dead in the hospital, where staff had no idea who to call because Granny had no phone and no ID on her – only a letter, made out to *me*, along with an empty plastic shopping bag.

And it was unbearable.

The pain of it.

Every moment sharper than the last.

When Reid told me what Dad had told him, Granny had already been dead for days. Knowing that was the worst part, definitely, aside from the realisation that I'd never get to talk to her again and the acrid taste of the knowledge that I'd not been with her during her final days, weeks, years.

I couldn't help but hate myself entirely.

I'd cancelled my visit because I hadn't wanted to bother flying over if I was moving home a month later.

The flight is only an hour long.

I could have gone home.

I could have been there for her.

She died all alone.

The night I found out, I crawled across Reid's lap and he leaned down to hold me, really tight, for hours. I couldn't say with any certainty how many days had passed since then for they'd all blurred into one another. Dad had to come through London on his way home for the funeral. He landed, without Sienna, and came to stay with me for a night – or I think it was a night. I was just drifting from moment to moment. But I remember that Dad didn't speak two words and mostly just sat out on our balcony on his own with his cigars for company. Rachel (without being asked) made us a home-cooked lunch and dinner, but neither Dad nor I touched them because we were sick and empty and nothing would fill us.

Thankfully, Rachel left me well alone to grieve.

So did Finn. He called up to us a couple of days after I found out – I'm sure Reid informed him of what had happened – and Dad turned him away at the front door. But not before Finn handed Dad an old mobile phone for me to use. He probably guessed how unimportant phone shopping seemed to me in the midst of everything but wanted to provide me with the means to contact him and the rest of Destiny's Child. I didn't deserve it after the way I'd stormed off on him, but the small gesture meant everything to me, and more.

19
The Wake

Erin: **I'm not going.**

Reid: **Your granny would have wanted you to go, Beggy. She loved a party. Finn, Rachel and I can come and stay in the house with you and your dad after the funeral, right up until the reunion, if you'd like? xxx**

Erin: **Dad won't still be here in a week – he'll have gone back to Sienna, wherever she is. Still can't believe she's not here to support him, at the very least. So it'll just be me here all week, probably. And anyway I won't enjoy the reunion. I'd rather donate my arms and legs than go.**

Reid: **You sure? xxx**

Erin: **Yeah. And, like, I know it's technically 'my house' now because of the will and all, but it doesn't feel like my house. I feel weird about inviting people to stay here. Granny's bedsheets still smell of her.**

Reid: I get that. What time is the funeral tomorrow? The three of us land late tonight and we'll be staying in some hotel near the airport Xxx

Erin: I can't remember. Early enough. Text my dad, he'll tell you. We're not really talking at the moment. He's kind of gone inside himself since it happened. Ugh ... this wake is going to be so shit. It's a real Irish thing to do. So you'd obviously hate it.

Reid: Only the Irish could have a tradition where a body is kept in the dead person's house overnight so everyone they knew and liked while alive can drink and eat in the body's presence. You're all as mad as bags of elbows xxx

Erin: You're not wrong. I get that it's supposed to be a celebration of her life and a nice send-off, but it's just creepy. She's literally dead in the sitting room and everyone is trying to act like that's normal. At least the coffin is closed because she's been dead for so long. If she was lying there all embalmed and that I'd probably do a Sienna and hide somewhere far, far away.

Reid: I wouldn't be able for that either. Did you get the flowers and the music all sorted for tomorrow? xxx

Erin: Yeah. Lots of Sinatra and Johnny Cash. She loved them. 'The White Rose of Athens' by Nana Mouskouri, too, for when her coffin is being carried. It's going to slay me. Honestly, they'll need to shove me in with her. I would have liked to add some cherry blossom from Mam's tree to the bouquets I ordered,

but it's dormant with the winter. The sight of the bare branches always makes me feel weird. Dad was in charge of contacting the undertaker and all that other horrible stuff. The grave, etc. Ugh. Reid :(

Reid: **Beggy :(xxx**

Erin: **I better go entertain the old biddies. I love you. I'll see you all tomorrow. Sorry in advance if I'm no craic.**

Reid: **There's that made-up word again. You mad cow. I love you, too. See you soon xxx**

A full house had never felt so empty. Floating, talking heads against the brocade wallpaper that held framed family photos of so many ghosts, and more around the elaborate oak coffin where Granny's wisp of a body rested. It sat atop some kind of cart, covered in a wine tablecloth; the cart stood out in the cosy room like scaffolding on a church. More heads hovered over Granny's furniture, spilling biscuit crumbs all over it, and yet more down the hallway and in the kitchen, where they ate sandwiches that smelled like the schoolchildren Granny once minded after she'd retired. One of the heads was surely Dad's, but I didn't want to talk to any of them.

Not even him.

Not then, not there, anyway.

My brain wasn't able for small talk. All I wanted to do was find the 'two bitches', Meryl and Molly, to bundle them up and hide in a bedroom with them, but they were way ahead of me and were nowhere to be seen. Like me, I'm sure they were deeply uninterested in a party at Granny's without Granny there to enjoy any of it.

'Erin, love. I see Peggy finally gave you her necklace! It's beautiful on you. We've all been admiring it.'

It was about an hour into the wake. I turned around, lazily seeking the source of the voice. A plump old woman sat in a wheelchair near the open front door, beside the entrance to the front room – the room with the coffin. It was Chrissy-with-the-bad-hip: one of Granny's friends from down the pub. I hadn't seen her in years.

'Ah, hi, Chrissy. She did indeed,' I replied, clutching the pendant. 'Don't suppose you know about this necklace?' I was grasping, hoping – not *praying*, but …

'That was once Great-Great-Grandmother Beglan's,' Chrissy sighed. 'Peggy was dying to give it to you for years. Always banged on about it. And now she's gone to join all the women who wore that necklace proudly through the centuries in the afterlife. I'm so sorry for your loss, love.'

Ignoring the last part of what she'd said, because all kinds of people (most of whom I didn't know) had said similar things to me all day long, I asked, 'Did Granny ever tell you about the bird? Did she … elaborate, at all?'

'Bird? What bird?'

Of course Granny didn't tell her. She didn't tell anyone.
'It's not of this world. People can't know.'

'Never mind,' I said. 'Sorry, Chrissy. I'm very tired.'

'To be expected. Are you going to come join myself and

the girls?' I imagined the five white and silver heads that likely floated just beyond the sitting-room door and how little I'd have to say to them.

'Would you mind if I didn't? I'm just … I'm struggling with … everything.'

'Of course not. If only we could sit and talk under better circumstances.'

My eyes opened a little wider. 'If only?'

'Aye. If only.'

'You *do* know, don't you?'

'I know you're *tired*, love. Go on. Up to bed. We'll all be here for hours yet.' I couldn't put my finger on it, but something in Chrissy's tone told me she was wise to the magic and was letting on that she wasn't. Either she knew, or I'd lost the plot entirely from my lack of sleep and my second Heartbreak Diet of the year. Maybe the starvation – broken randomly by gushes of chemicals and E-numbers – had me looking for clues that didn't exist. Maybe it was a complete coincidence that Chrissy said those exact words.

'Can I just ask you something first?'

'Go ahead, love,' she said.

'Was Granny happy?'

'Never met a woman happier.'

I exhaled. 'Why did she drink so much?'

'She loved the drink. It made her feel closer to James. That's what she told us. We didn't like to question her, love. That's how she felt.'

'Granny wanted more kids, though, right? To fill this house with more life?'

'She did. But she focused on what she had over what she didn't have. That's what we all loved about her. Your father. *You.*'

'I never got to have a grandchild for her to meet,' I said sadly.

'Believe it or not, she's looking down. You're asking an awful lot of somethings, love – are you sure you don't want to come and talk to the oul' gang?'

'No, honestly,' I said. 'I think I'll go take a nap. Thanks, Chrissy.'

Why can't *I* focus on what I have over what I don't have? Why didn't she pass *that* on to me instead of this useless lump of copper and stone that can't even bring her back from wherever she's gone? I held it out in front of me, staring at it, searching for … something.

What if I hadn't cancelled my visit?

Maybe if Granny hadn't been replying to my unexpected letter she wouldn't have fallen.

Or maybe it was just her time, and no matter where she was, she'd have left us.

I can't even try it because I'll just wake up in London, with no ability to call her! I always wake up on the day that's in it, and if she wasn't dead I wouldn't be here right now. I can't do it until a time I was due to visit … though, I suppose I could hop on a plane? Would I have enough money in my bank account? And even if it works, it'll break me into a thousand pieces. I'll still have to return to this version of the present, to this reality.

Chrissy's wheelchair creaked across the floor. I watched as she rolled into the front room where the coffin was, and I moved with her to peer inside. As I'd imagined, Granny's pub group were all sat on the chairs by the empty fireplace. They turned to look at me and wave as Chrissy joined them.

'Erin, dear. Fancy joining us?'

The coffin.

She's in there.

I need to see her, to talk to her, about the gift, about Finn.

My hands and feet and face went fizzy with hyperventilation. 'I'm OK. I – I need … some air. Sorry, ladies.' I headed toward the front door to step outside, to try to centre myself, to do the breathing exercises Granny always had me do, but the sight of a blackbird standing on the doormat stopped me dead. I could've sworn it was looking straight at me with its pencil-tip eye. Then it flew away, and I leaned against the living-room door frame in a cold sweat, light-headed, my heart pounding.

'She looks like she's seen the *púca!*' one of Granny's friends said. The words reached me through the chit-chat of other locals who'd come for the wake. I'd only ever heard that word during bedtime stories with my mam when I was really young. I'd never understood it, and I didn't want to.

Something about a bringer of good and bad fortune. Celtic folklore.

Ugh.

I want Granny.

I thought, again, about the pendant, but there was no way to be certain that using it to see Granny again would work. *What if I'd come home, as I'd planned to? Would she have had to walk into town that day? What if she needed bread and butter or more wine? What if she'd not left the house merely to reply to me? But ... what if she had?*

I found the two bitches in Granny's open wardrobe in her bedroom, and I ended up climbing inside there with them and breathing in the smell of Granny's tobacco-washed clothes, with the bitches curled up on my lap. I asked them if they thought her death could have been prevented, and if there was any significance to the blackbird's random appearance, or if I'd lost my mind entirely. Obviously, they didn't answer me. They just purred loudly as though hoping to soothe the agony and confusion I was feeling.

It actually helped.

I can't believe Finn isn't a cat person was the last thought to cross my mind before I drifted into a messed-up dream: I was being poked to death by a dozen blackbirds in the spot where Granny's coffin sat, surrounded by framed photographs of Granny and Grandad – only in the dream Granny looked a lot like Rachel, and Grandad looked uncannily like Finn.

20
Odd Socks

The funeral was bleak and black, like Mam's one when I was a child – and it was fast: horrid, like the sound of fingers clicking by your ear while you drift off to sleep. I couldn't bring myself to speak at it. I couldn't even pay attention to the people who *did* speak. All words about Granny's life and demise felt redundant in the pain I was caught in because that's all they were: words. They didn't change anything.

And as it all came to an end, I had that same feeling that comes after binge watching an epic TV show that lures its viewers to heavily invest their time and emotions before letting them down with the anticlimax of a lifetime, where the most-loved character is killed off for no apparent reason. Granny really had convinced me that she was Inishbeg's medical marvel and that she would live for ever.

Dad nodded at me several times throughout the day

– in the church and outside it, in the graveyard and at the reception – always from a few feet away, as if there were a thick stone wall separating us and preventing him from giving or receiving a hug. I wanted to hold him, but I didn't know how to – we never really did that, us Beglans. We probably hadn't hugged since Mam died.

People who knew Granny from around the place hugged me, though.

And Reid hugged me.

And Rachel hugged me.

Finn had hugged me too, and his hug lasted a good minute or so. I'd wanted to hold on to him for a lot longer. Finn was the past personified, on legs, stood here in the present and with an air of mystery that only the future could bring – and because such a huge part of my past was suddenly gone for ever, I didn't want to let any more of it get away. I didn't want to loosen my grip on Finn's massive warm body wrapped in a sad suit. I only did because Granny's hairdresser poked at me to offer her condolences and to say her goodbyes.

In the late afternoon I found myself in the back of some stranger's car beside Dad. We were two balloons deflated and both dressed head to toe in the kind of clothes we hadn't worn in years and years. The quietude of the long road where Granny's – *my* – house sat overwhelmed me. I peered through the car window at the house. It looked as it always did, yet still so very different.

'What a day,' Dad said.

'Yeah.'

'Will you … will you be alright?'

'I will,' I lied. I didn't want to have to beg him to stay with me for a few more days; I knew it would do him no good being in Granny's house. Besides, he'd clammed up completely, and he obviously wanted to be with Sienna. Even though I didn't like her, I could accept that Dad loved her dearly and that he probably needed to collapse into her arms after burying his second parent.

'I've transferred over some money to you,' he said out of nowhere. 'But I'm glad Granny left the house to you because you can sell it and get a bit of financial independence. Ye need that. Houses around here are worth a fortune right now, too.'

'I'm going to live in it,' I said firmly.

'Oh?'

'Yeah.'

'You're not going home? Do you need me to stay?'

I do.

'No, it's OK. But, yeah, I'll do it all up, obviously, before I properly live here. I'd actually already decided to move home, but, I wanted …'

'You wanted to be close to her.' My silence was my agreement. The thought that I'd be swapping one variety of loneliness for another hadn't crossed my mind. *That's what I'll be doing. She's gone.* 'I know the feeling,' he said. That was probably as much as I'd get out of him. That shadow of regret. Then he proved me wrong. He rubbed his palms against his black trousers, and he talked. 'This house, this *place* … just reminds me of how agonisingly in love with each other your mam and me were. The memories have me miserable, darlin'.' A pause. 'Some days I do be convinced I still feel your mam's thoughts floating around my head. She was everything. You're the only bit of her left. And Granny … well, she was most of the rest.' Another pause. 'I know I'm your da, and I should know what to say to make things better, I just—'

'It's OK, Da. Honestly. Just call me soon, OK?'

'I will. I'll see ya.'

'See ya, Da,' I said, opening the back door.

In the end, Reid didn't have to convince me to invite Destiny's Child to keep me company in the house. I only made it to 8 p.m. on the night of the funeral before I realised I was in no fit state to boil water for pasta, let alone to decide what to order from a takeaway. By 8.30 the whole gang were in a taxi back to Inishbeg from their hotel to stay with me. Finn and Rachel had originally planned to spend the week in Ireland together ahead of the school reunion (*bleurgh*), but Reid had decided to fly back to London the following day, after I'd told him I wasn't going to the reunion after what had happened. But I texted him from Granny's – *my* – kitchen table, where I sat with a growling stomach and a broken heart, to say I'd go if it would stop him leaving the country.

The three of them breathed so much life into the house

within moments of arriving. Bursting through the front
door with bottles of wine and bags of chips dripping in
salt and vinegar, they drew the first hint of a smile onto
my face in days. As they all removed their woolly hats
and their raincoats and their gloves and mittens, and as
Reid tried to figure out how to build a fire, something he'd
never had to do in his entire life – 'Beggy, why the fuck
didn't the woman just get an electric fire installed? How
the hell did she manage to carry in these big buckets
of coal every day? How did it take her eighty-six years
to die?' – I realised how lucky I was to have them there
with me. If I didn't have them, I'd be sitting there with the
smell of Granny and pictures of the dead and two cats and
nobody to call.

I'd probably resort to calling Dan and Josephine.
That's how shit it would be.

When Rachel was around, I noticed that I kept an
intentional distance from Finn. I talked to him, but just
like I talked to Rachel or to my colleagues in the café. I
also didn't look into his eyes for too long when Rachel was
in the same room. I didn't sit beside him or ask him any
questions. But I was so aware of it – like I was holding my
breath or something.

After we sat by the fire and filled our bellies with grease
and wine, after Reid recounted the many tales I'd told him
over the years about Granny to Rachel and Finn, I showed
them all to their beds. The cottage had three bedrooms. I
didn't want any of us to sleep in Granny's bed, because it

felt wrong, of course, but also because the two bitches had taken up residence on Granny's frilly pillows. So I gave them all a tour of the two free bedrooms.

'Two of us will obviously have to share each bed,' I said lifelessly, without realising how it sounded for a few seconds. It then dawned on me that if I wasn't situationally depressed I'd be laughing. They could probably sense that I wasn't going to crack a joke so we all said 'eh' and 'um' and 'ah' awkwardly on the landing until Reid saved me with, 'Well, obviously Finn and I will be snuggle buddies. Come on, beefcake, in here with me to Erin's dad's old room – he *wouldn't* approve, which makes it all the naughtier.'

Finn just laughed it off. Seeing how well Finn and Reid got along made me fuzzy inside. 'You and Erin have that room,' Finn said to Reid, pointing at my dad's old room. I twiddled my thumbs, waiting for him to confirm that he and Rachel would be sharing a room/bed. Sure, they were casual, and they spent most nights in their own separate beds back home, but I still prepared myself for the words *Rachel and I will have the other room* to come out of Finn's mouth. Then, 'Rach can take the green room with all the books, and I'll sleep on the couch. Sorted.'

I found myself watching Rachel, waiting for some hint of disappointment, but she seemed absolutely fine. I mean, I wouldn't have objected to them sleeping beside one another, but at the same time I was glad that he'd be sleeping in the room furthest away from her. My mess of feelings aside, it showed respect for the week that was in it. I could only hope that they wouldn't bump into one another during a midnight bathroom run.

Is it bad that I want them both to be here for me, but under a set of no-affection conditions?

Why should it matter if they want to cuddle?

Am I being selfish?

'Right, g'night everyone. Thanks a million. For coming,' I said to no one in particular while looking down at my odd socks against the worn floorboards. Finn had pointed out earlier in the night that my socks were mismatching, like his always were, but I'd quickly changed the subject. I'd told myself that I'd done it accidentally because I was grieving, that it had nothing to do with wanting to feel closer to him.

Finn reached across to clutch the top of my arm. 'We're always going to be here for you.' Rather than tell him that he didn't need to lie to me, I said goodnight again, went into Dad's old room, climbed into the bed and waited for Reid to come join me. I didn't even look for my pyjamas. I passed out before the boy had even finished brushing his teeth.

21
The Reunion

I'm convinced that grief is a time eater: that it literally swallows time whole or bites chunks out of days, making them shorter, making them bleed into one another.

I blinked, and it was the day before the reunion.

During the week gone by I'd visited Granny's grave a few times and kneeled by the freshly packed dirt, but I couldn't remember exactly when or for how long I'd been there each time. I'd called Dad a couple of times, too, and we'd squeezed out all of ten words to each other – what words, I've no idea. I'd even wrestled with the urge to reach out to Dan, but thankfully I could confide in Reid about that. He hid my phone and distracted me with Richard Curtis video tapes that Granny had stacked under her dusty cube of a television set.

Rachel and Finn weren't around the house much that week either. They kept going off on day trips to see Irish tourist attractions: Newgrange, the Guinness Storehouse, Trinity College's Old Library and all of the other not-too-distant spots I'd taken Dan to while we were together. Hearing about Rachel's excursions with Finn to places that reminded me of Dan was not high up on my how-to-pass-time-after-you've-lost-your-favourite-human-being list.

Somehow, already, as if the whole week had only happened in theory, the four of us were on a bus into Dublin City to go shopping for outfits for the debs-themed reunion. Reid and Finn had brought their suits, but they wanted to jazz them up with new shirts, shoes and belts, not least because they'd had to wear the jacket-and-slacks combos to the funeral and it would be rather morbid to wear the whole funeral look for a second time in the same week.

'I want you to buy me a corsage,' Rachel said to Finn. She sat beside him in the two seats opposite Reid and me down the back of the bus, which smelled of day-old sick that hadn't been cleaned up properly.

'What's that?' Finn asked, with his hands folded into one another in his lap.

'You know the small bouquet of flowers that women wear to proms? That they're given by their dates when they get picked up?'

'Nope, I don't know what you're on about. Beglan, did we do that back in our day? I don't remember giving my date a … what did you call it, Rach?'

'A corsage.'

'Yeah, the guys gave the girls corsages for our debs,' I said. 'This is why I didn't go with you, y'see. You were useless. I would have been the only girl without one. Even Georgie knew to get me one.' I kept my voice as light as I could so Finn knew I was only making fun of him, that I didn't mean it – Granny's death had literally changed my voice setting to 'serious'.

'What?' Rachel said.

'What?' I said.

'I wanted Erin to be my date to the debs. But she was mad for this total dick from school called George,' Finn said. 'Back when I was mad for her.'

Reid said nothing. He just looked out the window to avoid the tension, as if maybe it wouldn't exist if he couldn't see physical evidence of it. I was surprised that Finn's past feelings for me had never come up between him and Rachel.

Maybe he's surprised that it's never come up between Rachel and me either.

I looked at her to make sure she was OK. She seemed to be genuinely gobsmacked. Her doe eyes were so expressive. 'Really? You two?'

'No, we never—'

'Nothing ever happened between us,' Finn said, cutting me off. 'I wasn't enough of a scallywag for Erin.' He was trying to turn it into a casual chat, but it could never be that, not now.

'So, you had a little crush on *Erin*. My, you learn something new every day,' Rachel said carefully, looking from me to Finn and then back to me.

What is she thinking? I felt terrible. I didn't want her to be jealous. There was nothing to be jealous of. Was there? *No, of course not. How many times ...*

'We're here!' Reid announced in song, a good minute or so before our stop. We all stared at him. 'Sorry. I'm just really excited to try on fancy clothes. I've been tracking the bus route on Google maps for, like, twenty minutes.'

'You'll need to help me pick something, lad,' Finn said. 'We need to do these ladies proud.' He didn't look at Rachel then. He looked at me.

Flustered, I said, 'I'm sure you'll both do,' and then I stood up to walk to the front of the bus, to wait for it to pull in to the kerb along O'Connell Street, a blind woman playing with fire.

Rachel was definitely being off with me. We browsed for a while, leaving the boys in Ted Baker after window shopping for a while, with what felt like an ocean between us.

'Let's look in here,' Rachel said, gesturing toward a shop on a random corner.

'Eh, Rachel, that's a charity shop.'

'So? I don't support fast fashion anyway, and everything in the boutiques around here is *so* expensive. I'm not paying half a grand for elaborate stitching. Come on, babe.

We might find some gems in here! Neither of us are *above* charity shops – we're not exactly raking it in, are we?'

'I didn't mean it like that. I just – well, the lads are spending a fair bit on *their* outfits.'

'Tomorrow isn't about the money spent. It's about celebrating how far you've all come since leaving school.' I knew she didn't mean it as a dig, but that's what it felt like. Apart from my degree, I'd not done much else of note, but she didn't know how much that embarrassed me because I never talked to her about that stuff. Only Reid knew how far my regrets stretched. *He* knew I'd hoped to become a journalist with an award-winning blog and to be married with kids before showing my face at an event like a school reunion. I could confide in Rachel about a lot of things: my bad-brain days in relation to my body image, about sex and a lack thereof, about how coming off birth control made me a bit crazy. But not about deep shit.

Not about Finn.

Granny is the only person I want to talk to right now. Why did you have to fall, you old bat?

'You're right,' I said, forcing myself to get a grip. 'Let's have a look.'

We were in the door all of a minute and I gasped.

'What? What did you find?' Rachel said, darting through a bunch of clothes racks to look at what I was looking at. I couldn't believe my eyes. I swore the world was messing with me. It was *the* red dress: the same design I'd worn during my first tumble into a different reality with the pendant, donated by a perfect UK size 14 – my size – and so a lot bigger than the one I'd tried on in Selfridges with Reid. But it was just as beautiful. Long, strapless, skintight and with that slit up one side. *Ye look fantastic in dresses now, dear, just as ye are,* Granny had said, when I'd told her about slim-me.

I need to wear this.

It better fit!

'Damn, girl. Big change up from your usual. I love it. How do you feel about wearing bodycon? I know you said before how you don't feel comfortable in stuff like this—'

'I don't care if my rolls are visible in it,' I told her. 'I can't explain it – I just feel like I have to wear this.'

'It *is* gorgeous, and, babe, you've been doing yoga – you look awesome.'

'Haha. When's the last time I did yoga with you?'

Silence. 'Two months ago?' We both broke down in laughter.

I looked around for the shopkeeper. A bun of a woman in a silver scarf was down on her knees, folding freshly washed second-hand jumpers. 'Hi, can I try this on?'

She looked up at me. 'Sure! In to the right of the counter there, pet.'

I quickly squished myself into the dress, and while I did think I looked a bit like a hot dog in a too-small bread roll, I knew that was just my brain not being used to seeing so much of my body on show. I squinted at my reflection and tried to forget that it was *my* head attached to the body in the mirror before me.

If that person walked by me wearing this dress with those curves, I'd think, Shit, she looks good.

'Well?' Rachel whispered through the curtain.

'It's a success,' I said.

'Great! See, I told you bargain-hunting is the best. I think I've found something, too. It's lilac and backless, so I can show off all the pain I endured for my tattoo. Finn's a big fan of the tat.'

She'll absolutely outshine me. But that's OK. Because Granny would be damn proud of me, wearing this. I smoothed my hands over the outline of my tummy, accentuated by the red dress, and the flitter of anticipation in my chest set my soul soaring.

I was actually looking forward to the reunion.

It was taking place in the Inishbeg Sailing Club – the blocky white building that stood along the harbour – at 9 p.m. the following night. The view was breathtaking: a full moon and millions of bright stars dotted across a dark velvet canvas.

The organisers had hung sky-blue and navy ribbons from the ceiling in rows, like bunting, and they'd transformed the room – which was usually used for formal events – into more of a nightclub set-up by moving all of the tables and chairs to the sides of the room to make space for a dance section on the shiny wooden floor. The floor had been carpeted at our debs – I remembered it being sticky with spilled alcopops and fallen pints of cider. The hard floor was a liability – I imagined sixty-odd people getting drunk on it and some ending up with shards of glass through their feet come 2 a.m. The bar looked the same as always, and so did the stage, where a DJ was set to play hits from the noughties, from when we were in school, but very few of the attendees were instantly recognisable.

'No sign of my original debs date, anyway. Wouldn't be surprised if he's in prison or something now – he was nuts,' I said to Reid after ordering at the bar. 'The only ones I recognise so far are girls that Finn got his leg over years ago.' Reid looked at me with concern as I furiously scratched at the bit of my wrist under the satin corsage he'd given to me.

'Finn *insisted* that I give you that thing. It looks uncomfortable. You *can* take it off. Or you can throw it at one of the women you're death-staring at. I support either decision.' He sipped on the straw floating in his G&T, waiting for me to reply, with wrinkles in his forehead that told me he was worrying about me.

'I'm not death-staring. I loved school, mate – got along with pretty much everyone. It's … sorry. Ignore me. I'm just …'

'I know what you are.' I think he really did know. It just wasn't the time or place for that conversation. Finn and Rachel were just a few metres away, talking to who I eventually realised to be the members of Finn's old film club. They'd all gained a lot of weight over the past fifteen years and they'd grown a *lot* of extra hair, apart from one of them, who had no hair left at all – only eyebrows.

'She looks incredible,' I said of Rachel, pulling my eyes away from Finn and looking her up and down. We'd done our make-up together for the first time, in Granny's – *my* – bathroom, and I was astounded at how some lipstick and mascara took *her* from a nine to a ten, while it took *me* from a four to a six.

'So do you,' Reid said, his eyes alight with love. 'I'm surprised at how well you look, to be frank. You're usually so utterly hideous.'

After my drink arrived, the room had filled up some more, so Reid and I decided to do some laps. And even though I was happy to be there, I felt a bit … sedated. I think it showed. Reid frequently had to take over conversations for me; I kept running out of things to say and fidgeting and zoning out. Reid was great like that, a social butterfly. It's like he could sense that my mind was elsewhere and was taking exchanging-of-pleasantries bullets for me.

And at all times I knew exactly where in the room Finn was standing. We caught eyes a couple of times, and every time it happened it became harder to look away – I usually looked away first.

Because I had to.

'So, yeah, from student-union president to mother of twins and ex-wife to, essentially, a total fucking con artist,' Nuala, or Nancy, or whatever her name was (from the school choir practices I used to attend) said. 'Then you have lovely Sandra over there in the lemon. Her boob job nearly killed her, y'know. It went tits up … haha, *tits* – geddit?'

'Yeah, *mad* stuff.' Reid gave me our get-out signal: an obvious twirl of his straw, which meant 'Move, now, I hate this.'

'Lovely chatting, Nancy,' I said.

'It's Noreen.'

'Of course! Noreen. Sorry, I—'

'Beggy!' Reid put his arm up in the air as 'Survivor' by Destiny's Child started to play, the anthem that birthed the conversation that led to our group chat name. It was one of the few non-eighties songs I knew the words to – only because everywhere always played it to get angry women dancing. 'Let's reunite the group,' Reid joked. We looked around the room, and, of course, Finn and Rachel were dance-walking over toward us, miming along to the lyrics like they were in a music video.

I knocked back the end of my G&T, and I let loose with my friends.

When the song ended, Reid pulled me close to him, sparkling with sweat, and said into my ear, 'So, Beggy, I miss Martin. Obviously. I even sent him a picture of me in my new shirt, from the bathroom. He hasn't even opened it. And for a second there I wished he was here with us, giving it loads, so I could watch him and smell him and such. But you know what?'

'What?'

'Martin doesn't *want* to be here with me. That should matter to me. *You* wanted me here.' He trailed off. 'I'm so glad I'm here. I'm not even drunk – this is me being proper, real nice. You Irish people are fucking mental!' He glanced around at everyone we'd just danced in a big circle with. 'This is going to be a *night*.'

A few hours passed, and women swayed with their heels in their hands, and piles of people sat on top of each other in corners, hugging and reminiscing and crying, and the music had taken a turn for the worse. The DJ was scraping from the bottom of the barrel.

'Oi, Beglan,' Finn's voice called out. I was sitting on the floor near the stage talking to one of my old teachers, who'd likely been invited because everyone had loved her back in the day. She used to give out A+s like a priest giving out the body of Christ at Mass.

'Oi,' I shouted back. I smiled up at him with my eyes half closed. I needed to shield myself from his. I didn't want to let the universe implode.

Mrs A+ excused herself before Finn spoke.

Bet she senses the feels I'm feeling.

'Firstly,' Finn said, 'Reid pulled Gavin.' Gavin's older sister had babysat me a fair bit when I was younger.

'Eh?'

'Mm-hmm. They're being all flirty. Had a cheeky kiss, but they're *actually talking* too. So, secondly,' he leaned down beside me to continue, 'the three of us are each going to give you an eighties song option, and then we'll request whichever one you choose from Mister DJ up there.'

'That is the best idea any of you have ever had, ever.'

'It was my idea. I've been watching you from over there all night, see, and the smile has been sliding off your face ever since Kanye West came on.' I didn't know what to say. He'd rendered me temporarily speechless. Rachel and Reid joined Finn by my side. Reid was a lot mouldier than Rachel, who looked like she'd had one glass of wine at most. I thought about all we'd been through together and about a reality that likely existed in which I hadn't met any of them, and how bleak that probably was. So many friends had walked in and out of my life over the years, but these three had left clear and distinct footprints in the dirt. The connectedness between us in that moment was something special, rare, like an aurora.

'OK. I told her,' Finn said to them. 'Reid, you know her best. Go.'

'Too easy. 'Heaven' by Bryan Adams,' Reid slurred.

'No references to the afterlife tonight, please, mate?' I replied. 'Great song, but such a hard fail.'

'Ah, bollocks.'

'Rach?' Finn prompted.

'Hmm. Ooh. Oh! What's that one you used to play while you did the washing-up? You played it every single day for *weeks*.'

'Woman in Love' by Barbra Streisand,' I said. 'That brings back bad memories.' *Dan. Owen. Dan. Dan. Dan.* 'So, nah. Aw, guys, this is disappointing,' I teased.

'I want another turn!' Reid yelled.

Finn flashed that killer smile. 'Alright. Seeing as you're the best mate.'

'I've got it,' Reid said, so sure of himself. 'Bonnie Tyler! 'Total Eclipse of the Heart'!'

I nodded. 'Tempting. *Very* tempting. Finn? Can you compete with that?'

'No, wait! Wait,' Reid shouted. '*Flashdance* – 'What a Feeling'!'

'Right, pipe down you,' Finn warned, smiling. Then he bit his lip. I'd never wanted to hear a man name a song more in my life. 'Forever Young' by Alphaville.'

'Damn. Kelly *wins*,' I said, and I looked at him through heavy eyelids. 'That was our summer 2005 song.' Memories hugged me tight.

'I don't think I've heard it since then. Let me make arrangements. And, by the way, you're dancing with *me*,' Finn said, before climbing onto the stage to strike a deal with the DJ.

Rachel and Finn exchanged some kind of look then. They both seemed merry and … fine. Even Rachel. She didn't so much as flinch when Finn said it.

They must be solid.

She's not intimidated by me.

Fucking duh, but, God.

'Come on, sexy,' Reid said, taking Rachel by the hand and leading her to the middle of the floor to get ready to dance. I stood there like a deer in headlights. 'Forever Young' came on, and nobody else got up to join us. Confused moans erupted and eyes rolled into the backs of heads, but Finn was all that mattered in that moment. I swallowed a mammoth glob of spit and tried to fix my hair as he approached me.

Then I lost myself.

And somewhere during the song, with his hands around my waist, Finn found me. It was like he absorbed all of my fondness for him, my attachment, hopes and dreams I hadn't yet faced, but he said nothing, and shared nothing, just swayed with me, allowing my feelings to exist, safe in the space we briefly shared.

After the song ended, though, Finn was gone. Maybe grief was still nibbling away at time and taking chunks of it away from me; I don't know what happened. He walked out onto the balcony, linking arms with Rachel, and they stood at the opposite end to the smokers, and they talked, and I couldn't hear what they were saying. At some point, Reid tried to calm me down from an almost panic attack. I don't remember him guiding me into a taxi back to Granny's – *my* – house, but he did, and he held me as I sobbed for the first time since the funeral.

I lay awake fighting the urge to use the pendant to see if, in any life, Finn had ended up in my arms. Fighting it because I figured any more pain might actually kill me.

22
The Switch

Dad booked a flight for me to return to London so I could pack my things and arrange to have them sent overseas to Granny's house. I went back with Destiny's Child on an early morning flight two days after the reunion. I'd spent the entire day right after it in bed, feeling sorry for myself and rediscovering social media, which I'd forgotten even existed. It's like online-me died along with Granny. Mostly, I looked at pictures of Finn. Even though he was physically nearby, pictures were easier to deal with – the screen was the barrier that I needed to exist between us. My eighties playlist blasting my eardrums sealed me inside my mental cocoon, where I wished to dwell without interruption, and when Reid brought me cheese toasties or glasses of water, I kept the volume up full so he wouldn't try to ask me any questions.

We landed from a grey sky on a Sunday morning (one

of the ones approaching Christmas but I couldn't say the date if someone paid me).

Kenneth from the Sugar Pot was being difficult about my decision to quit. I'd requested time off after Granny died, and he cooperated because somewhere inside him existed a human heart, though, when I told him over the phone that I couldn't serve out my notice, I could practically hear the veins popping in his forehead. I'd assumed I wouldn't care, but guilt somehow managed to wedge itself in between all of the other awful feelings.

And packing up to move home to Ireland wasn't the relief I'd hoped it would be.

Is this a bad idea?

Was Dad right? Should I sell the house?

No.

Nothing's changed. London isn't for me any more.

Besides, the pub gang can't take turns feeding the two bitches forever.

I can start over.

Me, and my cats, and my house, and my blog – a new life awaiting.

Rachel was off teaching art classes, and I walked aimlessly around the apartment. I looked through the cupboards at all the healthy food she had sporadically fed me for months that I wouldn't miss but that my insides likely would. I picked up random ornaments and objects belonging to her that reminded me of various debates we'd had over wine and falafel – crystals and incense holders and books about productivity and spiritual healing and tantric sex and knitting and fermentation. And that's when I realised just how desperately I wanted only good things for her. She was a good person, one of the best I'd ever met. *So what if she bitches about people. Who doesn't? So what if she's nosy? She's been hurt, and she's a trooper – so independent despite the betrayal from her ex, with so much going for her. She deserves someone like Finn.*

I breathed out the jealousy for her that I'd carried with me for so long, just as Reid texted unexpectedly and recovered my spirits with a few words:

Beggy, meet at our spot in the sunken garden after lunch? At about 1ish? We need one last hangout there seeing as you're abandoning me and all xxx

I replied:

Hey, you know I'm going to visit loads. I mean it. I really do. And yeah, that sounds great. See you then.

It was the last time I'd cycle the route from Old Willow to the Palace Gardens on Rusty's back. I listened to 'I Want to Know What Love Is' by Foreigner. And I swallowed lungfuls of London air. I took in all of the familiar, busy sights and sounds. Then I was there, waiting for Reid, a sentimental lump on the step I'd miss as much as any human has ever missed a patch of space on the earth.

Reid didn't show, though.

It was a quarter past one when I took out Finn's phone

to call Reid, and I was sure I'd started hearing things. 'Beglan?' But it was so real. I looked up. Finn stood there inside a heavy black coat, hands in his pockets.

'Wha– eh … how … where's Reid? What are you—?'

'Reid was kind enough to let me in on this little secret place you two share. So I could talk to you somewhere … meaningful to you. Away from everything. All of it.'

'What do you want to talk about?' I still couldn't look directly at him.

'Can I sit down?'

I stood up before he could. 'What is it?'

'I'm no good at this.'

'At what?'

'Big talks.'

'It's one of those, then.'

'It is. I … it's …'

You're engaged to Rachel and you're moving into the apartment when I move out, and Bo will have my room, and you're glad I'm moving home, and you wish me all the best.

'Don't,' I said.

'Don't … what?'

'You're one of the most important friends I've ever had, or ever will have. And—'

'Friends.'

'I just mean, I don't care. Don't stand here explaining yourself to me. It's me. And it's you. And it's fine.' I wanted to add *I'm happy for you*, but I couldn't. Sure, I wanted to make it there, but I wasn't there yet, and I couldn't pretend.

He sighed, and waited, and watched me. Confusion flickered across his face. 'Sorry, Beglan. I'm being stupid. I'll tell Reid to come over now – he's just around the corner. I ... keep in touch.' Then Finn started to walk away.

'Hey. Finn, wait. *Wait* ...' Loss of him had me in a shell that had thickened and strengthened through the months, but then complete love for him broke through its surface as I chased after him. My body propelled me forward and I caught up to him after a few strides. 'Finn, stop. We've been friends for such a long bloody time. I'm being shit, and it's not fair. You've been there for me and now I need to be there for you. You can talk to me about anything, or, well, you should be able to do that. That's what friends are for. I've never been a great friend, not to Reid, not to anyone, really, but I'm trying and—'

'You're not my friend, Beglan.'

'I *am*, I ... I just—'

'You mean more to me than a friend ever has or ever could. I don't want to tell people that you're my old friend from school, or that you're the girl I wanted who never wanted me back. If you meant less to me this would be much easier to say, but ... well, you know me. And I know I've given you reasons to doubt what I'm telling you now.'

'What are you telling me?'

'That over in Ireland Reid drunkenly admitted that you're not in love with Dan any more. I didn't know for sure.'

'He—?'

'Just let me get this out. And *that* made me realise how unfair it is of me to date yet another person I'm not in love with. Hannah ... Rachel. *You* didn't go back to someone you didn't love – you spared both of you the hurt of that, even though I can imagine it wasn't easy. To turn your back on a ready-made life, the kind of life you want. So, yeah, I realised I shouldn't be with someone I don't love, either.'

'But—'

'I told Rachel at the reunion. And she felt the exact same. We're better off as friends, so please don't worry about—'

'*But*—'

'Stop. Let me finish. You want kids, and I already have my kid.'

'That.'

'I know. And I'm telling you how I feel anyway because that's something we can figure out. Because my need to tell you this right now is more important than who is living where, and who does and doesn't want kids. Neither of us is perfect, Beglan. But together, I think we could be. And I can't let you leave without telling you that. Now, please, say what you think.'

'Is this real?'

'It is. I've kept things from you before, and I can't do that, not any more.'

Again, I thought of clutching the pendant, then and there, to see how life would have panned out if I'd dated

Finn back when we were teenagers. Maybe Finn and I might have had a family of our own, or maybe we'd have broken up. But I didn't want to know – not how that life looked, not a reality where I'd not lived and loved and lost. I didn't reach for the pendant; I reached for Finn instead. And I leaned my forehead against his, like I had in his sitting room. And the kiss we'd already exchanged between our eyes reached our lips at long last.

Falling for Finn hadn't been like falling at all: it was as though I'd stepped into a house while house hunting, after brushing my shoes across the fifth welcome mat of the day, only to discover I'd found my home. I was there. And not with a prince that had saved me, like in the bedtime stories Mam read to me once upon a time – rather, with the person who'd been there as I fought to save myself, time and time and time again, and who looked at me no differently for all he'd seen me drag myself through.

23
Saudade

Time passed – so many tomorrows – until it was summer again, and Mam's tree was alive with deep rosy buds opening with single flowers in delicious creams and pinks, like cartoon cake frosting. I looked upon it fondly from the living-room window every time I travelled over the Irish Sea for a getaway and at the patch across the driveway where I'd planted a tree for Granny, just like she'd done for Mam. I'd brought back some *Prunus padus* seeds from a trip to Scotland with Reid for his thirtieth (as soon as I saw one fully grown I knew how wild Granny would have gone for it), and I hoped to help it grow into a healthy tree, with creamy white bursts of fragrant flowers.

Finn came up behind me while I looked out into the garden and wrapped his strong arms around my tummy. Over the months, during which we'd escape to Inishbeg for some quality time alone, his concerns and fears about having another child had started to unravel. 'Might be nice for Bo to have some company,' he'd say, and he'd often hold my stomach as though protecting a non-existent being that was ours, but I didn't want to discuss how and when we might have kids. Besides, Finn knew it might not happen for me because of my condition – something I was finally starting to make peace with. Time with Bo on weekends satisfied my hunger more than I could have expected. Sure, she wasn't *my* child, but I loved her as though she were.

He kissed my neck.

'Is this your way of asking if we can go to the cinema tonight?' I said cheekily.

'Nope. You just look amazing in this playsuit is all. But if it's on the cards, I won't say no …'

'Flattery will get you everywhere. Even if "everywhere" for you translates into a dark room full of strangers who don't speak a word to each other for two hours.'

'Score. C'mere, did you decide on that Skype interview with the personal-trainer guy? You gonna do it?'

'You jealous? He's kind of a ride,' I said of Jimmy Kitch, who'd responded positively to my request to interview him for my blog after the loss of his best friend to suicide. Talking to others who'd survived trauma felt so therapeutic to me after everything.

My blog had picked up steam since December. Not so much steam that it was paying the bills or anything – I'd found a lovely job working as a senior researcher

for MediaHQ, so I was actually *finally* using my degree
– but enough steam that I had a loyal following of about
eight thousand reading my posts, and I'd had this idea
to interview various people about how they coped with
grief after the loss of loved ones. Finn was so encouraging
when I told him about it. 'Saudade,' I read to him one night
in bed, from my dictionary, 'it's a deep emotional state of
profound melancholic longing for an absent something
or someone that one loves.' We talked together at length
about my grief, and he agreed that a blog focused entirely
on what I was going through would help me to process
things, to sort through them and organise them, to proper
Marie Kondo my heart. It also felt really great to be
working on little projects that people were actually excited
about – that they'd virtually engage with. It wasn't all that
I'd hoped for, but it was more than enough.

'Jealous?' Finn replied. 'Just a tad. The man's got the
kind of jaw that would break your fist if you had to punch
him. I know I'll be fine, though – I've never swung for
anyone in my life. Also, you're crazy about me, so ...'

I loved our repartee. I loved *him*.

'I think I will do the interview. The rest of the post so
far is just me harping on about Granny and Mam, pretty
much. Ugh, are you sure it's not going to be too—?'

'It's going to be fantastic. If it's not, I'll tell you. What
did I promise?'

'That you'd never keep things from me ever again.'

'Very good, Beglan,' he said and kissed my cheek. 'I'm

going to go pick up some wine for later, seeing as it's your granny's birthday. We need to toast her.'

He's so good.

'Wanna join me? Or do you need anything?'

'I'm fine. There's … something I've been waiting for today to do, and I sort of need to be alone for it. I need to do it today.'

'You're not gonna tell me?'

I laughed. 'It's the only thing in this world that I can't share with you, Kelly. It's between me and Granny, unfortunately.'

'Is that so?' He raised an eyebrow and turned my body to face him front on.

'It is. Do you trust me?'

He searched my eyes with his. When we looked at each other, two became a concrete one, and I knew his answer before he spoke it aloud. 'Of course I do.'

'Good. I'll see you in a while.'

'Right. I love you,' he said, so sure, with such heart.

'I love you too.'

Finn left, and I sat down by the fire and pulled the pendant out from my yellow playsuit and took a deep breath. I finally felt ready to give it a try. And it had to happen today because in *any* reality I'd be right here on Granny's birthday if she were alive.

I wasn't ready over Christmas, when I'd have been there with her, toasting Jesus and wearing paper hats and singing carols, pissed off my head at 2 a.m.

But I'm ready now.

'If only I'd not written to Granny to cancel my visit last
November ...'

I opened my eyes in the green room full of books, the
room I always slept in when I went to visit Granny from
London, the room I stayed in before Granny died and left
the house to me. Since then, I'd started to do the place up,
so I knew, within seconds, that it had worked and that in
this world she mustn't have taken a fall.

Happiness unfurled, there in the bed, like flower petals
in springtime.

My ears filled with the sound of sausages screaming
for their lives as steam escaped their skin from the red-
hot frying pan that Granny used to make 90 per cent of
her meals. The whistling of the kettle, the light baritone of
Frank Sinatra, the out-of-tune hum from Granny.

Granny.

I leapt out of bed and ran for the door, and through the
hallway, and to the kitchen, to the pocket-sized woman
with the wizened face that I still felt so much love for,
even though she no longer existed. Her green eyes and
her white whiskers and her blue rinse were all caught up
between my chest and arms and I didn't know where I
began and where she ended for all of two minutes, during
which she tried to say things through surprised laughter
and over my mumblings of half-nothings.

'Girl, would ye let go of me and tell me what's goin' on?'

'I can't believe you're here,' I cried, holding her shoulders, as with one hand she tried to keep the wooden spoon that dripped hot oil away from me without dropping her walking stick.

'Of course I'm bloody here, ye silly billy, now would ye let me finish making me birthday fry-up?'

'Let me make it – you go sit down! I'll bring it in. I'll make some tea, too—'

'Phhft, *tea*. If a girl can't kick off her eighty-seventh birthday with a glass of wine she doesn't *deserve* to be eighty-seven.'

'Oh, Granny, please go in and sit down – let me do this,' I said, wiping my eyes with the back of my sleeve.

'What's come over ye, eh? What's all this hospitality about? What's … what's that?' Granny pointed at the chain of the pendant, visible around the side and back of my neck. She started to pull at me, to get it out above my pyjama top.

'That's nothing, that's—'

'I bloody well know what that is. I wore it for ten years and I kept it hidden for forty-six more. God almighty and his million earths! Ye told me ye had decided to wear it only when ye were using it … so, that means …'

'Now, look, calm down. Go inside, I'll bring in the breakfast, and we'll talk. I just wanted to see you. I didn't want …'

But I didn't need to convince her or to calm her any further. She regrouped herself within seconds. 'Right. Hurry up. I'm starvin'.'

*

We exchanged few words while we ate. Well, while *she* ate – I had little to no appetite. I couldn't believe I was sitting with Granny. All I did was gawk at her. She ignored it. She knew.

She definitely knew.

'So, I'm dead, then,' she said, after wiping the ketchup away from her jowls. 'Some version of me is up in heaven, with my James.'

'Yeah. It's been horrible, Granny, I—'

'Did I suffer? Was it quick?'

'I … um … I don't know. You fell out along the road. You were posting a letter. Why you never let us get you a phone, I'll never understand …'

'I lived a long, good life without one of those *contraptions* sucking me up. Be glad of it. I certainly am.'

'But—'

'Did many people go to my funeral?'

'So many. Most of them I didn't even recognise, to be honest.'

She beamed with pride. 'I'd say a rake of them were from the soup kitchen where I used to volunteer. The girls down the pub would've invited them for me. That's nice. Lovely. How was your da with it all?'

I didn't want to lie to her, but I couldn't tell her the truth either. 'He was OK. He's OK.'

'And the house, did ye sell it? What happened to them?' She eyed the two bitches.

'I've been doing the house up, and they … they live

with me now, and my friend Rachel. In London. I stayed, Granny. I ...'

I wanted to tell her about how I was trying to come to terms with my my-flatmate-slept-with-my-now-boyfriend-before-me conundrum about the blog about how Dad (eventually) gave Finn and I his blessing, against all odds about how Reid left his job so he could separate himself from Martin ... FINALLY, and about how much cognitive-behavioural therapy was helping him to wade through his one-sided obsession; about how nervous I was about an upcoming lunch date I had pencilled in with Róisín so she could get to know the new woman in her daughter's life, and pretty much *everything* about Finn, but I could only gawk at her. No amount of daydreaming lived up to it, to her sitting there, all normal, alive and well, eating, asking questions.

'So you used up a whole go of *that* to sit here talking to me. Are ye mad?'

'If I am, so be it. I'm so happy to get to talk to you again.'

'Don't be tearin' up, now. Put those tears away. It's my birthday. It's a happy day. Even though this isn't reality to you, it is to me. And I won't spend my birthday cryin'.'

I snapped myself out of it. For her. 'We'll go to the beach, like we used to. And go to the pub with your friends. It'll be brilliant.'

'That sounds marvellous. I'll let ye ask me three questions today, about everythin', but can we just—?'

Three?

'Did you and Grandad really have no problems? Was it

all really the perfect fairy tale you made it out to be when I was a little girl? I'm sorry for cutting you off, it's just … it's been eating me up, really, it has. Things with Finn are great, but we do fight and, well, yeah. I need to know.'

Granny looked up at Grandad's portrait and kept looking for a couple of minutes before answering me. 'Ever since James passed I've had him on a pedestal because he was my world. But we had a load o' problems. Sometimes we wouldn't speak for days. It wasn't perfect. Nothing is. But the love was there. The love, the respect, the trust. I'm sorry if I ever let on otherwise, love. But ye were young. O' course I didn't talk about the fights.' She reached for her wine glass. 'Drinkin' takes me back to all the good times we had with wine and whiskies, y'see. And it takes the edge off the pain of missin' him.'

I exhaled. 'Alright. That makes me feel so much better. Eh, next, I suppose … I've been wanting your opinion on something.'

'Mm-hmm?'

'Do you think a woman can love another woman's child as much as her own? I ask because, well, I might not be able to have a baby.' I gasped for air. 'You know yourself, with the condition – it *might* happen, one of the sights even showed me so! But I've been warned not to get my hopes up. By, like, doctors. And, well, my boyfriend already has a daughter, a pretty wonderful daughter, too, and I love her to pieces, but … I don't know if it's the same.'

'Is he the one?'

'I told you before. I don't believe in "the one".'

'Is he the one you choose? Not one ye feel, y'know, lumped with? Is he the one ye want to commit to? Does he light ye on fire?'

'Well, when you put it like that, yeah. He's bloody great.'

'Then his daughter will become as much yours as she is his because ye love him, and that love will extend to her because he made her. And ye may just get over yer feelings about her birth mother now, I'm warnin' ye.' Reading my mind, just like she always did. 'Just give the girl yer love and all of it. And maybe adopt, if ye want to. Babies or animals. Whatever. Because ye have so much love inside ye. Granny knows.'

'Right. Last one. About that bird ...'

'Ah, don't use up all yer questions *now* – we've the whole bloody day ahead of us. I'll tell ye all about *that* on the beach.' Granny winked at me. I knew she wouldn't be there when I woke up in the morning, and that today's moments would become tomorrow's memories when the sun set, so I smiled and relaxed into her presence while I could.

Acknowledgements

Thank you to Thomas, to Andrew and to my father, Paul, for enthusiastically supporting me every step of the way while I was writing (and not writing) this book.

Nana (rest in peace) for gifting me the writing bug when I was only seven years old. I told you I'd get a novel on the shelves, didn't I?

Calum McSwiggan, my dear friend, for allowing me to pilfer your humour for various interactions in the book.

A collective thank you to all my viewers who regularly engage in insightful discussion under YouTube videos I make about topics related to story and plot points in If Only – many virtual conversations I had during 2018 fuelled ideas and developments in this novel.

I'm grateful to every author who inspired me to GET IT DONE via motivational tweets, to every film director who indirectly had an impact on my storytelling and to every musician whose music I listened to while writing/that I referenced in the book.

Finally, a huge debt is owed to my editor Joanna Smyth, whose guidance was invaluable as I first attempted to extract first draft ideas from my head. Without her, I fear the writing process would have taken me twice as long. Thank you for the peppermint tea, the encouragement, the editorial insight and the patience over the past year and a half! And to everyone else at Hachette Ireland for making my lifelong dream come true by agreeing to publish my fiction.